The
FELLS

An absolutely gripping British crime thriller full of twists

CATH STAINCLIFFE

Detectives Donovan & Young Book 1

Joffe Books, London
www.joffebooks.com

First published in Great Britain in 2024

Cover art by Nick Castle

ISBN: 978-1-83526-549-9

For Lan and Xi Lei,
Lynda and Joe

CHAPTER ONE

2019

The caver picks her way along the tunnel, stopping frequently to assess the best way to manoeuvre through the twisting limestone channel. The beam of her headlamp bounces off the pale rock, picking out the stippled patterns left by the water that has eaten into the stone. The mineral smell of wet stone is strong though not unpleasant.

The passageway is narrow; her slight frame means she's been chosen ahead of the rest to do this first pass. She takes care to survey each section, her helmet camera relaying the feed back to the guys at the top.

Beneath her feet, water gleams an inch or so deep, seeping through the stone. Tide marks on the walls either side of her, wavy brown lines, show how the gully will flood in heavy rainfall. They've waited for a dry spell to attempt this.

The passage tilts down and she sees a hole, maybe a metre in diameter, at the end. It is hard to tell what lies beyond.

Her pulse picks up as she realises the tunnel must connect to another cavity. The crawl hasn't led her to a dead end. Not yet anyway.

She approaches the opening with caution; there might be a thirty-metre drop the other side. She is harnessed to a guide rope that will secure her if she falls into nothingness, though a plunge into thin air might easily leave her with injuries from swinging and smashing into the rough rock.

On hands and knees she pauses at the entrance hole. Scanning her torchlight up and down she is elated to find a chamber of significant size. Her heart jumps in her chest. She estimates the space is as much as twenty metres across and the same lengthways. Perhaps fifteen metres high. The roof slopes upwards forming a dome. Stalactites and stalagmites decorate the fringes. The steady sound of dripping water echoes, magnified by the chamber.

The entrance is close to the floor of the cave. It will be easy for her to climb down and get back up again. She turns on to her front and lowers herself over the ledge, legs first, until her feet find purchase.

The cave floor is uneven, lumpy. She walks towards the centre, watching her footing and stepping over puddles of water.

Once there, she slowly performs a sequence of 360-degree turns, angling her helmet camera so the film captures each section of the cavern, the arcing roof, the walls, the floor.

She straightens and looks at the stalactites descending from the ceiling like giant milky icicles. Two metres long some of them. Below them, the stumpier stalagmites are growing upwards. Towards the back of the cave a limestone pillar has formed where the two have met.

No one has ever been here before! No human. She is the first. Her chest swells with the sense of achievement. She'll never hear the end of this. She imagines the lads above clustered round the monitor, shaking heads and swearing. The grudging admiration.

To think all this was once beneath a tropical sea. The rock formed by sedimentary deposits. An unaccountable number of sea creatures, shells, carboniferous plants settling on the ocean floor, laid down over millennia, compressed, fused together. Then thrust upwards by massive movements of the earth. Continually dissolving in the rainfall to form fissures, caves and potholes.

Turning, her eyes fall on a smooth, round boulder on the floor. She touches it with her toe and the rock tips, spins round to reveal a gaping nose, hollow eyes, a grin of teeth.

A skull.

Her mind clatters, scrabbles to understand. Close by she sees a scattering of other bones. Part of a ribcage. A femur.

She blows hard on her whistle, shock spinning through her, as her camera fixes on the human remains.

* * *

Vicky
1997

Vicky gets the train in Leeds with Melanie.

Vicky is as excited as a six-year-old.

She grabs Melanie's arm when the doors open to let them on. 'This is so sick.'

Melanie grins and they climb on board.

There's a scramble for seats, but Melanie is quick and slides past a clutch of boys laden with rucksacks to nab places for them both.

They left their bags with Robin; he's driving up later, bringing the others.

The chatter in the carriage is loud, everyone competing with the noise of the engine and one another, hyped about the festival and bragging over how wrecked they are going to get.

The group of lads are already on the booze, cans of special brew raised aloft in a series of rowdy toasts.

Freedom, Vicky thinks, leaning her head back against the seat and closing her eyes. Three whole days dedicated solely to having fun. Well . . . she has lines to learn for next week's practical. And revision after that for end-of-second-year exams. Still — away from uni, away from Leeds, out to the Dales with her friends to rave in the hills.

Each time the train stops, more travellers crush on. Most of them clearly festival-goers, but here and there are locals with bags of shopping, or hoiking a child in a buggy. Men with grey hair and flat caps.

Then the towns give way to the countryside, stretches of green and hedgerows frothy with blossom.

Outside of Hellifield, Melanie nudges her. 'Lambs.'

Vicky leans across her to look out of the window. The lambs, a pair, scurry away from the train, tails shivering. The tails remind her of catkins. And those Hawaiian flower garlands. Lei, is it? Or lie. Spelling is not her strong suit.

Leaving Ribblehead Vicky soon sees the viaduct rising in the near distance. 'Look, look!' The sun glances in the window, dazzling her for a moment. It picks out the dust streaks on the outside glass, the finger marks on the inside. 'It's amazing.' It's the picture on half the tourist guides, the arches of the great bridge marching over the green dale. Most of them show the viaduct with a steam train crossing, billowing clouds from its smokestack. But some postcards are more atmospheric, capturing the structure at sunset or in the mist of dawn.

Now they're crossing it, high above the land, and a cheer goes up in the carriage. Like when a plane lands safely after a package holiday. Or someone breaks a set of plates in the refectory.

Melanie cheers too, yelping a yi-yi-yi noise, her arms raised, shaking her head so her honey-blonde hair whips about. Vicky joins in, howling like she's Warren Zevon singing 'Werewolves of London'.

'I can't wait.' She squeezes Melanie's arm. 'This is so brilliant. And the sun's shining.'

'Of course. I told Robin to book decent weather along with the cottage.'

'Does Dee snore? I hope she doesn't snore,' Vicky says. They're sharing a room.

'You snore.'

'I do not,' Vicky says. *Do I?* Oh God, she hopes not. 'I don't, do I?'

Melanie gives a long snort and Vicky shoves her. 'I do not.'

'You'll be too pissed to notice even if she does.'

'True.'

Melanie rummages in her bag and puts on her mirrored sunglasses. Vicky can see herself reflected back. One of her in each lens. Her brown hair looks good, waves left tangled and streaked with neon pink and blue. It skims her shoulders, not long enough yet for space buns, which she wore last time she went to a rave.

'I'm starving,' she says.

'You're always starving.'

'High metabolism.'

'High maintenance,' Melanie says.

Vicky laughs. 'I am not. Look who's talking.'

Melanie lifts her sunglasses and glares at her, which makes Vicky laugh even more. It is true though, she thinks, Melanie is the one who'll complain if there are any problems with the cottage. Or if Robin's late.

'Food, drink, fags.' Vicky counts off her needs on her fingers. 'And theatre. *Featre.* I'm a happy bunny.'

Which is mostly true, though sometimes she wants more; she's just not sure what she wants more of. Not stuff, not money, though it would be nice to have enough not to worry about her overdraft. Maybe it's more of doing what she loves, of acting and directing. And that will come, won't it? Her marks have been 'exceptional' as Mr Hume says. She's heading for a first. Dee and Usha, her friends on the drama course, keep telling her she's really good. And she believes them. She knows deep down she's got talent even though she tries not to show off or behave like a diva. She cannot imagine ever wanting to do any other sort of work. She hates all the miserable statistics about how only five per cent of actors can make a living at it, or how they all have to have

5

day jobs to pay the rent. She *has* to make it, get the break that puts her in that five per cent.

The train slows pulling into Dent station.

'When you were little, did you always want to be a doctor?' she asks Melanie. Robin probably did, because his lot have been doctors for ever.

'I wanted to be an air hostess,' Melanie says.

'How do I not know this?'

'And then I wanted to be a showjumper. My horsey days.'

'God. I don't know which is worse.'

'Why?' Melanie bristles.

'Well, with your amazing scientific brain. Your stunning bedside manner.'

'Sod off.' Melanie shoves her with an elbow.

Vicky studies the sweep of the hills, which look like they're covered in green suede, and the grey escarpments that edge some of the tops. Liquid silver streams snake down the slopes.

'Memorial I', one of the poems she's learning for the play they've devised about Audre Lorde, intertwines images of nature, like these, with grief and lost love.

This is brilliant, Vicky thinks. *Already, totally brilliant.*

'I'm in heaven,' she declaims in her best theatrical voice. 'Heaven, I tell you.'

Melanie leans in. 'You really do need to eat, don't you?'

A hoot and the train gathers speed.

'Next stop!' Vicky says, the anticipation making her giddy. 'Yes, yes, yes, yes, yes.' She pumps her arms in the air five times in salutation. *Bring. It. On.*

* * *

Leo
2019

Leo is contemplating lunch and wondering whether to walk down to the river to eat his sandwiches when there is a sharp knock on his office door. *Rat-a-tat-tat.*

'Come in.'

She does. A short, trim Chinese woman. Hair in a shiny black bob. *Chinese?* She might be Japanese or Korean or Vietnamese; he's no way of telling. Is she even a full-grown woman? She looks about ten. He groans inwardly; he is turning into a dinosaur.

'Detective Inspector Donovan?' Her Yorkshire accent is as broad as his.

'Guilty,' Leo replies.

'Shan Young.' She thrusts out a hand and he reaches to shake it. His paw engulfs hers, but her grip is firm and swift.

'They've assigned me here.' Her eyes dart round the office. Not much to see. A couple of pot plants on the windowsill, a peace lily and a spider plant, the only personal touches. Thriving with his benign neglect.

'Shan?' he repeats. A short "a"; it rhymes with van.

'S-H-A-N.' She spells it out. 'It was a toss-up between Shannon and keeping Shan as my first name. I'm adopted.' She announces. 'From China.' Dark eyes steady on his, glittering like she is laughing inside.

'And how are you spelling Young?'

'The English way.'

'So English is your first language.'

Her reply is rapid. '*Bàoqiàn, nín shuō de yìjù huà wǒ tīng bù dǒng. Wǒ bù huì shuō pǔtōnghuà.*' A mix of vowels and hissing and shushing sounds, face working. Leo isn't sure how to respond until her face creases into a smile. 'I'm just messing with you,' she says. 'That means, "I have no idea what on earth you're talking about, I do not speak any Mandarin." It's about the only Mandarin I do know.'

She's a burst of sunshine, he thinks. Cheeky, and most people wouldn't get away with behaving like that with a senior officer. But she can carry it off; there's a warmth to her. *Why can't Luke be more like that?* Friendly, open. He squashes the treacherous thought. Tamps it right down. *Not here, not now.*

Leo clears his throat and gives a nod. 'So where were you before?'

7

'Chapel Allerton, uniform.'

'This your first time as a detective?'

'Yes,' she says. 'I think there's some paperwork. They said they'd send it through. Emails?'

'I'm sure there are,' he says. Probably lurking somewhere in the inbox that threatens to overwhelm him some days. 'David Jennings is our sergeant, he'll bring you up to speed on all the housekeeping, sort you out a desk. The room next door is a possibility. Not much bigger than a shoe box; it's storage at the moment.'

'Wherever,' she says.

'Let's see if he's in.' Leo rises. Then his phone rings. *DCI Booth*.

'Matthew?' Leo says.

'Job for you, Leo. Remains found in a pothole up on Lund Seat, beyond Garsdale Common. The forensics team are on their way.'

'Remains? In a pothole?'

'A caver found them.'

Leo feels his chest tighten, the sense of something dropping through him. 'That's only three or four miles from Tollthorpe,' he says. He tries to bring the missing student's name to mind. *Nicky?* Leo was twenty-eight when she disappeared and Ange had been pregnant with Luke. 1997.

Shan's eyes are on him. He can tell she's straining to work out what the call is about. Probably picked up on the change in his tone of voice, the fresh intensity.

'Indeed,' Matthew says. 'News embargo until we know what we're dealing with.'

They'd run an appeal, distributed posters round the area. *Vicky! Vicky Mott.* 'Understood. But what are the chances it's anyone else?' Leo says.

'I know. Poor kid.'

'I'll get over there now,' Leo says.

'Remains?' Shan asks as he slides his phone into his pocket.

'Underground. You've heard of Terence Bielby?'

8

'Fellside Strangler. He killed three women.'

'That's right.' Leo picks up his laptop and the bag with his lunch in. 'A fourth woman went missing six months before Bielby was apprehended. She was never found.'

'Till now,' Shan says.

'We need confirmation,' he cautions.

'But you think it's her?' She moves towards the door.

He grunts by way of assent, his thoughts turning to the missing woman's family. To those who have been waiting twenty-two years for news.

A life sentence.

* * *

Shan
2019

DI Donovan tells Shan to leave her car at the station. He'll drive. She'll have to come back this way at the end of the day anyway. She and Erin are living in Skipton.

He drives an old Peugeot estate. The back seats are folded down and the boot is half full of bits of wood and strips of metal. Maybe he's a handyman, or a DIY fan.

When they're in the car he pulls out a sandwich — a door-step, obviously homemade. 'I'll just . . .' He waves it about.

'Sure.'

'Do you want to go get something?'

She grimaces. Pats her stomach. 'A bit picky,' she says. 'Morning sickness.' He might as well know now.

He's bitten into his butty and turned, his mouth full, eyebrows raised.

'Almost three months. My girlfriend and I are so excited,' she says.

She sees the cogs turning as he processes what she's just said. He gives a slow nod. Then returns to his chewing. The news of her pregnancy doesn't seem to faze him. Or her family situation.

9

He eats quickly, swigging his food down with bottled spring water.

Shan scrolls on her phone while she waits for him, trawling through what's already online about Terence Bielby, and the missing student, Vicky Mott.

Bielby pleaded not guilty to the three murders he was charged with but the jury convicted him unanimously.

'He's still alive,' she says.

DI Donovan takes out a package of greaseproof paper. Peels it open to reveal a slab of flapjack, glistening with treacle.

Shan's mouth waters. 'In Wakefield,' she adds. *High-security prison.*

'How old was he when he was sent down?' DI Donovan asks.

'Thirty-eight. So sixty now.'

Shan had looked DI Donovan up too, when she was told of her new position. She discovered he was fifty years old. She'd have guessed he's about that; his dark hair is sprinkled with white — salt and pepper. He wears it short, and he has lines across his forehead and deep grooves down the sides of his mouth.

DI Donovan holds up the flapjack. Makes a noise that she reads as an invitation.

'Thanks. Just a small piece, sir.'

He swallows. 'Leo. Everyone calls me Leo,' he says, his words claggy with food. He breaks off a chunk of flapjack and passes it to her.

The sweetness is so intense she fears it will make her teeth ache but the taste is divine. Toffee, caramelised sugar. And some spiciness. Ginger? Cinnamon? Nutmeg?

'It's good,' she says. 'Where from?'

'Homemade. All my own work.'

'You bake?'

'Just flapjacks. Oh, and parkin,' Leo says.

'Respect.'

He looks at her sideways. Maybe he thinks she is taking the piss.

10

'I'll put an order in,' she says.

He smiles, a small smile, and the lines at the sides of his eyes crinkle like fans. There is a look in his eyes. It takes Shan a moment to name it. Sadness. He looks sad. Regret or loss in his expression.

He demolishes the rest of the flapjack and licks his fingers. He obviously decides that isn't good enough and opens the car door to pour bottled water over his hand.

Shan hopes it *is* Vicky Mott. Not because she'd ever wish anyone dead but because it will mean she can start on a proper case on her very first day. Yes, part of her feels a lurch of unease. Murder is horrible and, from everything she's learned, investigating it can be traumatic, but if the remains turn out to be some ancient Viking or a long-lost shepherd it will be such an anticlimax.

Leaving the town they manoeuvre through narrow streets thronged with visitors, half of them in walking gear. Pass cars waiting to find a space in the pay-and-display.

The shops here, like the rest of the Dales, cater to the tourists. Selling Yorkshire souvenirs, statues of sheep and woollen goods, walking sticks carved from hazel and blackthorn. Posters and tea towels sport famous Yorkshire sayings — *Ear all, see all, and say nowt* and *Where there's muck, there's brass*. They make her want to grind her teeth. Galleries stock handmade cards and paintings of nearby beauty spots by local artists. Other stores specialise in outdoor gear. Then there are the cafés, sandwich bars and pubs, in among the hardware shop, greengrocer, minimarket, butcher and estate agents.

The road outside the town heads north, skirting the valley. The river is hidden, fringed by a line of trees.

After a couple of miles the valley widens, revealing water meadows grazed by cattle. The Ribble is broader here, a wide brown ribbon, frothy where it tumbles over boulders or small weirs. Overhead the sky is blue and there are just a few small clouds on the horizon to the north.

'You know the area?' Leo asks as he slows to let a car coming uphill have right of way.

'A bit. Mainly the south. We had holidays here sometimes, in Kettlewell. I grew up in Leeds. You?'

'Born in Hawes,' he says. A stone's throw from where they are. 'I'm in Yockenthwaite now.'

'Globetrotter,' she says.

The road winds down between drystone walls to pass a substantial farm. A sign at the gate reads *fresh eggs, chickens, grass-fed beef*. And just beyond that hangs a camping notice. Shan can see a scattering of tents, orange and blue and green.

'Didn't you ever just want to be somewhere else?' Shan says. At eighteen she was desperate to leave, to spread her wings, be independent.

'Not really,' Leo answers.

At the T-junction at Ribblehead, within sight of the viaduct, they take the road northeast, into Widdale. Widdale Fell rises up on Shan's side of the road.

'I did two years with West Midlands, Birmingham. We thought we should try city life.' He shakes his head.

'I went to Bristol,' Shan tells him. 'For uni. Stayed for a year after, then moved on to Hendon for training.'

'But you came back up north?'

'Yes, I—' She breaks off, seeing the clutch of vehicles either side of the bridge below them. Police, mountain rescue, forensics van. Figures grouped around them and more on the track that leads up the side valley.

'Ready?' Leo pulls in to park on the roadside.

You bet, she thinks, feeling a tightness in her throat and a tingling in her fingertips.

CHAPTER TWO

Leo

The ascent is steep, nagging at Leo's knees and hip but he has his fell boots on. Those and trainers are the only footwear he can tolerate given his arthritis.

Shan keeps pace with him. They are both out of breath when they reach the plateau.

Leo introduces himself and Shan to the crime scene manager, Tom Bairstow, who's directing efforts near the pothole entrance. The area's cordoned off with tape.

'This is where they went down,' Tom says.

'The deceased?' Leo is astonished that Tom can deduce so much, so quickly.

'No, sorry, the caver.' Tom nods to the group gathered at the far side of the cordon.

A fresh breeze rifles the cotton grass and makes the bells of heather tremble. Leo drinks in the scent of bitter grass, the smell of stone. The sun is hot on the back of his neck but there is a cold edge in the wind.

'She filmed it all,' Tom says.

'And recovery?' Leo thinks of the remains locked away under the hill for decades. Shouldn't they leave them here?

13

Undisturbed. Perhaps this is as good a resting place as any. *What the hell are you thinking?* Vicky's not 'at rest'. She was *taken*, life stolen. There are people who want her back. *They* will lay her to rest. *They'll* choose the place.

'I'm talking to cave rescue,' Tom says. 'We want to preserve as much of the evidence as possible. Document as much as we can *in situ* before we remove anything so we'll be in lockstep with the forensics advisors.' Tom points to the cavers. 'You should see the video,' he tells Leo.

'Will do.'

Leo and Shan walk around the cordon to join the small group. Scattered on the grass around are rucksacks and hold-alls, ropes and bags, helmets and bits of kit that Leo can't christen.

'Leo Donovan, Detective Inspector. Detective Constable Shan Young,' Leo says. 'Who was it that made the find?'

The woman in the centre of the group raises her arm at the elbow. 'Me.' She is sitting on one of the boulders that litter the landscape. 'I didn't realise what it was at first.' She shakes her head.

A man beside her holds a computer tablet. He stands up. 'You want to see the video?'

'Please.'

He turns so there is less light falling on the screen. Leo and Shan stand either side of him. 'Do you want all of it or—' He breaks off, embarrassed.

'How long did it take you?' Leo asks the woman.

'About twenty minutes to reach the cave.' She shields her eyes as she looks up at him. Her face is solemn. 'The pot goes down pretty much vertically; that doesn't take long. Then I was navigating one of the tunnels at the base for most of the time. That led to the cave.'

'Could we see the part in the cave?' Leo says.

The man starts the film, scrolls through to the right point then taps his finger.

They watch as the woman climbs into the cavern. Leo sees the size of it, the arching roof, the pointed rock formations. He can hear her breath, the scuff of her boots on rock and dripping sounds in the background. She walks forward, turns in full circles, the footage showcasing the space. Then the angle of the camera swings down. The toe of her boot comes into view. Nudging a ball. A skull.

Ah, God. A sting at the back of his eyes. Leo hears Shan suck in a breath.

There's a gasp as the caver reacts and the picture shakes, swims wildly. Leo glimpses the other remains. But then the image settles, steadies on the skull. Naked, vulnerable, pitiful. The teeth exposed. *We'll be able to compare dental records.*

Questions flood his head. How on earth did she get there? Where are her clothes? Was she dismembered? Is it even a woman?

'Do you have a map?' Shan asks. 'Showing the tunnels, the potholes.'

'Sure.' The man opens a new file, a document with diagrams delineating the network of tunnels and shafts. 'We're here.' He touches the cross-section drawing. Then he flicks forward to give them a bird's eye view of the labyrinths below. 'This pot has two tunnels leading off. This branch hasn't been explored much before. It's too narrow. Some work was done back in the noughties, removing rock to increase access, but nobody ever made it through until today. So the cavern isn't logged. We thought there might be something there but it's never been mapped.'

Leo looks across to the woman. It dawns on him that her triumph in the discovery will forever be overshadowed by what else she found.

'Thank you for this.' Leo speaks directly to her. 'It will be a great help.'

She pinches her lips together, dips her head.

'We'll take your details.' He glances at Shan and she goes to talk to the woman.

Leo touches a finger to the tablet. 'We need to retain this. Have you made any copies?'

'No.'

'Good. If you can give the file to Tom Bairstow, over there.'

'Will do.'

Leo lets his gaze play over the land to the far horizon, where the purple of the heather gives way to the vivid green of grazing land on the slopes. In the low shrubbery close by, meadow pipits chase each other and take flight, soaring then parachuting down. Oblivious to the human activity.

When Shan rejoins him, he addresses the cavers. 'We'd appreciate your discretion. We need to identify the remains and notify the family.'

'You want us to say nowt?' one of the group splutters.

'I understand you'll want to share with close family and friends, but please don't put anything out on social media, don't speculate and don't speak to the press. At least until the family are informed. I'm sure you'll understand.'

'Yeah, of course,' the same man says, any heat gone.

On their way down the hill, they see a man coming up from the road with a camera sporting a large lens.

'Photographer,' Shan says.

'Shit.'

Once they're close enough to talk to him, Leo says, 'You need to return to your car, sir.'

'What's going on up there?' His face is alive with interest.

'I can't comment. This is a potential crime scene.'

The man raises an eyebrow. 'Well, there's nothing to show that.'

'Give it five and there will be,' Shan says. Then to Leo, 'We should establish an outer cordon down there.'

'Yes,' Leo says. It makes sense. People will come nosey-ing if there's no clear barrier.

'Is someone dead?' the man asks.

'Just return to your car,' Shan says, adding 'sir' after a beat. She sounds resolute.

The man gives a snort then swivels round and strides back down the path.

'Job done,' Leo says.

'Long as he doesn't try sneaking up some other way,' she says.

'Let him try, Tom Bairstow'll run him off soon as look at him.'

* * *

Shan

When they reach the roadside Shan asks the uniformed officer to set up a cordon at the bottom of the path.

She watches the photographer. He's leaning against his car, vape in one hand, thumb working his phone in the other.

'We should tell the family as soon as we can, shouldn't we?' Shan says to Leo. 'Even if it's not her. To warn them. It could well be all anyone's talking about by teatime.'

'That's right,' Leo agrees. 'I think there was just the mother. Soon find out. It's still an open missing persons case. The file will tell us who's next of kin.'

In the car, Shan calls up the file.

'Yes, the mother, Elizabeth Mott. Address in Bradford.'

'I can do this,' Leo says.

No! 'I'd rather come with,' Shan says. 'I can pick my car up on the way.'

'You sure?' He raises his eyebrows.

She knows most coppers avoid the job of breaking bad news if they can. But she doesn't want to be sidelined. She wants to be at the centre of it all, with Leo. She wants to learn the hard stuff, even the dull stuff — everything that's part of an investigation.

'Yes.'

'Okay,' Leo says.

Shan looks over at the photographer again. He's talking on the phone, animated. The uniformed officer is unrolling police tape between stanchions he's stuck in the grass verge. He approaches the photographer, and indicates for him to leave.

Shan recalls the Wikipedia page. 'Bielby was a photographer,'

'That's right. Freelance. He sold to the press, local papers. Did quite a bit for *The Dalesman*, too. Landscapes, life in the Dales, that sort of thing. But he also did the bread-and-butter stuff — schools and weddings, agricultural shows.'

'So he'd be well known?' Shan says.

'Yes. I ran into him a couple of times myself.'

She feels a swirl of uneasiness imagining that. 'What was he like?'

'Friendly, pleasant. Charming even.' Leo starts the engine, reverses to turn round. 'Can you order up all the historic case files for the Bielby investigation. Everything they've got, have delivered to us ASAP. And everything from the missing persons enquiry for Vicky Mott.'

By the time she's organised that they've reached the viaduct and are joining the Settle road.

Shan's uncomfortably hot. The heater dial is turned up high. 'Can I turn this down a bit?' she asks.

'Sure. Turn it off,' Leo says.

'How did Vicky even get there?' Shan pictures the maps they were shown, the pothole and the tunnels. 'No one even knew that cave existed, so how did Bielby, or whoever, get her there? It doesn't make sense. Someone knew a way in, even though the cavers didn't?' She tails off. *It doesn't add up.* 'The killer would have to get out again after leaving the body.'

'Perhaps the remains have moved over time. Twenty odd years,' Leo says.

'With flooding?' she says.

'That's a possibility.'

'But would they end up so close together like that?'

Leo grunts. 'Fair point.'

'Maybe there are other ways into the cave.'

'Could well be,' he says. 'It's like honeycomb, the whole of that area. Forensics will have a better take on that than you or me,' Leo says.

'Or it could have been an accident,' Shan says. 'She went exploring and got trapped. She fell down the pothole and couldn't get out again.'

'It could.'

They drive alongside a group of cyclists strung out along the road for a quarter of a mile, all in the same orange and black kit.

Leo makes a couple of calls, updating DCI Booth and asking the press office to prepare a press release to issue once they have spoken to the next of kin. 'Stress that we cannot yet confirm identity.'

Shan launches her browser, scans several pages about the Fellside Strangler until she finds what she's after.

'Bielby's other victims — two of them had been partially concealed. American tourist Martha Weiss in an abandoned grouse butt, on Darnbrook Fell in Littondale, discovered eight days after she disappeared. And Katie Fallows, marketing exec from Ripon, was hidden in a shallow cave on the limestone pavement at White Scar.'

'And the third?' Leo says.

'Veronica White, from Skipton. A-level student.'

'She was the fell runner,' he says.

'Yes. She was left on open ground on Conistone Moor. Perhaps he was disturbed before he had time to hide her? Or there weren't any places nearby.'

The sun is streaming in the front of the car, the glass thick with dust. Leo sprays the washers, obscuring the view ahead before the wipers clean the muck away.

Shan thinks it through. 'He targets women walking on their own. That must involve an element of chance, whether there'll be other walkers close by, runners on the hill. It's not like he could have planned it all, is it? It must have been opportunistic to some degree. Was there any evidence that he'd stalked those women, picked them out and followed them?'

'Not that I can recall. But he was organised enough to try and avoid leaving DNA evidence,' Leo says.

He brakes and slows. A flock of sheep are being herded across the road from one field to another.

'He strangled the victims but wore gloves,' Leo says. 'The victims were partially clothed, their jackets or tops missing, but there were no clear signs of sexual assault. The theory was he ejaculated on the bodies then removed the soiled clothing.'

'Oh, classy,' Shan says.

The cyclists have caught up with them. Shan sees them taking the chance to swig water.

'But he wasn't careful enough with Veronica,' Leo says. 'His skin cells were found under her fingernails.'

'How did that link to him?' Shan asks. 'He'd no criminal record, had he?'

'A fluke. Bielby was reported. He'd stopped a woman out walking on her own, he began making small talk and she got jittery. Everyone was back then. Three deaths and Vicky Mott missing. This woman ignored him and he followed her. But then he fell back when other walkers appeared in the distance.'

The sheep are safely across. The farmer raises a hand and Leo replies in kind and drives on.

'She told her boyfriend about it but she wasn't sure whether to report it, given that nothing really happened. He was a civilian in the police and he insisted she go in. When she described the man, that he had a camera with a telephoto lens and a tripod, that he was tall and wore a long leather coat, someone recognised him as Terence Bielby. Bielby was asked in for interview. He gave a DNA sample that put him with Veronica.'

Shan imagines the woman who escaped, how she must have felt during the encounter. All her instincts screaming at her that something was wrong, to run, to get away. Then how shaken she would have been when she learned how close she'd come. And how thankful that she'd trusted her gut.

Bastard.

'Eh?'

She must have spoken aloud.

'Sorry, sir — Leo.'

'No, I'm with you there.'

Shan rakes her hands through her hair. She thinks of all those times, too many to count, when men have approached her uninvited. All the catcalls and the slurs, the invasion of personal space, the smile that is really a snarl, the jokes that intimidate, the hand on her arm or the small of her back. The *darling*s and *sweetheart*s and *sexy*s and *girlie*s. The words especially for her: *Chinky, Chop Suey, Ting Tong*. The constant, relentless, low-level, thinly veiled hatred. And Erin. Erin last year. *My sweet Erin*. Assaulted at work.

Leo is talking and she yanks her attention back to him.

'A tricky balance,' he is saying. 'We need to prepare them for what *might* be established but it's all speculative until we have a proven ID.'

'Is there anything you want me to do when we get there?' Shan asks.

'I don't think so, but we'll see how it goes. It's a sensitive situation. We need to think on our feet. You never know how it will go, how they'll react. You step in if it seems appropriate.'

'I can do that,' Shan says. 'No probs.' A sudden nervousness at what's to come brings a rush of saliva to her mouth and a hollow churning in her belly. 'I'll probably pick up something to eat when I get my car.'

'No probs,' he echoes her, accelerating as a straight stretch of road opens out in front of them, the way ahead clear.

* * *

Vicky
1997

They all pile off the train at Garsdale. The crowd's too big for the backwater station. It takes a while to shuffle along the platform, with its wooden fretwork canopy and hanging baskets spilling ivy and red geraniums, and down the steps to the road.

'We go this way.' Melanie points to the south — the opposite direction to the rest of the visitors who are heading up to the festival site.

Vicky feels a little lurch of disappointment that they won't be camping. Enjoying the whole messy business of sleeping and eating and drinking and sharing toilets with fields full of strangers. Such a big part of going to a festival.

She'd tried to argue for it when Robin first told them he'd found a rental cottage close to Garsdale. They were talking about it over a lazy brunch at their shared house back in February. Robin had stayed over with Melanie. He did most weekends.

'It won't be the same.' Vicky shook her head as she stubbed out her cigarette.

'No,' Melanie said. 'It'll be even better. Best of both worlds. Clean toilets, comfy beds, food that won't poison us. We dance ourselves stupid then walk back there for a rest. A proper lie-in.'

The others, Usha and Col, agreed.

Well, Vicky thinks now, *no one is going to force me to go back to the cottage. If I'm having a good time I can always just stay and find somewhere to crash at the festival.*

The road narrows to a single track running between drystone walls. Sheep graze the fields, coats marked with muddy blue dye. Like tags. They've been graffitied.

It's so quiet. 'Listen,' Vicky says.

They stop walking.

'What?' Melanie cocks her head.

'Peace.' Vicky says. She can hear birds chittering and the bleat of a lamb, but no traffic, no constant din, like in the city. Not that she'd ever give up city life. But for a few days . . .

'Peace and quiet.'

Melanie scoffs. 'We came here to party!'

'Do you think we'll hear the bands this far?' It's a mile and a half's walk, is what Col told them. He measured it on an old Ordnance Survey map.

'There's the village!' Vicky spies the cluster of roofs.

'Hamlet,' Melanie says. 'Too small for a village.'

Vicky stops, speaks to the sky. '"O, that this too too solid flesh would melt, thaw and resolve itself into dew!"'

'Enough!' Melanie says.

'Race you!'

'Wait.'

But Vicky is off, her bag banging her hip as she runs. Her excitement surging with each beat of her sandals on the tarmac.

For a moment she thinks Melanie won't play. That she'll complain it's too hot or she's too tired or Vicky's childish, but then she hears the drumming of Melanie's footsteps behind her and as they reach the first building, the pub, they are neck and neck. Both reach out to touch the wall at the same time.

They are breathless and giddy as they go inside to collect the key to the cottage.

The pub is almost full already. Young people like themselves, eating, drinking. Smoke thick in the air. Not everyone has gone straight up to the festival. Or maybe these are early birds who've set up camp already and adjourned here until things kick off.

'Food,' Vicky groans.

'Key first,' Melanie says.

There's a young man at the bar pulling pints. They go up and wait their turn.

'Girls?' he says. Though he can't be any older than they are.

'We've booked Ivy Cottage. Robin Westwood.'

'Right, Robin.'

Melanie laughs. 'No, I'm his girlfriend.'

He flashes her a look of irritation.

'Are you now?' He waits, saying nothing. Just staring at them. Then, 'In that case, I'm not sure I can give you the key.' His ruddy complexion darkens.

'What?' Melanie says. 'Look, we came on the train. He's driving up later.'

'I'll be with you when this lot are served.' Two groups have arrived at the bar.

Vicky stares at Melanie. *What the hell?*

He takes his time, not just filling the order but chatting to the customers. Vicky feels her impatience grow. And she is starving.

'Right,' he says at last. 'Follow me.'

He moves to lift a section at the end of the counter and takes them down a corridor, past toilets and a staircase marked *Private* and into a small room. It's a cross between a lounge and an office. Sofa and telly, desk, phone, and shelves with files and papers on.

'Did Mr Westwood give you anything in writing to show us he's happy for you to take the key?'

'We've paid a deposit,' Melanie says. 'I don't see what the problem is.' Vicky can tell that she's trying to keep calm.

'*Someone* paid a deposit,' he says. He scratches his thatch of thick blond hair.

'This is ridiculous,' Melanie's voice grows crisper. 'I want to talk to the owner.'

'He's away.' The man is smirking.

'Wait, listen,' Vicky says. 'How would we know Robin had booked it if we weren't who we say we are?'

He surveys Melanie. 'So you're his girlfriend,' he says. 'And you?' Vicky feels her cheeks heat.

'Their friend.'

'Have you any proof of ID?' he says to Melanie.

She gets out her NUS card.

'Melanie Quinn,' he reads. 'Leeds University.'

'You can read,' Melanie says.

Vicky groans inside. *He's awkward enough. Don't make it worse.*

A flush reddens the man's neck. 'I'll take a key deposit just in case, twenty quid.'

'Fine,' Melanie spits. She pulls out her wallet, grabs a £20 note and thrusts it at him.

'You'd better sign here,' he says at last and passes a book to Melanie. 'Three nights, isn't it? Don't suppose you'll be getting much sleep.' He stares at Vicky. There's a leery sort of smile on his face.

'Not if I can help it,' she says.

He holds up a key fob. 'Yale for the front, with a spare, and mortise for the back. Instructions in the kitchen for the rest. Lock up. Normally we don't have to bother, but with all this rabble descending.' He gives a heavy sigh. Like a bad actor, he's learned the lines but the role doesn't fit.

'Thanks.' Melanie reaches to take the keys, but he moves his hand back. 'You've heard the police caution, have you? Down there in Leeds? That women up here shouldn't go anywhere on their own.'

'Yes,' Vicky says. *Prat.*

'The deposit doesn't cover that sort of thing, you see. Be an awful hassle to lose a guest.'

'We'll try and not get murdered then,' Melanie says. She practically snatches the keys from him.

Vicky shakes her head as they step outside. 'What a prick.'

'He's probably just pissed because he's stuck working here while we all get to go to the ball,' Melanie says.

'Or he's just a sexist shit,' Vicky says.

The cottage is next to the pub, the first in a terraced row of four. The frontage is right on the pavement. No fence or garden.

Melanie opens the door and steps inside. 'Watch your head.'

'I'm a hobbit,' Vicky says. Everything is crooked and small. Small windows, small rooms. It's cool in the lounge, almost cold enough for a fire, despite the warmth of the day. Nothing is set ready to light in the grate but there's coal in a scuttle to one side. Firelighters, too.

The kitchen is along the hall at the back. It's like Vicky's gran's — tiled with pictures of vegetables. There's a small fridge, an electric cooker with rings on top, a table with a set of stools. It's warmer this side of the house with the sun coming in.

A door leads to a storage and utility room. Coat hooks, baskets, ladder, brush and pan. A washing machine. It smells musty, catches at the back of Vicky's throat.

'Check out the bedrooms,' Melanie says.

They have to be careful going upstairs; the ceiling is low.

'Robin'll knock himself out, I swear,' Melanie says.

Upstairs the small bathroom has a toilet, basin and bath all in the same heavy white china. Rust marks stain the bath.

'Must be the originals,' Vicky says.

'Think the original would have been outside,' Melanie says.

'Always an option,' Vicky says. She'll pee anywhere when she's desperate.

Melanie rolls up the blind. 'Look. That's a bog. Handy, if it's still working.'

Melanie flings the door open for the back bedroom. She sits on the bed and falls back, then moves to compare it to the front one.

'About the same,' she says. They both have small double beds and a chair apiece. Chest of drawers. No wardrobes. But then, Vicky thinks, the ceilings are too low. A painting hangs on the wall opposite each bed. One of the pub in here, a waterfall in the back room.

Melanie bounces on the bed.

'So where are Dee and I going?' Vicky crosses the landing and checks the last room, above the front door. Bunk beds. A chest of drawers. 'We get a stool,' she calls. But it's fine. Luxury compared to a night on hard ground under canvas.

'I think we'll take the back,' Melanie says. 'The bed's not so lumpy. Usha and Col can go in here.'

'It's the selflessness I love about you,' Vicky says.

Melanie laughs. 'First come, first dibs.'

'Now can we eat?' Vicky says. 'I just need the loo first.'

'Go on then.'

'You know he'll probably spit on our chips,' Vicky says.

'Who? Mr Charisma?'

'Yeah.'

'Use lots of vinegar,' Melanie says. 'It's antibacterial.'

'Yes, professor.' Vicky makes the okay sign with finger and thumb. 'I'll be two minutes.'

* * *

Elizabeth
2019

Elizabeth is kneeling, small garden fork in hand, fighting to dig out the couch grass encroaching on the herb garden, when the cars pull up at the roadside.

She's not expecting callers. Perhaps they're visiting the neighbours.

The occupants get out. A man, tall, middle-aged. And from the smaller car, a young woman. Elizabeth sits back on her heels while she waits to see which house they're heading for.

She feels a prickle of sweat around her hairline and rubs at the scarf keeping her hair out of her eyes with the back of her hand.

She should divide the bluebells, too, she thinks. Put some round the back. They're over now. The flowers bleached, the petals curling brown at the edges.

The man reaches her gate, the woman by his side. They look up the run of steep stone steps to the top of the rockery. To Elizabeth.

The ground beneath her ripples as she gets to her feet, grunting with the effort. Her mouth dries and everything shrinks, narrows. Her vision, her thoughts, her hearing.

They climb the steps, twenty-four in all. She watches the tops of their heads, the man's dark speckled with white, the woman's a dense black, shining in the sun.

There is a tornado churning deep inside her, spiralling up from her bowels, from the pit of her stomach.

They step on to the terrace, first the man, then the woman.

'Mrs Mott?' he says. 'Elizabeth?'

No, she wants to say. As if that might make a difference. Say no and share a laugh about the mistake and watch them walk back down the steps and get into their cars and drive off.

And she will go back to weeding and divide the bluebells. Reward herself with a cold beer. Sit on the bench and gaze out over the valley, over the cottages and the new-build estate, and beyond the farms to the ridge on the horizon where the weather comes in.

She'll eat her tea outside in the back garden perhaps, reading as she does. She gets books online from the library. It's better that way — with paper books she was forever splashing salad dressing on them, or marking the pages with greasy fingerprints.

The man gives his name. All she hears is *detective*.

He holds out a hand.

Elizabeth looks down. She is still clutching the fork.

He flexes his lips, a tiny movement. Sympathy.

'Can we go inside?'

'No,' she says. Her voice sounds firm but the ground still ripples. The cyclone gathers force.

'A seat then?' He gestures to the bench.

The force with which she wordlessly collapses on to it takes her by surprise. He sits beside her, while the young woman stands at the end of the bench next to him.

As he talks, Elizabeth carves the soil from the tines of the fork with her thumbnail, the earth curling into whorls like snail shells. They fall and land between her feet on the paving stones.

The moss there is the brightest green. It glows.

He stops talking. All she hears now is the roaring in her ears; there's too much blood in her head.

'You understand?' he says.

28

She bends and sets the fork down on the ground. Then she turns to face him. Her chin itches. She wipes the tears away with both hands.

'No,' she says. 'No. Please, tell me it all again.'

* * *

Leo

It's almost dusk when he arrives home. The house is in darkness.

He wanders through to the back and sees a glow from the Velux windows in the roof of Ange's workshop. He crosses the garden, opens the door and peers inside.

There's a smell of pine and hot metal.

The lights above her workbench are on and she is bent over, hair caught up in a bobble. She wears a red boiler suit.

As Leo gets closer he can see she's using a hot glue gun. 'Ange?'

She turns, face blank for a moment, still lost in concentration, then breaks into a smile. 'Hi. I'm nearly done. You okay? You eaten?'

She puts the glue gun on its stand.

She moves to him. Gives him a kiss, a hug. She smells of machine oil and salt and the orange soap she uses. Grains of sawdust pepper her hair, coat her skin.

'Not yet. I'll heat something up,' he says. 'Is Luke here?'

A frown mars her face. She crosses her arms. 'No idea where he is.'

'Are you hungry?' Leo asks.

'Do me a half,' she says. 'If you're having casserole.' A glint in her eye.

He smiles. Then yawns. Dead on his feet. 'Quarter of an hour,' he tells her.

On automatic pilot he chooses a medium-sized Moroccan chicken casserole from the stack in the freezer and flatbreads from the larder. He puts the container in the microwave and turns the oven grill on. Lays out plates, cutlery, wine glasses, salt and pepper.

Their routine grew out of pragmatism. His hours were so often unpredictable. In the early days Ange would eat with Luke and save something for Leo. Whenever Leo had time off, he'd do the honours. But once Luke reached high school and would only eat shop-bought pizzas, and Ange grew more successful, taking on more demanding freelance projects, that all changed.

Ange would get caught up in her work and lose track of time and Leo would arrive home, late, drained and ravenous, to find nothing to eat. They'd had one of their few rows over food or the lack of it.

'I'm not your bloody cook. I'm working too but you expect me to stick a frilly pinny on and chop onions for you. To run to the shops every five minutes. To plan sodding menus.'

And then, with cooler heads, they'd agreed to take a different approach.

Once a month, she and Leo would make a batch of dishes to freeze and use later. They'd also bulk-buy staples and accompaniments that were quick and easy: basmati rice, pasta, noodles, tortillas and pitta, pesto and stir-fry sauces.

He sees the workshop lights go off as he turns the flatbreads.

Ange comes in and washes her hands, then pours the wine while he brings the food to the table.

'Did you pick up that timber?' she says.

'In the back of the car.'

'Ta.'

After a few mouthfuls she tilts her head to the side and says, 'So?'

Leo gives her the gist. The remains in the cavern, the suspected identity of the victim.

'The family?' Ange asks.

He tears more flatbread, folds it like a shovel and uses it to scoop up fragments of chicken and apricots in sauce.

'Just her mother.' The woman with long silver hair, a bright patterned shirt, faded blue corduroy trousers. The beaded earrings.

30

He thinks of the shock, the way she retreated at first, then how, with the second telling, she had regained her senses. Fired questions.

'What happens now? How soon will I know?' Leo had promised to keep her informed, that she'd be the first to know. Then she'd asked the inevitable: 'When can I see her?'

'She wants to see the body,' Leo says to Ange. 'Even though I told her it was skeletal.'

'She's still my daughter,' Elizabeth had said. Her voice wobbled but she spoke fiercely.

'Wouldn't we, if it were Luke?' Ange says. 'I think I would.'

'I don't know,' Leo says. The very thought of it, of losing Luke, makes his guts twist. 'The father died some years before Vicky went missing,' he says.

'God, that poor woman.'

'She married again. Lost him too.'

'Jesus, Leo!'

'Bloody atrocious luck,' Elizabeth Mott had said. 'Can't be trusted with anyone.' Eyes struggling to remain defiant.

Leo had given her a smile.

Shan had offered to make tea but Elizabeth insisted on doing it herself. Inviting them into the kitchen and carrying out the task with grim efficiency. Leaving smears of dirt on the cup handles, the surface liquid trembling as she passed them their drinks.

Leo drinks some wine, sighs. Stretches and sits back.

'I hope it is her,' he says. 'For her mother's sake. I hope we've found her.'

* * *

Elizabeth

Elizabeth doesn't go to bed. She sits vigil. That's how it feels.

She's spent.

She lets her mind roam wherever it will. Sometimes settling on Vicky, her girl, but at others on Phil or Mike. The house grows cold and she drapes herself in blankets. The lights in the houses on the new estate wink out, like dying tea lights. She switches her own lamp off and lets the stars in.

Elizabeth never closes the curtains. They bought the house, teetering on the bank of the hill, for the view. And they're so high that no one can see in the window. Though if she stood right in the bay, with her lights on, she'd be there on display.

A tragic figure.

She groans. She's fought so hard against the stereotype. The grieving mother who lives a half-life waiting for news, a widow twice over, the poor soul broken by such loss. She has resisted fiercely. Dragging herself into the light, to meaning, and purpose. Because *she* is alive. She must live for all of them. And she must hope. Hope that Vicky is alive somewhere too.

I don't know if this is her. Shouldn't she know, sense the truth? What sort of mother is she? And if this *is* Vicky? What will she do with her hope then?

A plane crosses the valley, red light blinking, a faint and distant roar.

Elizabeth closes her eyes.

The hope will be suffocated. Is that what she wants? Vicky won't be missing anymore; she will be found. *I'll know where she is. There will be an end to it.*

She is back in school with her Year Ones. She's teaching them to spell out words, to read. She writes the word on the whiteboard with a thick red marker. The lines squeal as she forms them. The children chant the letters. *D-E-A-D. Dead.*

Elizabeth turns from the board to see empty desks. And at the very back of the room, a figure slumped, head cranked to the side. Huge eyes in a skull. 'Dead,' it says in a thin voice.

She wakes abruptly, nerves sparking. She shudders, pulls the blanket up around the back of her neck, tightens it over her shoulders.

Outside, pale silver light leaks over the eastern horizon. The blackbird is busy already. Singing from the top of the alder. Elizabeth drinks in the sound.

She notices the moons of black soil under each finger-
nail. How old her hands look, knuckles like walnuts, crepey
skin, wriggly blue veins standing proud.

In a minute, she thinks, *I'll make tea. In a minute or two.*
And the blackbird sings.

CHAPTER THREE

Shan

When Shan arrives Leo is already at his desk, cardboard storage boxes piled up to one side.

'Bielby files,' he says. 'And the Vicky Mott ones.'

'What can I do?'

'Set yourself up next door and we'll divvy these up, go through them and get up to speed.'

'Sure.'

The small room is cluttered with piles of broken furniture; she can only just open the door.

Shan takes off her jacket and drops her bag and sets to work.

She moves two computer chairs, a wonky workstation and parts of a bookcase into the corridor, and is noisily dragging a small metal shelving unit out when a shout comes down the corridor.

'Oi, what's going on?'

Shan sees his stripes. The sergeant, David Jennings. 'DC Shan Young, sarge,' she says. 'Clearing this to use as an office.'

Leo's door opens.

'You can't leave it there,' the sergeant says.

34

'I'll take it downstairs,' Shan says. 'Might need a lift with it, like.' She sneezes, twice. The dust. 'Sorry.'

'You and me, David,' Leo says. 'It can go by the bins.'

Shan thinks about piping up with 'I can help'. But the men are better matched.

'To me, to you.' Leo rolls up his shirt sleeves. 'Chuckle Brothers,' he says to Shan. 'Before your time.'

'Paul and Barry,' Shan says. 'I remember them.' Sitting on the rug, drinking apple juice and eating toast and honey. Decompressing before she had to start her homework.

While the men do the shifting, Shan arranges the remaining items. The desk with drawers she shoves into place below the skylight to get the best of the light, the chair with it. She moves a trestle table to run along the wall next to a set of old wooden shelves.

She tears flyers and cards from an old cork board that she's discovered under the desk. The hooks for it are still in place so she hangs it back up.

It's weird how her energy comes and goes. Last night when she got home, she managed a bowl of noodles and a cup of tea before nodding off on the sofa. Erin woke her with a kiss and sent her to bed.

But then it had been a long, pretty intense kind of day.

Leo brings in a file and looks around. 'Not bad,' he says. 'Been a tip for years. We should have got you in sooner.'

'I charge extra for decluttering,' Shan says. 'What's that?'

'Case summary for Bielby. It'll give you an overview. When you've read that look at the Vicky Mott folder.'

His phone rings. 'Yes?' He looks to Shan while he listens. He has dark eyes, deep blue.

'Good,' he says. 'I see. Okay, thanks. Keep me posted.' He ends the call. 'Cave rescue are going in now.'

Shan wishes she could be there, taking part. But it's a job for specialists. Someone like her would just be in the way.

'Rain's forecast for tomorrow,' Leo says. 'That could mean flooding underground. They'll do all they can to carry out recovery before then.'

So they may have a confirmation of ID in the next twenty-four hours, she thinks.

'Is it possible that it's another of Bielby's victims but that it's not Vicky?' Shan asks.

'Anything's possible,' he says. But she can tell from his tone that it isn't likely.

* * *

Close to lunchtime Shan checks the latest news on her phone. It feels like the whole county, if not the country, is holding its breath.

They rehash old footage from the Bielby case and from the historic appeals for sightings of Vicky Mott. They must have used drones to film the hilltop site at Lund Seat where the white tent covers the pothole and figures in white coveralls are orchestrating the recovery operation.

Shan picks up the handwritten note from Vicky's file.

Gone to see the sunrise. Hippie? Moi? V xxx ☺

It had been left in the cottage the Sunday morning that she disappeared.

'We're getting a lot of coverage,' she says to Leo. The door between their offices is open.

'Everyone loves a serial killer.' His tone is dry.

'Are you going for lunch?' Shan asks. 'Or are we working through?'

'I'll stretch my legs,' Leo says.

'Did you bring any more of that flapjack?'

Leo laughs. 'As it happens.'

'Right then,' she says. 'I'll grab a sandwich on the way.' It suddenly occurs to her she might be intruding. 'Unless you'd rather be on your own, because—'

'No, company's fine.'

As they walk through the streets a number of people acknowledge Leo with waves and greetings, eyes sometimes flicking to her with curiosity, but he cuts off any further approach with a brief nod of his head, and if that doesn't work, adds, 'Can't stop, sorry.'

Will that be her one day? A familiar figure? Part of this community? She can't imagine it.

The day is still and hazy. Everything a little blurred. A sign of the rain to come.

Leo leads her up a cobbled lane to a rough track that climbs from the edge of town.

'This brings us back to the river,' he says. 'Takes about forty minutes. Is that okay?'

'Sure. There're no cows though, are there?'

'What?'

'It's the one thing . . .' Shan shakes her head, feeling slightly awkward.

'No cows. No. Not so's I remember.' There is a sparkle in his eyes. Is he laughing at her?

'Everyone's got something,' she says.

'That right?' He goes ahead and she follows. The path is narrow, running between a wall and a hedge, so they are forced to walk in single file.

'Go on,' Shan calls. 'You? Spiders, heights, ladders?'

He turns back to her. 'Ladders?'

'Or buttons? Some people have a phobia about buttons. Think of that. At least you know more or less where you might find a cow, but buttons . . . Go on . . .'

'I'm not that keen on snakes,' Leo says.

'They have adders up here?' she asks.

'No, they like the bracken best. More common places like Coverdale. Pretty shy even then.'

They reach a gate at the end of the passageway, a hand-painted sign warns *SHEEP AND YOUNG LAMBS IN THIS FIELD. KEEP ALL DOGS ON LEADS AT ALL TIMES. THANKS.*

Shan checks the field that opens out beyond, scanning the ground for cowpats. Her heart bucks when she sees dark splotches on the grass in between the thistles and a rush of

37

fear tightens her skin. She is about to call Leo back when she realises they are molehills. *Just molehills.* Soil, not shit.

She gives a long breath out before following him.

Flies come tickling her face. She keeps shaking her head, making her hair swing, and waving them away with her hands. When she looks at Leo he has a little cloud of them above his head too.

At the other side of the wall there's a meadow with donkeys and sheep grazing. Rabbits dart along the edge.

Leo takes her across another field and then they reach open country. Signs explain it is access land and they should observe the country code and keep dogs on a lead in the nesting season.

Underfoot the ground is springy turf, tussocky. Shan spots red clover and buttercups and wild thyme. Flowers her mum had taught her to identify. As a child Shan had a flower press and a scrapbook and built up a whole collection of paper-thin specimens. She was going to be a botanist when she grew up. Her mum used dried flowers sometimes to make greetings cards.

She does miss her. Still imagines ringing her up or texting whenever there is news, good or bad. It isn't the same with her dad, though they are close.

'You go walking much?' Leo interrupts her thoughts.

'Now and then.' Shan stops and says, 'What made Vicky go off on her own to watch the sunrise? The weather had turned; it was wet. There wouldn't be much of a display if it was all cloudy. And they'd been up half the night at the festival, then partying at the house afterwards. You'd be knackered.'

'Maybe she couldn't sleep?' Leo resumes walking with Shan alongside.

'Okay, so you get up, have a bacon sarnie or whatever, drink coffee. But to go off like that. Don't you think it's weird? What time was sunrise?' Shan stops again, looks it up on her phone. '5.05 a.m.'

'But the last sighting of her was later, on her return to Tollthorpe. The landlord's son, Christopher Hirst, saw her coming down the footpath from out of his window,' Leo says. 'That was at . . . half six?' He looks to Shan for confirmation.

'Yes. She didn't go back into the cottage as far as anyone knows and it was another six hours until her friends woke up. They found the note and realised she'd not come back.'

'Lunch.' Leo points to the small outcrop of blocky boulders, pale grey and splotched with lichen, that run along the slope. From here they have a vantage point over Settle. She can see the stone buildings with their pitched slate roofs, the green rectangle of the sports ground, a glimpse of the railway bridge between the trees. The police station on the edge of town, a converted mill, three storeys. She tries to work out which is her skylight.

Shan opens her cheese, cucumber and rocket sandwich. She holds it in both hands to prevent any of the filling spilling out.

She chews slowly — an unfamiliar habit, but she's developed heartburn for the first time in her life and eating quickly sets it off.

'So if Vicky was back in Tollthorpe at half six, where did she go then? How long would it take walking to get from Tollthorpe to that pothole at Lund Seat — Slack Pot, was it?' Shan asks.

'Yes. And a good couple of hours,' Leo says.

'Or someone took her there. They intercepted her coming back to the cottage or on her way out of the village,' Shan says.

Leo hands her a slab of flapjack in greaseproof paper.

'Whoa! Thank you.'

'But if she was put down Slack Pot, they'd have to drag her up that hill; there's no vehicle access,' Leo says.

'Unless she went willingly. You said Terence Bielby was charming.'

Leo's phone interrupts them. He wipes his fingers on his trousers before answering.

'Yes?' he says. 'Okay . . . Yes . . . That's right . . . I will.' He hangs up, his expression grave.

He doesn't look at Shan but stares straight ahead as he murmurs, 'Dental records are a match. It's Vicky Mott.'

'Right.' Shan gets to her feet. A surge of adrenalin jolts her pulse, dries her throat. She needs to act, to press ahead, to hurry back.

Leo pats the rock at his side. 'It's all right,' he says. His voice is soft and calm. 'Finish eating. Then we'll get to work.'

* * *

Leo

There is no sign of Elizabeth Mott when they arrive this time.

Leo knocks on the front door and listens for any sounds within. He is about to knock again when she answers. She is still wearing the same clothes.

She looks straight at him, reading his expression. He sees the loosening in hers. Something falling. A slow blink of resignation. He opens his mouth to speak but she raises a palm. 'Come in,' she says. 'Come through.'

She takes them into the kitchen. They sit at the scrubbed pine table. Shan at the narrow end, Leo facing Elizabeth. Behind her is the Belfast sink, the tall window with shelves full of potted plants casting a green light.

'It's Vicky,' Elizabeth says. A statement more than a question.

'Yes,' Leo replies. 'It's Vicky. I'm so sorry.'

She is quiet for a moment. The clock on the wall, like an old station clock, ticks the seconds away. Outside there is birdsong, a great tit, the trill of a robin.

'And now?' Her face is drawn, pallid beneath the broken veins on her cheeks, under the freckles across her nose.

'There'll be a post-mortem examination. The pathologist will try to determine the cause of death. But after so long that might be very difficult. We might not get an answer. It's possible Vicky died in an accident, even from natural causes. It's also possible someone caused her harm. We may

40

not be able to explain her death at all. But I promise we'll do everything we can.'

Elizabeth is pressing her knuckles together. Her mouth a grim line.

Leo gives her a minute then goes on. 'We're removing anything else we can find from the cave, anything that may be of forensic significance, but again after so many years it is likely to have deteriorated. Meanwhile an inquest into Vicky's death will be opened and adjourned until we have completed our enquiries.' He pauses in case she wants to ask anything then says, 'You want to see her?'

'I do.' No hesitation.

'Once the post-mortem is concluded we can arrange that.'

'How long?'

'A couple of days. You're welcome to bring someone with you, if you wish. And we can arrange for transport—'

'I have a car,' she interjects.

'You might not feel like driving and parking,' Shan says. 'And afterwards . . .'

Elizabeth looks at her and inclines her head. 'Okay. And then I can arrange her funeral?'

'Yes,' Leo says.

She moves the tips of her fingers along the edge of the table and back together, away and back.

'I am sorry,' Leo says again.

'I think it's best,' she says, a squeak at the edge of her voice. 'To know.' Her eyes fill but she does not cry. Her throat ripples and she swallows.

'Is there anyone we can call now?' Shan says. 'Anyone you'd like to be with you?'

'No. I can . . . I have friends. They'll come if I call. Come anyway, probably.' She tries to smile. Fails.

Leo clears his throat and straightens in his chair. 'One thing you may wish to consider, which we could do now, or arrange for someone to help you with later, is a statement from you. From the family.'

41

'"*Would like to be given time to grieve, and ask for privacy*"?' Elizabeth snaps.

'Exactly,' he says. 'It's entirely up to you but it gives them something to print, to broadcast, and it means you'll likely have less intrusion.'

Elizabeth looks weighed down at the thought.

'And people care,' Shan says. 'They want to help.'

That throws him momentarily, then he sees where she is going.

'That's right. People do care. And seeing you or hearing from you makes it more real. More personal. We'll be issuing an appeal for information and trying to jog people's memories, reminding them of the Vicky—'

'I understand' she says. 'I'll need a bit of time though.'

'Of course,' he says. 'I'll give you contact details for Jane, our press officer, and you can email her or talk to her on the phone. She can even come here. Whenever you're ready.'

'Yes.' Elizabeth gives a start and then begins to shiver. Presses her fingers to her mouth, a frown furrowing her brow.

'I'll make some tea,' Shan says.

'Yes, please,' Leo says.

He forces himself to stay calm and in control, to rein in his own emotions, while Elizabeth trembles and shudders, her breath ragged. Grief and shock rolling in.

His job is to sit and bear witness. To take the hands that reach for his across the table and enfold them in his own. The only comfort he can give.

* * *

Vicky
1997

Vicky is lighting her after-dinner cigarette when she sees Robin peering out into the beer garden. His face breaks into a grin as he locks eyes with her.

'They're here,' she says to Melanie.

Melanie jumps up and grabs Robin in a hug, while Vicky says hello to Col and Usha, who follow in his wake.

'You look amazing!' Vicky tells Usha. She's wearing a lemon slip dress, which looks great against her brown skin, and new platform sneakers. Her hair is plaited in two long shiny ropes and she has a choker round her neck.

'Ugh, I don't feel it. Just my luck to get my period at a festival.' Usha grimaces. 'Anyway, Dee's at the bar. What are you having?'

Vicky puts on a cod West Country accent. 'Cider, my dear.'

'Lager and lime,' Melanie says.

Usha turns to the others. 'Robin? Col?'

Robin draws back the curtains of dark blond hair that frame his face as he considers. 'I'll try the local draught.' He towers over Usha even with her platforms.

'Me too.' Col climbs into the picnic table bench opposite Vicky.

'How's the grub?' He swings his head round, not really waiting for an answer. 'What's the house like? You been to the site yet? Anything happening yet?'

He's out of it already, Vicky realises. His dark-lashed eyes have that plasticky gaze and there's a flush to his normally pale skin. He's speaking too quickly, too brightly.

'It's fine,' Melanie says. Robin sits next to her. 'Cosy,' she adds.

'Couldn't swing a cat?' Col asks.

'Or a mouse,' Vicky says.

'And Robin is bound to brain himself on the beams,' Melanie says.

There is no shade in the garden, no umbrellas for the tables, and Vicky can feel the sun on her shoulders and pinching at her forearms. A tan would be nice. She's brought some sunscreen so she can use that before they head up to the festival.

'We had to pay an extra deposit for the key,' Melanie says.

Robin frowns. 'What?'

'Lad at the bar,' Vicky explains. 'He's being a bit of a pillock.'

'You booked it so he's supposed to give the key to you, and you alone,' Melanie says.

'What did he think you are going to do?' Robin asks. 'Steal the place?'

'He needs a talking to.' Col looks belligerent, spittle at the edge of his mouth, face darkening. 'Bloody liberty.' He gets up.

Heads turn, voices lower. Vicky feels a prickle of unease run up her spine.

'Col, sit down,' Robin says. 'I'll sort it.'

'Yeah, but we're paying this twat—'

'Sit. Relax,' Robin says.

Vicky riffs on the Frankie Goes to Hollywood song, keeping it light.

Everything is full tilt, full colour with Col. The life and soul. It can be exhilarating but Vicky finds it increasingly exhausting. Is it just her? Usha is endlessly patient with him, smoothing things over in the house when he takes it too far. Taking him up to their room and giving him all the attention he craves. And Melanie isn't afraid to read him the riot act, like last month when she'd told him to 'Shut the fuck up and go to sleep. Some of us have got lectures in the morning.' And he had. Eventually.

'I'll sort it,' Robin says again. He is always steady, measured.

'Captain.' Col salutes. Some weird public-school code, Vicky guesses. Robin and Col went to the same place. Now they are both at the same school of medicine, in the year above Melanie.

Dee and Usha arrive, Dee carrying a tray of drinks while Usha holds a pint in each hand.

Vicky takes her cider and joins the toast.

Col is talking again, describing Robin's driving on the way up from Leeds. 'Then he starts changing down gears at least a couple of hundred yards from the lights, so we're at a crawl half the time.'

'It saves petrol,' Robin says.

Vicky glances around the courtyard, cast-iron mangers bracketed to the walls are full of brightly coloured bedding plants. Groups sit drinking and eating, smoking, gales of laughter punctuate the buzz of conversation. She can smell weed.

Then she sees the barman looking out of the doorway. Looking straight at them. It feels invasive, intrusive. Hostile. She doesn't like him. She doesn't like the way he acts.

She turns back to find Robin's eyes on her. He gives a quick, friendly smile and a bit of an eye-roll towards Col and she smiles in return. He's so kind.

She takes a long drink of cider, cold and sweet and so fizzy it burns her throat, then offers round her cigarettes. She's not going to let some skanky bloke with a chip on his shoulder spoil things. They're all here now, her friends all together, and this weekend is going to be totally sick.

* * *

Shan
2019

First thing in the morning, Shan drives to Harrogate to meet up with Leo and see the pathologist.

As she starts out the sun is burning off the dew. Here and there puddles glisten rose gold. The rain has cleared and mist lingers on the floor of the valleys and rises from the slopes in columns like smoke. Everything looks bright, rinsed clean. The colours sharper.

She lay awake last night listening to the drum and sizzle of the rain, to the clatter of water tumbling from the broken gutter above their bedroom window, to Erin breathing beside her, and thought of Vicky Mott in the cave. Had she been alive down there in the pitch dark? Unable to see anything, hearing the echoes of every sound bounced back by stone. Frantic for escape. Crying for help. Or was she already dead?

Nothing lives in caves without light. Shan had looked that up wondering if there were insects or even mammals scratching and sniffing in the dark.

It was a tomb.

Following her satnav Shan reaches the car park and finds a space near to the building.

She's not been there a minute when Leo arrives in his Peugeot and she gets out to meet him.

Once they're booked in, Leo leads the way to the mortuary waiting room, down in the basement.

The building is tiled like old prisons or schools or swimming pools. Rich green rows arranged like brickwork, white rows above, rolled dado tiles for the border. The stone lintels over the doors are carved with patterns of fruits and flowers.

'All the old tiles,' Shan says to Leo. There's a faint echo in the space, a reverberation to her voice, to their footsteps.

'Municipal palaces,' he says. 'Ideal at the time, aesthetic and practical, resilient, easy to wipe clean. They've torn it all out in the other rooms. Refurbished it. You'll see.'

A mortuary assistant appears bringing them protective clothing: aprons and gloves, caps and overshoes.

'As soon as you've got those on, I'll take you through,' she says. 'You can leave anything you don't need in here and I'll lock it up.'

Leo looks like a market trader in his apron and hat, with his craggy face — a fishmonger or a butcher. She supposes she looks the same but younger, with a smoother complexion.

Shan brings her notebook and pen. She sucks on two Rennies, her breakfast still burning her gullet.

The mortuary suite is like a room in a new hospital. Moulded units with curved edges to the floors and walls means there are no corners anywhere for dirt to hide. In the centre is a gleaming stainless-steel trolley, a sheet covering what lies there. A whiff of bleach tickles the back of her throat.

'Good morning.' The pathologist welcomes them. He's an elderly Black man with tight grey curls showing beneath his cap. He has pitted scars on his cheeks and forehead. Smallpox? Or acne?

'Dr Anthony James,' he says. 'You, I know.' He bows a little as he speaks to Leo. 'And who is this?' A West Indian lilt in his voice.

'DC Shan Young,' Shan says.

'Okay. I'll take you through what we've already established and answer any questions I can.'

He moves to take the sheet off the table.

The bones seem shocking here in this antiseptic, plastic room. Out of place. The contrast of something organic, natural but taboo, with the man-made sterility of the space.

'You will already have had the preliminary forensic reports and documentation of the remains *in situ*,' Dr James says. 'There was some displacement of smaller bones, some of those in the feet for example, and a few haven't been recovered. But all the major bones are accounted for. They weren't widely scattered. We have reassembled her and the skeleton is more or less intact.'

Shan makes notes. She looks again at the skeleton, familiar from horror films, from Halloween, from the grimmest newsreels, from X-rays. But still it is bizarre to be here staring at it, knowing it is real. This was a person. Vicky Mott, a twenty-year-old drama student.

'Of most interest in my examination were serious fractures to the right femur here, at the hip joint.' Dr James points. 'Also to the right humerus — the upper arm — and the right calcaneus — the heel bone.'

Shan thinks of the pothole. 'Caused by a fall?'

'*Consistent* with a fall.' Dr James stresses the first word. 'We have to admit other possibilities unless the evidence is incontrovertible.'

'How else could you break a hip like that?' Shan says.

'A car crash, a crush injury.'

'Did they recover the hyoid bone?' Leo asks.

'Yes, undamaged.'

'So she wasn't strangled,' Shan says. She knows if the small bone at the front of the neck is broken it's a clear indicator of this.

'Impossible to say. In fifty per cent of strangulation cases the hyoid remains intact,' Dr James says.

Shan glances at Leo. She has more questions but isn't sure if he wants to speak. He gives her a nod.

'Can you tell if her hip was broken before or after death?' She is trying to string together a sequence of events that makes sense.

'Not from these injuries,' Dr James says.

'Where were her clothes? Would they decompose, or had they been removed?' She turns to Leo. 'You said Bielby took clothing from his victims.'

'The bare minimum, to cover his traces.'

'There was no clothing on these remains,' the doctor says. 'However, other items recovered from the site tell us more.'

Dr James turns away from the table and wakes a screen on the wall using a remote control. 'These items were found south of her remains in the cavern,' he says.

Two rows of images appear, one above the other. The top row consists of photographs in the cavern, while the bottom shows the same items against a white background, presumably after recovery. In every shot a ruler provides scale and a unique number is attached to each piece of evidence.

Leo focuses intently on the screen. 'What are we looking at?'

Using the remote as a pointer the doctor selects the first picture. 'These are remnants of what appears to be a wax cotton parka jacket.' He directs their attention to the second image. 'We've also buttons. And moving on, here are fragments, possibly rubber, and assorted metal pieces. Samples are with the lab now so we should have confirmation soon.'

'How far from the body were these?' Leo says.

'Between nine and eleven metres.'

'Someone dropped her down the pothole and dumped her clothes too,' Shan says. 'The body must have moved after landing, been washed forward. But why didn't the clothes move as well? Wouldn't they be lighter, and thus move more easily?'

Dr James gives a small smile. 'Leo?' he invites.

'She moved herself. She was alive.'

Shan's pulse gives a kick. 'With a broken hip?'

'And the broken hip also gives us a potential explanation for why the clothes were separate from the body,' Dr James says.

'Hypothermia,' Shan almost shouts. She ignores the heat in her cheeks that follows. 'Can a broken hip cause hypothermia?'

Dr James smiles. 'Yes, untreated trauma of this degree can. And people with acute hypothermia may feel unbearably hot and desperate to shed clothes. We see the same at the end of life.'

Her mum, those last days, clawing at her nightdress, restless, frenetic. The memory pierces Shan and she turns back to Vicky's skeleton, trying to ground herself again.

'But we can't know for sure that's what happened?' Leo says.

'That's right.'

Shan winces. 'Could she even take her jeans off? Wouldn't it hurt too much?'

'It would be very painful but, if she became delirious, not impossible. However, denim is a natural fibre. Anything of that nature would biodegrade, whether she was wearing it or not. We are talking about a twenty-two-year period. Some metal studs were found close to the remains, potentially from denims. The lab's trying to identify them.'

'And cause of death?' Leo asks.

'I'd be speculating. It could have been organ failure, dehydration, starvation, sepsis.'

'How long could you live with no food and injuries like that?' Shan says.

The doctor shakes his head gently. 'It's water that's key.'

She thinks back to the underground footage. 'But there is some water in the caves.'

Shan sees Vicky underground, in the dark. Burning with thirst. Bracing herself for the agony each time she hauls herself forward. Dragging herself over the bones of the rock. The skin torn from her hands and feet.

The steely determination to survive, forcing her to keep looking for a way out. Sucking up water from small puddles, water tasting of the earth, of minerals. How long did she go on before she died? Days? Weeks? Alone and in pain. The thought terrifies her.

No one should die like that. And if someone was responsible for it they deserve to pay. She swears to herself that she will find them. She and Leo will hunt them down and get justice for Vicky.

And if it's an accident, just a chance stumble that sent Vicky plunging down Slack Pot, leaving her unable to find a way out? Shan's heart sinks. Immediately she feels uncomfortable. Does she *want* it to be murder and not just some random mishap? Is she that twisted?

After all, wouldn't it be far better to be able to tell Elizabeth that her daughter's death was simply a tragic twist of fate?

CHAPTER FOUR

Leo

They're in the corridor on their way out of the mortuary building when his phone rings. It's Tom Bairstow, the crime scene manager.

'There's something I'd like to show you, Leo. We've made some progress mapping the area further into the cavern. I'd like to talk you through it.'

'We can come up there,' he says. 'You're still at Slack Pot?'

'Better to meet me at Tollthorpe,' Tom says. 'At the pub, midday?'

'Tollthorpe?'

Shan cocks her head, mirroring his interest, eyes alert.

'Bring your walking sticks,' Tom says. Leo laughs.

As he parks in the lot at the start of the village, Leo sees they've had a playground built at the side of the pub. Something to attract families with children.

Shan pulls in next to him.

Leaving their cars Shan points to the row of small houses beyond the pub. 'One of those is the cottage where Vicky stayed?'

'That's right.'

The saloon is busy with tourists ordering home-cooked lunches. Smells of vinegar and fat and grilled meat fill the air. Leo's mouth waters on cue even though he's eaten his sandwiches on the drive over.

Tom Bairstow is at a table near the back with another man who is slightly built, like a jockey.

'This is Nat, our cave diver.' Tom makes the introductions. 'Do you two want drinks? Food?'

Leo is impatient to hear the news but he appreciates that it's their lunchtime and waits while Tom and Nat put orders in at the bar.

'The landlord's son, the last person to report seeing Vicky, does he still live here?' Shan asks.

'I don't know.' Neither of the bar staff fit the bill. A woman and a teenage girl.

Shan slips from her seat and weaves between the tables, goes out the front door and returns after a moment. '"Christopher Hirst, licensed to sell intoxicating liquor." Same name. We should see if he's in, talk to him.'

'We will,' Leo agrees. They need to speak to everyone who gave information back when Vicky went missing.

Tom and Nat return carrying drinks, and once they're seated attention shifts to the latter, who opens up a computer tablet.

'You know we found some items over here.' He indicates a point in the south of the cavern.

'Clothing and rubber and metal items,' Leo agrees.

'Right. Well further on we found a smaller chamber and off that were two openings. Tunnels. Here and here.' He shows them photographs, the flash glinting off wet rock, one hole low on the cave wall, the other about a metre above.

'We still need to do more surveying but they appear to travel in this direction towards Toller Fell. Now the area up behind here—' he jabs a thumb over his shoulder towards the hill — 'was the site of substantial lead mining. There are ventilation and extraction shafts all over.' He opens a map of the fell. 'You can see some marked here. And all around here.

There are some open swallow holes too, where streams have created a channel down through the stone.'

Leo runs his eyes over the symbols on the map, grasps what is being implied. The hairs on the back of his neck lift. 'Vicky never went to Slack Pot. She went down one of these shafts or holes and that leads to the cavern.'

'That's our theory,' Tom says.

Their sandwiches arrive and Nat turns his tablet over until the server leaves them.

'And to find out if you're right?' Leo says.

'We can use ground-penetrating radar to detect holes and tunnels here — and explore the tunnels further at that end too. Try and establish where the two might join up.' He takes a bite of his sandwich.

'Could she have fallen in, accidentally?' Shan asks.

Nat shrugs. 'It's rare but it has happened. Now and then you hear of a dog or a sheep needing rescuing.'

Shan takes a swig of her drink as she ponders her next question. 'So were the mines just left open?'

Leo blows on his coffee, then drinks. The espresso is black and bitter.

'The mines near footpaths would have been fenced off or covered with a metal grid and some would be backfilled and covered with wood, but that would rot eventually. A lot were just left,' Nat says.

'We were with the pathologist earlier,' Leo says. 'Talking about the placement of the remains and those clothing and metal remnants. One explanation is hypothermia — she removed some clothing after she'd made her way to the cavern. But in your opinion could the locations be accounted for by flood water moving the remains, and the clothes, after death?'

Nat shakes his head. 'No. The water flow in that section would find ingress from Slack Pot and travel through this area. See the pattern of the flowstone on the floor.' He shows them a photo of the cave, points out the rippled stretch of stone that runs through the front of the cavern close to where the first caver found her way in.

Leo shakes his head slowly, Nat's words dawning on him. 'So Vicky *was* alive and able to move to reach the cave from wherever she went underground.' It pains him. To think of the suffering she must have endured.

A scream from a toddler rends the air and silences everyone momentarily. Leo sees the father lean across the table to try and settle the child. The mother, her face aflame. He recalls that sensation with Luke. The irritation and the awkward shame. *Not just when he was a toddler, either.*

'We're going to walk up and take a quick look now,' Nat is saying. 'And then I'll draw up plans for a survey.'

'You can come with, if you like,' Tom says. 'But if you're busy—'

Shan sits forward, eager.

'We'll come,' Leo says. She's not the only one who's keen. He wants to get a sense of the geography. To walk in Vicky's last footsteps.

The path starts at a stile at the end of the small lane that runs between the pub and the row of cottages. The fell is open country, but most likely the route was an old drovers' trail and an access route for the lead miners.

Leo has fetched his OS Explorer map from the car so he can mark exactly where Nat takes them.

The climb isn't as steep as Lund Seat but the wind is stiffer, cooler today. Coming from the east. Puffy cumulus clouds move swiftly overhead, snow white against the summer blue.

Leo feels the familiar gnawing pain in his hip.

They reach a level plateau and Leo stops to look back at Tollthorpe. It hasn't changed much over the years. A couple more barn conversions perhaps, but this area is in the national park. Stringent planning laws limit new building. Young people can't afford to buy and struggle to find accommodation to rent, forced to compete with wealthy incomers looking to retire or set up artisanal businesses. It's a perennial topic for the parish councils and the national park authority.

He's not sure whether Luke will ever have the chance to leave home, never mind that his bed's empty half the time.

There have been cursory plans to find somewhere to rent in Keighley or Bradford, where prices are cheaper, but nothing ever materialises. And until Luke gets a job . . . Leo's guts churn as he's dragged into the same old worries. Chiding himself, he pulls his attention back to the matter at hand and checks where they are on his map.

The moorland rises again, another climb, and when they scale it the valleys and the village below, the railway and the road, pass from view.

Skylarks are busy burbling overhead and Leo welcomes the familiar lift to his mood that the sound always brings.

They keep to the path for another quarter of a mile, walking on packed earth threaded with worn-down heather roots interspersed with patches of rock. Leo spies bees criss-crossing over the grass, dipping to visit marsh violets.

'We go this way here,' Nat says when they reach an outcrop of rock close to a cairn.

'East.' Leo marks his map.

'She came to see the sunrise,' Shan says.

Such a simple pleasure, Leo thinks. *And then what?*

Walking is harder away from the path; tussocks like large cobblestones, some sprouting rushes, rise from boggy ground amid hidden pools.

There is a shallow incline and now Leo spots remnants of dressed stone, left from the mining era. The gold rush of its time. The influx of migrants changed the area. Not just the landscape of the hills but the settlements that grew alongside the industry. Accommodation sprung up to support the workers, as did places to pray — Nonconformist chapels, Methodist and Quaker — in an area that had previously been ruled by the monasteries and priories with their great abbeys. The little chapels have long since been repurposed — Ange's workshop, for one.

Nat leads them past a row of bell pits explaining how the miners dug down to reach vertical seams of lead. They look similar to natural sinkholes now, shallow bowls carved out of the ground. Perfect picnic spots on a windy day. But unless there was a further dramatic collapse of underlying rock, not somewhere a person could fall down.

Leo hears the cry of a curlew, loud and piping, and looks up to see a pair soaring over the land. The others watch too. The distinctive curved beak visible each time they pass.

'Good to see,' Leo says, and Nat agrees.

They walk on a little and Nat stops them besides a large crevice in the rock. 'We've a few natural holes like this,' he says. It's narrow but Leo thinks that a person could get down there at a pinch. And Nat points out what looks like a cave in the hillside that rises up further east. 'That's probably the entrance to a level, a horizontal tunnel, but natural caves were used as well.'

'Where will you start?' Shan asks. 'There are so many.'

'We'll try to identify the most likely shafts and any open swallow holes using the radar. See if we can make progress along either of those tunnels over at Lund Seat. But I can't promise we'll come up trumps. We'll keep you updated.'

Leo imagines the hilltop at dawn, light rain falling. Vicky reaching here. And what? Stumbling, falling in, slithering down? Or meeting Bielby? The man out with his camera, making small talk until he is close enough to grab her.

What happened to you, lass? Did you see your sunrise? Have that moment of joy?

A thought strikes him. Shan says the words before he can.

'How come she was seen by a witness coming *down* from here? It doesn't fit.'

'Let's find Mr Hirst,' Leo says. 'See if that's still how he remembers it.'

* * *

Shan

When they ask at the pub, the woman tells them Chris has gone to the cash-and-carry and shouldn't be long if they want to wait. Can she help? She's his wife.

56

Her eyes flick between Shan and Leo as if she's trying to come up with some explanation for them being together. It's a reaction Shan grew accustomed to growing up with parents who looked nothing like her. Her toes curl as she remembers the drunk who could barely stand, and his mate, accosting her and her dad as they queued for *Bend It Like Beckham* at the cinema in town.

'Mail order bride, pal? Thai, is it? Nice one.' And he'd leered at Shan, bubbles of spit in the corners of his mouth, reeking of booze. She was thirteen.

And her dad, her gentle, kind-hearted dad, his face flooded red as he drew back an arm, fist formed.

Shan had stepped between them, a palm on her dad's chest, then turned to the drunk.

'Yeah? Well, whoever ended up with you is due a refund, *pal*. Factory reject. Now fuck off, you Neanderthal.'

He had indeed fucked off, his mate in stitches. Ripples of consternation in the line of cinema-goers. Her dad shaking his head with laughter and giving her a hug. Oh, how she had wanted to punctuate her words with a judicious kick, shatter the pillock's kneecap or break his elbow, but she'd not got physical. Getting physical should only ever be a last resort. That was drummed into them by the sensei.

Now Mrs Hirst looks alarmed for a split second when Leo explains who they are, then her face clears.

'Ah, it's about Vicky Mott?' She gestures to the TV screen in one corner of the room. 'I saw that.' Her chin goes up towards the main door. 'Here he is now.'

Christopher Hirst is a solidly built man with short coarse blond hair, a ruddy complexion and a trim beard. He wears cargo pants and a blue and yellow Leeds Rhinos shirt. As he gets close Shan smells fabric conditioner, sickly like bubble gum.

Once he hears why they've come he takes them to an office up on the first floor at the back corner of the building. The window looks out past the end of the row of cottages to the hillside.

Hirst pulls out an executive office chair, swivels it away from the computer desk and sits.

'Take a pew.' He gestures to a stack of plastic chairs. Leo separates two from the pile and they both sit down.

The room is hot, baking in the sun that streams through the window.

'We're revisiting Vicky Mott's last movements, speaking to people who were witnesses when she went missing,' Leo says.

'Reet.'

'Can you remember what you saw?'

'She was walking down there, down t'path.' He nods his head to the window. His arms are folded, his legs stretched out and crossed at the ankles. Shan senses he is guarded but trying to appear relaxed.

'Do you remember the time?' Leo asks.

'Six thirty, thereabouts.'

'You were up very early?' Leo says.

'I'd work to do.'

'This was your bedroom?' Shan says.

Hirst glances over at her but doesn't make eye contact. He speaks to a spot over her head. 'It was.'

Leo stands and moves to the window. 'You've a clear view. It was like this back then?'

Shan goes to look.

'Yes. Bar the play area,' Hirst says. 'We put that in in 2010.'

From the window Shan can see the path they used earlier, a pale strip through the moorland. And to the right, across the narrow lane, is a partial view of the end cottage, the gable end, a lean-to ground floor extension and the backyard adorned with frothing hanging baskets, like the beer garden.

'She came down the path and went where?' Leo asks.

'Down the lane.'

Shan turns back to Hirst on his chair. 'How did you know it was her?'

'Seen her about. We were letting the cottage. They came in here.'

58

'But there were four women staying,' Shan says.

'Yeah, well, one were an Asian, so it weren't her.' There's a stress on the word Asian. A prickle in the air, a sense of things unsaid. 'Anyhow she had a red coat, like it said in the appeal.'

'You lost sight of her once she went down the lane?' Leo says.

'Yes.'

'Did you see her again?'

'No. I didn't.'

Leo moves closer, holds out his phone to Hirst. 'What about this man?'

'Terence Bielby?'

'Yes. Did you see him that day?'

'No.' He stretches his neck as if he's tired or bored by the questions. Shan puzzles over his attitude. A dislike of the police? Most businesses in the area have a reasonable relationship with the coppers, relying on them to keep the district safe enough not only for residents but for the tourists who are the local economy's lifeblood.

'Were there many people around that day?' Leo asks.

'Not at half six in the morning.' He speaks as if they are stupid.

'You didn't see anyone apart from Vicky?'

'No.'

'How about later?'

'Plenty. There were a festival on.'

Leo waits a beat or two, the man's churlishness expanding in the vacuum. 'You notice anyone acting suspiciously? Anyone you had concerns about?' Leo's tone is polite, mild. Shan's not sure she'd be so accommodating.

He shakes his head. 'I warned 'em,' he says out of the blue.

'Who?' Shan says.

'Those lasses, about not going out on their own. Supposed to be bright, in't they, students?' He doesn't look at her but studies his feet. 'She should have listened.'

59

It was her own fault? His callousness cuts through Shan but she gives nothing away.

'You think he's done it?' Hirst addresses Leo. 'Bielby?'

'That's what we're trying to find out.'

'He did the photos for our menus, back then. Everyone knew him.' He blows out his cheeks, rearranges his crossed arms.

'Have you remembered anything else since? Anything you might have forgotten at the time? Doesn't matter how small,' Leo says.

'No,' Hirst says without a moment's thought.

'Thank you.'

Hirst follows them downstairs and through the pub, where the girl clearing tables stops to gawp, to the front door.

'Donovan?' Hirst says on the threshold. 'Any relation to Luke?'

Shan sees muscles tighten in Leo's jaw, senses him stiffen.

'I'm his father. You know him?'

'Aye. Say hello from me.'

Shan didn't know Leo had family. Thought perhaps he lived alone given the flapjacks. She hasn't asked. In the job people volunteer as much or as little as they want to about their personal lives. But there is definitely an undercurrent to this last exchange with Hirst. Not simply two people finding a mutual connection and enjoying it. She is burning to know more but damps down the embers.

They stand for a moment outside the pub. Opposite a tractor is backing into the farmyard, a collie barking and nipping at its wheels, and a minibus makes its way down the hill, presumably bringing a late lunch party.

'If Nat's right then Vicky must have gone back up the hill after Hirst saw her at six thirty,' Shan says. 'Why?'

'She forgot something? Left something behind?' Leo suggests.

The minibus brakes make a squealing sound as it turns into the parking area. A flock of cawing rooks in the trees behind the farmhouse rise and circle.

'All that stuff about her being stupid, how he'd warned them.' Shan blows out a breath and shakes back her hair, as if doing do will somehow purge the unpleasant encounter from her system. Christopher Hirst doesn't like women; she knows that much. Might he have hurt Vicky? Invented the sighting to cover his tracks? But if he had anything to hide, surely he'd be less of a mardy sod. More careful, courteous with the police. Or is he simply arrogant, so sure of himself that he doesn't care?

It seems a bit of a leap, Shan thinks, promoting him from a witness to a person of interest. And she decides she needs to mull it over a bit more before deciding if it's worth sharing with Leo.

* * *

Vicky
1997

The place is heaving, a riot of colour. Flags and banners, people in costumes and face paints. The sun making everything glow brighter. The sky overhead a bowl of blue.

In the changeover between bands a DJ is spinning tunes. Vicky didn't know the last act but the next one is Cornershop. She adores them. After that will be James and tonight's headliner is Pulp.

Col and Usha have gone off to buy drinks. Melanie wanted the loo and Robin's gone with her. Dee has some weed and is rolling a spliff. She licks the papers, twists the end and fires it up.

Vicky feels the sun on her head. Maybe she should put some sunscreen on her parting. Or buy a hat? They'll probably have some cool hats — something to keep for a souvenir.

Dee takes a long drag, clenches her teeth as she holds it in, smiles at Vicky waggling her eyebrows.

Vicky laughs. Dee's a natural comic. She can act serious roles but her forte is comedy. She's single-handedly written a stand-up set for her practical, with Usha directing.

Vicky watches the crowd around them: a girl wearing a sort of antler headdress, a couple kissing, a lad blowing bubbles and his friend trying to pop them.

Dee passes her the spliff and Vicky has a few quick tokes, holds the smoke in then dragons it out. And again.

A hand on her back and Melanie is there, Robin behind her.

She glimpses Col and Usha returning through the revellers.

Melanie takes the smoke and gives a little bow of her head. All the colours of the festival dance in her mirrored shades.

Usha joins them, alone now, looking pissed off. That's not like her. She says something to Robin, and he looks back over the crowd then walks off. Vicky guesses it's something to do with Col.

Melanie nudges her.

There is a man with a staff pass and a camera, and he wants them to pose.

Laughing, they form a line. Melanie, then Vicky and Dee. Vicky calls to Usha. 'Come on! No wimping out.'

Arms draped over shoulders they beam for the camera. Then Vicky breaks contact, raises her arms and strikes a pose like a diva accepting applause. The others catch on. After months of joint improvisation classes she and Dee and Usha are on the ball. Melanie gets it too, so the four of them ham it up with outflung arms or blown kisses and the photographer laughs. Cheering them on, he runs off a series of shots moving closer in with each one.

'Cheers, girls,' he says. 'Live it large!' Which makes Vicky snort because it sounds a bit cheesy coming from someone his age.

'You too!' she says. 'And drink plenty of water.' Because that is being hammered into everyone so no one dehydrates and croaks after dropping Es and dancing like morons.

The DJ track fades away. Vicky turns to watch. The compere bounds on to the stage.

Beside her Melanie is fiddling with a lock of hair, snagged in her badge.

Usha has gone again.

'What's up with Usha?' Vicky says. 'Where's Col and Robin?'

Melanie shrugs. 'Search me.' Passes the spliff to Dee.

Then the band run on and Vicky jumps, arms in the air, and joins in the whooping as they launch into 'Brimful of Asha'.

* * *

Elizabeth
2019

Elizabeth sees Pam's Polo pulling in from her vantage point on the bench in the garden. She has locked up and been waiting here for a good half hour. Watching the day unfurl.

The daisies opening up as the sun touches their faces. The procession of cars on the school run and the parade of children and parents walking up from the new estate and on to the primary school. The great tit fledglings, three of them, leaving the nesting box in stuttering flight, landing bumpily, ragged baby feathers making them appear larger than the parents.

Today of all days? Seriously? She'd laugh if she didn't feel so hollow.

She waves to Pam, wanting to spare her old friend the climb. 'These bloody steps will be the death of me,' Pam complains whenever she visits. Pam is overweight and asthmatic.

'You could always park in the top road and walk down the alley and in the back,' Elizabeth has told her on countless occasions. But she never does.

At the top of the steps Elizabeth is suddenly vertiginous. She holds the rail tightly, finds she has to concentrate; all her muscle memory has flown away. The territory usually so familiar — the colour and shapes of each piece of York stone, the angle and elevation of each drop — is now treacherous. Her body not to be trusted.

'How are you doing?' Pam asks once Elizabeth is in the car. She shakes her head. No words.

'Okay.' Pam understands. She starts the car.

Pam doesn't trouble her with small talk or even turn the radio on. Though now and again she swears softly at other drivers with their video-game antics and breathtaking lack of road sense.

Elizabeth feels muffled when she tries to grasp what today is about, where she's heading, what she will find. Her brain is thick as though the synapses have corroded. Her mind slithers round the questions she poses, her imagination stalls, slack-jawed and puzzled.

They arrive and she looks at the solid stone building, golden in the sunshine.

They've agreed that Pam will come inside with her but wait while she has the viewing.

The viewing.

She remembers fetching clothes to the funeral director for Phil, and then in turn for Mike. Taking Vicky to see her father, giving her the choice, but advising she grasp the chance to say goodbye in person. To see him gone. It would help her comprehend his death. *Phil has left the building.* Vicky sobbing and saying he looked all plastic like an ancient Action Man with make-up on.

Of course, she isn't bringing clothes for Vicky. This isn't that sort of viewing. And there will be no slot booked in any chapel of rest this time.

The detective, Leo, appears with his young partner. She will stay with Pam if needed, but Pam says she's fine.

Another man explains that Elizabeth will be able to view Vicky's remains through a screen.

'No,' she says.

'Our policy—'

Leo cuts him off. 'The post-mortem is complete. Elizabeth's been informed of the preliminary results. There won't be any problem.' *Her broken bones, tearing her clothes off in delirium from hypothermia.*

The man looks as though he'd like to object, but eventually he says, 'Give me a few moments.'

When he comes back he gives Elizabeth a pair of disposable gloves, then they follow him to a room divided in two by a partition. The top half of the divide is glass. A doorway connects the two areas. In the inner room is a bier covered in a white sheet. There is a chair beside it. The man leaves them.

Elizabeth looks at the gloves. *Really?*

She looks to Leo. He shrugs his eyes, agreeing it's not necessary.

'I can wait here,' Leo says. 'Or I can come.'

'Thank you. Here is fine.'

'Take your time,' he says. 'As long as you need.'

'Thank you.'

She doesn't hesitate but walks through the door and closes it.

The room is cool but not cold, with lights in the ceiling. An artificial glow but not as bright as they might be, she thinks. Like those lights in hospital that you can dim.

She stands by the bier and takes the edge of the sheet in her fingers. It is soft and clean, fold marks visible. Taking a breath she turns it back once, then again until everything is exposed.

Oh Vicky. Oh my Vicky. Oh my sweet girl.

Her throat closes and her eyes burn. She breathes in again, consciously. Smells something chemical, astringent. A tang like vinegar. From the sheet perhaps?

These bones, formed inside her all those years ago. Laid out now in place. Some have become detached so several ribs are on the table inside Vicky's ribcage.

Gently Elizabeth places her palm on the top of the skull. The dome has a faint sheen, is lightly mottled. Fine lines wriggle across the sides where the bones fused. She curls her fingers round and closes her eyes. It feels smooth to the touch, cool.

My love.

Slowly, slowly she does the same with each set of bones in turn, tracing her fingers over them, touching, holding, stroking.

Down the arms to the hands. Ever so lightly over the ribs then around the wings of the pelvis. Down the long leg bones. At Vicky's feet are small, scattered fragments. These she tiptoes over with her fingertips.

She sits at last, moving the chair so she can cap Vicky's skull and rest her other hand on Vicky's sternum. Giving salutations to the places that housed her mind and her heart. In Elizabeth's head a mantra. *Oh Vicky. Oh love. I love you. I've got you now.*

Grief is a hard rock in her chest and round it flows a tide of memories of her darling girl. Each one bringing pleasure. And deep pain. For all that is lost. For a future that will never come.

Elizabeth sits until her back aches, sending daggers of pain up into her neck. What feels like hours pass, though she can't be sure — time has long since lost all meaning. The tips of her fingers go numb, her bladder protests.

Then she rises and kisses her daughter, her lips making a faint tacky sound. Once above each eye socket and a final kiss farewell on the top of her head.

* * *

Shan

Leo has told Shan that although Vicky's death may have been as a result of an accident, they need to explore all other possibilities and see where the evidence takes them. Rule out foul play. Or rule it in.

Shan works her way through the missing persons files on Vicky Mott. Skim-reads statements and documents relating to the appeal. Opens a large brown envelope of photographs, details and evidence numbers on the reverse of each one.

There are two pictures of the cottage where the students stayed, one each of its front and back aspects. And the photo used in the appeal: Vicky in her red coat, jeans and red boots. She's looking straight at the camera with a smile that reaches her eyes. Her light brown hair is streaked with bright pink and blue. She looks like the sort of person Shan might have enjoyed a drink or a night out with at the same age. She wears neon pink earrings like little aliens and a smiley badge pinned on her coat. The smiley has starry eyes.

Shan reads an A4 version of the appeal poster.

MISSING

Have you seen Vicky Mott?
Vicky disappeared from Tollthorpe on Sunday, 11 May 1997.
Vicky is 5' 8" tall and of slim build.
She has brown hair, coloured pink and blue, and hazel eyes.
Vicky was wearing a red waxed parka, jeans and red Kickers boots.
Please contact North Yorkshire Police with information.

Leo is in his office. She goes to the connecting door, opens it. 'Where did the appeal photo come from?' Shan asks.

Leo scrunches up his mouth. 'I don't know. What does it say in the file?'

She can't find a reference to the original source. 'Would it be from Elizabeth?'

'Possibly. We usually ask the family.'

Shan hesitates. Is it crass to bother Elizabeth now, with this query?

Leo second-guesses her thoughts. 'She'll want to help in any way she can.'

Elizabeth answers Shan's call quickly.

'One of her friends took it. Usha had it; it was her camera. The police cropped it so it would just show Vicky. Have you spoken to Usha?'

'No . . . not yet.'

'Well, she'll tell you if I remember right.'

'Are you still in touch?' Shan asks. It sounds that way.

'Yes. Christmas cards, that sort of thing. Melanie too. Usha rang yesterday. And Melanie sent a sympathy card.'

'Do you have their numbers?'

'Yes, just a moment.'

There's a crackle as Elizabeth moves her phone.

Shan is surprised they've kept in touch. Then wonders whether she's right to be. But wouldn't it be painful for Elizabeth to hear about her daughter's friends making lives, building careers, getting married, maybe having children of their own while Vicky stays lost, frozen in time? And wouldn't it be awkward for Usha and Melanie, wouldn't there be some sort of guilt on their behalf? Shan imagines most people would let the contact slowly fade away.

If something happened to Erin, would Shan still keep in touch with her in-laws? The thought of losing Erin makes her shiver, the room feels colder. *Of course you would*. Especially once the baby comes. They'll be its grandparents, after all.

'Hello?' Elizabeth is back on the line. 'Here you are.' She reads out the two numbers and Shan thanks her.

She goes through to Leo, tells him what she's learned. 'And I've contact details for them both.'

'Okay, we'll set up a time to visit them. Where are they based?'

'Not sure yet.' She should have asked Elizabeth, saved time. 'I'll find out.' She pauses on her way back to her room. 'No one could give Terence Bielby an alibi for when Vicky went missing. He was home alone, right? The other victims, were they walking at a particular time of day?'

'Early morning, you mean?' Leo says.

'It could be a pattern.'

It takes them a few minutes to get the details from the histories of Martha Weiss, the American visitor, Katy Fallows from Ripon, and Veronica White, the young fell runner. Martha and Veronica were out early but Katy Fallows only set off at lunchtime.

'You won't have had any GPS or mobile phone cell tracing back then?' Shan says.

'No. The only thing like that was that Bielby date stamped his photos, and kept copies on file. Some were used in evidence to prove he had at least been in the vicinity on the days of the murders.'

'He didn't photograph his victims?'

'No. He's not stupid.'

'Can we check the festival photos?' Shan asks. 'See what times they show?'

Leo points to the files and she brings them over.

They sit either side of his desk to go through the contact sheets from the festival weekend.

Leo gets out a magnifying glass.

Shan chuckles. 'Very Sherlock.' She wishes for a split second she hadn't said anything. *This is your boss!* But Leo just says, 'Your time will come.' And she relaxes.

The thumbnail images give a flavour of the festival, everything from shots of the crowd dancing, a sea of arms waving glow-sticks, to more individual shots — a couple touching palms and foreheads together, stalls selling burgers and curries and ice creams. A juggler with fire sticks, someone in a Teletubby costume, a woman on stilts wearing a periwig and frothy gown accompanied by a pantomime camel. Close-ups of unnamed individuals lost in music, or taking time out. A boy crying, his mouth a hole of misery, a woman with hennaed hands. A silhouette of a roadie in action. The guys on the sound desk. The stage a dazzle of light and dry ice.

Shan finds the series of shots that Bielby took of Vicky and her friends at the festival on the Friday afternoon. Usha wears a yellow dress. Her hair is long and plaited. She's pretty, with round cheeks and large eyes. Not as tall as Vicky and Melanie but not as short as Dee Price. Dee's in combats and a lime green string vest over a black T-shirt. Her head is shaved around her ears, longer on top, black tipped with bright green. A row of studs in her ears.

Shan keeps looking, reading the time stamps.

'These are the last ones on the Saturday.' She indicates the next series of shots. 'Well, early Sunday. The festival wound down about three. The final shot of the band is 2.30 a.m.'

'The following day, the first film puts Bielby back at the site at noon. Nothing before then.' Leo taps the sheets he has.

'That fits with his alibi,' Shan says.

'Which no one can verify.'

She frowns. 'What do we do?'

'We keep looking. We follow every lead until it's exhausted. And we talk to him.'

'To Bielby?'

'Yes, unless you—'

'No,' she interjects. 'I want to come.' Though the prospect makes her guts turn over. 'I want to meet him, see what he says.'

'It's all experience,' Leo says. 'Can't have too much of that.'

CHAPTER FIVE

Leo

Luke's motorbike is in the lean-to. But even if Leo hadn't seen it he'd know Luke was home as soon as he stepped into the house. A different energy in the air, a tension as though the molecules themselves have rearranged in reaction to Luke's presence.

Luke and Ange are in the kitchen.

She flashes Leo a look of warning. *He's here, go easy.*

Luke is opening a pizza box, the smell of oregano and garlic enticing.

'All right, Luke?' Leo says. 'How you doing?'

'Fine.' Luke tears the pizza into slices.

Leo wants to hug his son. That used to happen, a big hug, Leo's arms around his shoulders, Luke's head on his chest. He can't remember how long ago it changed but knows now he'd be rebuffed. Luke would either shrug away or stand frigid and unyielding. Instead Leo engineers a move to the sink, patting Luke on the shoulder as he passes.

Ange puts a container in the microwave. 'Nearly done,' she says to Leo.

He tries to read her words, her expression. Has she already talked to him? Is everything okay? Does she know

71

where Luke's been the last couple of nights? Leo fails to find any answers.

Leo sets the table.

Luke lifts his box; he's taking his food upstairs.

'Fancy a beer?' Leo asks. 'Eat with us?'

It's bribery. But it works.

'Okay.' Luke puts his pizza on its cardboard platter on the table.

'Ange, you want one?'

'Yes, sure.'

The microwave beeps and Ange gets their food out.

Leo fetches three bottles from the fridge and glasses for him and Ange.

'Cheers!' Leo raises a toast when they're all seated.

Luke rolls his eyes but clinks his bottle against their glasses.

He looks well enough, Leo thinks. Clear-eyed, clean-shaven. Wet hair, so he must have showered since he got back.

'Billy Ollershot's back in hospital,' Ange says. Their neighbour opposite. 'Ambulance came this morning. Still . . . ninety-five.'

'Is he ninety-five?' Luke's surprise seems genuine.

Luke used to tag along with Leo or Ange when Billy needed help, clearing snow or cutting back the trees that ring his garden. Fetching shopping when Billy's eyesight went and he had to give up his driver's licence.

Leo casts about for something to say, something neutral, a safe topic. When all he really wants to do is grill Luke about his whereabouts over the last days.

'Your mum's up for a prize. Did she tell you?'

Ange beams.

Luke shakes his head. 'What for?' He folds a slice of pizza, takes a bite.

'A new award. "Human + Nature". With a plus sign in the middle.' Ange makes the shape with her forefingers.

'Nice one.' Luke smiles. A glow that lights a fuse in Leo's heart.

Leo scoops up a forkful of ratatouille and decides it needs more salt.

'They longlisted my Ghost Trees project,' Ange says. Her pieces superimpose images and sculptures of trees on locations where they've been removed. 'They're looking for projects that address climate change.'

The temperature in the room plummets. Luke blinks slowly then takes a chug from his beer.

Leo braces himself for the coming snort, the lip-curling ridicule, the tirade. How global warming is a myth, a conspiracy cooked up by world financiers to control people.

But Luke just scoffs a laugh, returns to his pizza.

Leo and Ange have agreed that there is no point arguing anymore with him. Whether it's fake moon landings or chem trails or white replacement theory, he simply won't listen to reason.

Debates in the past have been so heated, seen Leo roaring with frustration, 'How can you be so bloody stupid?' Ange pleading, 'We didn't bring you up to hate people, to say those sorts of things. This isn't you, Luke.'

Luke, intractable, filled with a sense of teenage infallibility and rootless rage.

'He isn't just testing boundaries,' Leo said after one particularly vehement argument. 'He's building a wall with bloody barbed wire on top. We're losing him.' Ah, he had wanted to weep, to tear out his hair, his throat a ring of pain.

Now they operate in a sort of no-man's-land, neutral territory for the most part. Though Ange was clear: 'I will not censor myself. Those lunatic ideas, they're not just crackpot. They're harmful, they're dangerous.'

Leo wants to redeem the conversation, such as it is. 'Here's to a win,' he says to Ange. 'It'll pay for insulating the studio.'

'Sod that. It'll pay for a foreign holiday. Anyway, I need to make the shortlist first.' She turns to Luke. 'You been at Jack's?'

Leo holds his breath — will Luke answer?

'Yes.'

'How's he doing?' she asks.

'Same old,' Luke says. 'Their dog had pups. Five. Can't go near 'em yet.'

'What breed?' Leo says.

'Jack Russell. They got buyers lined up. Make a few bob.'

Outside, the sky is darkening to a deep and luminous blue and Leo sees the flash of bats darting past. He hears the call of an owl from the woods at the back, and a blackbird crooning.

'Oh, that reminds me. Can you lend us some money?' It occurs to Leo that this is why his son's come home.

'Of course,' Leo says. 'How much?'

'Fifty. I get paid next Tuesday; I'll give it you back then.' Pay is his Jobseeker's Allowance.

'Don't be daft.' Leo wonders what the money is for. He'd never begrudge Luke money to get by, money for treats even. But he's no idea how Luke spends his time when he's out of the house. He wonders what Christopher Hirst has to do with his son. He is half afraid to ask. Does he really want to know?

'Glad you're back. You can give us a hand with the poplars over the way,' Leo says.

'No, I'm off out.' Luke licks his fingers.

'Anywhere nice?' Ange says.

'Dunno.'

'Will you be late?'

'Dunno.'

And that's all they get.

'Drive safe,' Leo says.

Luke goes upstairs and Leo and Ange finish their meal, alert to the creaks of the floorboards above.

Then they hear Luke run down the stairs and the slam of the door. Moments later the bike growls into life, the note of the engine fading as he drives away.

'Jesus.' Leo draws his hand down his face. 'Is this it? Do we just get this for ever?'

'His brain's still developing,' Ange says. 'A few more years and perhaps he'll settle, come to his senses.'

74

Leo regards her, sceptical.

She draws back her hair then lets it fall. 'Maybe he needs to fall in love, meet some wonderful young woman who'll sweep him off his feet, re-educate him.'

'Like you did me?' he says.

'Precisely.'

Leo thinks of Shan. Which is ridiculous — she's pregnant and she's a lesbian. And Chinese. And Luke's a bigot . . . But someone like her. That sort of personality. Though why would anyone like Shan go anywhere near Luke once they knew his opinions?

Ange fetches them another beer. She stands behind Leo and kisses his head, wraps her arms around him, hands on his chest.

'It could be worse,' she says.

'I know.' Luke ill or dying. He could be off his box with a drug habit or suicidal with depression. Or violent.

'All we can do is look out for ourselves and keep on loving him,' Ange says.

The words bring tears to his eyes. He bends his head down, lifts and kisses each of her hands in turn.

'I'm going to have a bath,' he says at last. His joints are griping.

'God, you sexy thing,' she says. 'I might join you.'

He gasps in mock horror. 'No way.' They've tried it before. It's agony with two of them crammed into the old enamel tub.

She laughs and drops her embrace. 'Well, leave the water in. I'll come find you after.'

* * *

Shan

'You're going to see him in prison?' Erin is opening the takeaways.

'Yep.' Shan reaches for a falafel.

75

'Wait!' Erin knocks her hand away.

'Eating for two, here,' Shan protests.

'You're just greedy.'

'*I'm* greedy . . .'

Erin cocks her head. *Don't start.* A gleam in her eye.

'*You're* greedy,' Shan says. 'Was I the one who—'

Erin plucks up a falafel, reaches over and pushes it into Shan's mouth.

'Sho geedy,' Shan says. Her mouth waters and a froth of irrepressible laughter threatens to choke her. She slaps her hand on the surface of the counter until she regains enough control to swallow.

Erin's eyes flash that brilliant blue. It was what first drew Shan's attention. Those blazing blue eyes in a heart-shaped face.

Shan had stared at her across the dance floor and Erin had turned away. Not interested? Already with someone?

Shan told herself to leave it, forget her, but time and again Shan's attention was drawn to the curvy figure with her close-cropped hair.

When Erin next made for the bar, Shan had followed and found space next to her while they waited to be served.

Shan brought her face close to be heard above the music. 'Hi.'

Erin darted a glance at her and nodded then looked away. Those eyes! A rose bloomed on each cheek. Embarrassed? Because of Shan?

'You here with friends?' Shan persisted. It wasn't great but it beat *You come here often?*

'Yes,' Erin mouthed. She looked awkward; something was wrong.

'Anyone special?' Shan asked. *Last try.*

Erin leaned forward and gave her order then shook her head lightly. 'No.' She was studying the bar like she'd never ever seen a countertop before. Another quick glance at Shan but there was no invitation in it.

I give up.

One of the servers reached Shan and she asked for a bottle of Peroni. *Drink this then go.*

Erin disappeared back into the crowd.

Shan felt the night settle into disappointment. She kept up a good front, danced with the friends she'd come along with, finished her bottle then headed for the cloakroom.

Climbing back up the stairs she came face-to-face with Erin.

'Oh, hi,' Shan said. Fingers buttoning her coat.

Erin sat down on a step.

'You okay?' Shan said. She crouched on the step below her.

'There's no one special,' Erin said in a rush. 'If you . . . we could . . .' Her cheeks burned red; she was breathless.

Shan stretched up to kiss her, a gentle, hesitant kiss. Then pulled back to check if this was all right. Erin gave a smile, tremulous. Blue eyes dazzling. Erin reached for her and kissed her back, passionate, hungry. She tasted of lemons.

Shan soon learned that Erin was shy, painfully shy. Social anxiety some people called it. It'd taken Shan a while to understand how deep it ran, how even the simplest encounter could leave Erin feeling exposed, stupid, panicking. And how much it had meant for her to seek out Shan, a stranger in a club, like she did.

'I've never been in prison,' Shan says now.

'Good to know.' Erin hands her a spoon and begins to help herself to the food.

'See, once we nick them it's all down to the courts officers and the prison service.'

'Which prison is it?' Erin says.

'Wakefield.'

'You'll have time to get there all right?'

'Should do, the scan's at eight thirty?' Shan checks.

Erin nods. 'And we're not going to ask about the sex.'

'Correct,' Shan says.

'No gender reveal party?'

Erin's winding her up.

'Well . . . if you really want to . . .' Shan starts. Erin's face contorts, she blinks rapidly, runs a hand over her hair.

Shan laughs. 'Got you!'

They were having a baby — all they needed to know was that it was healthy.

'Oh, I bought you a present,' Erin says.

She disappears into the hall and comes back with a fat paperback book. *1,000 Baby Names.* 'Seeing as we've not got very far.'

'We've got six months to go.' Shan points out.

'All I'm saying is that we can make some lists. We can still wait to see what suits it, like you said.'

Shan knows that Erin already has favourites. May or Cara for a girl, Finn or Gabriel for a boy.

Shan thinks it's going to be impossible to find something perfect, that they both like, and that also reflects the child's mixed heritage: Chinese, English, Irish. Or maybe that should all be jettisoned. They choose a name purely on how it sounds, how it works with their surnames. They find something that has no associations for either of them. Or they invent a name.

What will the baby look like? Will it look Chinese? They'd picked a white sperm donor with blue eyes so there was a chance that it might inherit some of Erin's characteristics. They speculate endlessly.

There are echoes of other questions in Shan's head when they talk like this. Questions about her birth mother. Had she wondered what her baby would look like? Picked a name? Or had Shan just been a problem to be dealt with? Had she planned to give Shan up all along? To be dispatched to the orphanage as soon as she arrived? It was the orphanage who gave Shan her name, which means 'mountain' and also 'coral', depending on how it's pronounced. And if Shan had been a boy would that have made a difference? The one-child policy was in operation when she was born; traditionally boys were seen as more valuable than girls and many parents abandoned their firstborn if it was a girl, hoping to have a boy next time round.

Shan knows nothing about her birth parents. Not one hard fact. They are shadows. Her family history a black hole. Are they even still alive? Do they ever wonder about her? Impossible to know.

She tries not to dwell on it, but now and then the questions grow louder, bringing with them a feeling of utter sadness, of being lost, adrift. And then she feels treacherous because her adoptive parents have been wonderful, done everything possible to make her feel secure, have loved her unreservedly. So why isn't it enough?

* * *

Vicky
1997

Vicky jerks awake to shouting. Hears Melanie on the landing. 'Shut up, Col. Some of us are trying to sleep!' Then the slam of Melanie and Robin's door.

Dee groans and turns over in the bunk above her.

Vicky closes her eyes, tries to reclaim sleep but it's no good. The light is already stealing through the gap in the curtains. She's awake. She takes her duvet downstairs for warmth.

She uses the outside toilet. There are a few spider's webs and some dead daddy longlegs in there but nothing she can't handle.

She makes a cup of coffee and smokes a cigarette. Then settles on the sofa, huddled in her duvet.

Eyes closed she recites from the Audre Lorde piece she is learning in a murmur. She has a faint headache from last night's excesses and the smell of cigarettes in her hair makes her queasy, but it's too early to have a shower; she doesn't want to disturb the others.

She hears footsteps cross the landing and the gurgle of pipes. Someone using the toilet. Then footsteps on the stairs.

Robin appears.

'Oh, hi.' He yawns, scratching the back of his neck. He wears a skater T-shirt and shorts. His arms are covered in fine blond hairs. 'Bad night?'

'I've had worse. Revision.' She holds up her script. 'What about you?'

'Nothing a greasy fry-up won't fix. You hungry?'

'Always.' She smiles.

'Okay.' He goes into the kitchen. She hears the fridge open and then he calls out, 'Bacon, eggs, fried bread, tea?'

'Yes please. Coffee though.'

Robin shuts the kitchen door.

Vicky studies the next section, highlighted in orange marker. She reads it twice, working out the stresses, following the shape of the words on the page. Then closes her eyes and tries to recall them. She falters twice. Rereads it. It would be easier if she got up and moved around, fixing the words with gestures, but she doesn't want to give up the heat from the duvet.

The smell of bacon, savoury, reaches her and her stomach rumbles.

Robin puts his head round the door. 'It's ready.'

'Great.'

She follows him through.

'Wow!' Robin has made huge helpings.

'Well, Melanie and Usha won't need any bacon,' he says. They're veggies.

They sit either side of the table. 'You left them some eggs, though?' she asks, worried for a moment.

'I did.' He smiles. 'And there's plenty of bread and mushrooms.'

Vicky nods, already tucking in. The bacon is crisp and salty. She breaks one of her eggs, dips some in the yolk.

Perfection,' she tells him. 'My compliments to the chef.'

'Noted.'

She can see the hill out of the window, the slope a mix of tawny grass and splashes of green. It's another glorious day. Sparrows fly on to the back wall then off, squabbling audibly.

Somewhere in the village a car engine starts.

Vicky gulps down a mouthful of coffee. 'Is Col all right?'

He breathes out. 'Define all right?'

'Well . . . just . . . Usha seemed a bit—' *Fed up?* Vicky hasn't had the chance to talk to Usha on her own.

Robin grunts. Then swallows. 'She's good for him. He should see that. But yesterday he told her he had one mother and really didn't need another. She was suffocating him.'

'Jesus.' Vicky winces.

'She was only asking him to slow down. But he won't be told,' Robin says.

'Do you think she's right?'

'Yes, but I'm not getting involved.' Robin takes a drink.

'How does he cope with the course, with all the work, when he's off his box half the time?'

'The words "skin" and "teeth" come to mind.' Robin shrugs. 'Leave them to it, I reckon.'

'I don't want her to get hurt,' Vicky says.

Robin stares at her, an indulgent look in his green eyes.

'What?' she says.

'Nothing. So what are you revising?'

'Practical piece. For my exam. It's about this woman called Audre Lorde?' She makes the name a question but he shakes his head.

'Most people haven't heard of her. But she was brilliant. A Black American feminist. A lesbian and a campaigner for civil rights. She was always looking for common ground but she knew it was crucial to celebrate difference too.'

He's grinning.

'Don't laugh!' she says.

'I'm not laughing. I'm appreciating your enthusiasm.'

'Aka patronising me. It's like feminism is a dirty word. We rave on about other struggles. Like with race, we admire Martin Luther King and Gandhi and Nelson Mandela. But sexism, misogyny, anything about women's rights, it's boring and dull. We're shrill and humourless. Like there isn't this massive inequality. Half the human race.'

'I agree,' he says.

She meets his eyes. Does he mean it?

'So, how does it work for you?' He points to her script. 'How do you get it to stick?' He taps his temple.

'I mark it, see?' Vicky shows him the pages. 'Part of it is sort of photographic, along with the sound of the words. And movements.' She swigs more coffee. 'But you must have to memorise loads for medicine,' she points out. 'Biology, anatomy, chemistry.'

'True. It's similar, I guess. Though I've never had to learn speeches.'

'Thought you public-school boys were big into theatre.' She projects the last few words like a Shakespearean actor might.

'Never trodden a board in my life. Cricket, rowing. More my thing.'

'Did you have a whatsit — territorial army?'

'Cadets. Yes.'

Vicky shudders.

'Col got kicked out,' Robin says.

'Why? He shoot someone?'

'He shot a rabbit.'

'Is that bad luck?'

Robin shakes his head. 'More like a bad aim. We were supposed to be doing target practice.'

'Typical — you lot had rabbits, we had rats.'

Outside, the sparrows scatter as a mangy-looking ginger cat leaps up on to the wall. It settles and begins to wash itself.

'Thanks for breakfast. I'll wash up,' she says.

'Audre Lorde.'

'Well remembered. You ever read any poetry?' Vicky smirks. 'Or was it just Kipling and the war poets?'

'Now who's patronising? Yeats, Dickinson, Heaney, Hughes, Plath. Some women in there.'

They both laugh.

Robin rubs a knuckle across the tip of his nose. She feels a rush of warmth, then a jolt, as if she's tripped, stumbled, like those dreams that wake you. A moment where everything prickles, shimmers.

She distracts herself, telling him more about their set texts.

When Dee comes in Vicky feels they've been interrupted, that the conversation has to change.

Robin starts teasing Dee about her singing the night before as they walked back to the cottage with the roar of the festival drumming in their blood.

Vicky needs a cigarette. She pats her pocket as she stands up, picks up her coffee and escapes outside.

Idiot, she tells herself. *It's just this place, the lack of sleep, the high from last night. Just get a grip.*

* * *

Leo
2019

Leo picks Shan up in Keighley after her scan.

'How'd it go?'

'Fine, thanks. Pretty amazing to see it, the heart beating and—' She blows out air. 'Makes it real.'

'Yes,' he says. He remembers the grainy image of Luke they stuck to the fridge. All the hope and apprehension that came with it. And realising it was actually happening. There was no way back.

There's an iron sky, low and brooding. The day is warm, the atmosphere close and sticky.

'Monster Mansion.' Shan is reading about the prison's history on her phone. It's a category A prison, holding lifers in the main, notorious names among them.

'People do monstrous things,' Leo says. 'But I don't think the terminology is helpful.'

'Me neither,' Shan says. 'And monsters are made, not born.'

'What about psychopaths?' Leo asks.

'Well, most psychopaths aren't monsters, are they? They don't do terrible things. But the ones in Wakefield? I reckon they'll have abusive histories, traumatic childhoods. It's cycles, isn't it, trauma and violence going round and round.'

It's refreshing to be working with someone like-minded. Leo knows plenty of police officers are happy enough to enforce the law but couldn't give a monkey's about the causes behind offending. The nick-'em-and-stick-'em-inside brigade. Throw away the key. They've scant interest in the fact that the whole system's failing. Rehabilitation a joke. You'd be forgiven for thinking that Robert Peel had never placed prevention as the first priority in policing.

'Okay, so how d'you break the cycle?' Leo says.

'Lot of it is down to poverty and inequality. We need social welfare schemes, improve life chances, tackle domestic violence. It should all be joined up — welfare, education, security, work, housing.' Shan is waving her arms about, emphasising the points she makes. She catches herself and apologises. 'Sorry.'

'Don't mind me,' Leo says. 'All makes sense. Just need someone in power with the balls to shake things up that much. But I can't see that coming anytime soon.'

'Hopeful start to the day,' Shan says.

And he grins.

An accident on the A650 holds them up so by the time they reach Wakefield they are running a few minutes late. Shan has rung ahead at Leo's request to explain the delay. The last thing he wants is for them to be refused entry and have to make the journey a second time.

The prison is near the town centre and Leo parks in a multistorey.

A CCTV video recording of the meeting has been requested and Bielby has agreed to an interview under caution. He's waived his right to a solicitor. Leo goes over all these details for Shan as they walk through the shoppers to the jail.

'Love Lane?' Shan reads as they turn on to the street.

'Irony is not dead,' Leo observes.

The prison sits behind a formidable wall. Clock tower visible. Leo knows the place from a previous visit. Most of the buildings are Victorian, built in panopticon style, a K-shape. One long wing with radial wings running off at diagonals from the middle. Everything visible from the core.

The visitor centre is through the newer buildings at the front. Legal visits take place in individual rooms, each partitioned by a screen so there is no possibility of contact.

The security checks are rigorous. They leave their coats and bags, phones and keys in a locker. Walk through an X-ray scanner. Show their passports and have a photograph taken for a visitor's pass. The materials they want to bring — files, pen and paper — are examined and scanned.

In the waiting area Leo can hear the background noise of the prison. The cacophony of shouting that serves as communication between the inmates in their cells. The place smells chemical, like cleaning fluids with an undertone of body odour.

A prison officer leads them in and they find Bielby already waiting at his side of the partition. The room is plain, painted light blue.

'Mr Bielby,' Leo says. 'Apologies for the delay.'

Bielby nods. There is an unhealthy pallor to his skin, the result of being locked indoors, away from sunlight and fresh air. He has long, stringy hair, a thick moustache. It's possible still to see that he was an attractive-looking man in his time.

The video recorder unit is close to their seats. 'You know the drill?' the prison officer asks. 'This button to start and that one to stop it.'

Leo starts the recorder, reads out the caution and gives their full titles for the recording.

'We have recently recovered the remains of a woman called Vicky Mott. She disappeared in 1997 while visiting the festival in Garsdale. She was last seen in Tollthorpe village on the morning of Sunday the eleventh of May. Can you tell us anything about her death?'

'Me?' He feigns surprise. 'What makes you think I have anything to do with it?'

Leo ignores his question.

'Please take a look at this.' Leo produces the photograph of Vicky and her girlfriends at the festival. He reads out the evidence number. Then turns the picture so that Bielby has a good view through the partition.

'This is Vicky, second right,' Leo says.

'Pretty girl.' Bielby smiles. He slides a look at Shan, who is taking notes at Leo's side. Leo senses her tensing.

'You took this photo,' Leo says.

'Guilty as charged. But not a crime as far as I'm aware.' His eyes stay on Shan.

'This was taken on Friday the ninth of May. Did you see Vicky again after that?'

'Not a clue. There were thousands of them there.' As they talk Bielby strokes his moustache with thumb and fore-finger slowly. His fingers are stained brown and yellow with nicotine. Leo finds something almost sexual in the gesture. But tries not to be deflected from his purpose.

'What about the morning of the eleventh? Where were you?' Leo asks.

Bielby makes a show of remembering. Hoods his eyes then nods.

'Asleep most of it,' he says eventually. 'I was contracted to work from midday. You should have all this in your files. No?'

'Oh, we have,' Leo agrees. 'But stories change. People remember things after the fact.'

'It's not a story.' The smile disappears.

'Can anyone verify your whereabouts that morning?'

'I doubt it. I live alone. And I was too busy to be enter-taining.' He splits the last word into syllables, then wets his lips. 'Great atmosphere. Very long day but some decent bands.' He returns his gaze to Shan. Maybe Leo shouldn't have brought her, exposed her to this sort of attention. But she wanted to come, wanted to learn. And she's probably already had to deal with this sort of behaviour on the job.

Leo can barely imagine what life inside is like for this man or any of his fellow prisoners. The interminable monotony, the deprivations and degradations. Wakefield has a reasonable reputation according to its last report, but then again what's considered reasonable in the UK is a far cry from what's acceptable in most of Europe.

'You drove from home to the festival?' Leo says.

'That's right.'

'So what time did you arrive?'

'Ten to twelve?' Bielby says.

'You can't be sure?'

'It's twenty-two years ago. What were you doing?'

Supporting Ange who was expecting and sick as a dog, working shifts in uniform. Finding it all overwhelming: work, home, the prospect of fatherhood. Trying to keep on top of everything and not go under. Putting a brave face on as best as he could. Crying in the car on the worst days.

'That journey takes a quarter of an hour?' Leo estimates.

Bielby gives a nod.

'So you left at 11.35 a.m. You hadn't been out of your home earlier that day?'

'That's right,' Bielby says.

'You ever done any caving?' Leo asks.

'Caving?' He was thrown.

'Potholing?'

'Not for pleasure.' Bielby buys time.

'Go on,' Leo says. His heart pumps a bit faster. Is he actually on to something?

'I photographed Gaping Gill on occasion, and Stump Cross Caverns. For magazines, coffee-table spreads and the like.'

'What about Toller Fell? Anywhere up there?'

'No,' he says. 'I thought she was found in Lund Seat. Slack Pot, that's what it said on the news.'

'You have a TV?' Leo says.

'Model prisoner, Detective.' Meaning his good behaviour had earned him the privilege.

'You know the pub in Tollthorpe?'

'Yes.'

'You did some work for them, I believe.'

'What's that got to do with anything?'

'You were living in Sedbergh at the time so your journey to and from the festival would take you past the Tollthorpe turning, yes?'

Bielby doesn't answer.

'Is that right?' Leo says.

'Yes.'

'Did you stop in Tollthorpe on the eleventh of May 1997?'

'No.'

'Did you visit there that day?'

'No.'

'Did you have anything to do with the death of Vicky Mott?'

'No. Nothing.'

'Did you have any involvement in the disappearance of Vicky Mott?'

'No. And I shouldn't be here, you know. I never killed anyone.' He stabs each word with a forefinger pointed their way. 'It's a gross miscarriage of justice. I'm an innocent man. Write that in your book, sweetheart,' he spits at Shan.

Leo stares at him. 'You have the right to appeal, Mr Bielby. If new evidence comes to light. Has it?'

Bielby's look sharpens, his eyes drilling into Leo's. It's unpleasant but Leo waits before he looks away. He knows better than to appear unsettled.

'You pleaded not guilty; the evidence was circumstantial but there was no way of explaining away your DNA under the fingernails of Veronica White.'

'It was an error. Contamination. Must have been. Like I said, I'm an innocent man. But enough about me. How's the big bad world? And you, sweetheart, are you a trainee? He looking after you all right?'

'I think that's it.' Leo moves to turn off the tape.

'You've only just got here,' Bielby says. 'You can't go already. And there is something else . . .' He hesitates, suddenly coy.

Leo waits.

'It may be nothing at all, but there were rumours at the festival that some of the musicians were abusing their positions.' His gaze switches back to Shan.

'How do you mean?' Leo says.

'You always get groupies, nothing new there. But word was things got a little out of hand.' His face brightens as he talks. 'All hushed up, of course. Things went too far. Some girls got more than they bargained for. A lot more.'

'Which musicians?' Shan asks.

Bielby shakes his head. 'So long ago.'

'This is relevant how?' Leo says.

'Well, if your Vicky got sucked into something she couldn't handle — a party that got out of hand, say — if there was abusive behaviour backstage, who's to say that didn't spill over? Vicky takes a walk on the moors after too much indulgence. Leading someone on. Someone who was determined to take what he wanted. A predator. Pretty young thing, no one about on the tops. No one to hear her scream.'

There's a strain in his voice and he shifts position in his chair, and Leo realises with a rush of distaste that they are being played. Bielby is getting off on the tripe he's spouting.

Leo stands abruptly. 'Interview terminated.'

Shan looks up at him, disconcerted by the sudden shift.

Bielby laughs. 'Delighted. Loved our little chat. Do come again. Come as often as you like.' He slaps the innuendo on with a trowel.

* * *

Shan

It's been a waste of time as far as Shan can tell. And she's disappointed. But what did she expect? That Bielby would break the habit of a lifetime and actually confess? He came across like a disgraced, ageing rock star with his long, greasy hair, his gravelly voice and his *sweethearts*.

As they walk back to the multistorey, Leo dismisses his chatter about the dodgy behaviour by the bands. 'There were never any whispers. He was spinning a fantasy. His fantasy. See where he ended up — with a woman on the moors, a predator.'

'Ah shit,' Shan says. 'But shouldn't we check?' Imagine if they ignore his tale and then it turns out to have some connection to what happened to Vicky.

'Yes, we should. We'll talk to the local newspaper reporter at the time, Keith Sykes. If anyone heard anything dodgy about the festival it'd be him.'

The heavens have opened. Rain is coming down hard, rivers run in the gutters. People move briskly, many wielding umbrellas.

Shan sees a man sitting on a low wall with a supermarket trolley. She takes him for homeless, the old bags piled high in the trolley, a beer can in his hand. He hasn't looked for shelter but sits stoic in the teeming rain. She feels her heart dip with sorrow for him. Wonders what his story is.

At the car, they shed wet jackets and Shan shakes the worst of the moisture from her hair.

Driving out of the car park, Leo sighs. 'We've nothing from him, and the chance of his or anyone else's DNA being found on any of Vicky's things from the cave are pretty much zero.'

Shan feels hot and cross and suddenly hungry. 'So, what now?'

'We check his alibi, talk to his neighbours at the time, see if that turns anything up.' There's a flat tone in Leo's voice and Shan can tell he's pessimistic like she is.

'Today?'

'Good a time as any,' Leo says.

She gives her own sigh, stretches her feet out.

'No one ever said it would be easy.'

'I know.'

'You do what you can,' he says. 'Drive yourself nuts otherwise.'

She needs to pee again. 'Can we stop at the services?'

'Sure. There should be a place just outside Leeds.'

'I'll check.' She opens the maps app on her phone.

The rain grows even heavier so the wipers can barely cope. The world beyond the windscreen a watery blur.

* * *

By the time they arrive at Sedbergh the storm has moved off to the south and the rain has stopped. The trees are still dripping steadily, the ground beneath them littered with a green confetti of seeds and petals. Sprays of white hawthorn glimmer bright. Cow parsley bows in the verges. Everything looks lush, a thousand shades of green visible in the woods and fields. When they get out at Bielby's old address on the outskirts of the village, the air is a heady mix of floral scents and wet wood and stone.

Pebbledash bungalows are arranged in a cul-de-sac, half a dozen in all. The gardens are open plan at the front. Bielby lived in the first property on the left.

Of the residents they speak to, only one household, a married couple, lived there back in 1997. Eager to help, the Cotters welcome the detectives in, offering them tea and cake. But they can't remember what they were doing back in May of that year.

'Did you know Terence Bielby?' Shan asks.

'Good bloke,' the husband says. 'Or so we thought. The shock when it all came out. He'd do anything for anybody.'

'He had us fooled, good and proper,' the wife says. 'Sheer wickedness. Those poor women. You should talk to Ned Lister. If anyone saw something he'd be the one.'

'Postie,' the husband says. 'They always know what's what.'

'He was at number 2, opposite Terence Bielby's. He's in The Aspens now, the residential care home on the way to

Austwick. His legs gave up the ghost and he decided it was for the best. We go now and again for a get-together. Places there are like gold dust.'

'Aye, and you need gold dust to pay for 'em and all,' the husband says.

'So you'll not be putting me there, then?' the wife says.

'Workhouse for the likes of us, lass.'

* * *

The Aspens is smart, bright, like a comfortable hotel. Fresh flowers and houseplants everywhere. The upholstered chairs look brand new. The air smells of fresh coffee and baking bread. There's a buzz of chatter coming from one of the lounges off the large foyer. And a group of women coming out of the lift are roaring with laughter at something.

We should all have this, Shan thinks. The contrast with the home her grandma died in is striking.

A staff member in dark overalls pushes a woman in a wheelchair through the foyer. The care worker is Southeast Asian and there's a flicker of recognition, fleeting, almost hidden, between her and Shan as they pass.

Ned Lister welcomes the interruption to his afternoon and leaves the card game he's playing to talk to them in one of the conservatories at the back of the building. A cat reclines on the arm of a chair, opening one eye as they come in.

Outside, a bird feeder is alive with goldfinches and long-tailed tits while a squirrel makes fruitless ambushes.

The old man manoeuvres his wheelchair into a space between the other seats and listens intently as Leo outlines the reason for their visit.

'Stan Cotter said you'd talked to them. You reckon Terence Bielby killed the lass?' Ned Lister wears a grim expression.

'We're just trying to confirm whether he was at home on the morning of the eleventh of May. Up until half past eleven.'

'That's what he's told you?' He looks away as if disgusted.

'We know it's a long time ago,' Shan says.

'No,' he says. His hand tightens on the arm of his wheelchair. 'I saw him. Early. Six o'clock. Postman, I was. I remember he was just getting into his car and I'd never usually see him out at that time. So I stopped for a word. He was going up to the festival, he said. Get some photographs before the programme started. I told him my granddaughter was there with her pals. Lot of the local kids were. So I was glad to hear it was all going okay.'

Shan's mouth feels dry. 'You're sure it was the eleventh?'

'Yes, that's her birthday, our Lizzie's. I bought her the ticket as her present, see.'

Bielby lied! His alibi's not sound. Shan feels like whooping with joy.

'It's a poor do, isn't it? Lass like that, the family waiting all this time. I hope you nail the bugger,' Ned Lister says.

As they reach the car Shan gets a call from Melanie Quinn, a reply to the voicemail message she left.

'I'm sorry to not get back to you sooner,' Melanie says. 'And Vicky. I don't know what to say. I can hardly believe it.' There's a pause and then she goes on more briskly, 'Would tomorrow evening be any good, around six o'clock? I'll be in theatre until then.'

'Where are you based?' Shan says. Hoping it's not Bristol or Edinburgh or London, somewhere hours and hours away.

'York Hospital,' Melanie says. 'If you ask for me at the main reception.'

'Just a moment, please.'

Shan checks with Leo, who agrees. They've already booked a meeting with Usha Bhatti in Leeds for the morning.

'Yes, that's good,' Shan says. 'We'll see you tomorrow. Thank you.'

Leo's phone pings. He checks it. Nods. 'Report from the other items recovered from the cavern. Metal fragments have been identified as a belt buckle, rivets from denim jeans and a key.'

'The back door key to the cottage was never found,' Shan says. It all fits. But she's still thinking about the man behind bars. 'He lied. Bielby. His alibi doesn't stand up.'

'That's right.'

She senses reservation. 'But?'

'Look, it's a start but that's all.'

'Yes, but we can go back and challenge him.'

'And he can continue to lie through his teeth. We need more,' Leo says. 'He can turn round and tell us Ned's right, he *was* up early, he'd forgotten. He went to photograph before things kicked off. End of.'

Shan imagines it. Bielby out early, driving up from Sedbergh.

'Can you see Toller Fell from the main road?' she asks. 'Can you see the path?'

Leo narrows his eyes. 'I'm not sure.'

'Can we drive that way?'

They do. And as the road winds up around Toller Fell there's a stretch where the hamlet and the path up the hill are clearly visible.

'You're thinking he saw her? Opportunistic?' Leo says.

'Yes. Like with his other victims. He drives down to Tollthorpe and follows her.'

Leo is quiet.

'It could work,' she says.

'It could. It's a possibility but it's not the only one.'

She casts about for what they might do to flesh out her theory, or further dismantle any alibi of Bielby's. 'Can we find out if there was any record of Bielby arriving at the festival site? Would he have been checked in?'

'I don't know. But if we find out who the promoters were, see if they're still around, if there are records.'

Shan yawns, can't help herself, and apologises.

'Call it a day?' Leo says. He has to drive her back home before he can return to his.

'Yes.'

It's getting late. But the nights are light. She loves this time of year, the evening sky more beautiful than that in the daytime. If their little garden's dried off they could sit out for a bit.

She texts Erin with an ETA. Receives a row of hugs and kisses in reply.

Then she settles in to read through her notes as Leo drives. Making sure she's got everything down, adding any postscripts she might need to. And hoping tomorrow will bring even more progress.

CHAPTER SIX

Elizabeth

The rain sweeps down the valley in gauzy veils.

'Ghost rain', Vicky called it as a child. Her imagination was boundless, it seemed. As soon as she could string words together she was inventing stories, dreaming characters out of anything to hand. She spent half her childhood in fancy dress. Elizabeth regularly raided the jumble sales at school or charity shops for items to add to the dressing-up box. Hats and waistcoats, frocks from the 1940s and fifties with wasp-like waists — all several sizes too small for most of the women Elizabeth knew but perfect for a little girl. One time a red velvet jacket with a mandarin collar and faded yellow brocade trim — a marching band costume perhaps? An old morning suit. A Stetson and cowboy boots. An Indian tunic in rich turquoise, studded with tiny silver mirrors. A green fun-fur throw that became a dinosaur outfit.

With a simple cardboard box Vicky was a robot, a magician's rabbit, a pirate in a boat.

The house falls quiet as the boiling kettle switches off. Elizabeth goes through to make tea.

There are things she needs to do, arrangements to make.

She stirs the tea and dumps the used bag in the compost caddy.

A funeral. But what? Burial? Cremation? What would Vicky want? It's not a conversation she'd ever had with her daughter. Never imagined she'd need to.

She sits down and blows on her tea. She dredges her memories trying to remember whether Vicky expressed any opinion when Phil was cremated.

Phil's ashes were interred at the cemetery. It seemed important then that she and Vicky had somewhere to go, to take flowers, to remember him. A ritual. But that doesn't feel right now for Vicky.

She's already been buried.

It hurts to think of that, of her last moments. Leo has explained that they can't be sure when she died or what the cause was. And they still didn't know if anyone else was involved. But what is clear is that Vicky survived the fall, that she was injured and was alive for some time afterwards.

That stark reality worms its way round and round in her mind. It makes her heart ache but she knows there is no point trying to quash it. She needs to face it, unflinching. Let it burrow further, deeper, until the pain becomes familiar, until she is acclimatised to it.

Acceptance? Maybe. Who cares. She pushes the tea aside and makes herself a gin and tonic. Mainly gin.

I can't bury her again. Not even her ashes. She needs the light, the air.

Anger blindsides her, a wash of rage that makes her slam her fist on to the table and scream aloud.

This is so wrong. So unfair. She weeps furious tears; her nose runs with snot.

Oh Vicky, Vicky, Vicky.

She wipes her face, blows her nose on sheets of kitchen towel.

This is how it ends, she thinks. Her mind circling back over the years. All the fantasies she weaved to cradle her hope.

That Vicky had some sort of crisis, a mental break that made her leave her friends and family, leave everything behind. That she created a new life, joining new-age travellers or running off to the circus. Okay, a cliché, but it had helped.

Or Vicky had been kidnapped but escaped eventually, abused and damaged so that she'd not run home to Elizabeth. Not yet, but would someday find her way back.

She was working for an NGO on the ground overseas.

Homeless, itinerant, on the streets.

A letter. *Dear Mum, I'm so sorry I've not written before . . .* Elizabeth gasping aloud, eyes flying over the lines, Vicky's scrappy handwriting unmistakable.

The phone ringing, 'Mum?'

'Vicky?'

'I'm so sorry, Mum. I know I should have been in touch but things have been really hard . . .'

A knock at the door, Vicky there in the flesh. Looking just the same. Elizabeth opening her arms. Her daughter falling into her embrace. Clutching her tight. Breathing her in.

After all, there are people who went missing but turned up safe years later.

She'd be single and passionate about her work or married with twins and a baby on the way, a writer or an artist. She'd be an animator working in computer games, or voicing the characters. She'd be a Buddhist monk, her head shaved, radiating peace. She'd be mentally frail but volunteering at an animal rescue charity or a food bank, living on disability benefits.

She'd be alive. She'd be alive. She'd be alive.

When the gin begins to blur the edges, Elizabeth pours another then chides herself into making some food. Fusilli with mushrooms and garlic sauce.

She tears fresh basil from the plant on the windowsill to scatter over the pasta and breathes in the pungent scent.

She is crying again.

But she has made progress. *Baby steps for my baby.*

Vicky will be cremated. And her ashes scattered.

Elizabeth can't think where would be a fitting place.

Time yet for that. All the time in the world.

* * *

Nat, the caver, is almost breathless as he lays out what they've found for Leo and Shan. He's come into the station with Tom Bairstow.

'I was working in the tunnel that leads off the far side of the cavern and I reached a section where there was a partial blockage, a rockfall. I wasn't sure whether I'd be able to shift anything or whether we'd need to bring in some heavy-duty tools, use props to shore it up.'

He shows them an image of the boulders, only a slender gap visible. 'I decided to have a go.'

'I wasn't consulted by the way,' Tom Bairstow puts in. 'Or there'd have been a fuller risk assessment.'

'Yeah, exactly.' Nat grins. 'No, straight up, I knew what I was doing. I know the dangers. I could see this stone at the top, the blocky one, wasn't supporting anything. When I shone the torch I could see nothing was touching it. And when I pressed it there was some motion. So I levered it to the right and edged it back. It took a fair while but eventually . . .'

He shows them the resulting hole.

'I could just fit through. From there on in it's low but not too tight, almost level.'

They follow the footage. Leo finds himself holding his breath.

'Now look,' Nat says. 'This is near a bend in the tunnel.'

A small green tube, the size of a thumb and a blob of rust. *A shotgun cartridge? Too flat.*

'Disposable lighter,' Shan says. 'Did Vicky smoke?'

'We'll find out,' Leo says.

'Then it was another forty metres,' Nat continues. 'Took me a while, nothing of interest. I'll jump ahead.' Nat runs the film on, the limestone tunnel jerking here and there, twisting and turning until he hits pause.

'Okay. This spot here is below one of the abandoned lead mine shafts on Toller Fell. It was one of the most promising from the survey.'

'So this is where she fell in?' Shan asks. The timbre of her voice is high with excitement.

Leo has his map to hand. 'Where's that on the moor?'

It only takes Nat a moment to find it. 'Here.'

'How far from the path?' Shan says.

Nat pauses for a moment. 'Quarter of a mile.'

'Would you see someone over there from the path?' Leo says. He imagines Bielby on the moor spying on Vicky. Or did he follow her up from the village? He shakes the theories away, dissatisfied. How would Bielby know there'd be anyone around so early? That would be counterintuitive during the festival weekend, with visitors having such late nights.

'Yes, they'd be visible,' Nat says. 'Now, I tried to look up the shaft but I couldn't see daylight. It's blocked. Could be some collapse or an obstruction, muck falling in over the years.'

'How far's the drop?' Leo asks.

'Twenty-three metres according to the radar. I had a good look round, anyway. And . . . I also found this.'

He taps the tablet. The camera shakes as Nat crouches over the floor. He scrapes at some silt and picks up a dirty yellow button, turns it over. The back is brown and crumbly. 'That's the remains of a pin fastening.'

'A badge,' Shan says.

'It might not be hers,' Tom says.

'No, it is,' Shan interrupts. 'It's a smiley badge. They all wore one. Look.' She taps her phone, shows them the photograph that Usha provided for the appeal, the four women in their coats, badges visible.

'We don't know when it's from,' Tom says.

Leo sees a spark of intensity in Shan's eyes. 'Did you find any other things down there? Ring pulls or crisp packets, bits of plastic? Anything?' she asks.

'Only what you've already seen,' Nat says.

'So litter wasn't routinely ending up down there?' Shan points out.

'That's right,' Tom says.

Her eyes meet Leo's. 'Then it's hers. It's Vicky's, it has to be.'

'Probably.' Tom swooshes his eyebrows at Leo, who doesn't respond in kind. Shan is right; there's no need to undermine her enthusiasm like that.

'So that lasted longer than her clothes and shoes,' Shan says.

Leo shrugs. 'Plastic coating. It'll take years to degrade. Same with the lighter.' He turns to the men. 'Brilliant. Fantastic work. Well done.'

'We've logged it all in for evidence,' Tom says.

They know now where she fell. It's a critical part of the story.

Leo realises how anxious he'd been for Nat to bring them an answer. Because every morsel of information, every step of the narrative, is so precious, and they are likely to be few and far between.

* * *

Vicky
1997

'There's lead in the water. It rots your brain. Slowly. First your teeth go then—'

Vicky heads downstairs after a shower to see everyone staring at Col. There's a peculiar atmosphere, an undercurrent of tension. It chills her, makes the hairs on her arms stand up.

'Come on,' Usha chides him. 'A few cups won't do any harm.'

'Miners died horrible deaths, you know. And it was in paint and old pipes.'

Dee looks under the sink. 'These are all copper,' she says.

Col shakes his head. 'It's still in the water. It's not safe.'

'Have juice then,' Robin says. Does Vicky imagine it or can she hear a flicker of concern in his words?

Usha lifts her mug of tea and Col flings out a hand, sending the cup flying.

'Jesus, Col!' Melanie yells.

Usha stands, flicking the drops off.

'Did it burn?' Vicky asks.

'No, I'm fine.' But Usha doesn't look fine. She looks close to tears.

'Col, mate . . .' Robin says.

'It's not safe. I tried to tell you.' Col turns on Melanie. 'Why won't you listen?'

'What have you taken?' Melanie says.

Col doesn't answer.

Usha shoots Vicky a panicked look.

Robin claps his hands together. 'We'll get some air, yeah? You and me, mate, get out of here for a bit.'

Col looks over to his friend, indecisive, wary.

'Ten minutes,' Robin adds. 'Walk up the hill.'

'Okay.'

There's a communal sigh of relief as the men leave.

'You okay?' Vicky asks Usha.

'I'm worried.' She fetches a dishcloth and starts to wipe down the tiles where the tea has splashed.

'Here, let me,' Vicky says.

Melanie frowns. 'What's going on with him?'

'I think he needs a doctor.' Usha's face cracks. 'I think he's losing it. I've never seen him like this. It's like he's paranoid. I should get him to A & E, right?' she asks Melanie. 'Work out where the nearest hospital is.'

Vicky feels the day darken, a sinking feeling. Everything's going wrong.

Melanie is ashen-faced. 'A trainee doctor doing illegal drugs is not a great look.'

'But if he's ill?' Vicky asks.

'It could jeopardise his future.'

'Who'd have to know?'

'Maybe no one. I just think A & E's a last resort.' Melanie turns to Usha. 'Look, has he eaten anything?'

102

'Not since the pub yesterday,' Usha says.

'What about drink?'

Tears have begun to form in Usha's eyes. 'Just alcohol.'

'And he didn't sleep.'

'I'm sorry,' Usha whimpers.

'It's not your fault,' Vicky says.

'I told him to go easy yesterday, but he just slagged me off.' She looks so miserable.

Vicky throws the cloth in the sink. Goes to hug her.

'Food, hydration, and even if you can't get him to sleep try to keep him off the drugs,' Melanie orders.

Vicky scoffs. 'This is Col we're talking about.' They all indulge but Col is hardcore.

'Maybe he should stay here today,' Usha says. 'I'll stay with him, see how he is.'

Vicky hates the idea of leaving Usha behind. Should she offer to stay too? Oh God, she can't bear the thought of missing everything. To babysit Col, who is not her favourite person.

'Let's see what he's like when they get back,' Melanie suggests.

Usha nods slowly, wiping her sodden cheeks. 'Yes, okay. I'm going to grab a shower, is that all right? My cramps are making me feel rotten.'

'Go, go,' Vicky says.

'I've got some ibuprofen upstairs in my washbag,' Melanie adds.

'Thank you.'

When Usha's left the room, Dee starts rolling a spliff.

'Seriously?' Vicky raises an eyebrow.

'We'll smoke it in the bogs outside,' Dee says. 'Be like school.'

Vicky laughs. She can't deny it would be good to have something to calm her down, settle the jitters.

The three of them head out into the yard.

'Sunshine!' Melanie throws up her arms.

Vicky raises her face to the sky and turns to see the creepy guy from the pub at an upstairs window, looking directly down on them. 'Oh God.'

'What?' The other two speak in unison.

'We are not alone.' She jerks her head to signal to him. Vicky expects he'll turn away now he's been spotted, but he doesn't.

'Sit down,' Dee says. 'We'll be hidden by the wall.'

'Sod that.' Vicky faces him and waves extravagantly, shouting, 'Morning. Lovely day, isn't it?' She keeps waving.

The man's face hardens. Then he walks out of view.

'Sorted,' says Vicky. But she's feeling edgy about Col, and Mr Creepy isn't helping matters.

Dee sits on the toilet lid, leaving the door open for the other two to stand close while they smoke.

Vicky inhales the fumes, relaxes her shoulders. She tells herself that everything will be fine. She closes her eyes, seeking peace, but the rooks over the way are noisy, their constant cawing like a soundtrack from a cheesy horror film.

'That racket, it's not exactly bucolic,' Vicky says.

'That's the trouble with countryside,' Melanie agrees. 'The smells and the noise and the inconvenience.'

Dee gestures for Vicky to pass her the spliff. 'Bucolic . . . Sounds like an illness.'

'That's colic,' Melanie says.

'Melancholic,' Vicky says.

Melanie cracks a smile. 'Asystolic.'

'Alcoholic,' Dee adds and they all dissolve in laughter.

Col seems better when Robin brings him back. He's still chatting a lot but that's normal for him. At least he's talking about the bands and not poisoned water, so that's progress.

Usha cooks a cheese omelette on toast, which he accepts, and by the time they're ready to head for the festival the crisis seems to have passed.

The day is close to perfect. The only downside is the toilets.

She drinks cider and eats Caribbean food and then crepes when she gets a bout of the munchies. She is gloriously woozy. Not so drunk as to be sick or too stoned to dance.

When night falls she drops an E along with the others.

Each time the stage lights dip between the sets the stars explode in the vast blue-black sky. She can see the Milky Way. Diamond dust flung across the heavens. She can smell grass crushed underfoot and the scents of weed and fast food and people's bodies.

She loves them all.

The lights come up on M People. They open with their new cover of 'Itchycoo Park'. The driving drum beat then the soaring vocals. It's overwhelming.

Vicky is flying.

She's in a sea of people, hands akimbo. Glow-sticks rippling like the neon tentacles of some amazing sea creature.

Melanie on one side of her, Usha on the other.

It is all so beautiful.

She is crying. Crying with happiness. Because this is so fucking amazing.

And she will never ever forget it as long as she lives.

* * *

Shan
2019

Usha Bhatti lives in a large Edwardian semi-detached in a suburb north of Leeds.

'I work from home,' she'd told Shan. 'So any time suits me.'

When they arrive she shows them into a sitting room at the back of the house. Sanded floors, the wide boards a hazel brown. An original cast-iron fireplace with tiled surround houses a wood-burning stove. The soft furnishings and wallpaper are rich jewel colours.

She is recognisable from the photographs, though older, heavier, with grey streaks in her long hair. She wears a long-sleeved maxi dress in a black and white geometric print.

'It was such a shock,' she says. 'I couldn't believe it. Hearing they'd found . . .' She falters. 'And then that it was Vicky. And for her mum . . .' She shakes her head.

Leo asks her to describe the hours before Vicky disappeared.

She takes a breath, blows it out; it's obviously not easy for her.

'We all stayed till the end of the night. Vicky was mad for M People and they were headlining. I think it was about two when we walked back.'

'Just the group of you staying at the cottage?'

'Yes. Vicky, me and Col, Melanie and Robin, Dee. We were pretty noisy, I guess, on a high. Drunk. Dee was sick; she'd had too much. We got back home and Dee went up to bed. Col wasn't great. He was getting anxious again. Lashing out at people. He'd been like that earlier in the day. So we were trying to talk him down.' She sighs. Knots her fingers together.

'He had anxiety?' Shan asks. A warning bell sounds an alert at the back of her mind. There was nothing about this in the old files.

'Not usually, but he got all paranoid that weekend. He was taking all sorts, not just cannabis. He was imagining things, conspiracies, threats that weren't there. Robin and Vicky offered to stay up with him and Melanie and I went to bed. Col came to bed eventually. But I never saw Vicky again.' There's a wobble in her voice. She tucks her hands, palm together, between her knees.

'When did you realise she was missing?' Shan says.

'When I came down the next day. The others were talking about it. She'd left a note about going to watch the sunrise. This was a lot later, early afternoon. She should have been back. Melanie thought maybe she'd gone up to the festival, not waited for the rest of us. So we went to look. It was impossible. Like a needle in a haystack. We checked the first-aid station and left a message with them and got security to put out an announcement for her to find us at the meeting point. She didn't come. So Dee and I went back to see if she'd turned up at the cottage.'

'What time was that?' Leo's keeping notes this time, letting Shan focus on Usha.

106

'Teatime. About six o'clock. There was no sign of her but her stuff was in the bedroom. She was sharing with Dee. And her purse was still there. That's when we got really worried.' Usha looks ashen as she retells it. 'We went back up to the site and told the security people. They said they'd contact the police on the Monday morning if she still hadn't come back. We were still hoping . . . I don't know . . . hoping she'd roll up with a man in tow, or that she'd run into an old friend.'

'Was Vicky impulsive like that?' Shan says.

'Yes. We were young, we were just kids. She wasn't stupid or reckless, but adventurous, sure. And why not? I envied that about her. She was up for anything, you know? But she wasn't shallow or lazy. She worked so hard. If any of us were going to make it, it was her.'

'As an actor?'

'Yes. She had something.' Usha raises her hand, fingers cupped as if she's weighing something. 'I don't know, presence? Intelligence? But emotion too, a depth to her. She'd have been—' Usha stops talking, her eyes brim. 'Sorry.'

'Are you okay to carry on?' Shan asks.

'Sure.' She pinches the top of her nose and sniffs.

'Did you go into acting?' Shan chooses to ease her back slowly into the serious questions.

'I tried. But, God, it's brutal. I stuck almost ten years of auditions, working as an office temp to pay the bills. All that time I got half a dozen bit parts. And I was always either a doormat wife in an arranged marriage or a terrorist's sister. Oh, and a stint as a corner shop owner. I started my own business instead — creative holidays in the Balearics.'

Judging by the size and location of the house, that was going pretty well.

'We know that Terence Bielby took a photograph of the four of you at the festival. Do you remember that?' Shan says.

'Oh yes.'

'And did you see him at any point after that during the weekend?'

107

'No.'

'Would Bielby know where Vicky was staying? Did that come up?'

Usha considers it for a moment. 'I don't think so.' She looks wary. 'You think it was him, don't you?'

'Did Vicky mention him at all?'

'No. He took our photo, that was it. At least that's what we thought.'

'Was there anyone else around that weekend that caused any of you any concern?' Leo asks.

'Not really. There was the lad at the pub.' *Christopher Hirst.* 'He was a bit weird. It was like he was spying on us.'

Shan feels a bump in her pulse rate. 'How do you mean?' She remembers the vibe she picked up when they interviewed him.

'Well, a couple of times when we were outside in the yard we saw him watching us from a window upstairs. It could have just been coincidence but it felt more deliberate.' She stills. 'He was the last person to see her, wasn't he? I remember.'

'That's right,' Shan says.

'So?' The question hangs in the air.

'We're just gathering as much information as we can at this stage.' Leo sidesteps her query. 'It may be Vicky's death was accidental, we just don't know yet.'

'Can you tell us if Vicky smoked?' Shan says.

'Oh yes.'

'And she used a lighter?'

'Yes.'

'Any particular sort?'

'Disposable ones, I think.'

Shan recalls the lighter in Nat's footage. 'Did you see anything like that in her bag when you went back to the cottage?'

'I don't think so. I can't remember to be honest. We took everything back to her mum's after. Perhaps she could tell you?'

'Thanks, we'll check with her.'

Shan has a list of bullet points, things they want to cover in the meeting. She glances down to check what's left.

'We've contacted Melanie already,' she says. 'Do you know how we can get in touch with the others?'

'I've no idea about Robin. He left in the spring term the following year. Dropped out of medical school. But I can give you Dee's mobile number though whether it's still right I don't know.' She picks up her phone, scrolls through and reads out the number.

'You don't keep in touch?'

'Not for ages. I saw her at a friend's wedding, someone from our course, but that was years ago.'

'Thank you. And what about Col?' Shan says.

Usha flinches as if she's been slapped. She has a raw, wounded look. 'Col's dead. He killed himself.'

Shan gasps. 'I'm so sorry.' Should they have known this? She feels awful.

'Yes. He died that Christmas.' Usha frowns. 'He . . .' She raises her hand to her mouth momentarily. 'He crashed his car. He drove his car into a wall on an abandoned lot in town. He wasn't well.'

'Mentally?'

'Yeah.'

'Were you still living together?' Leo says.

'On and off. It was all a mess, really. Sometimes he stayed at Robin's. I think what happened with Vicky, or not knowing what happened to Vicky, made everything worse. Nothing was ever the same again.' She pointed to the door. 'Do you mind if I get a drink of water?'

'Sure.'

'You don't want anything?' Usha says.

They decline.

Shan and Leo don't speak while Usha is gone.

'Thanks for your help. I'm sorry, it must be difficult,' Shan says when Usha comes back. 'We just wanted to ask you about this photograph. Elizabeth said you gave it to the police.'

Shan shows her the snap. The four women in a row, not unlike the photograph Bielby took, though here they wear their coats and Dee Price at the end has a hat on. Vicky's bright smile draws the eye.

'That's right. We had to work out what Vicky was wearing, what was missing from her things. And it was those same clothes. So they asked to use this picture for the appeal.' She studies the photograph. 'I'd a new camera especially for the festival. Robin took it for us the Saturday night. Look at us.' Her voice quavers. 'I just hope she didn't suffer.'

Shan doesn't reply. It's not her place to disclose the forensics results to Usha. They're not yet in the public domain. When they are, or perhaps if Elizabeth tells her, then Usha will realise that her friend probably did suffer, that she'd likely lived for two or three days alone and in pain.

But she doesn't need to hear that now.

CHAPTER SEVEN

Leo

They enter York through the city walls. With its rich and tumultuous history, its castles and minster, boutique shops and river cruises, the place is a magnet for tourists. Leo can see two coachloads in the traffic ahead of them and, on the pavement, a tour guide carrying a pennant leads a group of sightseers. An open-top bus, passengers wielding cameras, passes in the other direction.

In the narrow winding shopping lanes, lined by half-timbered houses, hanging baskets spill a froth of flowers in between bright bunting.

The architecture is beautiful: ancient stone walls, medieval buildings. But Leo knows about York's bloody past, the darkest incident the massacre of the town's Jews in 1190 as part of the Crusades — religious wars that saw Christians encouraging the destruction of Jews in England and Muslims in the Holy Land. The Jewish people of York were besieged in Clifford's Tower, where they had sought sanctuary from the mob. Almost all died there, fathers killing their wives and children then themselves rather than waiting to be slaughtered.

'We came here to the Viking centre with school,' Shan says.

'I think every school in the county does,' Leo replied.

He remembers Luke's enthusiasm for the Vikings, him dressing up in a horned helmet, wielding a wooden axe. Ange had helped him build a miniature longhouse, sawing and fixing together the wooden structure. And Leo had constructed a model longship with him.

Leo had relished sharing his own love of history with his son. Telling about the Brigantes, the tribe who held the north until the Romans conquered them, the Anglo-Saxons who followed and the Vikings in turn, who made York the capital of their territory. Luke loved their gory names: Ivar the Boneless, Eric Bloodaxe.

Nowadays it pains him that Luke is happy to see that history twisted. Vikings as a mighty ancestral race, white warriors fighting 'barbarians', their signs and symbols appropriated. The same appropriation as the Nazis exercised. With the same flagrant disregard for the truth.

England for the English. The first racist sticker Luke brought home, plastered on his schoolbag. It had made Leo sick to his stomach.

'Everyone born here is English,' he'd said. 'Use your head. And British citizens are entitled to live here, to work here, because *we* were the colonial power. That was the deal. We ripped them off, took whatever we wanted and in return they were made part of the Commonwealth.'

Luke had retorted with something about pureblood.

'Luke, I'm half Irish. Your mother's got Scottish and Italian ancestors. You are not pure anything. English isn't a race. It's not a blood group.'

Leo parks at the hospital and puts the ticket into his trouser pocket for later. He still finds it galling that hospitals charge for parking, making money off people at their most anxious, the ill and their visitors.

At reception, Leo explains they have an appointment with Dr Quinn.

The receptionist frowns, glances at the clock. 'I'm not sure—'

'Non-medical,' Leo says. 'DI Donovan and DC Young.'

The woman nods and picks up the phone, relays the message. She asks them to take a seat, Dr Quinn will come down.

The wait stretches two minutes, three, four. Leo notices Shan tapping her feet, an edgy motion. She tucks her hands under her thighs, then between her knees. Before long she stands up and walks to peer at a noticeboard, swivels and retraces her steps, arms wrapped about herself.

'You okay?' Leo asks.

She gives an apologetic shrug. 'Don't like hospitals.'

'Never met anyone who did.' But perhaps she has particular reason to feel uncomfortable. A bad experience?

'What about the baby?' he says.

'Hates them too.'

He laughs, glad that she can make a joke.

'We're hoping for a home birth,' she says.

Before he can ask more, Melanie Quinn arrives.

'I'm sorry for the wait, it's just chaos sometimes.' She shakes hands with each of them in turn. A quick grip, her hand cool.

She looks frazzled, face lined with worry, dry lips, blonde hair escaping from a loose bun. Is it still called a bun, Leo wonders? Or is there some fancy new name?

She's rake thin. Leo notices the knobs of her wrist bones.

'Thank you for coming. Shall we go up?'

Following her they pass the lifts to access the stairs. Leo spots the posters exhorting people to do just that. She walks briskly. He gets the impression that this is how she lives her life — too busy, everything in a rush.

His knee twinges as he climbs, giving him gyp.

'Have you come far?' Melanie asks.

'Settle,' he says. 'But the traffic wasn't bad.'

Once they're seated in her office, Melanie says, 'I'm so, so sorry to hear about Vicky. There was always that sliver of hope, you know?' Her voice trembles slightly. 'Though after all this time . . .'

Her doctor's coat hangs on the office door. On the walls are framed certificates and a personal photograph sits on the filing cabinet. A man and a little boy. Husband and son, Leo guesses.

'I'm still finding it hard to take in,' Melanie continues. 'Have you any idea what happened?'

'We can't be sure yet,' Leo says. 'Could you talk us through that weekend?'

'Yes, of course. So, erm, Vicky and I went up on the train and the others came up in Robin's car.'

'You lived with Vicky in Leeds?' Shan's pen is poised.

'Yes, Vicky and me, Col and Usha.'

'And Robin?' Leo says.

'He had digs with some other medical students. Though he and I would spend time at each other's houses.' She pauses to see if they have other questions then continues, 'On the Friday, once everyone was there, we had drinks in the pub then went up to the festival. Vicky was fine. Everything was fine.' She gives a small shake of her head.

'On Saturday we slept in and went back up to the site. Stayed till the end. We were up half the night and the rest you know. When we surfaced on the Sunday Vicky had gone out for a walk but she never came back. I don't know why she'd do that.' Her voice is strained. 'We knew to be careful, that there was someone targeting women on their own. Why would she do it? I've been over it and over it.' She gives a sharp sigh. Her face is drawn, her expression pained.

'Might there have been someone else?' Leo asks.

'How do you mean?'

'Someone Vicky went to meet? Someone she'd hooked up with?'

Melanie shakes her head, light glinting off the golden studs in her ears. 'No. She'd have told me. We told each other everything.'

Leo asks her whether she remembers Bielby taking their photograph.

'Yes. And then when he was arrested . . . Oh God, seeing him on the TV. Recognising him. Realising it was probably him. It was horrific. The police came to talk to us again but eventually they said they couldn't find anything to link him to Vicky disappearing and he wouldn't be charged with that.' She sounds bitter. But Leo knows the evidence wasn't there. Still isn't.

'What can you tell us about Christopher Hirst, the lad who worked in the pub?'

'He was . . . a bit odd. In your face and I think he had a downer on students. He made a big fuss about giving us the key when we first arrived.' She pauses, looking off to the side, reaching for memories. 'He warned us about the murders, but the way he did it . . . it probably sounds ridiculous but at the time he made it sound like a threat. It's hard to explain. Almost gloating?' She looks between them and Shan nods.

Leo picks up on Melanie's revulsion. 'Did Christopher Hirst ever make any overt threats?'

'No. We saw him watching us a couple of times but that was it. Like I say, he seemed to resent students but we were paying good money for the accommodation and it's not like we'd trashed it or anything. At the time, when Vicky went missing, I had this awful feeling that maybe he'd hurt her but it seemed so far-fetched. I told the police about him watching us but—' She exhales. Curls a hand round the collar of her neck, as if seeking comfort. 'I think I was clutching at straws, anything to try and explain her vanishing like that. Then when Terence Bielby was finally caught, it seemed obvious he was responsible.'

'Christopher Hirst reported seeing Vicky coming down into the village early on the Sunday morning,' Leo says. 'But as far as you know she didn't come into the cottage.'

'No, but we were all out of it well into the afternoon. I will never understand why she went off in the dark like that.

Never. If only I'd still been awake, I could have stopped her or gone with her. I don't know.' Her mouth tightens in a line. She looks bereft. Drained.

'You said things were fine,' Leo says. 'But what about Col Green?'

A moment's pause. 'Oh, yes. Col got himself in a state. Looking back now I'd say it was probably drug-induced psychosis. And what came later — well, it was very sad.'

Leo recalls Usha's comment about Col lashing out. 'Was he violent at any point?'

'Well . . .' She hesitates. 'He didn't mean it, really.'

'Mean what?'

'He was . . . well, he was an idiot, to be honest, but he'd never have actually hurt anybody.' She seems reluctant to elaborate.

Leo leans forward. 'Tell us what he did.'

She plants her fingers on the desk, hands raised like a pianist. 'He whacked a cup of tea out of Usha's hand, and he pushed Vicky. He was jumping at shadows. Imagining things. It was us he seemed to take against, Usha and Vicky and me.'

'The women?' Shan says.

Melanie nods. 'Especially Vicky.'

'What about Dee Price?' Leo asks.

'She'd been sick and gone to bed. She slept through the worst of it.'

'How did he take against you?'

'Saying we weren't to be trusted. We were plotting against him. He was talking rubbish. Pointing the finger at Vicky and shouting—' She broke off. 'You can't think that Col had anything to do with it.' She looks puzzled.

Leo doesn't. Or hasn't up till now, but he won't rush to any snap judgements.

'After Vicky went missing, how was Col?' he says.

Melanie frowns. 'I can't remember. We were all getting a bit frantic by then. And I think Robin was keeping Col out of the way as much as he could, in case he started on at us again.'

116

'You didn't mention this to the police?'

'It wasn't relevant. Seriously. Col was delusional, he thought he was being persecuted, but he wouldn't . . . He couldn't . . . He was barely functioning.'

'And you all went back to Leeds on the Monday?'

'Yes, it seemed to take for ever for anyone to take us seriously. At last they listened and we had to give statements to the police first, then we all piled into Robin's car. God, it was awful. We had to call Elizabeth and she came over to Leeds—' She clasps her hands together, touches them to her mouth. 'It was unreal, like a waking nightmare. Just awful.' Leo imagines Melanie having to explain to Vicky's mother that her daughter has disappeared.

'And Col died in a car crash?' Leo says.

'That's right. I don't think any of us realised how very poorly he was. Usha was devastated. Vicky was still missing . . . It was a terrible time.'

'And you and Robin?'

'I think it changed things. He felt responsible, almost blamed himself for Col. Robin decided to take some time off, but they really don't like that in med school and he never went back. He left Leeds. We'd split up by then anyway. I did what I could to help but he said he just needed to get away. Time to sort his head out.'

'Do you know how we can get in touch with Robin Westwood?'

'No. He made a complete break of it. I don't know if he ever went back into medicine, I've never come across his name. You could try his family perhaps. They were in London back then; his father was a consultant at the Royal Free. But . . .' She opens her palms, indicating how uncertain she is that the information is still correct.

She takes a breath in, a hand to her chest. Leo can see she's close to tears. He waits, giving her space. Eventually she says, 'As soon as I heard you'd found Vicky, and where you found her, I just assumed it must have been Terence Bielby. That you'd finally be able to convict him of her murder too, but Elizabeth says you don't know how Vicky died. That it might have been an accident?'

'That's right,' Leo says.

'I hope so. I do hope that is the case.'

'We might never know. But we're doing everything we can to try and find out.'

* * *

Shan

Shan is shattered and it will be another hour's drive home. Keeping busy will distract her from the tiredness. She flicks through her notebook to find Dee's number.

'I thought I'd call Dee Price,' she tells Leo.

'Good idea.'

Shan sets the call to speakerphone, and after she's introduced herself and Leo, explained who they are and why she's calling, there's a silence. Has she been cut off? 'Hello?'

'Can you say that again?' Dee sounds shaken.

Shan repeats herself.

'Oh my god, I didn't know. Oh God,' Dee says in a rush.

'You didn't see the news?'

'I'm living in Germany. I don't usually bother with the news in the UK. I'd no idea.' Shan can hear the astonishment in her voice.

'I'm sorry, it must be a shock,' Shan says. 'Are you okay to talk?'

'Yes, thank you. So what happened? Where did you find her? Jesus!'

'Vicky's remains were recovered from a cave close to Lund Seat, near Garsdale Common.'

'A cave?' There's a pause. 'And was it that man, Terence Bielby?'

'We don't know. There's a chance it was an accidental death. But we would like to go over the events of the night Vicky disappeared.'

'I don't know that I can help. I was asleep. I'd got really drunk and gone to bed. I'm sorry.'

'You didn't hear anything?' Shan says.

'No, I'm sorry.'

'Do you know if Vicky went up to bed at all?'

'No.' She moans. 'God, it's just like back then, I felt so useless because I couldn't tell them anything then either. Oh God, poor Vicky. You think she died, then? That she was already dead when we were looking—' She coughs. 'Jesus.' Dee's voice is raw, full of emotion.

'Close to that time, yes,' Shan says. 'Is there anything you can tell us, anything you've remembered in the years since, that strikes you now?'

'No. I'm sorry.'

A string of bikers are coming the other way. Machines gleaming, bristling with accessories and flags, riders clad in elaborate leathers. Shan watches them pass, the roar deafening.

'We're aware that Col Green was unwell during that weekend. There were a couple of incidents where he acted aggressively?'

'Yes. I wouldn't have wanted to be alone with him,' Dee says.

A tingle runs up Shan's spine. 'Go on.'

There's a sigh down the line. 'What happened to Col was terrible, really sad. But he was . . . can I be frank?'

'Please do.'

'He was a right bastard. One of those public-school boys who can't see beyond their own privileged little world. Completely selfish. He treated Usha like his own personal servant. He could turn on the charm but there was this vicious side that came out sometimes when he was drunk or off his head. He was really good-looking and boy, did he know it. Life was one big, long party for Col; everything was a joke. But it was actually really self-destructive. Col Green was a nasty piece of work. And I know he's not here to defend himself but . . .'

'And Robin?' Shan is curious; the men were friends.

'Robin wasn't like that. I mean, yes, he had the posh schooling and a career in medicine lined up and money in the bank. Probably stocks and shares somewhere, too, but I think he was just more intelligent, considerate.'

'Was Col violent in his relationship with Usha?'

'Physically? No. I don't think so. These things can be hidden, can't they — often are. But I never heard any rumours. Never saw anything till that weekend.'

'And what did you see then?'

'He hit a mug out of her hand and got hot tea all over her — that I did see. And he shoved Vicky.' Shan tries to imagine how that must have felt. A close friend turning nasty like that. If anyone came at Shan they'd soon be sorry. But she'd had training. And if Col was ill at the time perhaps Vicky didn't take it personally.

'Vicky and Col, how did they usually get along?' Shan asks.

'She thought he was a pain, like I did.' She lowers her voice to a whisper. 'We were hoping Usha would get tired of him and . . . well . . .'

'Did you believe him to be dangerous?'

Leo clears his throat, raises an eyebrow. He probably thinks she's putting words into Dee's mouth.

'I don't know. I just didn't trust him. I didn't feel safe around him when he was drunk.'

'You didn't report this to the missing persons enquiry?' Shan says.

'No. I mean, the others were babysitting him that night, making sure he didn't do something stupid. So it's not like Col could have done anything.'

Shan pictures the group. Dee, Usha and Melanie have gone to bed, which leaves Robin and Vicky with Col.

'One last question, do you remember Christopher Hirst? He worked at the pub.' Shan says.

'Yes. I remember Vicky took the piss out of him and he deserved it. He was the eyewitness who said he'd seen her that morning.' Her voice shifts tone, curious, as if she thinks Hirst might be involved. 'Why?'

'No particular reason. We're just building as full a picture as we can.'

'God.' Dee's tone is clearly contemplative.

'Please do get in touch if anything else occurs,' Shan says.

'Is Vicky's mum still around?' Dee asks. 'In Bradford?'

'Yes.'

'I should write.' Dee groans. 'But what on earth do you say?'

Shan has no answer for that.

'So what are you thinking?' Leo says when Shan's finished the call.

What is she thinking? The three men — Terence Bielby, Christopher Hirst and Col Green. Her mind is circling round them.

'Was there ever any suggestion that Bielby might not have acted alone?' she says.

'Not a dickie bird. Why?'

'Christopher Hirst. The women say he acted strangely — well, intrusively — and that he was watching them.'

'Go on.'

'Well, could he have been watching for Bielby? Like a scout?'

Leo turns, taking his eyes off the road for a fraction. 'Christopher Hirst was only eighteen at the time. Very young. There was no proof he was involved, and we've no record then or since of any criminal behaviour.'

Maybe it's a stupid idea but Shan can't just leave it. She needs to share all the niggles of suspicion that snag in her thoughts.

'But him reporting the sighting of Vicky coming down the hill put everybody off looking for her on Toller Fell.'

'True. Though the sunrise was long over by the time her friends knew she was missing, they assumed she'd gone to the festival.'

'Yes.' It's all sticky, tangled in her head. 'Hirst could have made up the sighting, a way to cover his tracks.'

'Not necessarily. The last person to see someone is always of interest in the case of a suspicious death. That's partly why we paid him a visit. But like I said before — no criminal record, no shred of evidence against him.'

'What about Col Green, then?' Shan says. 'Both Dee and Melanie told us his paranoia was directed — violently — at Vicky. He could have followed her. He was delusional.'

'He and Usha were sharing a room,' Leo says.

'But Usha wouldn't know if he crept out when she was asleep. He catches up with Vicky and he loses it, there's a struggle. He hurts her and then has to hide what he's done. But he can't live with it. Hence the suicide.' *It could work. Could it work?*

Leo makes a doubtful sound. 'Bit pat. And it still doesn't account for that sighting by Hirst.'

'Okay. What if Vicky comes down to the cottage, Hirst sees her, then Col goes with Vicky back up to the tops.'

Leo shakes his head. 'Look, I'm no expert but we do see a lot of mentally ill people in the course of this work. Most of them are a danger to themselves, not anyone else. More likely to be victims than attackers. And those few who do commit crimes, they don't generally have the wherewithal to conceal what they've done. In fact they're more likely confess. Or we learn they've been asking for help all along and not been able to find it.'

Shan thinks of all the enquiries launched when someone has been killed after friends and families had begged for better care, for any care, for a hospital bed, for a section. When people have tried to warn the authorities that their relative is in danger and poses a danger. The tragedies that then unfold when they are not heard. Services stretched so thin that people fall through cracks wide as chasms.

'You're right,' she agrees. It's not likely to have been Col Green. *But not impossible.* 'So — what are you thinking?'

'I'm thinking that if this Transit doesn't get a move on we'll be here all bloody night.'

122

The white van is pootling along at ten miles below the limit. Someone has written *WASH ME!* in the grime on the back.

Shan giggles. *The old ones are the best.*

The road is taking them through the Vale of York. Flat farming land, fields full of crops, though Shan is not sure what they are. Potatoes? Kale? A stand of trees edges the road, a group of magpies above are dive-bombing a seagull.

'I'd like to talk to Robin Westwood,' Leo says. 'From what we've heard, Col and Robin and Vicky were the last people up. Though leaving a note implies that everyone else was asleep when Vicky went.'

'True,' Shan says.

But was someone else awake and watching, Shan thinks? Christopher Hirst at his bedroom window. Or Terence Bielby stealing out of his house hours before his shift, taking the road to Tollthorpe, hunting a new victim.

* * *

Leo

'Look at the state of them! They're ruined.' Ange's voice carries. Leo can hear her as he's putting his key in the door.

He finds her in the hall with Luke. She's flushed, a frown carving lines in her forehead. Luke stands sullen, shoulders drooping, head angled off to the side.

'What's up?' Leo asks.

'His boots. They cost over a hundred pounds, those did,' Ange says.

Luke's leather boots are speckled with red dots.

'It might come off,' Luke says.

'It won't. It's spray paint. It's permanent,' Ange tells him. 'The only way to get that off is if you shave the leather.'

'How did you get paint on your boots?' Leo says.

Luke gives a theatrical sigh. 'Helping Jack re-spray his bike.'

'Well, you're not getting any new ones,' Ange says. 'You'll have to wear them like that.'

'I know!' Luke retorts. 'Fuck's sake! Just give it a rest.'

'Hey!' Leo admonishes him.

Luke turns away and stomps upstairs. They hear his bedroom door slam shut.

'Welcome home.' Ange looks weary, her eyes full of regret.

Leo opens his arms and holds her, closes his eyes. Rests his chin on her head. Her hair tickles. It smells of oranges with a tang of garlic.

'I'm going for a run,' she says after a minute.

'Good idea,' Leo says.

* * *

He eats, then showers.

It's still light. A crescent moon slices a sickle in a high blue sky.

He chooses a bottle of beer, a Ribblehead bitter, and takes that and the Robert Macfarlane book he's reading outside and sits on the bench by the pond.

There's a hush in the air, as if everything is holding its breath waiting for the dark. The poppies in the grass and the morning glories scrambling along the trellis are closed now the sun has dropped below the horizon. Night-scented stocks and nicotiana perfume the air, mixed in with the piney aroma from the cypresses and the mineral smell from the pond.

Only the blackbird sings and occasionally there's a scream from one of the swifts above. The swifts are nesting in a box on the workshop gable end and the parents are busy feeding their young. Quick black arrows scissor in and out bearing insects.

He tries to read but the themes and stories in *Underland* — of the world beneath our feet, of burial chambers and legends of the deep — feel too close for comfort. He'd no idea when he started it that he'd be investigating the death of someone in an underground cavern. He should pass it on to Ange; she's keen to read it.

Movement catches his eye beneath the shrubbery. There's a snuffling noise and he watches a hedgehog move at a fair crack through the wildflower lawn to the border on the other side.

Leo's neck is stiff. He rolls his head round slowly trying to gently stretch the muscles. He knows he should do this exercise more regularly, consistently, same as he should for his legs, and build up the surrounding tissue to compensate for the way his bones are crumbling, but there never seems to be enough time. *Or inclination.*

His thoughts roll back to the investigation. *What did we learn today?*

He has a sense of being burdened. That for all their efforts they're not going to be able to solve the mystery. That Elizabeth will be left not knowing, never really knowing the full story.

Defeat talking, he says to himself.

Your Eeyore side, Ange calls it.

'I prefer phlegmatic,' he'd said when they first talked about it. His tendency to see the dark side, his downbeat nature. 'Or philosophical.'

'Or depressed?' She ventured, worried about him.

'A bit, perhaps.' He was as honest as he could be. 'It comes and goes. You know, melancholy is one of the humours according to Ancient Greek medicine. All based on imbalances of the four bodily fluids. Melancholy is too much black bile.'

'Like the black dog,' Ange said. 'And the others?'

'There's choleric — too much yellow bile; sanguine — that's blood; and phlegmatic — phlegm.'

'Delightful,' Ange had said. 'What am I then?'

'Sanguine, definitely. Positive, sociable.'

'I'll take that.' She'd grinned.

Luke's choleric, he thinks now. Hot tempered, angry.

Why can't we make him happy?

He wonders if his own low moods have played a part in Luke's state of mind. Leo thinks he hides them pretty well. He functions, goes through the motions until something

125

shifts. But perhaps over the years his son could sense Leo's withdrawal, his air of anxiety or sorrow.

Leo stretches again. He sees the stars glitter faintly behind the blue heavens, in the wings ready for their cue.

A fox barks from up the road somewhere and the Whitakers' dog gives a volley in return.

Leo doesn't want to think about Luke because he feels helpless. He can't change his son's opinions, he can't change his mind and dwelling on it is like picking at a scab — a vicious circle of irritation and pain.

He searches for any nuggets of comfort. Luke was helping Jack do up his bike — that's something positive, constructive. Not just video gaming. And Luke has friends, Jack for one — that's good too. He isn't isolated in his room all day, every day, encountering who knows what online.

They don't know Jack well. Have seen him a handful of times since he and Luke met at sixth-form college.

Perhaps they should encourage Luke to invite Jack over, instead of always the other way around. They've a spare room.

He'll suggest it to Ange when she's back and see what she thinks.

He's twenty-one, the voice in his head whispers. *And you want to plan sleepovers for him?*

Same age as Vicky and her friends, give or take a year. Coming together at university, all knowing what they wanted to do, to be. Studying hard to make it happen.

Luke had resisted all attempts to persuade him to apply for a degree. 'What and end up fifty grand in debt? There's no point.' He didn't even know what he wanted to do.

Would that have made a difference? Meeting a wider range of people, gaining confidence and skills? Or would Luke still have drifted towards those people who saw conspiracies everywhere, who united against imaginary enemies, preaching fear and hatred, who revelled in a misplaced sense of victimhood?

Although, Leo thinks, from what they've learned only Melanie has thrived in her career. Col Green died; Robin

Westwood dropped out. Usha Bhatti changed direction after years of disappointment. They didn't ask Dee Price if she makes a living through her drama. Perhaps she does.

And Vicky, the one they all agreed was the brightest star, had her life snuffed out. The ripples from her disappearance spreading to change the course of so many lives.

* * *

Vicky
1997

The rest of M People's set was amazing but their opener, 'Itchycoo Park', is the earworm lodged in Vicky's head. She leads her friends in the chorus as they walk back to the cottage.

Except for Usha, who lags behind with Col. Col is rabbiting on, a stream of nonsense. Vicky tries to zone him out. She doesn't want him to ruin what's definitely been the best night of her life.

She starts the call and response part, and Dee and Robin sing out the answers. Then they all holler the chorus together. Vicky and Melanie applaud and whoop.

There aren't any streetlights here, but the moon, even behind hazy cloud, throws enough light so they can make out the strip of tarmac and the pale grey drystone walls either side. The dew has fallen and the smell of the earth is stronger. A bird calls somewhere, a harsh scrape of a sound that Vicky can't name. The quote from *Macbeth* comes to her:

> *The raven himself is hoarse*
> *That croaks the fatal entrance of Duncan*
> *Under my battlements.*

Her head is full, full of words and ideas and songs. Full of love. She wants to run but spins instead, arms out for balance.

The lane climbs a final time before the descent to the village and Dee starts to complain but then makes a gulping sound and bends over, spewing up on to the ground. Vicky leaps away just in time.

'Oh, gross!'

'Better out than in.' Melanie fakes a Yorkshire accent.

Dee snorts, stands, then lunges forward and vomits again.

'Whoa!' shouts Robin.

'Christ, it's like *The Exorcist*,' Melanie says.

Col and Usha reach them.

'You need to listen, though,' he is saying. 'If nobody listens, nobody hears the messages, and the messages won't get through. You need to listen. It's important that we're on the right frequency to hear that.' He seems oblivious to Dee being sick, to the rest of them.

'Let's go home,' Usha says.

Vicky sees Col's grip tighten on Usha's arm.

'Are you listening?' he hisses. 'Open your ears.'

'Hey.' Vicky says. Both what Col's saying and the manner in which he's doing so concern her.

He whirls round. 'I'm not talking to you!' he screeches.

'Hush,' Melanie whispers. 'Keep it down.' Even though they're still a quarter of a mile from the houses.

Col lunges at Vicky and shoves her breastbone with the heel of his hand. 'Fuck off!'

She staggers, stunned. Her heart thuds fast, fear sizzling along her nerves.

'No. Hey, Col, no.' Robin grabs him, guides him away.

'Fuck's sake!' Melanie seethes.

'Come on, mate,' Robin is saying. 'There's some of that keg left. Let's get back and chill out.' He says it so normally, like Col isn't having a meltdown.

'Are you okay?' Usha asks her. 'Vicky, I'm so sorry.'

Usha looks wretched.

'I'll be fine,' Vicky says, though she's shaken, hurt. 'And it's not your fault.'

Back at the cottage they crowd into the kitchen to get beer and glasses. Col and Usha stay in the living room. Vicky is determined not to let this ruin her weekend. She pours herself a glass.

Dee says she's going to bed.

'Take some water,' Vicky says. 'And a bucket.'

'I don't need a bucket,' Dee slurs.

'You might need a bucket,' Robin says.

'*There's a hole in my bucket*,' Dee sings. She sways to the sink and pulls a large saucepan out from the cupboard there.

'No!' Melanie objects. 'Skanky! You are not throwing up in that.'

Vicky looks in the little utility storeroom and finds an oatmeal-coloured rectangular washing-up bowl. She gives it to Dee who staggers off upstairs.

'Do you think Col's okay?' Vicky asks Robin and Melanie.

'Not really,' Robin says.

'Does he need a doctor, then?' Vicky's stomach twists with unease.

'I'll get him to see his GP when we get back.'

'Good luck with that,' Melanie says. She looks pissed off.

Robin and Melanie take their drinks through and Vicky goes out into the yard for a cigarette. Her ears are still ringing from the music.

She smokes, closing her eyes to try and recapture the feeling of being swept up by the power of the evening, the amazing buzz of the crowd, the atmosphere of affection for the bands, for one another. Being part of something immense, creative, beautiful, the energy of the experience.

But she feels really shaky, like she's had way too much caffeine or cocaine.

Her tongue feels peppery, her mouth dry from the long day and too much alcohol and cigarettes, but she slakes her thirst with a few large swigs of bitter.

The moon slips behind some shreds of cloud then emerges, washing the hillside silver. Vicky feels a pinch of sadness. It had all been so perfect, but now it's spoiled.

When Vicky goes inside, into the lounge, Col freezes like he's seen a ghost.

Usha tries to distract him, talking about the next day's lineup, but he barely listens to her.

'Where have you been?' Col says to Vicky.

'Just for a smoke.'

He looks so pretty, with his thick dark mop of hair, his fine bone structure and long lashes. But the curl of his mouth and the cast of his eyes are ugly.

'Don't lie to me.'

'Col!' Usha remonstrates.

'She's a fucking traitor,' he says. 'She's passing messages. She's listening and telling them. She's telling everybody, don't you see?'

'Telling who?' Usha says. But Melanie shakes her head, shoots a look. Vicky realises they shouldn't encourage his delusions. She feels scared. She's never seen anyone she knows like this, raving and unpredictable.

'Don't pretend you don't know,' Col rounds on Usha. 'I told you to listen. Stupid bitch.'

Usha gasps and gets up, walks through to the kitchen. Vicky goes after her.

'I don't know what to do,' Usha says. Tears brim in her eyes.

'Robin says he'll get him to the GP on Monday,' Vicky says.

Usha sniffles. 'What do we do till then?'

Vicky sees her friend is exhausted.

'Why don't you rest? We'll keep an eye on him. Take turns.'

Melanie comes in. Vicky tells her about the plan.

'What do you think?' she says.

'I think he's a pain in the fucking arse,' Melanie replies. 'He should never have come.'

Vicky is shocked by the callous remark. Worse because Usha is there.

'Brilliant bedside manner,' Vicky snaps. If any of them can understand what Col is going through, shouldn't it be Melanie and Robin, the medics in training?

'Fine!' Melanie spits. 'There's no point in us all babysitting him. You go and sleep if you can,' she tells Usha.

Usha looks torn.

Vicky wonders again about A & E but they only have Robin's car and he's drunk too much to drive anywhere. She has no idea what a taxi might cost. Is Col bad enough for an ambulance?

'Should we call 999, get him taken to hospital?' she says.

Usha looks alarmed.

Melanie shakes her head. 'Not unless he gets worse. Look, he's talking garbage but a lot of that's the drugs and the drink. It's not like he's running around with an axe. He's just a fucking idiot.' She's so dismissive. Vicky wants to be reassured. Why does Melanie have to be like this?

'You go up,' Vicky says to Usha.

'Okay. Thanks. I don't think I'll be able to sleep.'

'Just rest, then. Breathing and relaxation.' Vicky places a palm on her diaphragm. It's a practical class they do on the drama course.

Usha rolls her eyes, a wan smile on her face.

'I'll see if Col will come with,' she says.

In the living room, Col refuses, so Usha tells him she's going for a lie down.

Vicky tries to ignore the way Col is staring at her.

Melanie takes Robin aside and tells him they've agreed to take turns to give Usha a break. 'This is such a fucking shitshow,' she complains.

Robin scowls at her. 'That's really not helping.'

'Do you want to go up too?' Melanie asks Vicky.

'I'm fine. I'm not tired,' Vicky says.

'Okay. I will then. See you later.' Melanie leans in to kiss Robin but he offers her his cheek and Vicky catches a twist of distaste on his face. Then she feels guilty for seeing it. Melanie leaves.

Col is whispering something Vicky can't hear, staring at her. She needs to get away. It feels as if her being there is making things worse. And the vibes from Col's paranoia make her feel edgy and frightened, like something bad is going to happen.

But she doesn't want to desert Robin.

'How about some toast?' she says.

'Good idea,' Robin agrees. 'Tea and toast all round.' He nods, telling her to go, and says, 'Col, you must be hungry, mate. Soon get you sorted.'

As Vicky steps into the kitchen, she overhears Col whisper, 'She's listening.'

'It's all right,' Robin says. 'Everything's okay. I'm here, yeah? You sit and have a rest and I'll stay with you.' He sounds so kind and relaxed. She prays that it will work on Col and soon things will be back to normal.

CHAPTER EIGHT

Shan
2019

The alarm wakes her and she lies for a moment trying to capture her dream as it dissolves. It was a tunnel, wasn't it? A hallway? But she can't grasp anything else, only the residue of emotion. She was scared in the dream, or disturbed — certainly not excited or happy as she sometimes is.

'Time to get up,' Erin murmurs.

Shan hauls herself up on to her elbows, leans over and kisses Erin on the nose.

'You can have a bit longer,' Shan says.

'No. I'll call at the gym before work.'

'Whoa, fit woman.'

'In every sense.' Erin looks at her lazily, a shimmer of blue eyes.

Shan giggles. 'I'm tempted. Can you wait till tonight?' She kisses Erin again.

'I suppose.'

'Okay. I need a shower.'

Breakfast is half an orange, a bowl of muesli with oat milk, and a cup of tea, plus the supplements she's been told to take for the pregnancy.

'I had some good news yesterday. I passed my probation,' Erin says.

Shan stops mid-mouthful. 'Why didn't you tell me!'

'I was going to but you were half asleep, so thought I'd wait till you were more receptive.'

'I would have been receptive, if you'd just told me. Or you could have messaged me,' Shan says.

'No way! I wanted to tell you in person.'

'Well, it's brilliant!' Shan picks up her cup of tea for a toast. 'Congratulations. Not that I had any doubts.'

'So more money per hour. Paid holidays. Permanent contract.'

'And it's much better there. Thank God you walked,' Shan says. Though it still rankles that the man who assaulted Erin at her last place was given a warning and moved to a different section rather than being sacked for gross misconduct.

He argued that he was unwell, going through a difficult divorce in the wake of his father's death, when he grabbed Erin's bum in the corridor and made horrible comments. It was just a light-hearted prank he realised was inappropriate.

Shan had talked to Erin about pressing charges, reporting him to the police if her employers wouldn't do anything, but Erin couldn't face it. She found a new data import job at a logistics firm in walking distance of their house.

'I'll do Morrisons later,' Erin says. 'You need anything else?'

'More antacids,' Shan says. 'And that long-stemmed broccoli.'

'That's on the list.'

'Data queen.' Shan teases Erin about the spreadsheets she has set up for their grocery shop and their bills but it actually makes life a lot easier. When Shan lived at home with her parents they were forever running out of things and having to improvise meals or make a dash to the shops.

While Erin scans the news on her phone, Shan flicks through the baby names book. Idly she looks up her father's name, Richard, and reads the entry. *Old German origin . . .*

powerful leader, strong leader. Then her mother's, Fiona. *Gaelic word* 'fion'... 'white' or 'fair'... *Irish name Fíona, meaning 'vine'.*

How she'd love this, Shan thinks. To be here for this. To be a grandma.

She closes the book.

'You okay?' Erin has an uncanny ability to read Shan's mood.

'Thinking about my mum.'

'Yes.' Erin reaches over and squeezes her hand.

'Oh, and almonds,' Shan remembers. 'Whole ones as well as flaked.'

* * *

Tracing Robin Westwood proves harder than Shan thought it would be. He has no online presence, which is very rare. There are a few Robin Westwoods on Twitter and Facebook and LinkedIn and Insta but most are easy enough to discount by their appearance or age. She contacts the one that might be a possibility, asking if he studied medicine at Leeds University in the late nineties. Gets a no in reply.

She looks for the family next and finds that Professor Andrew Westwood is still working at the Royal Free.

She calls the hospital and leaves a message with his secretary asking him to return her call. Then she joins Leo in the business of updating their files on the case, typing up and logging statements they've accrued so far.

The front desk buzzes up to tell them Keith Sykes, the reporter who used to work on the local paper, is here. Leo goes down to meet him. Shan fetches a spare chair from her office and puts it in Leo's room.

Keith Sykes is a short, stocky, white-haired man with a bulbous nose riddled with broken veins and enormous white eyebrows. He greets her warmly when Leo introduces them.

'Long time no see,' he says to Leo. 'So when d'you get your carriage clock, then? Not long now, I reckon?'

Leo smiles. 'A while yet. How's retirement?'

'Not bad. I thought I'd go doolally at home but Sheila has me trotting off here, there and everywhere. Japan, Thailand, New Zealand. Even a dreaded cruise — Norway. Some amazing sights. Wouldn't have missed any of them. Anyroad—' he slaps his knee — 'these rumours you heard, bad behaviour backstage?'

'Yes,' Leo confirms.

'I never heard anything like that. By all accounts the festival was very peaceful. Your lot didn't make any arrests, did they?'

'No. Light touch policy, I believe.' Leo hadn't been on duty at the festival. Instead he was on day shifts that week-end, available to attend any other incidents in the district.

'There were a couple of cautions for disorderly behaviour, but that was about it,' Keith says. 'Now, the other question . . . I had a look into the promoters of the festival. The company doesn't exist anymore but I tracked down one of the site managers. He said security would have checked in festival staff like Terence Bielby but there'd not be any record left now.'

'Long shot,' Leo says.

'Aye,' Keith Sykes agrees. He braces his hands on his knees, elbows out. 'That bastard. You think you know a person.'

'He worked with you?' Shan asks.

'Did a lot on the paper. Lot for the town. Talking to him you would never have had a clue.' His outrage feels fresh, still keen. Re-awoken, perhaps, with the discovery of Vicky's remains. A feeling shared by the whole community, Shan sees. Like Ned Lister at the retirement home and the other neighbours.

Shan thinks of the man in prison, his stringy grey hair and the way he leered at her.

Of the women: Katie Fallows from Ripon who never got to go home to her three-year-old; Martha Weiss whose trip to the UK had ended so brutally; and Veronica White, only sixteen, raising money for charity on her fell run.

And Vicky?

Shan's phone rings and she leaves the men to take it in her office.

'DC Shan Young,' she answers.

'Andrew Westwood here. You asked me to call.'

'Yes, thank you. We're trying to contact your son, Robin.'

'Ah, we haven't been in touch for some time,' Andrew Westwood says.

'Could you give me his last address and phone number?'

'Afraid not. He left the last address I knew about.'

'Is he homeless?' She remembers the man with the shopping trolley near Wakefield prison. So many people like that. Too many.

'I can't tell you.' He sounds resigned to the estrangement. Not bitter or even particularly worried but regretful. 'You could try his mother. We divorced.'

Shan writes down the number. She wonders why he no longer has contact with his son.

When she reaches Meredith Westwood the woman volunteers the information without being asked.

'When Robin decided to drop out, he didn't just drop out of his university degree, he dropped everything. Friends, family, the lot.' Her accent is crisp, cut-glass.

'Does he work?' Shan asks.

'Odd jobs. Usually out in the sticks somewhere. Such an awful waste.'

'What made him drop out?'

'The million-dollar question. By his account he saw the light, wanted to be close to nature and self-reliant and I think there was some Buddhism in there somewhere along the way. So off he goes and never mind who it affects.' There's a hitch to her voice. 'I presume this is about Vicky Mott?'

'Yes. We want to talk to Robin as one of the witnesses.'

'I can't be sure where he is, I'm afraid. There's a village near Kielder Water, in Northumberland, called Staunton. It has a shop with a post office. I write to him there. I don't know if he still collects his mail there. He never replies.'

'Never?'

'No. We tracked him down with a private investigator. This was years ago. Robin was furious. He was so angry. He's never been an angry person. So I promised we'd never do anything like that again if I could just send letters. I promised I wouldn't harass him, as he puts it, but I needed to communicate. Even if it was one-way.'

It seems so brutal to Shan. To cut your parents off like that. Like disappearing into a cult. A cult of one. She wonders whether there is anything in the family history to warrant it. A difficult childhood, or abuse of some sort?

Shan writes down the address of the village shop and sets about tracing the phone number for it. She wonders if Robin Westwood is still in the vicinity and what sort of welcome they are going to get if they track him down.

* * *

Elizabeth

When Elizabeth answers the door, Melanie's face softens with sorrow, or maybe pity.

'I am so sorry.' She has tears in her eyes, and Elizabeth feels her own eyes burn in response.

Elizabeth steps forward opening her arms and embraces Melanie, who hugs her back with a fierce squeeze.

'Tea? Coffee?' Elizabeth says.

'Coffee would be lovely but I can get it.'

'No, you sit.' Elizabeth needs a moment alone.

In the kitchen as she waits for the percolator to bubble she feels the weight of grief pressing down on her, on the crown of the head, the yoke of her shoulders, through her spine and in her belly. A hot, leaden burden.

Elizabeth has never forgotten the moment she heard her daughter was missing. The phone call.

She'd popped home for lunch — one of the bonuses of living so close to school — and had snatched a quarter of an hour to tie in the tomato plants in the lean-to greenhouse by the back door.

She almost hadn't heard the phone and ran inside to answer it.

Melanie, Vicky's housemate was on the line, her voice breathy and stuttering. The poise that she'd demonstrated on the couple of occasions they had met now flown.

Elizabeth struggled to decipher the message. 'You're still at the festival but Vicky is missing? You're with the police?' The blood in her veins ran cold. *Missing?*

The smell of tomato leaves on her hands as she clutched the phone was pungent.

A police officer came on the line telling her the same as Melanie and talking about an official missing persons report and Elizabeth grew numb. Her skin was taut, frozen, her tongue swollen and rubbery, useless. But inside everything was seething, fizzing, chattering.

Every time she hears from Melanie or Usha, every time a Christmas card arrives, the memory crashes over her as fresh as daybreak. And she smells the spicy tomato scent.

The pot is burbling when there's a second knock at the door.

Melanie rises and follows Elizabeth as she lets Usha in.

'Oh, Elizabeth.' Usha reaches out a hand. She is crying, dashing away the tears. 'I'm sorry. Stupid.'

'It's okay,' Elizabeth soothes. 'You cry all you want.' They hug. And then Usha and Melanie do the same.

'I've made coffee. Or there's tea,' Elizabeth says.

'Coffee's fine, thanks,' Usha says.

Elizabeth brings through the drinks and a jug of milk.

'How are you both?' she asks when they're settled. 'Tell me what you're up to.' Does her voice sound brittle? She's on edge but wants to put them at ease. The prospect of going to pieces horrifies her.

Usha and Melanie trade glances. *Who's going first?* Melanie inclines her head. 'Okay. Busy. Not enough hours in the day. Not enough staff. Our lists get longer.'

'You're still working in York?' Elizabeth says. 'The change of address?'

'Yes. Same hospital but we moved further out in January. A new build. Still a building site.' She smiles. 'It's a longer commute but a lovely spot. Fields all around.'

Elizabeth has seen Melanie a handful of occasions in the years since Vicky's disappearance and each time it's been a surprise that Melanie has aged. Because in her mind's eye Melanie is still twenty-one just like Vicky will always be twenty.

She had barely known these housemates. Why would she? They shared her daughter's student house. They shared her life. In phone calls home Vicky would mention them: *Usha and me saw* The Crucible *at the Playhouse*, or *Melanie is planning a barbecue for her birthday*. They were shadows, extras, bit parts. And then afterwards they were all she had left.

Elizabeth had gone to the house in Leeds with its shabby sofas and grubby paintwork and listened while they told her about the weekend. Elizabeth hadn't shed many tears by that point. She was anxious, horribly worried, yet resolutely hopeful that Vicky would soon be back, convinced it was some sort of grotesque misunderstanding. But as Usha described the note and the hill that rose behind the cottage, a stone lodged in Elizabeth's throat, and heat rose behind her eyes. *To see the sunrise. With a serial killer on the loose?* At that moment she had wanted to shake Vicky. Grab hold of her and drive some sense into her.

Elizabeth had left with Vicky's holdall. A month later she would return to collect the rest of her daughter's belongings. Her clothes and textbooks, make-up and shoes. Her collection of hats. Bedlinen and towels. Melanie and Usha helping her to box it all up.

Usha had cried then too, and Elizabeth had reassured her. 'She'll be back. I know she will. You need to believe in that.'

Usha had nodded. Dark smudges ringed her eyes; her skin was dull. Melanie's fair hair was greasy, stringy, her lips chapped, sclera bloodshot.

140

'And how's Kieran?' Elizabeth asks Melanie now. Melanie signs her Christmas cards to Elizabeth with the three names: Melanie, Graham and Kieran. Usha simply signs her own name, did so even when she was married. Always just the one name. The marriage was short-lived.

'A handful.' Melanie gives a rueful smile.

With a sudden pang Elizabeth realises that she will never be a grandmother. Vicky will never have a child.

'How old?' Usha asks.

'Just turned ten.'

'When Pam arrives we'll go in the kitchen if that's okay,' Elizabeth says. 'We can spread the photos out in there and I can make lists.'

'Sure,' Melanie says.

Elizabeth hadn't known if they'd agree to help plan Vicky's funeral. She had dithered before asking them because wouldn't it be hard for anyone to say no to a request like that? But her desire for their contribution, the friends who knew Vicky best in that last part of her life, the ones she may well have gone on to be lifelong mates with, overrode her doubts.

Vicky's friends from her schooldays had drifted away over the years. The two closest ones had both emigrated, to the USA and to Japan, and were no longer in touch.

Elizabeth wanted whatever ceremony they planned for Vicky to reflect her as a young woman and a friend, not just a daughter.

'It's hard to believe,' Usha is saying to Melanie. 'All that time and she was—' She breaks off, a guilty look flashing over her face.

'It *is* hard to believe,' Elizabeth agrees. 'Waking up in the morning, there's still that moment before I remember.' *And all those years of hope, dissolved like a dream.*

'And the police?' Melanie says. 'Will they be able to charge Terence Bielby?' Both pairs of eyes fix on Elizabeth, hungry for information.

'They have to be cautious, be certain. And rightly so. And of course they can't tell me everything.'

141

'They said it might be an accident.' Usha's words are threaded with hope.

'Yes.' Elizabeth swallows. Clasps one hand in another. 'She was alive for some time after she fell.' Not dead already and dumped by her killer.

'Oh, God,' Melanie says. 'And she was hurt?'

Elizabeth guesses at the words unsaid: did she bleed to death, hit her head? Did she starve?

'She had broken several bones.' Her tone is matter-of-fact. 'They won't be able to specify a cause of death. It could have been an infection or a lack of water. We'll never know.' Elizabeth feels the goosebumps prick on her arms and the familiar burn of nausea at the stark facts of Vicky's last days.

Pam's knock interrupts them.

Elizabeth is relieved her friend is here. Pam bustles in, a bottle of gin in one hand and an overnight bag in the other.

With introductions made they assemble round the kitchen table.

Ever the teacher, Elizabeth has done her prep. Headings for them to discuss.

Coffin and flowers.

Service — celebrant, eulogy, readings/poems, music.

Celebration — venue, numbers, invitations, food, photo display.

'I've decided on a cremation,' Elizabeth says, 'so I'll look to book at one of the crematoriums in Bradford. But I still don't know where to scatter the ashes.'

'Here?' Pam suggests. 'In the garden?'

Vicky spent most of her life here and Elizabeth imagines she herself will live out her days here. Prays she will not be shipped off to some care home at the end. But Vicky? Shouldn't Vicky be free of that? Out in the world somewhere, on the wind?

'I don't know,' Elizabeth says, and her friend gives a nod.

'It's not like you have to decide now,' Pam says. 'Some people hang on to them for years.'

Keep her close? In an urn on the mantelpiece or on the dresser in the kitchen? Elizabeth's mind slips to slapstick scenarios of someone opening the container thinking it's a biscuit jar or flour and she is privately appalled at her warped imagination.

When she asks Usha and Melanie if they have any ideas they both look unsettled.

'It's difficult.' Usha looks at her then away. 'Because we didn't really know her for very long.'

'What about the Dales?' Melanie says. 'Not Garsdale—' Elizabeth notes how rapidly she adds this — 'but she talked about you and her dad taking her camping there.'

'You did.' Pam smiles. 'We all went together some summers.'

'Hawkswick Cote, Littondale,' Elizabeth says. 'Wait.'

She picks up one of the photograph albums and thumbs through. Finds pictures of one of those trips. Vicky, gap-toothed, scruffy in shorts and a *Ghostbusters* T-shirt. Tattoo stickers on her arms. She is crouched beside Phil, who is tending their campfire. Sausages on skewers.

'Oh wow,' Melanie says. 'That's lovely.'

'She wanted to camp when we went to the festival,' Usha says. She turns to Melanie. 'Do you remember?'

In the silence that follows, as they all perform the *what ifs* and *maybe thens*, rewriting history, Elizabeth decides that Melanie's suggestion is right. Vicky would be happy there.

She tells them she has already considered coffins and is going to find the most environmentally friendly option. 'Though I'm not quite sure how green cremation is, but anyway. Probably something in cardboard or willow.'

'That sounds great,' Usha says.

'And Pam has a friend, Suzy, who's a celebrant, so I'll ask her to conduct the service and that means we can do whatever we like. Nothing religious,' Elizabeth says. 'I want to write a eulogy for Suzy to read and if you could both send me a paragraph or so about Vicky to put in that — any special memories or how you met or an anecdote.'

They both nod in agreement.

'It would be nice to have a couple of poems as well. Not necessarily something about losing someone, though it could be. But something to suit Vicky.'

'One of the sonnets?' Usha suggests.

Shall I compare thee to a summer's day . . . 'Perhaps,' Elizabeth says. Her mind snags on all the times she tested Vicky while she learned her lines or memorised her audition pieces. The way Vicky would collapse in giggles when she stumbled, then berate herself and try again.

'Could we email ideas?' Melanie asks. 'All come up with suggestions and you can choose.'

'Yes, good,' Elizabeth says. She takes a breath. 'I'd like you each to read one out but only if you want to.'

'Absolutely,' Usha says.

'Of course,' echoes Melanie.

Elizabeth is so grateful for their generosity. She knows she cannot trust herself to stand up and speak at the service.

The talk moves on to music and Usha and Melanie relax as they throw out suggestions — bands Vicky loved, tracks she danced to. Most of them Elizabeth recognises but nothing strikes her as right for the ceremony.

'Let's keep thinking,' she says. 'Lots of those would be good for the celebration afterwards.' She doesn't want to call it a wake; that word makes her think of open caskets, of sitting vigil with the dead.

Elizabeth expects half of Thornton will turn out to welcome home the girl who went missing. And part of her is tempted to throw a big reception. To make up for all those parties, the birthdays and opening nights that never were, the wedding and christenings, the award nights and New Year bashes.

She runs this past the others. Money isn't an issue; she has a pension from teaching and the house is paid for. She has savings in the credit union.

Pam's eyes gleam. 'Why not? Go for it.'

Melanie nods, smiling.

'Vicky would love that,' Usha agrees.

'And dancing!' Melanie says.

Pam laughs. 'I've never been to a funeral with dancing.'

'Well, now you shall.' Elizabeth is warmed by the thought of it. 'We'll dance and we'll get pissed and we'll make a bloody good night of it. Talking of which, I could do with a drink now.' She fetches the gin that Pam brought. Finds four glasses.

'I can't, I'm driving,' Melanie says.

'I'll just have a small one,' Usha says.

'Make mine a double.' Pam makes them all laugh. She will stay and eat with Elizabeth and spend the night in the spare room.

'Melanie, tonic or elderflower cordial?' Elizabeth asks.

'Elderflower, please.'

Elizabeth organises the drinks, tearing sprigs of mint from the plant on the windowsill, almost giddy at the progress they've made and the sense of common purpose. Love, even — the love of Vicky that has brought them together.

She raises a toast. 'To Vicky, in our hearts.' Her voice thickens with emotion. And the glasses chink as the four of them reach across the table, repeating the words.

* * *

Leo

On his drive into the office, Leo sees the leaves on the sycamore trees blowing back, exposing their undersides. 'A sign of rain,' his grandma used to say. That and cows lying down.

'Maybe they're just tired,' was Luke's response when Leo passed on this country lore to him.

'Maybe so.'

Leo likes the quality of light on days like this. The bruised slate colour of the sky setting off the vibrant baize of the sloping fells, with the network of pale drystone walls glinting in between. There is a drama to the contrast.

The rain is spitting by the time he reaches Settle. The tourists sport pac-a-macs. The hikers have their Gore-Tex on.

Shan is there ahead of him, intent on her laptop. Papers spread across her desk. She flashes him a welcome grin.

'Tea?' he offers.

'Got some.' She tips her chin to a mug on the desk.

They have arranged to visit Elizabeth to look at the possessions of Vicky's that her friends brought back from the festival. But first Leo wants to spend some time making sure that all the case files are completed and uploaded so he can apprise his boss of the story so far.

Jane from the press office has been in touch as well. They are trying to keep the story alive in the public realm and she would like to release a new appeal.

Leo explains what he'd like Shan to do and they agree to combine efforts in an hour or so.

'And the press appeal?' Shan says. 'I was thinking we could focus it, now we know where Vicky fell, and ask for information of sightings in the vicinity of Tollthorpe and Toller Fell. People or vehicles.' She wrinkles her nose. 'I know it's a long shot. How can anyone remember anything from twenty-two years ago? Not unless it sticks out for a reason, like Ned Lister's encounter with Terence Bielby. He could remember that but only because his granddaughter was at the festival for her birthday.'

Leo agrees. 'I'll check with DCI Booth and Dr James but I think we can also disclose the likely narrative of Vicky's death: the fall, the injuries, and the fact she crawled to the cavern. That's compelling — heartbreaking, really. People will want to help if they possibly can.'

'Can we release that information before an inquest?' Shan asks.

'I don't see why not. Dr James will tell us,' Leo replies.

The milk in the fridge downstairs looks dodgy and smells even worse, making him gag. He tips it down the sink, rinses the container and puts it in the recycling. Heads out to the butty shop for a pint of semi-skimmed.

'Any news, Leo?' Marjorie has been there for ever. Snowy white hair and pin thin, she looks like she'd break if you sneezed in her direction.

'Nothing yet,' Leo says.

'Poor do.' She tuts as she takes his pound coin.

'Going as fast as we can,' Leo says.

'Not you, you daft apeth,' she scolds.

'I know.' He gives a half-smile and tells her to take care.

Outside it is cool, fresh. The wind is coming from the east and sharp showers are forecast.

Back in his office, Leo waters his spider plant and picks off two yellow leaves from the peace lily before sitting down to work.

The time passes quickly. An hour and a half later they are ready to speak to DCI Booth. Leo dials, puts the phone on speaker.

'Leo!' Matthew Booth answers with a cheery energy and Shan gives a little jump at the blare of sound.

'Matthew, morning,' Leo says.

'How's the new girl working out? Any problems? These youngsters with no life experience, can be a steep learning curve.' *For them or us?* 'She fitting in all right?'

Leo winces and across from him Shan opens her mouth in a silent scream, closes her eyes and holds her hands cupped over her head as if for protection.

'She's here with me now,' Leo says. 'You're on speaker-phone, if you'd like a word with her directly. I've been very impressed so far.'

'No, no. That's fine,' Matthew says. 'Good morning, Miss . . . erm . . .'

'Young,' Leo says.

'Young, yes.'

'Morning, sir,' Shan says. Leo can see the laughter in her eyes. But her tone is serious, respectful. Which is wise. It won't do to antagonise a superior like Matthew. If he feels undermined it will be Shan, not Leo, paying the price. The rigid police hierarchy makes sure of that.

'So, Leo, what have you got for me?' Matthew asks, all brisk business.

'You've had the forensic report and we now know where Vicky entered the cave system. We've established some doubt over Terence Bielby's alibi, with an eyewitness who saw him early on the morning in question. We've also come across information not received by the missing persons investigation about one of the party at the cottage. He was suffering from paranoia that weekend and exhibited some hostility toward Vicky.'

'Really?'

'We're not leaping to conclusions and unfortunately the man in question died back in 1997 so we're not able to talk to him directly. In addition we have questions about the last sighting of Vicky coming down into Tollthorpe from Toller Fell. That counteracts our evidence about the location of her fall so implies she went back up there. Now, there could be any number of explanations for that but it does raise questions. I think that's it.'

Leo looks over to Shan, inviting her to add anything.

She spreads her hands palms down and moves them apart. *Done. Cut.*

'All good,' Matthew says. 'Any progress, keep me briefed as a matter of course.'

'Will do, sir. Thank you.' Leo finishes the call. The 'sir' wasn't strictly necessary given they're on first-name terms but he hopes it will mitigate any awkwardness that Matthew might have felt.

'Well, that was only slightly embarrassing,' Shan says. 'For all concerned.'

* * *

'There's an accident on the A629,' Shan tells him as they near the junction for the road to Bradford. 'Forty-minute delay.'

'Good to know. We'll take the old road through Keighley.' The journey is slow, a car towing a caravan in front of them.

As they near the town centre, Shan looks across to his side of the road. 'Oh, fuck.' Then adds, 'Sorry.'

148

A taxi company, Azed Cabs. Thick red graffiti sprayed on the walls. *PAEDO SCUM*. A wobbly drawing of a noose.

'Jesus!' Leo breathes.

In front of the shop stand a cluster of Asian men and a patrol car is parked up.

The ugliness of it, the stupidity, the cruelty.

'Where do you start?' Leo says. A rhetorical question. He tries to imagine what that would feel like, turning up to work, maybe after dropping the kids at school, ready to spend the day ferrying people from the supermarket home or to the airport or the hospital, to see a wall full of hate. Monstered. Threatened.

He drives on and tries to shake off the feelings of revulsion and despair.

Hope, Ange is always telling him. Just a sliver; it's all you need.

But sometimes it's hard.

The vicious words ring in his head. He can imagine faces chanting them, angry white people full of spite and bigotry. People like Luke.

Blood-red paint.

His heart gives a kick and his stomach drops like a stone.

'Helping Jack re-spray his bike,' Luke had said.

He was telling the truth, wasn't he? *Wasn't he?* He'd never have gone this far. He wouldn't. Surely, he wouldn't.

* * *

Vicky
1997

Robin goes out to the car, leaving the front door ajar, and comes back with a bottle of brandy.

'Whoa. Well sneaky!' Vicky whispers. 'You been saving that?'

'Strictly medicinal,' Robin says. 'I think this counts.'

Col is quiet now, dozing on the sofa but twitching fitfully and making soft noises in the back of his throat.

Robin gestures they should go through to the kitchen.

'A nightcap?' he offers.

'Please.' She feels shattered but not sleepy; the buzz from the ecstasy still simmers in her veins. She hopes the booze will dampen everything down. Let her rest.

'Will he stay asleep?' She takes the glass from Robin. A water glass with lemon dots printed on it, half full.

'No idea. I'll wait up with him. You can go to bed if you like.'

'Maybe. I'm still all . . .' She splays her fingers wide, waves them, a cartoon gesture. *Wired.*

She takes a swig of brandy. It's powerful, burning her tongue, her throat. Leaving a pleasant afterglow. The fumes fill her head.

'We have cheese,' she remembers. She moves to the fridge and peers in. 'And grapes!' Large purple ones. 'Who brought the grapes?'

'Don't know.' Robin shrugs.

'Usha probably.' She's good at that, presenting food. Always making big colourful salads with loads of different ingredients. Cutting recipes out of the paper. Trying new dishes.

Vicky gives the grapes a quick rinse under the tap and brings them to the table with the cheese, a knife and plates. She cuts some of the cheddar into small cubes.

'Now all we need is pineapple and cocktail sticks,' she jokes. 'They were the highlight of my birthday parties as a kid.'

Robin shakes his head. 'Rice Krispies squares. And cocktail sausages.'

Vicky pushes the plate to the centre of the table so they can both reach.

She hears a sound outside. An owl calling. A proper *tu-whit tu-whoo*. 'Listen!'

They wait, Robin's head tilted, a half-smile on his face. Nothing.

'Owl,' she says. Then it calls again and they both hear it. There's something magical about the sound. Haunting, plaintive.

'We had them at school.' Robin picks off a couple of grapes.

'What, like, for falconry?'

'No.' He laughs. 'Like in the woods. Tawny owls.'

'Bet you had sword fighting?'

'Fencing? Yes. There was a club. I never learned,' Robin says.

'We've got a course coming up next term.'

'Why?' He looks puzzled.

'All those costume dramas,' Vicky says. 'Not that there'll be that many women cast in them, I'm guessing. Not swash-buckling anyway.' She chews a piece of cheese and reaches for more grapes.

'Would you do costume dramas?' he asks.

'I'd do anything,' Vicky answers without hesitation. 'It's all I want to do — acting. TV, radio, theatre, tacky adverts. Sell my soul. What about you?'

'What, me in a frock coat and a big floppy shirt with lacy cuffs?'

'No,' she snorts, though she likes the image. 'Did you always know you'd be a doctor?'

'Pretty much the family line.' He sounds resigned, with none of the passion that Vicky has.

'But you like it?'

'Yes, sure I do.'

'And you'll specialise?'

'I'm thinking of ENT.' Robin lifts his glass and drinks.

'Well, you're a good listener.'

Robin guffaws, a spray of brandy coating his hands. He rubs it away. 'I'm not sure that'll wing it,' he says.

Her arms feel heavier, looser, and her neck is tingling. She loves the sensation of being intoxicated. The way the edges become all fuzzy.

'But do they do that, teach you how to deal with patients?' Vicky says. Her experience with doctors has been mixed. Some attentive, empathetic, others supercilious and remote.

151

'Yes, role-plays. There's a module coming up. A group of actors come in and pretend to be the patients. You could do it.'

'I could!' she says.

Melanie's harsh reaction to Col's behaviour flashes in her head. 'Maybe Melanie should get some of that,' she says. Immediately she feels awful for slagging off her friend. 'Sorry. I didn't—'

'You're right.' He suddenly looks serious. Not worried but burdened. He shakes his head, mouth crimping, a shadow in his green eyes.

'What?' Vicky murmurs.

He looks at her straight on for a moment. Two. 'Things aren't that great.'

Melanie's not said anything. But Vicky recalls her goodnight kiss, Robin's expression. She feels a clutch of unease, a tension in her stomach.

'I'm sorry.' Robin waves a hand. Reaches for the bottle. 'I shouldn't—'

'No,' she says. Not sure what she means. No, he shouldn't talk to her about Melanie like this? Or no, he shouldn't apologise for doing it?

Robin pours the drinks.

Then he reaches over, touches her hand. A jolt like electricity runs through her. His eyes on hers. There is no air and she feels dizzy.

'Vicky, I—'

'Bitch! Devious fucking slag.' Col is swaying in the doorway, eyes livid.

Vicky's heart clatters. Robin pulls his hand away. Vicky scrambles to her feet. Robin moves to intervene, putting himself between them.

'You get some air,' he says. His back is to her; his eyes remain on Col.

Vicky grabs her brandy and snatches her coat from the back of the chair.

'She'll destroy you,' Col says. 'She's a cheating bitch.'

'Come on,' Robin is coaxing Col. 'Come sit down.'

Outside she gulps cooler air. A fine soft drizzle is falling and the moon is shrouded in cloud. When the clouds part momentarily it shines with a diffuse glow.

Vicky can smell the night, the earth, the rock. She sniffs her wrist and catches the faintest trace of sunscreen from earlier.

She listens but the little village is silent. Not even the cry of the owl disturbs the peace.

With trembling hands she lights a cigarette and goes into the outside toilet, out of the rain.

She smokes and drinks and listens, hoping to hear the owl again. Counting it a sign, an omen, that everything will be okay.

* * *

Shan
2019

Driving into Bradford, the city centre is spread out below them in the bowl of surrounding hills. It hasn't been developed like Leeds has, no rows of skyscrapers bristling heavenwards.

The sandstone warehouses and mills and streets of terraced housing are all a warm honey colour. Closer in, Shan can see the signs of neglect and austerity. Boarded-up shops and run-down houses. Peeling fly-posters and scrawls of graffiti. A woman with a brood of children pushes a buggy laden with shopping uphill. The children's clothes are faded, worn. Thin wrists and ankles peep out. Litter swirls in the gutter, skitters across the road.

The village of Thornton where Elizabeth lives is four miles from Bradford, among green fields. It's renowned for being the birthplace of the Brontes, the old centre carefully preserved. A desirable location.

Elizabeth is on the phone when she answers the door to them. She mouths, 'Sorry,' and waves them in.

'It doesn't matter if it's morning or afternoon but we can't do the Wednesday,' Elizabeth is saying.

Leo and Shan hover in the sitting room. Leo moves to the window and Elizabeth gestures, inviting Shan to take a seat.

Shan chooses the sofa. Her phone chirps. A message from her dad: *We still on for Sunday?* He's cooking lunch for her and Erin. A walk with the dog first. They do it every few weeks.

Yes. 10.30? She adds emojis — a plate of food, a dog, a tree, a heart. He lives alone in the family home. Shan worries that he's lonely, but he has a handful of friends he meets up with, other men his age. And there are people he sees at work during the week.

Elizabeth ends her call. 'Funeral director,' she tells them.

'Have you got a date?' Leo turns back to the room. He's been quiet on the drive from Keighley. Preoccupied. Shan's not sure why.

'Two weeks on Thursday,' Elizabeth says. She presses one fist into her other palm, takes a deep breath, eyes shut, then claps her hands together. 'So, you wanted to see Vicky's things from the weekend. I've got them ready. Would you like a brew?' Bright and practical. Has she been able to move beyond the shock that consumed her on their first two visits? Or is she functioning in spite of it?

'Tea,' Leo says. 'Thank you.'

Shan is bursting for the toilet. It doesn't feel professional to ask but she can't wait much longer. And the last thing she wants is another bladder infection. 'Tea would be great, thanks,' Shan says. 'Please could I use the loo?'

Elizabeth smiles, 'Of course. Upstairs, first on the right.'

Sweet relief.

The bathroom is a generous size, homely, quirky. A whitewashed wooden floor and walls, a mirror ringed by seashells. Mosaics in a wave design run around the bath and shower. At one end of the bath an enormous palm plant reaches halfway to the ceiling, and across the window sits a shelf with a row of coloured glass balls placed on it. Shan imagines them catching the sunshine at the right time of day, sending discs of colour on to the wall opposite.

The towel's thin, crisp and smells fresh as if air dried. The mirror is old and a little mottled. Shan face looks fuller. She wonders if she's gaining weight. She touches her stomach. Is there even a bump yet?

Shan wonders whether the room was like this when Vicky was here. How much has Elizabeth changed things over the years? Or has she felt obliged to leave things untouched? Vicky's room perhaps? But this room, the house downstairs, doesn't feel like a mausoleum. Doesn't look tired or outdated. Elizabeth must have revamped things in twenty-two years.

Downstairs, Elizabeth hands round tea, then kneels by the large coffee table. It's made of reclaimed wood. Erin's parents have a similar one. Elizabeth begins pulling items out of the holdall and placing them on the table.

'This is everything that came back?' Leo asks.

'Just about. Some sweets I didn't keep, and some underwear that needed washing.'

There's a pause, slightly uncomfortable, and Shan and Leo exchange a glance.

'What?' Elizabeth says. 'You don't think I should have? No one said.'

'No, that's fine,' Leo says. Shan sees that there could possibly have been traces of DNA on Vicky's pants, if she'd had sex with someone before the Sunday morning. But with a houseful of friends and everyone's accounts following more or less the same lines, that wasn't likely.

Shan leans forward to look at the items and has a lurch of déjà vu. Sorting through her mum's bag after bringing it home from the hospice. The pathos of the collection, the things she'd had with her at the end of her life. A photograph of the three of them together, a half-full bottle of Chanel Coco Mademoiselle, her brush and comb, even though her hair had been patchy for weeks. Vaseline for her lips. The

155

shawl Shan had bought her, fine cream wool shot through with gold. Her engagement and wedding rings. Keys and purse. Her phone and charger.

Shan shifts in her chair, pushing the memory away. She sips her tea, watching Elizabeth separate the items. Clothing, a bundle of paper rolled up. 'One of her scripts,' Elizabeth says. An unopened pack of cigarettes, Rizla papers. Purse, a canvas wallet in a zebra print.

'There was no lighter?' Leo checks. Shan remembers the crime scene photographs they've seen, the green plastic tube discovered near the bottom of the shaft.

'No,' Elizabeth says.

Shan picks up the purse, looks inside. Credit and debit cards, library card, Blockbuster video card. *Rave from the grave.* The thought in Shan's head before she can censor it.

Mortified, she concentrates on Elizabeth still laying things out. Body Shop White Musk perfume oil, Ambre Solaire sunscreen. Toothbrush, make-up bag.

A badge.

Shan reaches out and turns it over. A smiley badge, the same yellow face as the one from the cave. She feels a prickle of shock, like touching a bare electric wire.

'Her smiley badge,' Shan says. She turns to Leo, searching his face for understanding. 'We thought the smiley badge at the bottom of the shaft was Vicky's, but hers is here.'

'Everyone wore them,' Leo says. 'And she could have had more than one.'

'Not these,' Shan says. 'They have starry eyes, look.' Like scribbled asterisks, slightly spooky.

Elizabeth is still, intent on following their conversation.

'Have you got that copy of the photo of the four of them, from the festival? The one Usha had,' Shan asks Elizabeth.

Without speaking, Elizabeth gets up and goes to one of the shelves in the alcove. Brings out a manilla envelope and fetches the photograph.

'See.' Shan points to the badges that each of the women wear. 'The same design.'

And the men, Shan thinks, Robin and Col? Did they wear them too? Col in particular.

'Someone was there with her,' she says. *They lost this badge.*

Shan sees it, Vicky falling, snatching at air, her fingers catching on the smiley button, tearing it off. Plunging.

Alarm flares in Leo's eyes. She's speculating, and in front of Elizabeth, who has lost so much and should only be told hard, incontrovertible facts. Elizabeth's face is drawn, ashen, her cheeks hollowed. A shard of fear in her eyes.

'Sorry,' Shan mutters. 'I'm guessing. We don't know that. Vicky might have just borrowed someone else's badge or picked it up by mistake.'

Does Elizabeth believe her?

Shan doesn't believe her own words — not for one moment. She knows with a sense of absolute certainty that someone else must have been on Toller Fell with Vicky that day. And it's down to them to find out who.

CHAPTER NINE

Leo

'I'm sorry,' Shan says. 'I shouldn't have reacted like that. God knows what Elizabeth's thinking.'

'Along the same lines as us would be my bet,' Leo says.

Shan looks crestfallen, eyes cast down, jaw taut as she gets into the car and fastens her seat belt.

Leo sighs. 'You know what they say about mistakes.'

She glances at him.

'Opportunities for learning. It might be tea towel wisdom but there is some truth to it.'

'I'll know next time?' She meets his gaze.

'That's the spirit. So let's see what we can find out about these badges, eh? And get this one logged in evidence.' Shan has the smiley button in an evidence bag.

'Okay, I'll ring Usha Bhatti.'

Shan gets busy on her phone while Leo drives back into Bradford. The rain has stopped and there are patches of summer blue between the clouds. The drops on the trees glint like diamonds. The streets shine gold.

Leo once dated a girl from Bradford, travelled in to concerts at St George's Hall, followed by a late-night curry. Her parents were Latvians. Wool capital of the world, Bradford was in its day. Relying on immigrants to staff the hundreds of mills and warehouses, or do the dirtiest jobs. The Irish first, then Polish and Russian Jewish refugees. Eastern Europeans after the Second World War then South Asians and people from the West Indies.

'No answer from Usha,' Shan says. 'I can try—'

Leo's phone interrupts them. *Ange calling.* His stomach cramps. *Luke?* Accepting the call, he braces himself for bad news.

'Can you talk? Is this a good time?' Ange, in his earpiece, sounds bright, not anxious.

'Yes, I'm in the car with Shan.' Making that clear in case Ange is planning to discuss anything that should be kept private.

'Leo, I got through! I'm on the shortlist.'

It takes him a second to catch up.

'The award?'

'Yes.'

'That's brilliant, Ange. Blimey, that's fantastic.'

'I know! There's going to be a ceremony at Yorkshire Sculpture Park on Monday evening. Remember we had to keep the date free? I don't know if you can still manage . . .'

'I'll be there,' he says. 'Is it black-tie?'

'Shouldn't think so. But sod that anyway,' Ange says. 'We'll wear what we like.' She has always hated dress codes, especially formal wear. Wouldn't don a skirt when she temped in an office, refused a traditional wedding dress when they got married.

'So, I'll see you later. I just had to tell somebody.'

'Of course. And well done. That's fantastic.' She hangs up.

'My wife, Ange.' Leo is aware Shan may only have heard his side of the call. 'She's an artist and she's up for a prize.'

Shan's eyes light up, sharing his pleasure. 'That's great. What sort of art does she do?'

Leo takes a breath. He finds it hard to summarise because Ange's projects are so wide-ranging.

'Environmental projects, mainly,' he says. 'To do with landscape and the natural world. Climate emergency.'

Shan is nodding but he can tell she'd like more of an idea.

'So, the year before last year she created a trail in an old quarry in Coverdale, carving images of locally endangered species into the rocks. Sort of reverse fossils.'

Leo stops at the traffic lights. A tall, thin, pointy man walks a tall, thin, pointy dog across the road.

'And before that she set up an installation in a far-flung part of the grouse moors in East Arkengarthdale. Wove slips of willow into a giant image of a goshawk and planted it so it'd come into leaf. She used sand and stones to write a slogan round it, "One Land, One World", and filmed it from a drone.'

'Sounds amazing,' Shan says.

'Goshawks are often killed by gamekeepers,' Leo adds. 'They were driven to extinction. Had to be reintroduced. Ange's project was all over the local news. It got lots of publicity. Landowners were not best pleased.'

The traffic is heavy, funnelling them past roadworks up the hill to the Keighley road. Impatient drivers tailgate and even overtake with little space to do so.

Shan calls Melanie Quinn on speakerphone. Leo isn't expecting an answer given the doctor's workload but she picks up. 'DC Young?'

'Good morning,' Shan says. 'We wanted to talk to you about the smiley badges that you wore at the festival. You remember them?'

'Yes. Okay.' She sounds intrigued.

'Where did they come from?'

'Oh, Dee made them herself,' Melanie says. 'She gave us all one.'

'All six of you?' Shan asks.

'Yes.'

She must be burning to ask why they're interested, Leo thinks.

'Do you know how many she made in total?' Shan says.

'No, sorry, I'm not sure.'

'Okay. Well, thanks very much.' Shan hangs up.

Dee Price sounds breathless when she answers Shan's subsequent call. The line is noisy with the roar and rumble of traffic.

'Hello?' Shan says. 'Can you hear me?'

'Yes . . . sorry . . . I'm out running.' There's a scuffling noise and then a few moments later Dee comes on again. 'I've found a quieter spot,' she pants. 'Can you hear me now?'

'Yes, thanks, that's better.'

Leo is trying to weigh up the odds that the badge is as significant as Shan thinks it is. If Dee made dozens of them, will that alter Shan's conviction that this one belonged to one of Vicky's friends?

'We want to ask you about the smiley badges that you wore at the festival. You made them, is that right?'

'Yes. I ran a badge-making stall for a Women's Aid fundraiser at the student union. I made them then. Why?'

'I'm sorry, I can't go into any details. But how many of that particular design did you make?'

'Six. For those of us going to Garsdale. I took them with me,' Dee says.

'And they were identical?'

'Yes.'

'Can you remember if everyone wore theirs that week-end?' Shan asks. Car horns sound down the line.

'I don't know whether Robin actually wore his, but . . . well . . .' Dee sighs loudly. 'They have more than one purpose.'

'Sorry?' Shan says.

Leo can't follow either.

'See, it's an easy way to smoke hash.'

Leo catches on.

'You put the badge on a postcard or something, with the pin bent, and stick a piece of hash on that, light it and cover it with a glass. Move the glass just enough to suck in the smoke from the bottom edge. You've no need for tobacco.'

161

'Right, I see,' Shan says. 'Well, apart from Robin, can you remember if the others had their badges on that weekend?'

'I'm sorry. I've no idea. It's so long ago. Has there been any news?'

Shan looks to Leo, who gives her the nod. They've okayed a fresh press release with Jane and it will have been distributed by now. In the public domain.

'You'll find an update online,' Shan says. 'We've released further information today.'

'Have you charged him?' Leo knows she means Bielby.

'No,' Shan says.

'Arrested someone else?'

'No. The information relates to what we've established about Vicky's death and an appeal for any sightings of people near Toller Fell early on the Sunday morning.'

'Right, okay.' She sounds disappointed.

Shan ends the call. 'So the badge must belong to one of them.'

'Agreed,' Leo says. 'But we don't know how it ended up where it did.'

There's a flash of irritation on Shan's face but she recovers quickly.

Leo elaborates, 'Yes, there could have been someone there with Vicky but there are any number of other possible explanations. Vicky used it to smoke cannabis like Dee described. She picked it up thinking it was hers.'

Shan opens her mouth — to argue, he thinks — but he gets in first. 'Remember, these kids were drinking most of the day, taking drugs left, right and centre. They were off their heads.'

'So what now?'

'Robin Westwood. At the very least he should be able to tell us if Col Green left the cottage at any time that night. Or if he himself did.'

'Kielder Forest — it'll take us all day,' Shan says.

'It will. Does tomorrow work for you?'

'Yes, that's fine.'

Leo hears her energy return at the prospect of moving forward. Of having a task to complete with the hope of filling in another part of the picture.

* * *

Ange is in the workshop. As Leo crosses the garden he can hear the whine of a power tool. *A drill?*

It's a jigsaw. Ange is bent over the workbench, goggles on. A sheet of plywood is in the vice and she's cutting along a wavy line.

Leo waits, not wanting to startle her.

She reaches the edge of the board and the top section falls to the floor with a clatter. The sound of the tool's engine dies.

'Congratulations!' Leo says.

Ange pushed the goggles up on to the top of her head, face beaming. 'I can't believe it! Just to be shortlisted—'

'I'll hug you later.' He points to the coating of sawdust on her boiler suit and then to the black daub on her cheek. 'Charcoal?'

Ange pulls off a glove and swipes at the mark, examines her fingers.

'Oil. And muck.'

'How many on the shortlist?' Leo asks.

'Four of us.'

Leo whistles. 'Good odds.'

'Oh, Leo!' She's bubbling with excitement.

'We should celebrate.' He's tired but a trip to the pub or out for a meal won't kill him.

A sceptical look in her eye. 'We will, but not tonight, a work night.'

He's relieved.

'Narrow escape,' she teases.

He laughs.

'Let's do something next weekend. I'll know if I've won then. I can see if Bryn and Jenni are free.'

'Sounds great. Okay. Now — food?' Leo says.

'Yes, please.'

'Luke's in?' His bike's here, which is the usual sign.

'In his room, I think.' Ange pulls the goggles off, shaking her head when they snag on her hair.

'Have you told him?'

'Yes. He actually congratulated me.'

'Good. And the do, the ceremony — will you invite him?' This could be a bridge, a truce. Luke sharing in his mum's success. The family together. Even if only for an evening.

'You think I should?' Ange says.

'He can say no. But at least the invitation's there.'

'Yeah. Yes, I will.'

'Okay. Twenty minutes till tea,' Leo says.

He chooses vegetable korma and naan. Sets the table, his mind rehearsing how to broach the discussion he needs to have with Luke. His guts tightening, twisting at the prospect.

Just to rule him out. Silence the whispers in his head accusing his son of a crime. Put the lid on his suspicions. Echoes of work — all the times he has questioned people *in order to eliminate you from our enquiries.*

But how to start? *Where were you last night?* Or, *Did you hear what happened at one of the taxi firms in Keighley?*

Something more direct?

Leo dips his hand under the tap and sprinkles water over the breads. Cuts them into pieces small enough for the toaster.

You could leave it for now?

But Leo knows that buying himself time will only let the worry mount. He needs to nip it in the bud.

He washes his hands and walks up to Luke's room.

He can hear voices, snatches of music, but can't tell if Luke's talking to someone or gaming. Or both.

Leo knocks, swallows, consciously lowers his shoulders.

Hi, Luke . . . Luke, listen . . .

He knocks again.

'What?' Luke calls.

'Can I have a word?' Leo says.

164

Luke takes his time, pausing whatever he's doing, and then comes to open his door. Face impatient.

Did you do it? Were you involved?

'This is a bit awkward,' Leo starts.

'Why?' Already an edge of belligerence sharpens Luke's tone.

Leo takes a breath. 'Because I was in Keighley today and I saw that somebody had spray-painted the words "paedo scum" over a taxi firm. An Asian taxi firm. And I want to see if you know anything about it.'

'What?' Luke's face creases in derision.

'You heard me,' Leo whispers.

Luke shakes his head. 'Aren't you supposed to be investigating a murder? A serial killer, yeah?'

'Was it you?' Leo says. He feels heat across his chest and back, his heart unsteady.

'No.' The denial sounds automatic. 'What you accusing me for?'

'It's a hate crime, Luke.'

'That right? Well, whoever done it, they deserve a medal, if you ask me.'

'Those men had nothing to do—'

But Luke withdraws, shoves the door shut.

Leo imagines barging through it, demanding his son give him a straight answer, insisting on seeing his phone to work out his movements. Wanting proof that he is telling the truth.

Helping Jack re-spray his bike.

Really?

He doesn't want to tell Ange about his suspicions. Not when that is all they are. Not today when she is relishing the recognition of her talent. They don't keep secrets. And he's learned over the years to be more open with her than he is naturally inclined to be. There are still times when he gets depressed and it's Ange who will drag it out into the light. Like she can smell it on him.

She does understand that when he's down it's harder to initiate communication. The negative spiral of his mood is accompanied by a chorus of voices in the wings telling him that he's not worth the bother, that he shouldn't burden anyone else with his troubles, that it's tedious and needy and self-indulgent. That he's a worthless piece of shit.

Ange isn't having any of that. 'If I don't know, I can't help. From my side of things you're shutting me out. Sure, I won't be your therapist and I don't expect you to tell me everything. Just tell me the one thing: that you're not feeling well. That's all.'

In the kitchen Leo empties the dishwasher, grunting as he bends and the sting of pain stabs through his knee.

He'll tell her tomorrow, he decides. Soon anyway.

She comes in. 'That smells good. I'll just get changed and wash my face. Oh—' She stops in the doorway. 'I saw a hare today.'

'Yes?'

'Up near Buckden Pike. Not seen one for years. Pretty big,' she adds.

'Great.'

'Traditionally associated with rebirth and physical love.' She winks.

'And madness,' Leo says. 'Go. Wash. Two minutes.'

She turns and leaves.

Leo braces his hands on the sink and takes a moment, looking out at the trees silhouetted filigree-esque against the dull steel sky. Drinking in the beauty of it all.

* * *

Shan

When Shan sinks into the warm bath, it feels like she's shedding the weight, the dirt, the tension of the day.

She closes her eyes and leans back, breathing in the steam with its spicy, smoky aromas of vetiver and bergamot from her bath oil.

She tries to empty her mind, to let herself relax in the moment, but thoughts from work, from the case, dart through her mind like minnows.

Or piranhas.

The badge. The kick when she saw the badge. *What if we can't find Robin Westwood tomorrow?* His mother was uncertain if he'd still be in the area.

'Shan?' Erin calls up. 'You want a drink before I go?'

'Cranberry soda, thanks.'

Shan sits up, scoops palms full of water on to her face. Her breasts are tender. She peers down. There are crease marks imprinted on her skin from her bra straps. Perhaps she needs a bigger size.

Erin comes in with her drink and puts it on the shelf at the edge of the bath. She kisses Shan on the cheek.

'Do you think my breasts are bigger?' Shan asks.

Erin looks. 'Maybe. A bit? I don't know.'

Shan puts her hands over them, testing. 'Feels like it.'

'Perhaps they are — given your condition. Look, is all that stuff in the bedroom for the wash?'

'Not sure. I'll have a look.'

Erin hesitates as though there's something else. 'Okay. I'll see you in a bit.' One of Erin's nights at the gym.

Shan drinks half of the glass in one go, burps, then lays back again. She hears the front door close.

She thinks of Elizabeth Mott's big bathroom. How with somewhere like that there'd be space for a chair. Erin could sit and chat to her while she soaked. And vice versa. But maybe that'd get irritating after the novelty wore off.

Will they ever be able to buy somewhere bigger? They could only afford this place because Shan had a lump sum from her mum's life insurance that her dad insisted she take then rather than waiting until he died too.

Their house is *cosy* in estate agent's speak. It's tiny. Built as a mill worker's cottage, there are two rooms downstairs, which previous tenants knocked into one, a bedroom, box room and bathroom upstairs, and a backyard.

The baby will be fine sleeping in the box room but the living room already feels cluttered with just the two of them. What will it be like once they add in all the baby gear and toys? There's no storage they can use.

167

Mind you, she thinks, *this place probably housed a large family in years gone by, crammed together, all sharing beds. And we're lucky to be able to buy at all. Most of our friends are still renting.*

Whose is the badge?

Shan groans. She can't turn off for half an hour even.

She finishes the drink and bends her legs and sinks lower in the water. Just her face and knees sticking out.

There's a tingling sensation in her belly, like a bubble, and she expects to fart. But that doesn't happen. The fluttering comes again.

'Oh, jeez,' she breathes. She put her hand to her stomach and waits.

And waits.

Did she imagine it? Is it just wind after all?

She tries to remember what she's read — a quickening sensation. Any time after thirteen weeks but usually later with first pregnancies. *Is it too soon?*

There it is again! Nothing to feel on the outside but a twirling, flipping motion deep inside her. The baby moving.

She wants to run to the gym and tell Erin.

Or call her dad.

She wants to tell her mum.

She wants to dance and eat cake and make love.

Then she starts crying, which is stupid.

She doesn't know why she's crying, because she's happy. She's happy. She is.

Of course she's happy.

She's having a baby.

* * *

Leo

'It's the next exit?' Shan checks.

'Yes.'

The satnav agrees.

The run up from Yorkshire has been pretty smooth, the M6 surprisingly quiet though it got busier around Carlisle.

The route now takes them into Kielder Forest proper — new territory for Leo. He's been to Northumberland before, to Alnmouth and Alnwick on the coast, but never to the forest.

'The largest man-made woodland in England,' Shan informs him. A plantation. 'And the largest artificial lake. Oh — going by capacity.' A reservoir that along with the forest has been developed for leisure: camping, walking, canoeing, stargazing, nature trails, fishing, cycling. 'They've got badgers and pine martens,' she says. 'Ooh — and adders.'

'Now you tell me,' Leo says.

The hamlet they are heading for is off the beaten track, away from the main tourist areas, the lodges and outdoor pursuit centres.

The woodland either side is mainly spruce. Ranks of the tall conifers take much of the light but here and there dappled sunshine falls on the road ahead. Signs warn of deer and red squirrels. 'The Dales were forested once upon a time,' Leo says.

'People cut them down,' Shan says.

'That's right. Buzzard!' Leo spies the bird soaring overhead. Then another joins it.

The road twists and turns, twice they cross cattle grids, which Leo assumes must be to contain the deer.

After a false turn leads them to a dead end and what looks like an abandoned forestry cabin, Leo reverses and a quarter of a mile further on they find the hamlet of Staunton.

A row of six cottages, a shop with a post office. And next to that an abandoned pub, roof slates missing and the boards over the windows bloated with damp and mottled with mould.

'How does this place stay in business?' Shan wonders. 'It's the middle of nowhere.'

But even as she finishes speaking a small van appears from the other direction, stops outside the shop and a family climb out and go inside.

'Visitors would be my guess,' Leo says. 'Four miles that way is a campsite. It's probably worth a trip here if you don't need a supermarket. And having the post office will be an asset, year-round.'

A few minutes later the family emerge, parents each holding a bulging carrier bag and the two children eating ice cream cones.

Inside, the shop is bigger than it looks from the frontage. The premises have been extended a fair way at the back. There is a small section of fresh food amid aisles carrying groceries, hardware, drinks. Chiller cabinets and freezers line one wall.

The post office counter adjoins the cash desk. Cigarettes and vape material lie out of sight behind sliding doors.

No one is immediately evident but a voice calls out, 'Hello, with you in a minute,' from somewhere inside, and shortly a youngish woman emerges wearing a dusky pink linen pinafore over her clothes.

'Help you?' she says.

For a moment Leo thinks she has earbuds in but realises they're hearing aids.

He introduces himself and Shan and explains they're trying to trace Robin Westwood.

'We know he used to come in here, that his mother sent letters to him care of this address.'

'Yes.' She volunteers nothing further. He senses she is weighing them up.

'Has he been in recently?' Leo asks.

'About three weeks ago.'

Leo is relieved to hear it, pleased that they have not come all this way on a wild goose chase. 'You know where he lives?'

She looks troubled, grimaces. 'If this is about evicting him—'

'No.' Leo jumps to reassure her. 'It's a historical case we are looking into. We want to talk to him as a potential witness.'

'He's not good with people,' she says.

'Okay,' Leo says. 'We'll bear that in mind. If you can give us directions . . .'

'Well — I'm not exactly sure of where it is. I've never been. But one of my boys told me it's about three miles due west near a stream. There's not much of a path. Toby could maybe show you but he's not home from school till after four.'

Leo looks at Shan, who gives a quick shake of her head — they'd have to wait for half the day.

'West and by a stream,' Leo says. It's not a lot to go on.

'Yes. Oh, and you pass an old cottage about halfway there. Just the walls are left.'

When they are outside, Shan takes her phone out. 'I've got a compass app on here. And we can measure how far we've got with GPS.'

'If there's a signal?' Leo says.

Shan checks. 'Okay here. Whether there'll be one further in I don't know.'

A scant trail leads into the forest from the roadside. The tree cover here is a mix of birch and oak, beech and rowan. The air is rich with birdsong. Leo makes out great tit and chiffchaff and the hollow drilling tock of a woodpecker.

Soon they are having to forge a path of their own, crushing the grass and brambles underfoot. The smell of mulch, of wet bark and sap, is pungent. The scent reminds Leo of pencil shavings.

Shan checks her compass frequently.

They reach a particularly impenetrable section. 'Should've bought a stick,' Leo grumbles.

Shan moves away. 'Go around,' she suggests. 'It's not so bad here.'

Occasionally they find narrow animal trails that disappear off among the trees.

Sun glints through the gaps in the canopy, throwing blotches of gold on the trunks and the vegetation. Bees and hornets are busy around the tall stalks of foxgloves and the tiny violas that lie close to the ground.

Leo stops where an old beech has fallen, the wood crumbled like honeycomb. 'This is a mile and a half.'

Shan, a couple of steps ahead of him, freezes. She raises a hand to quieten him, directing with her eyes.

A roe deer within a stand of trees. Movement, and a smaller one, a fawn, steps in beside it.

Shan looks to him, smiling.

The deer are browsing, tugging at leaves within reach. Caramel-coloured fur. Black noses contrasted with white fur around.

Slowly Shan raises her phone to take a photograph, though Leo thinks they are too far away for it to be worth doing.

Either her action or something else spooks the deer, who bolt, a rustle of grass and leaves the only noise they make.

A blackbird shrieks an alarm call in the trees above.

Moving forward Leo wonders if they've strayed from the route, *Ten minutes*, he tells himself. *If it isn't clear in ten, we rethink.*

They are picking their way through a copse of silver birch when Shan suddenly starts. 'There.'

The old house — three tumbledown walls coated in vegetation. Bright green ferns are growing round the base. Patches of wild garlic, with spiky white flowers, cover the woodland floor and scent the air.

A hundred yards ahead they meet a shallow stream, too wide to ford in a stride. The water is a peaty brown and flies hover over the surface. Sphagnum moss hangs over the banks.

Shan checks her compass and they continue west, keeping close to the stream.

Occasionally there are small waterfalls, mini rapids, where rocks interrupt the flow of the water.

Leo feels a pricking at his cheek and brushes away a gnat.

Further on, he misjudges the proximity of the nettles and is rewarded with a sting across the back of his hand.

They circumvent a dark pool rife with tadpoles, who dance frantically at the edges while water boatmen skate on the surface. Fringing the far side of the pool are long, lance-like leaves that Leo recognises as bulrushes. It's too early in the season yet for the rushes to bloom.

He realises they've reached their destination before Shan. It's the haze of smoke that first catches his attention. A campfire, a ring of stones, flames, a figure seated there. Perhaps thirty yards from them.

'Shan!' he whispers. Points.

They draw closer to the clearing.

Behind the campfire, the land rises up sharply and Leo spots with a jolt that there is a cave mouth carved into the face of the small cliff.

He sees the grainy footage from the caver's headcam in the cavern beneath Lund Seat again. Vicky's skull on the ground.

Vicky Mott died in a cave; Robin Westwood has made his home in one. Does this signify something? Is it because Robin knew that was her fate? Is it some sort of penance?

Before Leo can untangle his thoughts, the figure rises swiftly. Startled. Putting Leo in mind of the deer. The man has a full grey beard and long grey hair. Head lowered, his eyes flash on to them. He is poised, ready to spring.

And in his hand he holds a large silver knife.

* * *

Vicky
1997

Vicky hears the creak as the back door of the cottage opens and she freezes, alert in case it's Col coming out. A flush of fear sizzles through her veins like hot metal. Her throat is suddenly parched.

She forces herself to move, prepared to slam the toilet door shut and scream for help.

Then she hears Robin's voice. 'Hey. Vicky?'

Her bones go rubbery with relief. She gets up and steps out to meet him.

The light from the kitchen window makes it possible to see him holding up the brandy. 'Top-up?'

'Thanks. What about Col?'

'Asleep. Snoring his head off.'

He sits down on the bench that butts up against the outside wall of the toilet. An overhang from the toilet roof gives some shelter.

Vicky holds out her hand, palm up, testing. The rain has stopped.

Joining Robin, she offers her glass, lets him pour.

He lifts up a spliff, half smoked. 'I could save this for tomorrow?' he says. His voice sounds rough, croaky.

'Or we could make a night of it?' she tries to joke. But she feels wounded inside, the horrible feelings when Col shoved her, when he screamed in her face, still raw.

She passes Robin her lighter, and as he flicks the wheel, she sees his fingernails are bitten down. She's never noticed he bites his nails.

He releases a stream of smoke and passes her the joint. She lifts her head as she smokes. The moon is still behind a gauze of cloud.

She wants stars, a million stars, a whole Milky Way. She wants the rain to stop for good and the sun to rise, and the fresh day to be perfect again. Like tonight never happened.

There's an ache in her stomach, not hunger but something else gnawing at her. She's felt it before. She tries to place it, name it, and realises with a lurch it's the sensation she had when her dad died. A tension, a weight and pressure. A hollow sadness.

Her bossy, sometimes bad-tempered dad, who loved her so much. More conventional than her mother. His face, eyes rolling, when he accused the pair of them of ganging up on him.

'Just live a little, Phil.' Her mum's refrain.

They'd spat and squabbled but they adored each other. And then he was gone.

Vicky sniffs, squeaks. She doesn't want to cry. She won't cry.

Robin turns, alarmed, as she waves the spliff at him, wanting rid of it.

'I'm sorry,' she blubs.

'What is it? Is it Col?'

'No . . . yes . . . I don't know.' She can't stop the tears and feels herself getting snotty. She hasn't even got a tissue.

'I don't know,' she repeats.

'Hey.'

He reaches out, puts an arm around her shoulders, pulls her in so that her head rests just below his collarbone. She can smell detergent and woodsmoke on his clothes, a trace of sweat too. Musky.

She lets herself cry, wiping at her nose with the heel of her thumb, and gradually the clenching in her belly melts away. She sniffs hard, lifting her head and shifting away from him. 'Sorry. Your top's probably all soggy now.'

Robin smiles.

A late tear tickles as it runs down the side of her nose and he moves to wipe it with his thumb. His touch burns and a feeling of panic, of excitement, ripples through her.

She shouldn't. She knows she shouldn't.

But the burning sensation in the pit of her stomach, the heat that rises in her, is intoxicating.

She reaches up and touches his hand, cupped against her face.

He stretches a finger to touch her bottom lip.

I can't. But the words remained unsaid.

Everything is slow. Frozen.

She sees the pulse on the side of his neck below his ear. The blood beating there.

This is wrong.

But it feels so good, so right. Her body is singing, humming, vibrating.

She tries to draw away. His eyes, his sweet green eyes, are hard on hers. His face is solemn, open.

'I'm leaving her. It's over. I've been planning to tell her as soon as we get back to Leeds,' he says.

She reads his look. Sees no guile, but no expectation either. *We should wait*, she thinks.

She looks at his lips then back to his eyes.

She craves his touch. The heat of his body is making her dizzy. Giddy with lust. In every inch of her body there is a gathering, a growing hunger.

She stretches the tip of her tongue to circle the point of his fingertip. Tastes tobacco and salt. The tang of alcohol.

A wash of desire sends her head spinning, full of stars. Skin tingling. Aching for him.

She closes her eyes, stretches her neck.

He bends to kiss her.

* * *

Shan
2019

Shan sees the knife. Feels the bristle of fear. Checks her stance, her balance. Assesses the obstacles between her and the man holding the blade.

'Robin Westwood.' Leo's voice is soft. 'We're police officers. I'm Leo Donovan and this is Shan Young.'

The man remains coiled. *Will he run or attack?*

'We'd like to talk to you,' Leo continues. 'You might be able to help us.'

Robin looks strong, wiry. Shan can see the tendons on his bare forearms, the toned muscles.

The smoke from the fire drifts to her, the rich, savoury smell of roasting meat. She can see a scrawny lump of something on the spit. Rabbit? Pigeon?

'You need to put the knife down,' Leo says.

Robin's eyes are wild still. Glittering. Dancing between Leo and Shan.

In her mind she rehearses the moves she'll need to disarm him. But first she'll have to get close enough to grab his wrist.

She straightens her spine, rolls back her shoulders a fraction.

In the glade, flies and moths dip in and out of sunlight. The stream makes a shushing sound, punctuated by the high squawks of a bird that silences the trilling of others. Spider silk gleams and shivers on the bushes.

The meat starts to char, the smoke grows thicker, darker. Leo coughs.

Shan sees Robin Westwood flex his mouth and swallow, the ripple of his throat almost hidden by his beard.

'Go away,' he says. His voice is hoarse.

'We've come a long way,' Shan says. 'We'd really like to talk to you.'

'What about?' His hand on the knife is steady.

'About Vicky. Vicky Mott.'

Robin Westwood blinks. Reeling slightly. 'Vicky's missing.'

There's a crack from the fire as a nugget of burning wood is spat out beyond the ring of stones.

'We found her,' Leo says. 'We found Vicky's remains.'

Robin starts as if he's been slapped. He gulps air, turns and paces away, still holding the knife.

Shan prepares to chase after him, shifts her weight.

Leo looks at her. *Wait.*

The roasting meat catches fire, tongues of flame licking round it.

Robin turns back towards them, his eyes pained. 'Go. Please go.'

'We're trying to find out what happened to Vicky,' Leo says. 'We've been talking to her friends, your friends.'

Robin shakes his head. His eyes catch on the burning food, the meat like a torch now. He keeps staring at it but he's not really seeing it, Shan thinks. He's somewhere else.

'Robin?' Leo says.

'I don't know anything. I can't help you.'

Why hasn't he asked any questions? Isn't he curious about where Vicky ended up? How she died? Or does he already know?

A wood pigeon coos somewhere in the trees behind them. Robin is unmoving, gazing at nothing.

'Let's just talk,' Leo says. 'Put the knife down, come and sit. We'll talk about what happened.'

'We know Col Green was unwell that weekend,' Shan adds.

Robin looks up at the name. Eyes clouded.

'We know he was hostile, aggressive towards Vicky,' she says.

'Col's dead.' His tone is clinical. *Befitting of a doctor*, Shan thinks.

'Yes.'

The meat, charred through, slips from the skewer and lands in the fire with a hissing noise, sending up a cloud of ash.

The birds fall quiet.

'But if Col had anything to do—'

'No.' Robin cuts Shan off. 'It's my fault.'

Shan's heart gives a jolt. Her ears ring. *He's confessing?*

'It's all my fault.'

CHAPTER TEN

Elizabeth

The milk has turned. When Elizabeth adds it to her tea, cream-coloured globules float to the surface. There's a sour smell.

She feels a rip of rage, followed by a slump of defeat. *Why me? Why now?* She cannot face the walk to the shop, the inevitable conversation. The chess game of question and answer as people try to navigate this appalling situation.

She refills the kettle, rinses her mug and makes a green tea. While the drink cools she lugs the rubbish out to the wheelie bins. Her recycling bags consist almost entirely of wine and spirit bottles and tonic cans.

Back inside she savours the first hot, grassy, slightly bitter mouthful of tea.

Her to-do list has sprouted offshoots. Is growing like bindweed.

She scans the tasks, looking for something she feels capable of tackling today, something she can achieve, when there is knocking at the back door.

Someone who knows her, then.

It's Caroline from school. Thirty years younger than Elizabeth, Caroline inherited her year group. Caroline never knew Vicky, or Phil. Elizabeth has seen her at work and she's an excellent teacher. Always confident and upbeat. Plain-speaking, which occasionally ruffles feathers in the staff room.

'I'm sorry to hear about your daughter,' Caroline says. 'You're probably drowning in casseroles and flowers but I'm doing a big shop today if there's anything you need.'

'Oh, thank you. Yes. There's not much but that would be really helpful.'

'Great.'

'Come in,' Elizabeth says. 'It'll only take a minute.'

She tears paper from her jotter. Writes, *semi milk 2 litres*. Then, after a quick look in the fridge and vegetable rack, *mature cheddar cheese, new potatoes, red onions,* and *Yorkshire teabags*.

'I love your kitchen,' Caroline says. She lives on the new estate. Elizabeth imagines her kitchen is all shiny grey or ice-white units and weird taps. Maybe a fridge with an ice dispenser. *Who needs that much ice?*

'I think a tenner should cover it.' Elizabeth gives her a note.

'Lovely. It'll probably be about half five when I'm back.'

'Thanks. You can leave it by the back door if I'm not in. It'll be fine there for a bit. And thank you again.'

'No worries.'

Elizabeth's phone has pinged, and once Caroline has gone she checks her messages.

Emails. From both Usha and Melanie. *Doing their homework.* She reads Usha's first.

Dear Elizabeth,
I'm still looking for pieces but one possibility that I've attached is by a poet called Audre Lorde. Vicky was learning this for her practical exam when we were at the cottage. I'll keep looking for other ideas and get back to you tomorrow.
Love, Usha

Elizabeth reads the title but that's all.

She feels a swirl of claustrophobia, too confined by the house, by her to-do list. She needs fresh air.

Within minutes she is walking along the back road to the edge of the village, where she takes the footpath to the viaduct.

The sky is drab, an oyster grey dimpled here and there with darker smudges. A light breeze stirs the aspens, making them whisper.

At the start of the bridge she reaches the place where she first met Mike, not long after the viaduct was opened as a trail in 2008. She saw him fall off his bike, his cycle skidding from under him and across the path. Mike skinning his knee and elbow. Elizabeth had rushed to help. He'd reassured her it was just a scratch. His knee gouting blood.

'A phantom pothole,' he joked.

'It could do with dressing,' Elizabeth had said. 'I'm not far from here.' She signalled towards the village. 'I could fix you up with something.'

She thought he'd refuse, carry on dripping blood like a real man, but he looked at his knee, the stream of red running into his sock and then back at her. He'd given a warm smile and thanked her.

They married within the year. And he was dead within five. Vicky never met him. She had never known that Elizabeth remarried.

Dead. Everybody dead.

Sorry for yourself?

Haven't I the right? Just for a few hours? Christ, if not now when?

She passes a dog walker with three different breeds on leads, nods a hello.

The path reaches the start of the viaduct, giving views of the Pinch Beck valley below.

The wind is stiffer here. And Elizabeth feels a chill. She should have worn another layer.

The valley floor is a swathe of grass, the narrow beck snaking through.

A flock of birds, starlings judging by the way they fly in such close formation, spin and wheel, painting patterns.

Her mind veers back to the police visit, showing them Vicky's things. The young officer, Shan, seizing on the badge. *Someone was there with her.* She had backpedalled quickly after that, obviously worried that she'd spoken out of turn, but Elizabeth had seen her expression when she turned over the badge. Her eyes sharp with suspicion, face fervent.

There had been two men staying with Vicky's group at the festival. Elizabeth had met one of them briefly when Vicky was moving in, Elizabeth's car crammed with her daughter's bags and boxes. Usha's boyfriend, he was a medical student like Melanie. The other man was too. Melanie's boyfriend. Did the police really suspect one of them of involvement in Vicky's death? One of those friends? But what about Terence Bielby? Elizabeth shakes her head, oppressed by this line of thought, and irritated that she can't find out more.

She reaches the first bend of the S-shape of the viaduct.

Here she stops. This is her place. Maybe she should get them to stick a bench here when she's gone. Wouldn't be allowed, though. The viaduct is clear of obstacles; it's just a sterile tarmac strip between the low parapet walls.

She rests her elbows on the wall.

Looking down 120 feet or so she can make out the movement of water in the stream, spies rabbits grazing.

A fall from here would kill you.

She thinks of Vicky falling, down into darkness. On to rocks, not grass. Down to her tomb. *Oh Vicky.*

She sucks in a breath. Another.

I am so lonely, she thinks. *For all my friends, such good friends and neighbours, I still feel alone.*

Don't we all? Really?

She acknowledges the self-pity, allows it for now.

A gull flies overhead, its plaintiff cry echoing down the valley.

She should go to the sea. When this is all over. Perhaps with Pam, if Pam would like. If not, on her own. Somewhere

182

warm where she can walk on hot sand and pick her way through pine and olive groves. Sit at a rickety table to eat chewy bread and heaps of fresh salad washed down with dry local wine. Float on the sea with the sky in her eyes, let the salt dry to dusty patterns on her skin. Sit and read, lose herself in other people's stories. Count the stars.

She takes out her phone, increases the brightness level so she can see properly, and opens Melanie's message.

Dear Elizabeth,

Thank you again for inviting us to help plan Vicky's funeral and celebration. She was such a good friend even though we'd only known each other a short while since starting uni. Full of life and funny, such good company. I saw her perform a couple of times and she was amazing. She was really kind, too. Getting to know her and then living together made the whole university experience so much easier for me. I'm so glad I knew her.

I've found a couple of poems by Christina Rossetti you might like. They are traditionally used for funerals but you may prefer a more original piece. Please do let me know if you want something different and I'll try again.

Take care,
Melanie

A trio of cyclists whizz past, wheels ticking. Elizabeth catches a snatch of conversation, 'He said it wasn't practical so we decided . . .'

She waits a moment before selecting the first attachment. She opens the file and reads.

WHEN I AM DEAD, MY DEAREST
When I am dead, my dearest,
Sing no sad songs for me;
Plant thou no roses at my head,
Nor shady cypress tree:
Be the green grass above me

183

With showers and dewdrops wet;
And if thou wilt, remember,
And if thou wilt, forget.

I shall not see the shadows,
I shall not feel the rain;
I shall not hear the nightingale
Sing on, as if in pain:
And dreaming through the twilight
That doth not rise nor set,
Haply I may remember,
And haply may forget.

Elizabeth gazes over the valley, her eyes burning and the green, all the glorious green, swimming before her.

* * *

Shan

Should they caution him? A confession without a caution is inadmissible.

'Why do you think that?' Shan says.

Robin doesn't answer.

She looks to Leo.

'Let's sit down,' Leo repeats. Gesturing to a boulder and a fallen trunk at their side of the fire, then to the seat that Robin was using when they arrived.

Robin still holds the knife, dangling from one hand as if he's forgotten it's there. He looks bewildered and much older than his forty-three years.

He moves slowly and takes his seat.

'Can you give me the knife?' Leo says. 'While we talk.'

Robin looks at him for a long minute then adjusts his hold on the knife and stretches out his arm so Leo can approach and take it by the handle.

Leo and Shan go to sit down. The log is covered in plush green moss; she expects it'll be damp.

Leo settles on the boulder and places the knife close to his foot on the ground.

A puff of wind tugs the smoke directly at Shan. Her eyes sting and she blinks to pinch away the tears.

Robin's gaze is cast down, staring into the fire.

Shan wonders if he's going into shock.

'Why was it your fault, Robin?' Leo asks.

Robin's shoulders move, taking a breath, but he doesn't reply.

Shan glances at Leo. *Can I?*

Leo agrees with a blink.

'You and Vicky were looking after Col, in the early hours of the Sunday. He'd become disturbed, paranoid.'

'Yes,' Robin whispers. He clears his throat.

A movement to Shan's right. A squirrel digging in the undergrowth.

'And the others were in bed?'

'Yes.'

'And then?'

'Col had gone to sleep. We'd been outside for a break and . . .' His voice wavers and he stops.

'Yes?' Shan gives him a bridge to the next part of the story.

'When we went back in, he wasn't in the living room anymore.'

Shan's skin tightens. *Col disappeared? Then what? They tracked him up the hill? Vicky found him? But the note . . .*

'I went upstairs and checked and he was with Usha. He'd gone up and was asleep again.'

'And then?' Shan's mind swivels to juggle other scenarios.

Robin leans forward to pick up a slender branch, one end of it blackened. He stirs the fire, which is close to cinders now, the wood glowing coals.

'We stayed downstairs. We fell asleep. I fell asleep.' He pauses. 'I heard the door in the night; it woke me. I thought Col

185

had run off but then I heard him snoring. And once I knew that Col was okay, I didn't even wonder who'd gone out. I didn't think. When the others came down she was gone and—'

He shakes his head over and over.

'She was gone,' he repeats. He lets go of the stick. Hugs his knees, head bowed.

'Why was that your fault?' Shan says.

He doesn't reply.

'Did you hurt her, Robin?' Shan keeps her voice soft, non-judgemental.

'I don't . . .'

Shan's feet are pressing down into the grass and mulch. Her back rigid. She can feel the damp soaking into her trousers, the back of her thighs.

'I thought it was all right. She was all right. Then she went off like that. She shouldn't have gone like that.'

Shouldn't? Shan can't tell if he's trying to justify his actions. Did he go after her, punish her for some perceived wrongdoing?

'Did you follow her?'

He looks directly at Shan, brow creased.

'No. I told you. I fell asleep. When they woke me up I knew something terrible had happened. She'd been out there for hours on her own. She was upset, she must have been. To go like that. Not to wake me, not to tell me.' He looks at them, tears threatening to brim in his eyes. 'I thought she wanted it the same as me.'

'What? Wanted what?' Shan says.

Robin rubs at his face, combs fingers through his tangled grey hair.

'What did you do?' Shan says.

He steeples his fingers and braces his head, not making eye contact.

'Robin?'

'We slept together. We had sex. And then she disappeared.'

For a few moments the only sounds are those of the forest, the chatter of birds, the burble of the stream, the whisper of leaves on the aspen trees.

Then Robin coughs, makes a sound halfway between gasp and a groan. He is leaning forward, elbows on his knees, head braced between his hands, palms cupping his forehead, shielding his eyes.

'Robin?' Shan feels hot, clammy, a pressure inside as though there is too much blood pumping through her. 'Where did this happen? In the cottage?'

'What?' He looks up, stupefied, mouth slack, eyes glazed. 'Where?'

'Outside, in the yard.'

'Did Melanie know you and Vicky slept together?'

'No.'

That can't be right. She must have known. 'Are you sure?'

'I never told her.'

'And Vicky?' Leo's words carry a weight after his pro-longed silence. 'Did she tell Melanie?'

Robin stays quiet.

'Melanie and Vicky were close friends, weren't they?' Shan says.

'Yes. I shouldn't have . . . we shouldn't . . .' Robin falters.

Did Vicky go upstairs and wake Melanie, tell all, beg her forgiveness? It doesn't seem likely to Shan.

'Where were you and Melanie sleeping?' she asks.

'In the back bedroom.'

Overlooking the yard. Shan swallows. She imagines Melanie looking out, seeing the figures in the dark, recognising with a dizzying sickness just who it is and what's going on. Shan's mind skitters ahead, building scenarios. Melanie distraught, confronting Vicky, begging her friend to come with her, *let's get out of here, have a talk.*

But the note?

They knew the note was in Vicky's handwriting. Had Melanie asked her to write it? *Just so no one worries.* Wouldn't Robin have woken if all this was going on?

In the tangle of grass and weeds around the log Shan sees ants scurrying, shiny and brown, stopping to communicate with one another as they pass.

'You were asleep in the living room. Did anyone disturb you in the night?' she says.

'No. Only when I heard the door. If I'd known it was her going out. If I'd only thought about it—' He bites off his words.

There's a flash of black and white as a pied wagtail crosses the stream.

'And afterwards, did you ever tell anyone, Melanie or anyone else, that you'd had sex with Vicky?'

'No.' His expression is strained.

A fresh puff of wind sends a tremor through the woodland. Shan lifts her hair away from the back of her neck, welcoming the cooler air. The smell of soil is sweet and earthy; the musk of the trees grows stronger.

'You and Melanie split up after the weekend?' Shan says.

'Not straightaway.'

'Go on.'

Robin presses his fingers to the centre of his forehead. Then curls his hand into a fist, tapping his knuckles on his brow. 'I . . . she was so upset about Vicky going missing, it would have been a shitty thing to do. But then, I was struggling with the course and, um . . . Col was all over the place. He needed . . .' He gives a huge, shuddering sigh.

When he makes eye contact with Shan she sees he's now in tears. 'It was all a mess.'

'Who broke it off?' Leo says. 'You or Melanie?'

'It was mutual. I said maybe we should take a break and she agreed. Then with Col . . .' He clears his throat. 'She was really great when he died. She came and stayed and helped. As a friend though. That was it really.' He shrugs. 'We never got back together.' He stills. Then his head flies up, face alert, apprehensive. 'You're sure it's Vicky?' He's clearly clutching at straws as he looks from Shan to Leo.

'Absolutely,' Leo says.

'You and Vicky, when you came into the cottage everyone else was upstairs. How long was it before you fell asleep?' Shan asks.

'I've no idea. Not long, I don't think.'

'Did Vicky go upstairs?'

'I don't know.'

'And how was Melanie when you realised Vicky hadn't come back?'

'She was worried. We all were. But we hoped we'd find her at the festival.'

'Was it Melanie who suggested looking there?' Shan says. *Leading you all away from Toller Fell.*

'Yes. Why do you keep asking about Melanie?' He freezes. A look of repulsion alters his face, lips parted, teeth bared. 'You can't possibly . . . No. That's insane. There was a serial killer. You can't . . . why would . . . how? No . . . that . . . this—' He's agitated, words breaking up.

'We're just gathering information at this stage.' Leo's tone is level, controlled. 'Putting together all the facts. Establishing evidence. Filling in the details.'

Robin still shakes his head.

A gust of wind stirs the embers in the fire and shivers the bracken.

'Melanie loved Vicky,' Robin says. His shoulders are raised, head lowered a little as if he might spring up and charge at them.

Shan checks the knife is safe by Leo's foot. Leo sees her glance. Gives a blink of reassurance.

'She loved her,' Robin repeats.

'Yes.' Shan agrees. An ant crawls over the toe of her boot. She shakes it off.

But loving someone means you're open to betrayal. And jealousy is a powerful motive.

* * *

Leo

Leo silently considers the encounter as he navigates the route back towards the M6. Senses Shan doing the same alongside him.

189

'It gives us a motive.' She breaks their quiet introspection.

'A *potential* motive,' Leo corrects her.

'But with the badge though—'

'Yes. I'm not discounting it. Not by any means. On Monday we sit down and consider if we have reasonable grounds to speak to Melanie as a person of interest.'

'Okay,' she agrees.

Leo knows that in the right circumstances anyone can be driven to violence, but if Melanie Quinn was involved in Vicky Mott's death the more remarkable aspect is that she has been able to live with that since, to create a successful life for herself and not be destroyed by the guilt and the secrecy.

'Can you imagine living like that?' Shan says.

For a moment Leo thinks she's talking about Melanie.

'Like Robin, completely off-grid?' she continues.

'It has its appeal,' he says.

'Really?' She swivels to look at him. 'Could you do that?'

Could he? Be without Ange? And Luke? He feels a prick of guilt that Luke is an afterthought. 'Not sure I could do it on my own.'

'But wouldn't you miss stuff? Electricity? TV? The internet? Heating? Taps?'

A flash of glowing red scoots across the verge, into the trees. A red squirrel. It's gone before he can point it out.

'Not so much. My bed? Now *that* I'd miss. And a hot bath.'

'Slippers?' Shan laughs.

'Comes to us all,' he says. 'You're laughing now but . . .'

A camper van passes, going the other way. Kayaks on the roof and bikes strapped to the back. Maybe that'll be him and Ange, one day. A road trip. They've talked about it sometimes. Canada, or Italy.

'And you?' Leo says. 'Doesn't it appeal?'

Shan shakes her head. 'No. Not one bit. I like people, need people around. And stuff. Lots of stuff.'

* * *

190

Sunday morning and Leo is restless. Yesterday he was up early and spent the day doing chores in the house and helping Ange to get Billy's house opposite ready for his discharge home. Throwing away old food rotting in the fridge and replacing it with fresh. Cleaning the kitchen. Hoovering round while Ange changed the bed and put sheets on to wash, sorted out the bathroom.

Leo fetched over a helping of chicken stew for Billy to heat up, and a couple of his freshly baked flapjacks.

It wasn't mentioned. Not beyond Ange telling Billy that they'd had a tidy round and left him a bite to eat, when the ambulance brought him home. The man is of an age and persuasion to feel demeaned by accepting help in the house, while he is completely happy for assistance with his garden or his car. The intimacy perhaps of the domestic sphere.

Where will I end up, Leo thought? *Like Billy, clinging on at home? Like Ned Lister, in a fancy retirement home? Or a no-frills place with budgets slashed to the bone, the staff paid peanuts, and never enough cover so it's all they can manage to keep on top of toileting and feeding their charges. Maybe I'll be dead before all that. Before Ange.* The thought was strangely reassuring.

Sunday Ange has work to do, preparing information for the awards. 'They're lining up several interviews for us, and I need to print off photos for the exhibition.'

'Singing for your supper?' Leo says.

'Something like that. But I think it's canapés, not a sit-down dinner, so you'd better eat something first to keep you going.'

'I might go for a walk this afternoon,' he tells her.

'Good idea.'

What he doesn't say is that he's planning to visit the area up round Buckden and Starbotton. Which just happens to be in spitting distance of the farm where Jack Sherringham, Luke's friend, lives.

He'll have his walk first, he decides, use the time to figure out how to approach the task of verifying Luke's story.

It's a fresh, blue, breezy day and the wind, coming down from the northeast, has a nip to it. Rags of sheep's wool, snagged by thistle and gorse, flutter in the wind.

There are a fair few folk up on the trail, including some mountain bikers. All exchange greetings with him as they pass, often a comment about how fine the day is, how beautiful the place.

Leo skirts the outcrops on the hillside and finds himself working up a sweat as he climbs. Sheep, raggedy-looking, regard him with baleful eyes. Crows bounce and fossick on the ground.

Crossing a boggy section, Leo uses the rushes as stepping stones. He misjudges a step and his foot plunges into the bog, cold water seeping down the ankle of his boot. A pang stabs through his bad hip.

He tugs his hat lower to keep the cold out of his ears.

All he needs to do, he tells himself, is pass by Jack's house and see for himself. Put his mind at rest.

And if the bike's not in view?

Call in, then? Claim he's looking for Luke? *Clumsy.* A phone message from Jack to Luke would tell Jack that Luke was home in bed (maybe surfacing now) and tell Luke that Leo was checking out his story.

There's no elegant way he can think of to do this. Not without spinning elaborate lies: *car broken down, looking into poaching, thefts in the area, killing of peregrine falcons, have you seen anything?*

What if Jack's out?

A mewling cry catches his attention. He's pleased to see curlews again, watches them wheel and dance for a few moments.

Leo meets a couple, a man with a toddler in a backpack and his partner carrying a baby in a sling. They ask him if they are still on the right route for the Dales Way and Leo reassures them, tells them they'll see a finger post before long showing them the turning.

He can't place their accents. Dutch? German?

For the minute's conversation he forgets his worries.

Rounding the rocks, he loses any shelter and the wind is fierce, making his eyes water and his nostrils run. He stops to blow his nose and drink from his water bottle, before taking the path down through a small copse in a steep-sided valley. The slopes are littered with the last of the bluebells. His knees remind him that going up is always easier than walking down. He makes his way back over several stiles to join the road and walk along to where he's parked.

The toes on his right foot are cold, sodden. At the car he swaps his hiking boots for an old pair of trainers, no socks.

The Sherringhams' farm is halfway up the hillside, with views across to the opposite side of the dale. The road is straight on this stretch and the farm comes into sight when Leo is still a mile away, marked by a ring of trees, shielding the farmhouse and garden from the worst of the weather. Lombardy poplars occupy one side, the spiky sentinel row an unfamiliar sight in this landscape, while the rest of the boundary is a mix of broadleaf and conifers. Two huge old forest trees rise either side of the entrance.

The road widens at the farm, giving enough room for tractors and trucks to turn. And slightly beyond the farm there's a lay-by with a yellow grit bin for icy winter days.

As Leo approaches he sees a van at the gates, by the two oak trees, back doors open. A figure there. Leo draws closer and the man is shutting the doors, a box at his feet. Something familiar about his stance.

Closer still, Leo slows down to twenty, no one behind him to care.

There by the gate, meeting the van driver, is Jack Sherringham astride a motorbike. Helmet under one arm, bright blond hair. The bike is black, liveried with flashes of blue on the fuel tank and mudguards. No red. Not a spot.

As Leo passes, the van driver turns and says something to Jack. Face alive, smiling. Christopher Hirst. *Donovan? Any relation to Luke?*

The landlord in the pub at Tollthorpe and the last person to see Vicky Mott alive.

* * *

193

Erin is loading the dishwasher when Shan comes down for breakfast.

'I was going to do that,' Shan says.

'Yeah, but you didn't, did you.' There's a flatness in Erin's voice that signals she's pissed off. And Shan can sense the tension in the air, feels it stiffen her muscles. Erin continues shifting cups and plates, keeps her back to Shan.

'I can do it now.'

'Don't bother, it's nearly done.'

'Come on,' Shan says. 'I was tired last night.'

'You're always tired.' Erin turns, a jug in her hand, the orange and yellow one they bought in Palma. Erin's eyes are hard with resentment. 'And I end up doing everything.'

'One night's dishes,' Shan retorts.

'No, Shan. Most nights. And the bathroom. When did you last clean the bath? Change the towels? Even tidy up, for Chrissake? Look at the place.' Erin slams the jug down on the worktop and the handle comes away in her grasp.

Shan almost laughs. For a millisecond she hopes the mishap will derail the argument, till she sees Erin's face.

'Okay, it's a bit of a mess,' Shan says.

'A *bit*? I try to keep on top of it but you swing in from work and it's like living with a bloody student. Or a teenager.'

Swing? Swing in?

'Okay. Okay.' Shan raises her voice — hands too — in surrender. 'I'll do it, I'll clear up and . . . Maybe we need a rota.'

'That says what? It needs doing every day, as you go. You make a mess, you clear it up, you put things away. You don't leave it till Saturday or whatever. But *you* don't even notice and I end up doing it all. I'm sick of it.' Erin looks mutinous, mouth screwed tight, eyes stony blue.

Shan takes in a quick sweep of the living room. She wants to say, 'It's not that bad. It's just a bit of clutter,' but that's not going to help. 'So what needs doing now?' Shan pushes up the sleeves of her robe.

Erin gives a little laugh, dry as dust, not a speck of humour in it. 'You ask me. You see, right there, that's the whole thing. You just can't see it. Don't see it. We've talked about keeping the house clean before—'

Argued, more like.

'And nothing changes!' Erin grabs the jug and shoves it, and the handle, in the bin.

'Maybe we should get a cleaner, then?' Shan suggests. She's no idea what a cleaner charges but it can't be that much, can it?

'No way,' Erin says.

'Why not? Pay someone the going rate.'

'No.' Erin shakes her head, arms folded. 'We should be able to clear up our own mess.'

'But—'

'And cleaners *clean*. You'd still have to tidy everything away before they came.'

Shan hates this, hates to fight. But she doesn't know how to fix it. And she feels hurt too, resentful, not ready to make up, even if Erin were. Which she clearly isn't.

'If we had more storage we—' She doesn't get to finish as Erin swears under her breath and moves towards the stairs.

'Fine! I'll start now.' Shan hates the way she sounds. 'I'll do the rest in here.' She waves at the collection of items jumbled on the coffee table and half of the sofa, along with the pile on the floor by the window.

'There isn't time.' Erin is marching upstairs. 'We need to set off for your dad's in half an hour.'

Shan's stomach is churning. She feels queasy but she knows she ought to eat. She pours a bowl of muesli and makes a cup of tea. When she's eaten she thinks, for one unforgiveable moment, of leaving her dish in the sink. A dirty protest.

Act your age, woman.

She puts it in the dishwasher, adds powder and sets it running.

* * *

Erin streams one of her Spotify lists as she drives, avoiding any chat.

Shan feels a rush of emotion when she sees her dad. Tearful. She blinks it back.

He greets them each with a bear hug, and once Shan has used the loo they set out with Banjo, the dog, for a walk.

Erin is at the command of the dog. Throws his stick repeatedly. Banjo, a medium-sized brown mongrel with a foxy face, is a fast runner. But he has no interest in other dogs or rabbits, only in his stick — and whichever human is wielding it.

Shan tells her dad about feeling the baby move. And seeing the roe deer. He's curious to know why she went to Kielder Forest but she explains it was for work and she can't say more.

For lunch he has made aubergine parmigiana. One of the three vegetarian meals he has had in his repertoire since Shan turned veggie in her teens. Next time it'll either be roast root veg and halloumi, or mushroom risotto.

Erin shares her news about passing her probation and he keeps them entertained with stories from the office. He works at a print and design firm and collects tales of typos and gaffes in design that bring him and his listeners endless amusement.

Shan will drive back, which means that Erin can share the bottle of red wine with Shan's dad. It's his mission to try all the budget varieties at Aldi and Lidl, in search of a hidden gem.

Can he tell we've had a row? Shan watches him pour Erin another glass. *Is he oblivious? Are we putting on a convincing act?*

Shan tries to come up with a solution to the housework issue on the way home. She doesn't see how on earth they can bridge the gap between what's acceptable to Erin and what suits Shan. What can she say beyond promising to do better? Though why Erin is dead set against getting someone in to help, Shan's still not sure.

Erin is busy with some game on her phone and doesn't volunteer any conversation beyond agreeing with Shan that her dad seemed in good form.

As they pull into their road, Shan puts her hand out, touches Erin's forearm. 'I'm sorry,' she says. 'I will do more. And if it gets bad again, please just tell me before . . . you know.' *You start going off on one.*

'Okay.' Erin gives a half-smile but Shan finds a shadow in her eyes, as though something has been lost.

Before bed a text comes from her dad: *Everything okay with you and Erin? xx.*

Yes why? xx.

You seemed a bit subdued. xx.

She types, *We're fine. Long week.* Then deletes that and puts, *Bit of a tiff about housework. We'll be fine. xx.* He deserves her honesty.

I can guess who's in the doghouse. xx.

You know me so well. Nite Dad xx.

Night night xx.

Of all the stupid things to get stuck on, she thinks.

She turns off the lights and heads upstairs. Then groans aloud, retraces her steps and puts her plate and mug in the dishwasher and lines her Kindle up neatly on top of the books on the coffee table.

1,000 Baby Names sits there like a reproach. Okay, she's not had time to pick it up, but why does it feel like it's now part of the argument between her and Erin?

CHAPTER ELEVEN

Elizabeth

It's too short notice.

Elizabeth has tried three of the hotels on her list, looking for a space to hold the funeral reception. But they're all booked up.

'People tend to choose venues a long way ahead, for weddings and parties,' the last person tells her. Has she tried Fairmount Park, in Nab Wood, the Clubhouse there? They do a lot of funerals.

'Yes, thank you, I'll look at that.' Phil's reception had been there, and Mike's at Little Horton Social Cycling Club. She wanted something else for Vicky. High ceilings and moulded plaster cornices. A sprung dance floor. Great big windows draped with velvet. A sense of occasion. The place buzzing with chatter, alive with music.

She draws a line through the hotel on her list. Perhaps she should consider something more bespoke, DIY. Hire a marquee and find a green space to stick it. But then she'll need to find toilets too . . . all the effort.

Is she being too ambitious anyway, exaggerating numbers?

She turns to a blank page in her jotter and tots up the categories. Her friends, Vicky's, people from school and from the village who knew Vicky. Because although people who had no personal relationship with Vicky might attend the funeral out of a show of sympathy, they'd not come to the reception.

The afterparty? Vicky's voice, wry in her head.

Maybe somewhere more modest? Thirty people or so.

She has scrolled past those places on her browser, but now she goes back. West Bradford Golf Club. That's pretty close.

A golf club? Vicky sneers.

'That's inverted snobbery,' Elizabeth says.

Better than the other sort, Vicky shoots back.

'Blimey, I'm going barmy here,' Elizabeth mutters.

She writes out the phone number, and also one for a place at St Ives in Bingley.

If one of those is free she needs to ask if they can provide catering. And what about the music? Usha and Melanie had plenty of ideas for that. But practically, what will they need? A sound system of some sort? And the music itself?

She rings Usha and puts the questions to her.

'I think those places have a PA so you can usually play digital music through that. It's just a question of checking if we bring a USB stick or a laptop. I tell you what, I'll talk to Melanie. Between us I'm sure we can put a playlist together. And if there are any particular pieces you'd like, just let us know.'

'I'll have a think,' Elizabeth says. She sees Vicky, a little girl, singing and dancing to 'The Lion Sleeps Tonight', as a teenager leaping round the house with the B-52s' 'Love Shack' at full volume. Rehearsing the doo-wop songs from *Little Shop of Horrors* for her high-school show. Vicky signed up for drama classes at Stage 84 in Bradford as soon as it opened when she was eight. Already intent on becoming an actor.

Elizabeth stops to make lunch. She surveys the casseroles in the fridge. Some must be past their best by now. They'll need chucking, the dishes soaking, returning to their rightful owners. *Later.*

She decides on bruschetta. Halves a ciabatta roll and smears it with garlic, drizzles olive oil over. Grills each side until it starts to crisp. Then piles chopped tomatoes and red onion on top, a sprinkle of oregano, a splash of balsamic vinegar, and puts it under the grill for another couple of minutes. Tops it with torn basil leaves.

She is just finishing the last mouthful when Melanie calls.

'How are you?' Melanie asks. 'How's everything going?'

'Okay. Yes. Fine, thanks.' Because it is. Even though her heart feels like someone's been at it with a tenderiser. And there are moments when panic and fear grab her by the throat, rendering her temporarily numb and dumb. Times when she feels as if her very self is separated. Split into the woman who acts and thinks and breathes and continues to see the sunrise, and her doppelganger, howling at the moon and clawing at her skin, a wild anguish like a bottomless pit inside her.

'Usha called me about the music,' Melanie says. 'We can deal with that, no problem. Graham is a dab hand with streaming and downloads and we can use his Mac to play everything through the PA. That way people can see the track list and pick something out if they want. Like asking the DJ and getting an immediate response that's not a no.' She laughs.

'That sounds great,' Elizabeth says.

'All you need to do is find out what inputs the PA system has. If it's Bluetooth-enabled, or takes a jack or USB.'

'Just a sec, I'm writing this down.' Elizabeth scrawls the options. 'Okay. And thank you for the poem. It's lovely.'

'Oh, good.'

'I'm hoping to sort the venue out today. I'll email once it's confirmed.'

'Thanks. Bye-bye. And please let me know if there's anything else I can do.'

For a split second Elizabeth considers asking Melanie about the men, Col and Robin, about the police finding Vicky's badge among her things and another badge underground and suspecting that meant one of those friends was with her when she fell. But if the police do have a new suspect, Elizabeth doesn't want to start blabbing about it and possibly mess things up. Though it's hard not sharing, she thanks Melanie and hangs up.

Elizabeth writes a large tick next to *Music* on her main list. 'Progress.'

A wave of fatigue washes through her as she stands up. An after-dinner slump.

Briefly she contemplates going to lie down, having an hour sprawled on the bed, dozing, drifting. Why not?

But she's resistant. Some throwback puritanical streak that tells her to motor through and that she'll not sleep so well at night if she sleeps now.

Mike used to do it. Napping in the armchair for half an hour after lunch at the weekends. It irritated her, truth be told, but she couldn't explain why. Something about indolence. Or the smugness, the sense of contentment, that meant a person could relax so very easily, just dissolve into sleep at will.

Supposed to be good for you by all accounts, naps. Pam swears by them.

Not for me.

Elizabeth notices the bird feeder is empty but she's run out of seed. At least the blue tits have flown the nest. And her neighbours both sides have feeding stations. She just hopes the birds will come back when she stocks up again. Not shift allegiance and ignore her offerings. It would be a really rotten time to lose anything else.

* * *

Shan

Shan sits opposite Leo at his desk. The room smells of coffee from his drink and the sun pokes stripes through the slatted blind, illuminating the dust dancing in the air. There is an occasional tick from the wooden floors and wall panels expanding in the heat.

'So—' Leo begins.

'Can we open a window?' Shan interjects. The scent of coffee turns her stomach. She can't drink it, not since she became pregnant.

'I think they're painted shut. Let's see.'

He lowers the blind and tugs on the cup handles at the bottom of the sash once, twice, then with a screaming sound the window moves up, a six-inch gap. And the volume of noise from outside doubles.

'Great, thanks.'

Leo swings back the blind and sits.

'Melanie Quinn, we have to talk to her,' Shan says. 'She had motive, she had opportunity and the badge at the bottom of the shaft could have been hers.'

'*Could*,' Leo says. 'Equally it could be any of the other friends. We'll not be able to prove provenance, ownership.'

'But—' Shan breaks off. She knows he's right.

'And . . .' He sighs as if he's about to break bad news. 'We have no evidence that Melanie Quinn knew that Robin and Vicky had sex. We can't prove motive either.'

'So what do we do? What *can* we do?' Her frustration surfaces. She sounds irritable and tries to dial it down. 'There must be something else?'

A blare of sound, the roar and whine of motorbikes passing, fills the room. Leo winces, waits for it to fade. 'There is. We'll talk to Melanie but we have to be realistic. The likelihood of finding any other evidence — forensics or eyewitness or anything else — at this stage . . .' He shakes his head, turns his coffee cup, a half-circle and back. 'It's not going to happen.'

'She might confess,' Shan says. 'If she sees we're on to her and she's been hiding what she's done all this time . . . well, it must have been hard. To lie like that. To be able to function. Live a normal life. You'd need nerves of steel, wouldn't you? A stone-cold heart. They were best friends.'

202

'Which would make Vicky's betrayal so much the worse.'

'But do people do that? Can people really do that? Ordinary people, not career criminals or people raised on violence. Just take a life and then concrete over it? What would that do to you?'

'I can't imagine,' Leo says. 'Perhaps you compartmentalise, big time. Or you find justification for what you did and for concealing it. "I was provoked", that sort of thing. "No point in causing further damage; it won't bring them back". Or maybe Melanie was there but it was an accident?'

'Then why wouldn't she have fetched help?'

'Perhaps Melanie wasn't there at all. Vicky was alone and—' Leo's phone rings. He picks it up and frowns as if he doesn't recognise the number. 'Leo Donovan.' Listens. 'Yes? . . . What? . . . Oh God . . . Yes, I see.'

Shan feels goosebumps break across her arms and the fine hairs on her neck prickle at the urgency in Leo's tone.

He stands, continuing the call. 'But he's conscious? . . . Yes, yes, of course. Thank you. I'll be there as soon as I can.'

He turns to her. Face drained of colour. 'It's my son, Luke. He's been in an accident. I need to go.' His breath is ragged.

'Yes, of course. An accident?'

'Motorbike.' His eyes dart side to side. He gathers his things together. 'I'm not sure when I'll be—'

'No, it's fine,' Shan says.

'Just handle what you can. We can talk about strategy for Melanie Quinn when I'm back. Okay?'

'Sure. Let me know if I can do anything.'

'Thanks.' His face is haggard. 'I've got my phone.'

Then he's gone, banging the office door, his steps loud and quick on the stairs. She hears the thump of the outside door.

Shan sits, stunned for a moment, her own thoughts scattered. At sea with the sudden turn of events. She consciously takes a long, slow breath in and slowly out to calm herself.

The sound of a child wailing in misery rises from the street. Shan places her palm on her belly. And breathes again.

* * *

Leo

Leo's mind swarms with questions as he drives to Airedale General. A motorbike accident? What accident? Where did it happen? How? What went wrong? Was anyone else hurt?

He knows next to nothing about the circumstances but revisits the phrase 'He's conscious' time and again. A mantra.

He had intended to talk to Luke yesterday, to confront him with his lie about spray-painting Jack's bike, but by the time Leo got home from Buckden, Luke was already out. Leo tried texting him. *Where are you today? Are you back tonight? Please let us know. Dad.*

There'd been no response. Leo had rung after an hour, left a voicemail along the same lines. Nothing. When Leo left for work this morning Luke's bike still wasn't there.

What if Luke crashed on purpose? The sickening thought makes his guts churn. What if Leo's mistrust drove Luke to hurt himself? Like Col Green had. Suicide by motor vehicle.

He recoils from the idea. Besides, Luke has never done anything like that, never harmed himself, never seemed to suffer from the black dog that haunts Leo. And given the grim statistics for mental illness in young people, for the prevalence of self-harm, Luke's been surprisingly lucky.

The hospital car park is busy and Leo has to drive around twice to find a space.

He's familiar with accident and emergency. Been here before when Luke broke his arm on his trampoline, and when Ange crashed one winter, her car spinning on black ice and ploughing into a hedge. Whiplash and bruising but nothing worse. And of course, several times work has brought him here, dealing with people who needed urgent care.

At reception Leo gives Luke's name and date of birth and explains the hospital called him. 'I'm his father.' They must have got his number from Luke's phone.

He's asked to take a seat.

He spots an empty row and makes for that, passing people quietly waiting. A man with a tea towel wrapped around his hand. An elderly woman, face cut and bruised, shivering violently beside her companion who keeps patting her hand. A teenager in green football strip, her swollen foot raised. Others, old and young and in-between, have no visible injuries but sit with the silence and stillness that betrays pain.

He should call Ange. He will. Once he knows what the situation is.

He stares at the posters about flu jabs, and respecting NHS staff, and domestic violence, and wills the time to pass.

Nurses circulate in and out from the triage area. Every so often a patient is called through. Other staff come from the corridor that leads to the rest of the hospital. One nurse wears shoes that make a screeching noise with each step, setting Leo's teeth on edge.

The time crawls by. Leo tries to distract himself, browsing on his phone. He reads again the web page about Ange's award and follows the links to find out about the other three contenders. He checks out the website for the inn where he and Ange will stay for tonight's ceremony. *Might have to cancel.*

Luke had turned down Ange's invitation to the event. 'Nicely though,' she'd reported to Leo.

New patients arrive, among them a little girl in her mother's arms. The child sobbing, a bandage over her eyes. Her mother panicky, calling for help.

Rapidly assessed, they are taken through ahead of others with less urgent need.

Leo is staring blankly at some page about coaching inns in the county when his name is called.

In an anteroom a doctor explains that Luke is in the X-ray suite. He has several suspected fractures and will likely be admitted to an orthopaedic ward. They are monitoring him for concussion.

'He'll be all right?' Leo asks. A prayer as much as a question.

'There's nothing else of concern at the moment. He's a fortunate young man,' the doctor replies.

'Do you know what happened?'

'Only that he crashed riding his motorbike.'

'And no one else was hurt?' Leo says.

'No.'

'Do you know whereabouts it happened?'

'Near Hawes, I think. That's all I was told.'

Near home.

'A passing motorist called the ambulance,' the doctor adds.

'Thank you. Can I see him?'

'Once he's back up here from X-ray, we'll call you through.'

He's going to be all right. He's going to be all right.

Leo feels as though the relief will knock him over. As he stands to go, dizziness blurs both sound and vision. The room spins black. He grips the back of the chair to balance. The doctor, already at the door, doesn't notice.

Back in the waiting area, Leo pours a cup of water from the dispenser and takes it to the entranceway. Breathes in the air.

There are houses across the road, beyond a fence and a line of shrubs. They have dormer windows on the roofs. Those rooms will have a great view of the comings and goings in the emergency department. Presumably they've got used to the sound of ambulance sirens night and day.

Leo looks away beyond the hospital grounds where trees mark the beginning of farmland.

He drains his cup and returns to wait, still unsteady on his feet.

* * *

His first sight of Luke, flat on his back on a trolley, stops his throat.

My boy.

Luke's on a drip. A blanket covers him. His eyes are half closed.

'He's a bit groggy,' the nurse who's with him says. 'Fracture to his collarbone, which is very painful so we've put him on something to help with that. He's also got a break to the right tibia and wrist. Those can be set with plaster. But the collarbone will need a sling. He's been referred to the plaster room and it shouldn't be too long a wait. You're welcome to stay until he's taken down.'

'Thanks,' Leo says.

'And his clothes and possessions are in the bag underneath.'

'Have you any idea how long he'll be here?'

'Three or four nights would be my guess.'

'And visiting times?'

'I'd check with the ward. It's likely to be trauma ortho and they usually run eleven in the morning till eight in the evening, but I've no idea when he'll be admitted there so you'd best ring tomorrow and confirm that he's up on the ward and what the times are.'

She leaves him to it and Leo draws a plastic chair up to sit by Luke's side.

'Luke?'

Luke's eyelids flutter. His face is unmarked.

Thank God for the helmet.

'Luke?' Leo repeats.

'Dad.' His voice is hoarse. He's barely awake.

'You just rest. I'm going to sit with you a while. You're going to be okay.'

Broken collarbone. Tibia. Wrist.

Leo has an image of Vicky Mott's bones laid out for her mother. He shakes it away.

Luke gives a sharp breath in, his face creases in pain.

Leo lays a palm gently on the crown of Luke's head. Feels the heat there, and the hair, thick and damp.

'It's okay,' he murmurs. 'It's all right, Luke. You rest.'

He watches as his son's face relaxes and softens. Soon after, his breath comes and goes in the slow regular rhythm of sleep.

* * *

Shan

'Shan, I just had a call from a Ned Lister, wanting to speak to Leo.' Sergeant Jennings is standing in the open door to her room. 'I offered to take a message or get someone else to call him back but he hung up on me. Seemed to be in a state. You know the name?'

'Yes, he's an eyewitness, a neighbour of Terence Bielby's back in '97,' Shan says. 'He saw Bielby up bright and early on the day Vicky Mott disappeared.'

'Did he now!' The sergeant tips his head in interest.

Has he remembered something else? 'I'll go see him,' Shan says. 'Find out what he wants.'

'Okay. Good. Any word from Leo?'

'No, nothing.'

'Right.' He gives her a nod and returns downstairs.

* * *

Shan is glad to get out of the office and the drive is pleasant, apart from a near miss with a car ahead of hers that doesn't bother signalling for a right turn. The hard stop floods Shan with adrenaline, and leaves her wrists prickling and her heart thudding painfully.

A breeze pushes high clouds across the sky and the sun is hot. Walkers are out and about wearing shorts and T-shirts and hats with brims.

At The Aspens she sees several residents on the large, canopied veranda that wraps round the building. Glimpses others in a gazebo on the lawn.

She asks the receptionist where Mr Lister is and is told to try the main lounge. She gives it a quick scan but Shan can't see him among the groups there.

She wanders through to the conservatory where she and Leo spoke to him before. The doors are open on to the garden today.

A woman poring over a crossword looks up, her expression contemptuous 'I've been waiting fifteen minutes for assistance but take your time, why don't you.' She puts the newspaper down and moves forward in her chair, mistaking Shan for one of the care workers.

Shan gives a silent sigh. Sees the call button on the pillar next to the resident. 'You'd better ring again. I don't work here.'

The woman makes a tutting sound, offers no apology.

Back at reception Shan asks if Mr Lister might be in his room.

'Number eight. First floor, to the left.'

A cleaner is wiping the banisters as Shan goes upstairs, there's a smell of lavender and something chemical that catches the back of her throat.

Ned Lister's door is closed and Shan knocks. Hears, 'Come in.'

It's a good-sized room. The living area has two high-backed chairs, bookshelves and a large TV, and across the other side stands a bed, a run of drawers and a wardrobe. The furniture is all built in some dark, solid wood. Another door, by the bed, leads to the en-suite, Shan guesses.

The television is on; a man on a yacht talks to the camera. Ned Lister switches it off. Looks at Shan. Looks irritable.

'You rang the police station,' Shan says.

'I wanted to talk to Mr Donovan.'

'Perhaps I can help. As you know, I'm working with DI Donovan.'

Ned Lister's mouth works, his breathing sounds rapid. It takes her a second to realise he's pent up, angry about something.

'I'd rather talk to him,' Ned Lister says.

Because he's a man? Because he's white?

'I don't know when he'll be available again,' Shan retorts. 'But if it's not urgent, then fine, I'll leave you—'

'You issued an appeal!' He bursts out. 'But I already told you I saw him! Why haven't you done anything yet?' His face reddens as he talks.

'If there are any other witnesses we hope to find them too and—'

'But it was him. It were Terence Bielby!' Ned Lister insists. He bounces a fist on the arm of his chair. 'We all know it was him. Why the hell are you pussyfooting around?'

He's increasingly agitated. Shan hopes he hasn't got a heart condition or high blood pressure. That he's not going to make himself ill.

Why so upset? Guilt?

Something strikes her. 'Mr Lister you never came forward before. Not when the missing persons appeal was made back in May 1997, and not when Terence Bielby was later arrested for the three murders.'

'But no one knew back then that he killed the student Vicky an' all, because you lot hadn't found her.'

'I believe the appeal would have asked for information of any unusual sightings or activity on that particular day. You didn't think to mention seeing Mr Bielby even though it was so early for him?' Shan says.

'Why would I? We didn't know then. And he'd got this cover story about going early to the festival. But now we *do* know. He killed that lass just like he killed those others and you lot, you're sitting on your hands. Incompetent bloody cowards.' Spittle gathers in the corners of his lips.

Shan feels a prickle of annoyance but speaks calmly, hoping to reduce the charge in the atmosphere. 'The evidence we have—'

'Who else could it be?' he seethes. 'Veronica White were sixteen years old. Sixteen! Twin brothers a year younger. She was running to raise money for Cancer Research when that bastard took her. She wanted to be a teacher like her mum. Biology.' His eyes, pale grey, gleam like cracked ice.

'And Terence Bielby was convicted of Veronica's murder and is serving his sentence.' A worm of suspicion wriggles into her thoughts. 'You seem to know a lot about Veronica White,' she says.

Ned Lister doesn't answer. Jaw rigid, he makes a chewing motion.

Ned Lister had known they were coming to talk to him about Bielby. Shan remembers his words: *Stan Cotter said you'd talked to them.* He had warning from his old neighbours.

Time enough to fashion a story for us? Shan's pulse stutters, her mouth goes dry. *Is he lying?*

'Mr Lister, did you have a personal connection to Veronica White?'

'What if I had? She were our Lizzie's best pal. Grown up together. Like that, they were.' He raises his arm, fingers crossed, his hand shaking. 'And when Veronica . . . It tore our Lizzie apart. Devastated. It broke her heart. It made her ill.'

'And you want . . .' *Vengeance?* 'You want Bielby to pay for Vicky Mott's death too, whether he is guilty or not?' Shan knows she's taking a chance, accusing him like this. But it all adds up. 'That's why you claim to have seen him on that Sunday morning and—'

'I *did* see him.'

He's not looking at Shan now. His fist, tightly curled, taps at the chair arm.

'Mr Lister, perjury is a serious crime. And giving false information to the police is considered to be perverting the course of justice. A criminal offence.'

He doesn't respond, though his throat ripples and his jaw flexes. Somewhere out in the grounds there's an explosion of laughter and a smattering of applause.

Shan shifts her weight. Speaks again. 'It also makes it significantly harder for us to establish the truth. Vicky Mott's family deserve the truth, don't you think? Wouldn't you want that for them?'

Ned Lister picks up the remote control and points it at the television. His hand is quivering and it takes him two tries to turn on the set.

'Mr Lister?'

He raises the volume to a deafening level.

Shan gets the message and leaves.

* * *

Leo

Luke is asleep. Flickers of movement twitch across his cheeks, around his mouth. Ripple over his eyelids.

Leo rubs his own face. Tired, he wonders about going to find a coffee, but they might come to fetch Luke at any moment.

He'll need stuff bringing, Leo thinks. Fresh clothes — shorts and T-shirts'd be best, if there're going to be casts on his wrist and leg. Toothbrush and flannel. A dressing gown; he's got a Leeds Rhinos one that he likes.

From what Leo's heard they try to get people mobile as soon as possible after treatment for fractures or replacement joints, anything to do with bones. Encourage them out of bed and start them on physical therapy.

Leo pulls out the hospital bag with Luke's clothes in. He can take these to clean. The helmet is dented and grazed, hatch marks on the black fibreglass. He'll not be able to use that again.

Will he ever ride a bike again? Be fit to? Be keen to? Leo doesn't know which of the prospects is worse: that Luke won't be able to do something he loves, that Luke will have lost his nerve, or that he'll return to an activity that is so horribly dangerous.

They had all argued about it when he first wanted to buy a bike, with Leo the more concerned between him and Ange. But Luke's persistent arguments — that he needed transport, that he was stuck out in the sticks, that he wanted to be

independent, that he'd do all the training, always ride safely —
eventually brought her round. And Leo went along with it. Was
he wrong? Weak to agree? But what else could he have done?
And what might Luke have done if they'd refused?

Leo pulls out the clothing. With a frisson of shock he sees
the leather jacket and trousers are cut apart. *They cut him out of
his clothes.* It slams home the truth of how close Luke came to
critical injury or worse. Life-changing, they say nowadays. Life-
changing injuries. The leathers smell of petrol and earth and
something coppery. Blood, Leo realises. Blood on his clothes.

Oh, Luke. Oh God, if they'd lost him.

Leo squeezes his eyes tight, takes a breath, another.

A porter wheels a patient past on a trolley. Old, an ash-
grey face. Hard to tell if it's a man or woman. *We're all just
bags of skin and bone and blood in the end.*

Luke's boots are in the bottom of the bag, speckled red.
His socks stiff with sweat.

His phone. He'll need a charger. Leo hefts it in his palm.
The screen is cracked. He presses the button to wake it. At
least it works.

Without giving himself time to make up excuses or
rationalise his actions, Leo taps in Luke's PIN — his birth
year — and touches the text messages folder.

His own text is there. Not even opened.

He feels the burn of resentment.

The call log is the same. *Missed call from Dad.*

There's no voicemail notification so presumably Luke
did actually pick up Leo's message. And then ignored it.

Leo rubs at the back of his neck.

Luke sleeps on.

Near Hawes, they said he'd crashed. But Luke knows those
roads inside out. And the weather's been fair enough today. So
what happened? A distraction? Luke swerved to avoid a stray
sheep and lost control? Or a blowout, perhaps? Leo knows
nothing about the state of the bike. Had something failed?

Leo taps the contacts folder and finds Jack Sherringham.
The messages sent and received are brief, practical. *See you at 5.*

What time tomorrow. You coming tonight? Jack is also on WhatsApp. Leo presses the green symbol and finds their chat there. More of the same. Photos, too. The pups that Luke mentioned. Jack on his bike. The pair of them, a selfie in leathers, helmets on and the light reflected off their shields obscuring their faces.

Luke sighs and Leo stiffens, anxious that he'll be caught snooping. But Luke's eyes remain closed and Leo concentrates on the phone again. He launches the main WhatsApp. Luke's latest exchanges are with someone called Crusaders. A group chat.

At the top of the thread is a photograph posted by Luke. Nighttime, the glare from the flash illuminates the dome of a mosque and on the stone wall beneath runs graffiti, large capital letters dripping green paint: *TERRORIST SCUM.*

'Ah, Jesus,' Leo breathes.

CH14 replies: *Good work.*

Jack replies: *Red would have been better, blood on their hands.*

CH14 replies: *Message is good, loud and clear. All that matters.*

Hate messages.

You stupid—

Leo's head hurts.

The exchange was yesterday. With a miserable sense of dread Leo scrolls up the chat and finds another photo. The taxi firm. All the evidence anyone could ask for.

Above that, a photo of another building, not defaced. It takes Leo a moment to identify it as a synagogue from the menorah above the entrance. A future target?

So, Jack Sherringham's involved. And CH14?

He taps the group info. Sees CH14 is listed as admin but there is no other information. Their phone number is not in Luke's regular contacts. There is no photo for CH14 but a symbol, a square cross in a circle. An emblem used by white supremacists.

CH? Crusader something?

It hits him, a thump in the gut. *Christopher Hirst.* He was at Jack Sherringham's. And he knows Luke. Three of them. An ugly little cell of right-wing hate merchants.

214

Leo's racing thoughts are interrupted by the arrival of a porter. 'Luke Donovan?'

'Yes.' Leo nods to his son.

The porter checks the bracelet on Luke's arm.

'Okay, they're ready for him.'

'Thanks.'

Leo stands, slips Luke's phone into his pocket.

He touches Luke's cheek. Aching for him but full of anger too. And despair. At his ignorance. At his cruelty.

You stupid, stupid, bloody fool.

* * *

Vicky
1997

Robin is asleep; he doesn't wake when Vicky moves off the couch.

She can't settle. And anyway, how awful would it be if she had done and they were discovered like that by Melanie.

She feels wretched, confused when she thinks of her friend. Of what Vicky has just done to Melanie. But it's weird because she also feels elated. A giddy excitement for Robin. For the prospect of being with him. Of making love again. It's not just lust, she tells herself. Yes, the sex was wonderful. Amazing, really. But everything else, their conversation, the way his eyes shine with affection, with what feels like admiration, when she talks. His gentleness.

She never imagined being the other woman and certainly not betraying her best friend. The thought of facing Melanie when they tell her the truth makes Vicky sick to the stomach.

Should they admit that they cheated? Would it be kinder for Robin to just break up with Melanie and wait some time before Vicky starts seeing him? Even then Melanie will hate her. It will destroy their friendship.

Her head is pounding, a sickening mallet blow to her temples, over and over. The brandy perhaps?

Is it all a horrific mistake? Should she tell Robin that? Keep secret what they've done and stay friends with Melanie. Forget it ever happened. But the way her stomach sinks when she imagines that is all she needs to know.

At least it's nearly the end of term. Most of her courses are over so she doesn't need to be in Leeds every day. She can get her practical done next week and then move back to her mum's.

It will mean a real trek in and back again for the few classes she still needs to attend and for the exams but it's probably better to have a clean break.

Oh God, Melanie will hate her. And Usha? What will Usha think? Usha, who's already beside herself with worry over Col. The last thing Usha needs is for their house to break up and the support from her friends to disappear.

Vicky's throat aches, feels raw. Too many cigarettes. She goes through to the kitchen for a drink of water.

Outside the sky is just beginning to lighten. A pale grey glow edging over the silhouette of the fell. Dawn. A new day.

Vicky feels claustrophobic and cold. She imagines Col racing downstairs, his head full of crazy notions that Vicky is evil. Usha, miserable and anxious. Melanie. How can she face Melanie? How can she act halfway normal feeling like this? She needs to clear her head, work out what to do.

Vicky puts her coat on, cigs and lighter in the pocket. She tears out the title page of her script and writes a note on the back: *Gone to see the sunrise. Hippie? Moi? V xxx.* She adds a smiley face. But she wants to cry.

She leaves by the back door, locking it behind her. When she opens the back gate it makes a horrendous squealing noise. Startled, she turns back, anxious in case she's disturbed anyone. But the house is quiet, she sees no movement, and only the kitchen light spills into the yard.

Not wanting to make any more racket she leaves the wooden gate ajar.

A fine rain is falling, like a sea fret, and everything looks hazy in the dim light.

The air smells cool and clear, of minerals and water. Vicky drinks it in, hoping it will ease the thumping pain in her head.

The path beyond the stile is easy to follow, gleaming pale grey. The crunch of her boots is the only noise apart from a *tick-tick-tick* sound that she guesses is the plants reacting to the moisture, the ground waking up.

Each time Robin comes to mind a lurch of desire spins inside her, a wash of warmth, licks of excitement. It makes her nauseous, febrile.

Can you trust him?

Yes. Her gut reaction. Instant. Unthinking.

Based on a one-night stand? The cynic in her head raises an eyebrow.

It's not that, she thinks. It's more than that. Much more.

I want you. I want to be with you. He said those things and she believed them. Believed him. She still does.

She is warmer now, the climb steeper. She stops to get her breath.

There is rustling in the heather. She isn't sure exactly what lives here — shrews and voles and mice perhaps? There must be plenty of small animals because there are always birds of prey in the skies in the Dales.

She remembers camping with her family, driving out of the city on a Friday after her dad finished work. Pitching the tent and heating up tins of beans for their evening meal. Beans and hunks of French bread slathered with peanut butter that her mum bought from the baker that morning. The smell of the bread filling the car on the journey.

The Saturday night's tea was bangers and hot-dog rolls or a trip into the nearest village for fish and chips. Rice pudding from a tin. Club chocolate bars.

There's something magical about sleeping under canvas and waking in a pyramid of orange light to the sound of sheep bleating on the hills. Hearing the murmur of other campers, the familiar *swizz* of zips being opened and shut. The smell of the soil and the grass.

That's what they should have done for the festival. Camped on site. Next time she'll insist.

But there won't be a next time, will there? Not like this.

The group will fall apart once Robin breaks up with Melanie. And Col? Vicky doesn't ever want to go anywhere near Col again. She wishes she were more sympathetic — he's ill — but he frightens her and even before he got sick she was tired of his excesses, his need to be the centre of attention. Will that be a problem for Robin? Can the men keep up their friendship and leave Vicky out of it? Might that work once Col's better? Couples don't have to do everything together, after all. When Vicky's dad was alive her mum had friends that only she saw.

Vicky climbs the incline; the exertion aggravates her headache. She reaches a plateau.

From here, the path heads west where the sky is still dark. But she wants to go east. She *does* want to try and see the sunrise. It's still drizzling and she isn't sure what'll be visible with the cloud, but she should at least try.

A few yards ahead she makes out a narrow track through the ground cover and sets off to follow that. Spiders' webs cover the heather, beaded silver. The cotton grass hangs damp in the still air.

It's hard to tell how far it is to the edge of the plateau and she can't see the valley or any of the dales beyond it. Maybe when she gets closer. Or maybe the plateau will stretch on for ever like some walks she's been on.

Ahead are miles of moorland and not another soul.

Vicky feels as if the whole world is asleep except for her. Like those fairy tales where all the people are frozen in time apart from the protagonist, or the stories of toys that come to life in the night.

She is glad to be alone with so much to think about. There is this strange feeling churning inside her telling her that today is a special day. Everything has changed because of the events of the last few hours. There's a new part of her life beginning and nothing will ever be the same again.

CHAPTER TWELVE

Leo
2019

Leo tries calling Ange from his car. Gets voicemail. He has a moment's panic, mouth dry. How can he leave a message? Too blunt. He needs to speak with her, reassure her.

'Hi,' he says. 'Call me when you get the chance, yeah? Okay. I'll see you later.'

A bee careens into the windscreen, veers away. Leo blinks, sees Luke falling from his bike, slamming into the road.

'Thank God.' He says it aloud, though Leo has no God. Luke's alive. He'll recover.

He rings Shan.

'How is he?' she asks.

'Broken bones but they say he'll be okay, eventually.'

'That's good.'

'Still not sure what happened. Anyway, I'm not going to be back in today,' Leo says.

'Sure, fine.'

Leo feels drained, weak and tired. He drives home more slowly than usual, worried about his concentration, response times. He keeps the window open for fresh air, picks up regular wafts of stinking silage from the farms.

A man driving a white SUV tailgates him and, eventually frustrated, swerves out to overtake on a blind corner.

Leo swears. If anyone had been coming the other way . . .

Drawing into their road he sees Billy Ollershot sitting outside his house, in the teak captain's chair that his daughter brought him, taking the sun.

Billy raises a hand to beckon Leo over.

Leo's heart sinks. He hasn't time to help Billy out today. He needs to get ready and get to the sculpture park. But first he needs to eat.

'Billy? You okay?'

'Fair to middling. Your lot were here earlier, in a patrol car. Said they were looking for Luke.'

Leo's bowels loosen. 'What time was this?'

'Half ten, thereabouts.'

About an hour before Leo got the call from the hospital. Was there a connection?

'Everything all right?' Billy says.

Leo looks away, can't bear the concern in Billy's pale eyes.

Can he tell Billy before he's even told Ange?

He watches a robin flit down to the grass from the yew hedge.

But how can Leo not say anything? He glances back to the old man. 'Luke's crashed his bike.'

'Good grief.'

'He's in Airedale, broken bones.'

'Here.' Billy makes to stand. 'You'll be wanting a brew.'

'No, thanks. I'll get one at mine. There're things I have to be getting on with.'

'Sure, sure.' Billy shakes his head. 'It's a reet to-do, in't it?'

Leo's eyes sting.

He pictures the photo that Luke took, the defaced mosque. 'Aye,' he says. 'It is that.'

* * *

220

Leo makes himself a pile of scrambled eggs on toast with grated cheese on top, and a large mug of tea.

His mind loops back time and again to the phone call from the hospital, to the sight of Luke on the trolley. The smell of his ruined clothes.

He devours a slab of flapjack, swigging his tea to dissolve the clumps that stick in his back teeth.

A commotion from the birds draws him to the window in time to see the dull orange brush of the fox sliding out of view beyond the trellis.

He hopes it's not been after the frogs in the pond.

The garden is a haven, inviting him to go and sit among the grasses and flowers. To rest, step apart from the world for a while. Breathe the perfumed air and let the sun warm his skin. Be soothed by the hum of insects and the songs of the birds.

He draws in a sharp breath, pushing the idle fantasy away.

Luke's phone sits on the table. A burden. Silent. Sinister.

It'll want charging, he thinks.

And you need to report what you know.

Or give Luke the chance to own up first? If the police are looking for Luke, have they already linked him to the graffiti? Luke must have crashed around the time they were here. A chase? But no other vehicle was reported to be involved.

Leo groans. He can't see any way back from this. From turning in his son. Besides, if Luke's not stopped, what happens next time? A Molotov cocktail through someone's window? Petrol through letterboxes? Fists and boots and bricks? Fire or knives?

He leaves the phone to charge and goes to shower. He smells rank, the stress of the day expressed as toxins in his sweat.

After dressing in a fine-checked shirt and chinos with dark trainers, he puts a change of clothes in an overnight bag with his toothbrush and shaving kit.

Luke's phone chirps as Leo enters the kitchen.

A new message from Jack: *Dad says if u still want a pup u need to let us know soon.*

Oh Luke.

He's not said a word about wanting a puppy. The juxtaposition of messages and photos about puppies with the hatred and thuggery of his Crusaders group seems obscene.

When Leo checks his own phone, there's a voicemail from Ange, 'Hi . . . all good here. We're just going into a recording for *Look North. Look North!*' Her words are thick with exaggerated excitement. 'Telly, Leo! So my phone will be off for a while but text me if you need. And Leo . . . if it's work and you're calling to say you can't make it, you owe me *big time*.'

Ah, Christ. If he leaves soon he should just have a chance to talk to her before the ceremony starts.

* * *

Leo finds Ange inside the new gallery building where guests are mingling. She's entertaining a group of people with some anecdote. She smiles a greeting to him but doesn't break her stride. Leo hovers on the outskirt of the circle.

'Drink, sir?' A youngster in black holds a tray of bubbly drinks. 'Prosecco.'

Leo demurs. He can't stand the stuff. Acidic pop.

'There will be soft drinks coming round, too.'

'Thanks.'

Leo would kill for a pint — a hoppy pale ale or a hearty bitter. Or a glass of red wine.

A gale of laughter signals the culmination of Ange's tale. She nods to her group and excuses herself.

'Okay?' She beams at him.

Leo opens his mouth, closes it again.

She reads his face, expertly. Her own smooths into apprehension. 'What?'

Leo looks to the side. For space, for privacy.

She understands. 'Here.'

He follows her through a set of glass doors that lead on to a wide terrace. The parkland rolls away on all sides, dotted with sculptures.

'Leo?'

He takes her hands.

'You're scaring me.'

'Luke's been in an accident.'

She gasps. Her hands tighten in his.

'He came off his bike. But he's okay. He's all right. He's in Airedale General, with broken bones.'

'Oh God.' She pulls a hand free to cover her mouth. 'Broken bones?'

Leo lists them. 'They're putting casts on his arm and leg.'

'We should go.' She tries to move. He holds her.

'Listen. They won't let us visit till eleven in the morning.'

'What!' She scowls.

'I've seen him and he's okay but they need time to get him admitted to a ward. Visiting hours are eleven till eight. But we can ring first thing,' he says. 'Find out how he is then, check which ward he's on.'

Her mouth works, tears stand in her eyes.

'Oh God, Leo. So when did you . . . what did . . . ?'

He details the sequence of events. Her eyes are clamped on his and he begins to feel ashamed that he hadn't called her soon enough. He might have contacted the venue and told them Ange needed to speak to him urgently.

'I couldn't leave a message . . . I couldn't tell you like—'

She pauses. 'No.' She gets it. She always gets it and he is so thankful for that understanding. For what they share.

'I could ring him!' Hope lights her eyes.

'I've got his phone,' Leo says. He's debating whether to say more now, to burden her with all the rest, when someone calls her name.

'Ange, five minutes.' A face in the doorway, a woman clutching a clipboard.

'Sure, fine. Thanks.' Ange's words are rapid. She turns back to Leo. 'I don't think I can—' She waves her hand back towards the hall. 'I don't . . .'

'You can. We can't see him till tomorrow but we'll ring at breakfast. And we'll go in for eleven. This is your work, Ange. All your work. You deserve this.'

She nods. 'Oh, Leo.'

'I know.'

She pinches the bridge of her nose. He sees her fix her resolve as she straightens up, pulls back her shoulders.

'I need a drink. And the loo.'

'I'll find you a drink,' he says.

She turns and Leo catches her arm. 'Hey.' He pulls her into a hug. He breathes in her hair, feels the shape of her. So familiar, so comforting. 'It'll be all right,' he tells her. Something to say, something to cling to even if he's not sure whether he really believes it. Before he lets her go, he plants a gentle kiss on her forehead. 'Good luck.'

* * *

She wins. Ange wins and his heart soars for her. She smiles and clasps her hands to her chest as if she needs to contain herself. She gives a short, sweet, witty thank-you speech.

And then there is more mingling. Ange accepts all the congratulations with charm and Leo wonders if anyone else can see the splinter of pain in her eyes, sense the residue of anxiety in her bright talk.

People start to leave and Leo asks Ange, 'Is there a bar at the inn?'

'I don't think so. But I brought some wine with me, just in case. And some beer for you.'

He grins. 'What are we waiting for?'

It is growing dark as Leo drives them to the inn. Trees silhouetted against a velvety blue sky. The first stars glimmering pinpricks in the east.

No sooner have they entered their room than Ange delves into her bag and holds aloft two bottles. 'There's a terrace downstairs,' she says. 'We could check it out?'

They do, and meet another couple who are just leaving.

'Lovely night,' one man says.

'Kept the chairs warm for you,' his partner jokes.

Ange pours herself a large glass of wine while Leo opens his bottle of ale.

He toasts her. 'You're bloody brilliant, you know.'

She smiles.

They sit quietly for a few moments.

She reaches for his hand and he clasps hers.

'I can smell honeysuckle,' she says.

'Jasmine.' He nods to the side where the climber, with its tiny white starlike flowers, scrambles up a pillar.

'He'll be laid up, won't he? For weeks. He'll need looking after. He won't be able to get dressed or anything,' Ange says.

'Probably be living in his dressing gown for a while,' Leo says. 'We should get more idea tomorrow.'

'Crutches?'

'Not sure how that works with his shoulder being on the same side.'

'The bike?'

'No idea.' Leo thinks of the helmet, scratched and dented.

He drinks more beer and gazes up. Isolated patches of cloud, like slate-coloured rags, move slowly across the sky. The stars glitter brighter now, sharp.

Ange's face contorts, suddenly overwhelmed. 'It's the not knowing.' A rush of emotion. 'Where he was, what happened. And is he okay in himself? I just want to see him.'

'Yes.' Leo agrees.

He feels the weight inside him, heavy in his core. The things he hasn't told Ange yet.

Leo drains his beer. Sets the bottle down. Takes her hand.

'Ange, there's something else I need to tell you about Luke.'

* * *

225

'How's your son?' Shan says when Leo arrives at work.

'Okay. We spoke to the hospital earlier, they said he had a comfortable night. They've got him on pain relief. Just a question of getting the fractures to heal.'

'*Just*,' Shan says. Then adds, 'Good he's okay, though.'

Leo gives a tired smile.

'Tea, coffee?' she offers.

'I can—'

'No. I'm doing mine anyway.'

She makes their drinks and they sit in Leo's office. Shan has a moment's déjà vu from the morning before, the back of her skull tingling.

'So, I met with Ned Lister yesterday,' she says.

Leo pauses, reaching for his mug.

'How come?'

'He rang here in a state: why hadn't we charged Terence Bielby? Anyway, it turns out that Ned Lister *knew* Veronica White. Veronica was best friends with his granddaughter.'

Shan waits to see if Leo will guess where this is heading.

'He never said.' Leo's eyes sharpen.

'Right. And he never mentioned seeing Bielby back when the missing person's appeal was launched. Only now. He got very agitated with me.' The TV blaring, his mutinous rebuttal.

'You think he lied?' Leo says.

'I know it.'

'Did he admit it?'

'No.'

Leo takes a drink, put his cup down, fingers dancing lightly on the rim as if he's weighing up what she's told him. Does he not agree? She must convince him.

'Look, he knew we were coming to talk to him,' Shan says. 'He told us himself, "*Stan Cotter said you'd talked to them*." Remember?'

Leo gives a slow nod.

'His granddaughter was devastated when her friend was killed. Lister said it made her ill. He wants vengeance. He's not satisfied that Bielby is already doing time for that — he wants to pin this on him too. He'd have seen us go after the wrong person. I asked him, what about Vicky's family? What about the truth? He didn't like that. His supposed sighting was the only shred of evidence we found that came anywhere near implicating Bielby for Vicky. Without that, we've nothing.'

'Agreed,' Leo says.

Yes! With the surge of relief, Shan notices the tension she's been holding in her shoulder blades. The pressure in her chest.

Leo pauses for a minute. 'We shut down the line of enquiry into Terence Bielby. He's no longer a suspect.'

The field is narrowing.

'So, Melanie Quinn?' Shan says.

'Go on.'

Leo shifts, stretches in his chair. He massages his shoulder as he stretches his neck.

Shan wonders if he's slept, with all the worry about his son.

She begins to lay out her theory. 'Melanie finds out that Vicky has slept with Robin.'

'How?'

'Maybe Vicky tells her. Or she sees them. Melanie was staying in the room that overlooks the yard.'

Shan pulls out the photograph of the rear of the Tollthorpe cottage. Yesterday, after speaking to Ned Lister, she spent the rest of the afternoon building a case to present to Leo.

'So Melanie goes with Vicky to see the sunrise, or perhaps she follows her. Whatever happens by the old mine shaft, whether Vicky trips and falls, or there is an altercation, Melanie loses her badge. Two of them go up there but only Melanie comes back. And when the friends realise Vicky's missing, it's Melanie who insists they check the festival site.' Shan taps the statement from Robin Westwood that she's typed up. 'Deliberately leading them away from Toller Fell.'

'Except—' Shan's heart contracts — 'we have a witness statement made at the time in 1997 from Christopher Hirst saying Vicky Mott came back to the village at about six thirty in the morning. That doesn't fit. And it's solid evidence. It's the only eyewitness testimony we have. It's our last sighting.'

Shan is about to protest Leo's counter, to try and wriggle round the obstacle ruining her narrative, when her mind sparks and clears. A chill runs over her skin. She feels a rush of blood, a tilt of vertigo.

'It fits if that was Melanie!' she says. her voice rises. 'It fits perfectly. And it makes sense.'

Leo frowns. 'Hirst identified the woman as Vicky. She was wearing the same clothes as described in the appeal.'

Shan sees Hirst, sullen, abrasive. *She should have listened . . . Supposed to be bright, in't they, students?* Shan had felt his dislike, his hostility, throughout the interview.

'It *must* have been Melanie,' Shan insists.

'You can't ignore the evidence we have, Shan. Christ knows, we've little enough. But that sighting put Vicky in Tollthorpe that morning. How can you explain that?' He is intense, pushing her but not in an aggressive way.

'I can't. I don't know!' Shan realises she's waving her arms about but she doesn't care. 'Maybe he was mistaken. Or maybe he made it up to get attention. Maybe he's colour-blind and it was Melanie he saw, not Vicky.'

She sits back, desperate to be right but out of ideas.

Leo's face changes, his mouth opens as if in shock.

'What?' Shan says.

'Jesus Christ.' He rubs at his face.

'Leo?'

He drags his palms down to cover his mouth but his eyes are steady, bright.

'You're killing me here, what is it?' Shan says.

'Quickly. What colour was Melanie's coat?'

Without waiting for an answer, he scrambles to find the folder containing the original appeal photo. On locating it, he thrusts the picture at Shan and plants his hands on the desk. 'Colour-blind,' he says. 'I think that's it. You're right. I think Christopher Hirst is colour-blind.'

* * *

Leo has gone to visit his son in the hospital, leaving Shan to look further into the science of colour-blindness. Especially with red and green colours, he's told her.

She feels a jolt of certainty as she reads that red–green colour-blindness is a thing, and the most common type.

It's possible, it works! Vicky's coat was red, Melanie's green. Similar styles — lightweight parkas with hoods.

Shan thinks of traffic lights, flow signals. How would you manage? But then traffic lights are always in the same order, aren't they. And other signals, like the ones in lanes or through tunnels, always show the red no-go zone in the shape of an X, a red cross.

Shan is buzzing with excitement, a fizz in her bloodstream at the breakthrough. A small voice urges caution, telling her not to count her chickens, that they have could have got it wrong, but it is drowned out by the louder chorus cheering her on.

She wants to go for a run or ring Erin up and crow down the line. But then, things still feel out of kilter with Erin. She might not share Shan's jubilation. Maybe a quick jog, Shan tells herself. Once this is all prepped.

They need to test the theory on Christopher Hirst. Using the computer and fancy printer downstairs she scans in the photograph of the four women taken by Robin Westwood then selects and copies the figures of Vicky and Melanie, making sure to capture as much of their coats as possible.

She isolates the coats themselves, removing anything else from the images. That means bits are cropped off the garments — the neckline of Melanie's where her hair fell, the forearm of Vicky's that was hidden behind Usha's hand.

When she is satisfied she prints off a copy of each coat. Then she manipulates the colours so she can print several versions of each garment in shades least likely to be confused by someone with red–green colour-blindness. The same coat in pale lilac, lemon, mushroom and baby blue.

She cuts each one out. Remembers an old game one of her primary-school friends had. A cardboard cut-out doll with sets of thick paper clothes to dress it in. Folding little tabs over to attach the costumes.

Using the scanner again she creates two sheets, each with a row of coats in different colours. When the ink is dry she numbers the images A–E and F–J, slides them into protective sleeves and labels them with evidence numbers.

Returning the original photograph to the files, she studies their faces. They look genuinely happy, carefree. Usha has turned slightly towards Vicky as if Vicky has just spoken. Usha's mouth is wide with laughter. Vicky looks forward, smiling. Her hair streaked with bright pink and blue. Melanie, head tilted to the side, mirrored sunglasses on her head, stares at the camera, presumably at Robin. Dee Price at the end, next to Melanie, wears a hat. Her mouth is pursed as if she's whistling, or blowing a kiss.

The image captures the sort of friendships that might last a lifetime. Independent of childhood and home, of school. Relationships forged as young adults.

And a few hours after the photograph was taken, Vicky was gone.

* * *

Leo

'Where's my phone?' Luke says.

At this, Ange ceases putting away the clothes and provisions they've brought in. looks up at her son. At Leo.

'Here.' Leo holds it up. 'And your charger. The screen's cracked but it still works. I checked. Your messages, your chats, they're all there.'

There's a moment of stillness. Luke's eyes, wary, on his. Leo doesn't smile or make any move to soften the exchange. Let Luke know that Leo has seen the content on his phone.

What Luke might not suspect is that Leo has taken screen-shots of the incriminating material in the Crusaders' group chat. Or that Leo's been in touch with the police in Keighley.

Still, Ange and Leo have agreed that they will not confront Luke directly with what they know today, but give him some time to recover.

'What will happen to him?' Ange asked last night when Leo had described what Luke had been involved in.

'It's a hate crime,' he said. 'There is a possibility of custodial sentence. Perhaps a referral to the Prevent programme.'

'Oh God, Leo. Prison? No, no.' He tried to comfort her but felt as wretched about the prospect as she did.

The irony was that, although Luke needed to take responsibility for the crimes he'd committed, a spell inside was more than likely to crystallise his extremist views. There he'd find plenty of like-minded people ready to take him into their fold, feed him a diet of bile and misinformation, incite him, continue the process of radicalisation.

'Prison,' Ange said again. 'Everything you've ever said: the conditions, the culture. It'll destroy him, Leo. Jesus. They'll eat him alive. He'll go crazy.'

What could he say? Prison *did* destroy people. And in an era of austerity and political posturing, rehabilitation no longer really figured. Now and again there were heartwarming stories of people who turned their lives around, found education or religion, and against the odds used prison to recalibrate, to change. But most people? Prison harmed them.

'He might get a community sentence as a first-time offender,' Leo had said. 'And the shock of being caught could be a wake-up call.'

'I guess we have to hope he hears it,' Ange said. 'And we have to believe people can change, don't we? We have to hope. Else there's bugger all, isn't there?'

'Whatever happens won't happen quickly,' Leo said. 'With the backlog in the courts. If they are prosecuted it'll be well into next year before anything starts.'

* * *

'How did you crash?' Ange is asking Luke now.

Luke blinks. 'Skidded.'

'On what?' Leo says. 'The roads were dry.'

'Don't know.'

Luke is bleary, his words slur. He is still on the drip but the nurses have him propped up in bed.

'Where were you?' Ange says.

'On the brow, coming home.'

It all slots into place for Leo. From the crest of the hill Luke would have a clear view down to the village. Would have sight of their house, would see in a flash that a patrol car was in the street outside. *Then what?* He spins round to get away, heading back downhill too fast, not concentrating clearly enough, and before he can correct his position the bike is sliding sideways, churning out of his control, hammering across the road, flinging Luke to the ground.

'Is there anything else you need?' Ange says. 'We'll come back this evening.'

'A card for the TV,' Luke says.

'Sure. Doubt they'll have Netflix though.' She keeps her voice light but Leo hears a brittle edge. He half expects her to lose her composure.

There is an awkward pause.

At the next bed, an Asian man about Leo's age has his leg in traction. He has been dozing but now a visitor arrives and wakes him. 'Daddy? I brought you lunch.'

'Your mum won her award.' Leo feels the urge to puncture the silence.

'Great.' Luke sounds like he actually means it. But perhaps he's just grateful that he's no longer in the spotlight. 'So you'll get to go on that holiday.'

The simple normality of it, the fact Luke retained the dinner-table chat, unmoors Leo. He wants to weep.

He stands up and rearranges Luke's drink on the tray table.

'Not while you're laid up like that, we won't,' Ange says.

'Three to six months, the doctor says, for the leg. Six to eight weeks for the collarbone and the wrist,' Luke says.

He sounds sanguine. Leo wonders if the reality of this incapacity, of the trauma he's suffered, has yet to hit home.

'You'll have to stick with the physio,' Ange orders.

Leo can barely breathe. The ward is too hot. There's a smell of bleach and something else, a sweaty, rubbery smell making him nauseous.

'I'm going to head off,' Leo says.

'Okay.' Ange nods.

'I'll see you later.' Leo bends to kiss Luke's head.

A Judas kiss.

* * *

Shan

'There something you need to know about Christopher Hirst.' Leo says.

'What?' Shan says.

Leo keeps his eyes on the road as they leave Settle. He takes a breath before replying.

'I'm almost certain he's involved in far-right activity. The damage to the taxi company we saw and also to a mosque on Sunday night.'

Shan's confused; she was expecting something about their investigation.

Leo sighs. 'And my son Luke's caught up in it.'

His son? 'Oh, God.' She doesn't know what else to say. She feels uncomfortable. Shan has policed some of those gatherings in Leeds. Faces contorted with hatred. Speakers dressed up to appear respectable, spouting venom. Always a few drunk and seething, out for blood.

Worse, she had known that some of her colleagues covertly shared those views even if they disagreed with the tactics. Felt it, like an undercurrent at work. All those times when conversations stopped as she entered a room, her fellow officers exchanging smirks. The occasions when her contributions were ignored, and she was deliberately given

233

the worst jobs. The constant sense of not being included, of being other, different, outside. Not one of them.

'The investigating officers have CCTV footage of Luke leaving the mosque,' Leo says. 'They traced his number plate.' He shakes his head. He looks devastated.

'So the accident? Was it a pursuit?' Shan asks.

'No. I think Luke had seen the police; they came to our house.' He glances over to her, his expression bleak. 'I think he was doing a runner and crashed. They'd not made the connection to Hirst yet, so I told them I thought he was part of it. And that I was speaking to him on an unrelated matter.'

'How did you find out?'

'Luke's phone. They have a WhatsApp group. Crusaders.' Shan groans.

'One of them's a friend of Luke and the other uses the handle CH14. I think that's Hirst, it's his initials. And something they wrote in the messages about the paint they used chimes with the colour-blindness.'

'Fourteen,' Shan says. 'It figures.' It's one of the numbers in the pamphlet circulated by the service about signs and symbols, names and numbers used by different extremist groups. Extreme right-wing symbols, like eighty-eight for '*Heil* Hitler', twenty-eight for Blood & Honour.

'Sorry?' Leo says.

'Fourteen, the number of words in that white supremacist quote. You know, white replacement theory.'

'Right — got you.'

She tries to remember the phrasing. Something about *the existence of our people . . . a future for white children.*

'Of course, this is completely separate,' Leo says. 'I've no idea whether Hirst knows about the crash or any of that but if he does, if he raises it, we shut that down. That's why I'm telling you. So everything is out in the open.'

Would he not have mentioned anything otherwise? Would she have wanted him to?

'Transparency and so on. Bloody nightmare.' Leo increases his speed. 'How could he? We never raised him—' He cuts himself off. 'Sorry.'

He's obviously distressed. Shan tries to imagine her child growing up to become a misogynist or a racist or a rapist and fails. She cannot even imagine being a mother. Not beyond rerunning scenes from her own childhood.

'Okay.' Shan feels tense. The day is close, a lid of steel cloud seals the sky. There's a chance of thunder.

A small tortoiseshell butterfly lands on the wing mirror, bright orange and black wings scalloped with blue edges. It clings on, vibrating in the current, then is swept away.

They reach the viaduct, the great arches striding across the moorland. Cars parked all along the roadside, a tea van in a lay-by. A horse and rider cantering over the turf.

Shan tries to set aside what Leo has just told her, that Hirst is a white supremacist, and focus on the job in hand.

If this goes right, if they can prove Hirst is colour-blind, then they will have new evidence. An eyewitness who saw Melanie Quinn return to Tollthorpe on the morning Vicky Mott vanished.

* * *

Leo

The van Leo had last seen at Jack Sherringham's is at the side of the pub. Although the day is dull, the sky a sickly grey, there is no shortage of customers. Most of them are finishing lunches, judging by the crockery on the tables.

Christopher Hirst is in the cellar changing a barrel when they ask for him, and his wife goes to fetch him.

They wait at an empty table close to the bar.

Hirst arrives eventually, wiping his hands on an old towel.

'Well?' His tone is flat.

'We'd like another word,' Leo says.

'What?' He continues to rub at his nails and knuckles, not giving them the courtesy of his full attention.

'In private, Mr Hirst.' Leo is all formality.

'Caz, I'll be upstairs.' He throws the towel on to the bar and walks off. Leo and Shan exchange a glance and follow.

Leo tries to dampen the rage simmering inside, to silence the questions in his head: does Hirst know Luke's in hospital? Does Jack Sherringham know? Hirst is forty years old; the lads are almost half that age. Who initiated the Crusaders group? Did Christopher Hirst pollute Luke's mind, send him material, links to websites? Make Luke feel — what? Valued? Brave? Special? Righteous?

In the same corner office, Hirst's old bedroom, Leo looks out briefly at the fell. It looms closer, the land darker, beneath the lowering cloud.

Hirst sits in his computer chair as before. Leo and Shan stand.

'We want to talk to you about the sighting of Vicky Mott,' Leo says.

'I already told you.'

'We need to clarify your account. You couldn't see the face of the person coming down from the hill at the time but you recognised the coat as the red coat from the appeal photo?'

'Yes.' Hirst sounds impatient, as if they're asking him something idiotic.

'DC Young?' Leo invites Shan to proceed, deliberately using her full title.

'Mr Hirst, we'd like you to look at these pictures and tell us if you can see the coat you noticed that morning.'

He scowls. 'You what?'

Shan holds out one of the sheets of A4 with a row of coats on.

'Can you identify the coat on there?'

He gives a long sigh before reaching slowly to take the sheet from her. He runs his eyes across the page, stabs at the central image, making the sheet crackle.

'There.'

'Item C. Thank you,' Shan says. She doesn't betray any reaction as she takes the sheet from him and hands him the second one.

236

Leo's apprehension grows as Hirst surveys the second sheet. The green coat is last, at the end of the line.

Red would have been better, blood on their hands.

Leo reckons Christopher Hirst supplied the paint that Luke and Jack used. Perhaps he'd been delivering another batch when Leo saw him at Jack's.

'That one.' Hirst picks out the green coat. Leo feels his own shoulders drop in relief.

'Item J,' Shan says. 'So that is Item C on the first sheet and Item J on the second.' She tucks the papers back in her folder.

'What's all this in aid of?' Hirst asks.

'We needed to double-check you'd seen the same coat,' Shan answers.

'Yes. Well, I had, so if there's nowt else—'

'They were different coats,' she says.

'What you on about?' He snaps like he might at a tiresome child.

'The ones you've picked out. Different coats in different colours.'

He gives a harsh laugh. 'Don't be thick.'

'One is red, one is green,' Leo says. 'But you can't tell the difference.'

'Bullshit.'

Leo fights to quash the mounting urge to lamp the man. 'That's all we need for now. We'll be in touch if we need anything else.'

And they leave, Shan first.

She turns to Leo on the stairs, face alive with excitement. *Yes!*

Leo tips his head to her; he doesn't need to see what she's mouthing to know she is full of joy.

It's not a lot but it's something solid. An eyewitness. Enough to try and crowbar open the truth behind Vicky's death.

CHAPTER THIRTEEN

Leo

'Robin Westwood thought he heard Vicky go out. He heard the door. What if he actually heard Melanie?' Shan says.

'How would we know?' As soon as the words are out, it strikes him. 'Ah, different doors. Vicky went out the back door, locked it, took the key with her. Anyone else leaving would have to go out of the front.'

'If he only had a phone, we could ring and ask him.'

Leo fleetingly thinks about sending a message to the shop. Perhaps the boy who lives there can take a note to Robin's cave. Come back with a reply.

Hardly acceptable police work.

There's no way round it.

'Early start?' Leo says.

* * *

It looks like the camp is abandoned. No fire burning, no noise save for the rustle of leaves and the gurgle of the stream. The birds. Leo picks out the drilling of a woodpecker again.

'Robin?' Leo calls. The forest swallows the sound.

'Check the cave?' Shan suggests.

A sense of fear grips Leo, a falling sensation inside. Robin Westwood had been desolate, ridden by guilt when they spoke to him. Had it all been too much? Had he come to harm?

He holds his breath as they approach the cave mouth.

They peer in. Daylight illuminates the first few feet. To the left, rough shelves rest on blocks of timber. Some hold tins and jars of food. Others carry tools and rope, candles, a lantern. There are books, too, and a small radio. At the other side is a woodpile of stacked logs, and a couple of large wooden crates with lids. A three-legged stool, a ladderback chair and a large trunk.

Further back Leo makes out a pallet bed, a pile of blankets. The cave beyond is all shadows.

He steps forward, mouth dry, when a snapping sound outside jerks him round.

Robin Westwood holds a brace of dead rabbits by their hind legs.

He stares at Leo and Shan, unspeaking.

Leo moves out of the cave, heart settling. 'Hello, Robin.'

Robin gives a wary nod.

'We've something else we'd like to ask you. Can we sit?' Leo gestures to the empty fireplace.

Robin walks over to one of the silver birch trees and slings the rabbits over a fork in the branches. Taking off the canvas shoulder sack he's wearing, he hangs that up too. He walks to an enamel pail and dips his hands in, rubbing them clean then wiping them dry on his trousers.

The three of them settle in the same places as before. 'The last time we were here you told us you heard Vicky leave the cottage, that you heard the door,' Leo says.

'Yes, that's right.' Robin's voice sounds dry, whispery. Lack of use? Does he talk to himself, sing to himself, here in his isolation?

'Think back to that, to hearing the door. Now, which door was it?'

Robin's eyes reach up and back to the memory. 'The front. I was in the living room, close by.'

Yes!

'If I'd only gone after her,' Robin says. 'I didn't even think. Once I knew Col was okay, I didn't even wonder who it was. She wasn't safe out there and—'

'You didn't hear Vicky go,' Leo says. 'We believe that you heard Melanie.'

'But—'

'Vicky used the back door,' Shan explains. 'She took the key. Anyone else leaving the house would have to go out of the front.'

Robin's frown deepens as he considers the revelation. 'Melanie?'

'That fits with other evidence we have,' Leo says.

There's a further pause. Robin studies Leo then looks up to the trees that encircle the glade. He shuffles and says, 'But why would she—' He looks appalled. 'You honestly think Melanie killed Vicky because she found out that we slept together?'

'Yes.'

Robin covers his mouth, shaking his head, eyes shining with pain. 'I told you it was my fault,' he says. 'If I hadn't—'

'You're not to blame. Melanie is,' Shan says.

Robin won't have it. He keeps shaking his head.

'And this, living like this? Is it some sort of penance?' Leo asks.

Robin gives him a glance. 'Being here . . . it's . . . it's just best for me.'

'Really?' Leo can't tell if the man finds peace in this place or if it's actually a form of punishment. 'From everything I've heard about Vicky, I don't think that she would blame you, or hold you responsible for what happened. Not for one minute.'

Robin knots his fingers, studies his knuckles.

'You should know there's going to be a funeral. Vicky's mother and Usha are—'

'No, I couldn't . . . I can't . . .'

A moment's quiet, then Leo continues. 'Perhaps you could write, to Vicky's mother, if you want to.'

'Why would she want to hear from me?' Robin's bitterness and self-loathing are palpable.

'Because you loved Vicky. She might like to hear how Vicky was, those last hours at the cottage. What you talked about,' Leo says. *And it might help you too*, he thinks. *To face those memories. To reach out to someone. To see beyond yourself.*

'You can write care of us, and we'll check with her before sending anything on,' Shan says.

'Maybe.' Robin's nose has reddened and tears stand unshed in his eyes.

Leo gets to his feet. 'It wasn't your fault any more than it was Vicky's fault. There's only one person responsible for what happened. She made a choice. Now we want her to pay for that.'

* * *

Shan

Melanie Quinn arrives promptly for her voluntary interview at the police station.

Leo had called her the day before and invited her to attend while Shan listened, the phone on speaker. 'We'd like to talk to you in light of new evidence,' he'd explained.

'Yes, of course, anything I can do to help.'

'You are welcome to bring a legal representative with you if you wish. Or we can supply one.'

'A solicitor?' Melanie said. 'Why on earth would I need a solicitor?' Puzzled amusement in her voice.

'I'm just informing you of your rights,' Leo said.

'Do you think she'll bring someone?' Shan asked Leo.

'She'd be a fool not to. And she doesn't strike me as a fool.'

'But the optics?' Shan said. 'She might think it looks better if she doesn't see the need for a lawyer.'

Shan was wrong.

The smartly dressed woman with Melanie introduces herself as Abigail Shaw, Dr Quinn's solicitor.

Melanie greets the detectives warmly, smiling and shaking hands with Shan and then Leo. She wears a cream blouse, camel-coloured slacks.

She appears relaxed while Leo goes through the protocols with her in the interview room. Shan is at Leo's side, with Melanie directly opposite her and Abigail Shaw facing Leo.

Once the recorder is working, Shan reads out the caution and Melanie agrees that she understands it.

Shan is nervous, tension in her calves, toes pressing into the floor. She takes a slow breath in and smiles at Melanie in a concerted effort to mask her nerves. Shan was excited when Leo suggested she lead the interview. And daunted too. Although she's done the training, this is the first time she's been responsible in such a serious situation.

'We spoke to you previously about the disappearance of Vicky Mott and the events of that weekend. Is there anything you'd like to change or correct or add to the account you gave us?'

'No,' Melanie says. Her expression is open, pleasant, eager even.

'Robin Westwood was your boyfriend at the time?' Shan says.

'Yes.'

'You rented a cottage as a couple and invited your friends?'

'Yes.'

'How was your relationship with Robin at the time?'

'Fine. We were very happy.'

'No strain? No arguments?' Shan thinks of Erin, how she becomes cold and critical when they row. How that tears into Shan, lacerates her. Being shut out.

'No,' Melanie says. 'We were fine.'

'Until Robin slept with your best friend, Vicky?'

'What? He didn't. They didn't.' She laughs, incredulous. 'I don't know where you've got that from but it's wrong. It's not true.' She is completely convincing in her denial.

Is Shan wrong? She feels a jet of fear and guilt. *No.* The evidence is there. *Melanie is a good liar*, Shan tells herself. *Keep going.*

'It would hurt wouldn't it, to be betrayed like that?' Shan says.

'It didn't happen,' Melanie insists. 'Vicky would never do that. They were friends, that's all. We all were.'

'We have information to the contrary.'

'From whom?'

'Whom?' Do people really say that? It feels like Melanie's using the word to distinguish herself, to make a point. *I'm cleverer than you. Better educated.*

Shan sees Melanie's calculating possibilities.

'Has Robin told you this?' Her voice softens. 'It's not true. It must be some sort of sorry fantasy. I don't understand why he'd make something like that up.'

'In our statement you told us that you left your friends to go to bed in the early hours of the Sunday and remained there until lunchtime,' Shan says.

'That's right.' Melanie moves her hand, fingers smoothing above her ear as if tucking away a stray lock, but everything is in place, her hair neatly drawn back in a French plait. She wears make-up, a little more than when they met at the hospital but still subtle.

'You're absolutely certain about that?' Shan says.

'Yes.' A faint frown gives her a bemused look.

'We have an eyewitness who says otherwise.'

'What?' Melanie stirs in her chair. Disbelief in her grey eyes, in the curve of her mouth.

'You were seen coming into Tollthorpe village from the fell at six thirty on the morning of the eleventh of May 1997.'

Melanie makes a gasping noise, looks briefly at Abigail Shaw shaking her head. 'That's ridiculous,' she says. 'They're mistaken.'

Leo moves, flexing his shoulders then writing in his notebook. He doesn't need to say a word to convey an air of weary scepticism.

'It's a credible account,' Shan continues. 'We have no reason to doubt it.'

'But it's wrong—' Melanie begins. 'Don't you see? They can't possibly have—'

Abigail Shaw lays a hand on her forearm. 'My client has answered your question.'

'You wore this coat that weekend?' Shan shows her the picture Robin took at the festival.

'Yes.'

'And you wore a badge like this?'

'Yes. We all did.' Melanie appears quieter now, hurt. But has no problem holding eye contact with Shan.

Shan lays down another picture — the photograph of the rusted badge.

'This badge was recovered from the bottom of the mine-shaft where Vicky fell.'

'It must be Vicky's.' There's an indulgent tone in Melanie's voice.

'An identical badge was found in Vicky's belongings, the ones retrieved from the cottage,' Shan says.

Melanie freezes for a fraction of a second, composes her-self quickly. 'Well, it's not mine. It can't be. Not unless Vicky took it with her?'

A pause.

'When you realised Vicky was missing, why didn't you go looking for her in the most obvious place?' Shan says.

'What?'

'Vicky left a note. She'd gone to watch the sunrise. It would make sense for her to go up Toller Fell directly from the cottage, to see it. So why didn't you go look for her there?'

'Because it was hours later.' A flash of temper, incandes-cent. Shan almost flinches. For a moment Shan can imagine Melanie turning this volcanic fury on Vicky. Losing control, lashing out, strangling her or hitting her over the head, drag-ging her to the mine shaft, hiding the body.

244

Shan continues, 'But she could have been lying on Toller Fell, injured or even a victim of Terence Bielby. You'd all been warned a serial killer was active in the area. Why on earth would you not look for her close by, first of all?'

'She said the night before she didn't want to miss Catatonia. They were opening. We just assumed she'd gone there to catch them.'

'I don't think that's the case,' Shan says. 'I think you deliberately led people away from Toller Fell because you knew Vicky was there. You'd been there with her.'

Melanie inclines her head, pushes herself back slightly from the table. 'You don't . . . you can't even think—' She breaks off. Her mouth trembling, her palm rubbing the top of her chest. 'This is ridiculous. A terrible mistake. Vicky was my friend. This is horrible.'

'Yes,' Shan says. 'Vicky fell twenty-three metres down a shaft and broke her hip, and her arm and her heel bone. She crawled through underground tunnels, probably trying to escape, alive and in pain for hours if not days. You left her there to die.'

'No. This is wrong. Completely wrong. These are false allegations. I was asleep. I've told you.'

'Let's look at the evidence. And I'd like to remind you that anything you say can be given in evidence. A transcription of this interview will be available to the court.' Shan is careful to keep her voice measured, to avoid any possible accusations of bringing undue pressure to bear. 'So please, think very carefully. During the night you became aware that your boyfriend Robin Westwood and your best friend Vicky Mott had sexual relations. When Vicky left to go see the sunrise you followed her. A witness heard you leave. At or near the site of the abandoned mine you met Vicky. Vicky fell or was pushed down the shaft . . .'

As Shan speaks Melanie keeps her eyes cast down, her fist resting on her mouth, refusing to engage.

'. . . as did a badge we believe to be yours. A badge that Vicky Mott grabbed in the course of an altercation or struggle. Soon after this, we—'

Melanie shakes her head.

'We have an eyewitness who saw you coming down the path and over the stile to the cottage.'

'No.' Melanie says a single word.

'Are you denying that you learned about Robin and Vicky having sexual relations?'

'Yes.'

'Do you also deny that you met Vicky Mott on Toller Fell in the early hours?'

'Yes. I was asleep. I've told you. This is outrageous.' Her fury is cold and contained. 'I'd like to go.' She turns to her solicitor. 'I can do that?'

'You can,' Abigail Shaw says. 'This is a voluntary interview.' She looks over to Shan and Leo. 'Unless you're going to arrest my client?'

Screaming inside, Shan glances at Leo. They have already agreed that they will need to speak to CPS before making an arrest. Because once an arrest is made they'll be up against the ticking clock, with only twenty-four hours to question the suspect. Better to make an arrest when they are on firmer ground.

'Interview terminated,' Leo says and stops the recorder.

Melanie Quinn stands. She's trembling lightly. Simmering, Shan sees, exuding indignation and a fierce sense of injustice.

Me too, Shan thinks. Though she nods and musters as much politeness as she is able. 'Thank you for your cooperation. We may well be back in touch.'

Melanie looks over at her. Something in her eyes makes Shan want to curse and fly at the woman: the sharp, bright pride of triumph.

* * *

Vicky
1997

Vicky sits on the edge of the depression, feet resting on the slope, and smokes a cigarette. It's almost stopped drizzling; she tilts her face up to the sky and can't feel any drops now.

Ahead of her a wash of deep orange floods the horizon, tinting the underneath of the clouds. It looks like an oil painting: rich, majestic.

She blows out a stream of smoke and watches the vapour disappear.

The air is damp and mild and the first light picks out beads of dew and rain on the grasses and heather. A sheen on the tips of her boots.

The dome of the sun, blurred and diffuse, rises.

Vicky stares at it. It doesn't hurt to look but when she blinks the afterimage is there, not gold but dark green.

Her stomach rumbles. Hungry again. She smiles at the thought of the fry-up Robin made her. Her mouth waters. She'll have some toast when she gets back. And then she should probably grab some sleep; there's time for a few hours' kip before the action starts.

She studies the hole she's sitting by. Is it the site of a stone-age house? Or just an old shallow pit where they dug out metal or clay or something? The sides slope down and the centre is obscured by straggly grass and reeds. But it looks like there is an opening there. A well, perhaps? Deep?

There's a patch of bare rock to her side and she finds a loose piece of angular stone the size of a matchbox. She throws it into the middle and it disappears. She hears a chink, another one fainter, then nothing. She laughs because that has told her absolutely nothing about how far down it goes.

A flock of birds fly above the plateau. Too far away for her to tell what they are.

Now the sunlight spreads, the disc of the globe clears the horizon. Streaks of red fading to yellow, rose gold in the clouds.

I'll remember this, she thinks. *This special day.*

She draws in smoke.

And tomorrow? Tomorrow will be home and back to reality. The city and the campus. Their house.

Her heart tightens as she thinks of that, cooped up with Melanie and Usha, and Col — depending on what the doctors say.

She *will* go back to her mum's. That decision still feels right, feels safe. It loosens the knot in her guts.

She can make up some story about feeling fluey or needing somewhere quiet to do her revision. Tell them her mum's not well and Vicky is going home to help out. But she hates lying. The revision excuse is probably—

A rustle behind her sends a jolt of shock through her nerves. She turns, ready to scrabble to her feet. An awful thought in her head: the creepy guy at the pub, *You've heard the police caution, have you? Down there in Leeds? That women up here shouldn't go anywhere on their own.*

But it's not a stranger, it's Melanie.

'Hi.' Vicky stubs her cigarette out. 'You scared me.'

Melanie doesn't say anything. She's not smiling, her face looks . . . blank. Impassive.

She knows. Oh God, she knows.

Vicky swallows. Her mind racing. What to say? She stands up.

I'm sorry?
I never meant to hurt you?
Are you okay?
Shall we head back?
I never knew he felt like that about me?
It just happened?
I'm sorry?

Nothing is right. Nothing fits.

For an instant she wants to jump back in time, to be best friends, telling each other everything, dancing with arms around each other. Nursing hangovers together on the sofa. Braiding Melanie's hair, Melanie running Vicky's lines with her.

But Robin — Robin is the future.

'So . . .' Vicky says. She coughs, clears her throat.

'You bitch.' Melanie's words are pure venom.

Vicky feels it like a slap. Tears ache behind her eyes.

'I'm sorry,' she says.

'Sorry?' Melanie sneers. 'You fucking slag.'

Vicky bows her head. She deserves it, she knows she deserves it.

'Shagging in the yard like a couple of dogs.'

She must have seen them. Vicky is mortified. It sounds so ugly. It wasn't. It wasn't ugly.

'Melanie.' She can't think what else to say.

'How long?' Melanie says.

'What?'

'How long have you been fucking my boyfriend?'

'It's not like that. It's . . . Tonight was the first . . . we've never—' Her words are all jerky, and her face is burning and she starts to cry. A horrible blubbering sound. 'It just happened.' She wipes her nose.

'I'm supposed to believe that? Well, you can fuck off,' Melanie shouts. 'Get your stuff and get out of here.' Her eyes shine with fury. 'And you can look for somewhere else to live. How could you?' she screams. 'How could you? Just get out of our lives and leave us alone. Leave us alone.'

Vicky rubs at her eyes. She is about to comply, feeling bloodied and bruised. But she can't just leave it like this.

'Have you talked to Robin?' Vicky says. Her words are thick, her nose blocked up.

'That's my business.'

'You should talk to Robin.'

'Why?' Melanie steps closer. Her face is deeply flushed, her breath rapid. She's so, so angry.

I'm sorry. I'm sorry. 'He'll tell you. Talk to him.'

'Tell me what?'

A beat. Vicky's heart thuds in her throat. 'He's leaving you.'

'You fucking liar.' Melanie grabs her by the shoulders. Shouts, 'You lying slag.'

'Don't!' She wants to escape this angry, hurt Melanie. 'It's true. We want to be together. Robin said—'

'Lying bitch!' Melanie shoves Vicky hard.

Vicky stumbles, reaches out to Melanie, her fingers catching her coat trying to hold on. She feels the badge peel away. Vicky wheels her arms. Tries to throw her body weight forward, away from the dip in the ground. Her feet skitter on the side of the hole. The ground is wet, slippery. She looks to Melanie, pleading, a moment that stretches for ever. The sun glinting on Melanie's blonde hair. Melanie's face wild with hate. Melanie stepping back.

Vicky slips. She falls feet first, she tries to scramble back up the slope but there are only stalks of grass and bracken and old thistles that break, and air, and emptiness. She plummets, feet first, smacks into stone, falls further. A vicious helter-skelter, a brutal marble run.

She hits rocks. A massive jarring snaps her bones and she bites through her tongue, tasting blood. Pain floods her. Pain. And all is dark.

* * *

Leo
2019

They spend the afternoon putting together all the documents in a case file for the CPS.

Leo has scant hope that they will get the go-ahead to charge Melanie Quinn. Though he agrees with Shan that with everything they've unearthed she is now the key suspect.

'I've spoken to the lab, asked them if there's any chance of recovering DNA from the smiley badge,' Shan says.

Unlikely, Leo thinks and he reckons Shan knows that too. But there's no harm in asking the question.

The strongest plank of their evidence is Christopher Hirst's sighting of Melanie. The rest is theoretical — that Melanie had motive, that the badge was hers. The criteria for bringing a charge are stringent and rightly so. There has to be enough evidence against the defendant and a realistic prospect of conviction.

The defence could argue that Hirst's evidence is unreliable because he cannot be certain whether he saw Melanie in a green coat or Vicky in a red one.

Leo's phone rings. *Elizabeth Mott.*

'Elizabeth?'

'I've just had Melanie Quinn on the phone. What the hell is going on?'

Leo doesn't swear, much as he'd like to. He looks over to Shan and gives a shake of his head.

'I don't know what you've been told—'

'Nothing from you, that's for sure.' She cuts him off. 'You *promised* you'd keep me informed and next thing I'm hearing God knows what.' Her voice almost breaks. 'This is my daughter we're talking about.'

'We'll come over now,' Leo says. 'Tell you what we can.' He looks to Shan who nods.

'Good.' Elizabeth hangs up.

Leo blows out his cheeks. He's dismayed that Elizabeth has been upset like this and angry that Melanie has seen fit to go running to her.

'Elizabeth Mott, very agitated,' he tells Shan. 'Melanie's been on to her.'

'Why would Melanie Quinn tell Vicky's mother that we'd been questioning her? Wouldn't you want to keep a lid on that?'

'She gets there first,' Leo says. 'Plays the innocent. The wronged party. It undermines whatever we then tell Elizabeth. It looks like Melanie is transparent and open, and we're not.'

Shan nods. 'She wants Elizabeth to trust her, to feel sorry for her. To doubt us. So what do we do?'

He picks up his bag. 'We reassure Elizabeth as much as we can. And we see exactly what she's been told.'

* * *

Elizabeth

Leo Donovan looks sombre, even a little sheepish. And his colleague Shan Young seems more formal as she greets Elizabeth and takes a seat at the kitchen table.

Elizabeth is bubbling with impatience, with annoyance. She doesn't offer them drinks as she normally would. And when Leo starts, 'So we understand that Melanie contacted you—' she rounds on him. 'And why didn't you? You gave me your word when we first met. Whenever there was any progress, I'd be the first to know. You promised you would keep me informed.' She's so angry her throat aches and it's hard to keep her voice in check.

'And we have.' Leo is calm. 'But one thing we don't do, one thing we simply won't do, is share lines of enquiry with you when they remain inconclusive. That would not be ethical.'

'So what was all this with Melanie? You never mentioned anything.'

'Because we were still investigating.'

'What did Melanie say?' Shan speaks up. She looks . . . angry, Elizabeth thinks. Or intent, eyes quick and bright.

'That you were insinuating she knows more about what happened. That Vicky slept with her boyfriend, Robin, behind Melanie's back. And the eyewitness who saw Vicky has suddenly changed his story, saying it was actually Melanie. You were insisting the badge you found belonged to her.'

Shan nods. 'That's right. But we weren't insinuating or insisting. We were asking her to answer questions based on the evidence we've gathered.'

They're serious. Elizabeth feels dizzy, sick. The room seems to ripple. She swallows, saliva thick in her mouth. She had hoped for apologies and talk of misunderstandings or crossed wires. Reassurances.

'You don't really think—' But she can see the truth plainly in Leo's eyes. And something else — sympathy or sorrow. Pity.

'She couldn't,' Elizabeth says. 'She . . . they were . . .' She buries her face in her hands and struggles to hold on to her thought processes. She needs to understand this even if it seems nonsensical.

She takes a breath, sits up taller. 'This sighting. It was the boy from the pub?'

'That's right,' Leo says.

'Then why did he say it was Vicky in the first place? He identified Vicky.'

'He identified a woman wearing the same clothes as Vicky, the red coat. But he's colour-blind,' Shan explains. 'He can't tell the difference between red and green. Melanie wore a similar coat in green. We interviewed him, showed him a set of images. That proved he couldn't distinguish between those two coats.'

Vicky loved that coat, Elizabeth thinks. Elizabeth gave her the money to buy it for Christmas. A stupid, irrelevant thought. She must concentrate. She has to concentrate.

'No,' Elizabeth says. 'No. I can't believe . . . this is—' She wants to stop them talking, tell them they are wrong. Completely wrong. She exhales. Finally, resigned to face the facts, she motions her hand weakly for them to continue. 'Go on.'

'Once we found Vicky, that sighting became an anomaly. But if that *was* actually Melanie . . .' Leo says.

'It changes everything,' Elizabeth whispers. 'And is it true that Vicky had sex with Melanie's boyfriend?'

'Yes, according to Robin,' Leo says.

'We believe Melanie found out but we don't know whether Vicky told her or she caught sight of them,' Shan says.

Elizabeth sits, absorbing this.

'And the badge, can you prove its Melanie's?'

'No,' Shan says. 'I've just checked. There was no DNA present.'

'And even if we could,' Leo says, 'we can't prove how it ended up where it did.'

Melanie? Melanie who rang Elizabeth to tell her Vicky was missing. Who helped Elizabeth pack up Vicky's belongings. Who's kept in touch over all the years. A loyal friend. Who Vicky loved.

'Was it consensual, the sex?' Elizabeth asks. Another shift in the story occurs to her.

'As far as we know. Robin Westwood says that he and Vicky had planned to carry on seeing each other. And he was going to end his relationship with Melanie.'

Elizabeth drags her hair over one shoulder, twists at it. 'He dropped out, didn't he? Moved away?'

'That's right,' Leo says.

'If he had spoken up at the time. If he'd just said something then. Why didn't he?' Now her ire is suddenly directed at this man.

'He didn't think it was important,' Leo says. 'He didn't believe Melanie knew anything about it. He thought Vicky had gone off to see the sunrise because she was flustered by what had just happened. He assumed she'd probably been a victim of Terence Bielby.'

'We all did! He should have said!' Elizabeth argues. 'He should have.'

But Melanie? The emails, the Christmas cards. It can't be true or Elizabeth would have known. She would have been able to tell if Melanie was lying, pretending. *I'm not an idiot.*

'I don't know what to think,' Elizabeth says. 'Tell me, honestly. Please be frank with me. Can this really be true?'

'An eyewitness puts Melanie on Toller Fell at dawn. Something she denies. Until that can be explained we consider Melanie to be a person of interest,' Leo says.

Elizabeth closes her eyes, presses her fingers to her forehead. She can hear the squabble of sparrows from the hedge at the back. She feels as though her head is full of static, interference buzzing and shocking.

'What happens now?' she murmurs. 'Will you arrest her?'

'It depends on the CPS. Whether they consider the evidence strong enough to bring a charge of murder.'

Her heart burns as he says this. A dry sob breaks in the back of her throat.

'Could they decide not?' she says.

'Yes. That's something to be prepared for.'

Shan stirs, gives off an air of frustration.

'And then?' Elizabeth says.

Leo's shoulders rise and fall. He looks at her, ruefully. 'The police investigation would remain open. The case on file, as we call it. Revisited periodically.'

'You give up? You give up on my girl?'

Shan's mouth tightens, lips compressed, as if she shares Elizabeth's exasperation.

'Having done everything we can, exhausted all possible lines of enquiry,' Leo says.

'Is that a phrase they teach you from the manual?' Elizabeth fights tears, loses. Wipes roughly at her cheeks and eyes.

No one speaks for a moment. Then Leo says, 'We will do everything we possibly can. That's not a platitude. I told you that at the beginning. It was a promise. It still is.'

Elizabeth, her eyes brimming, jaw aching, looks from him to Shan.

'I know,' she admits. Because they have, she knows they have.

But this . . . the thought of Melanie, of Melanie leaving Vicky down in the bowels of the earth, of her lying, possibly getting away with it . . . .

Elizabeth is horrified. She has been duped. And it's so sordid, ugly and cruel. And unbearably sad.

* * *

Shan

'Can we stop at the services?' She needs to pee. Again. And her back aches. Too much sitting around maybe. There's never any time to do her exercises, stretching and relaxation, or the warmups that she carried on even after leaving martial arts classes.

'Sure,' Leo says.

It was her mum who persuaded her to try martial arts, to join her in a family class. Fiona had been going to the dojo long before they adopted Shan.

Sometimes her mum would surprise her at home, turning from the worktop or the table and taking a stance, giving one of the cries they learned. Shan would mirror her. It became a game. How quickly they could ape each other. A conversation in space and movement that usually ended with them both in stitches.

Shan stopped training when she moved into the house with Erin. It was too far to go into Leeds. She could have found somewhere new but she liked the familiarity of her dojo and she knew the sensei so well.

Besides, they were crazy busy sorting out the house.

Erin still goes to the gym, though. Has Shan changed to accommodate Erin? She turns the thought over. Has she? Isn't there bound to be some give and take, some adjustment to living together?

What has Erin changed?

She doesn't like to think like this. She hates to doubt the relationship. It rarely happens, but when it does, like a snake rearing from a hole, it makes her panic. Brings a rush of thoughts about walking away. Selling the house.

But the baby?

It was the same in an earlier relationship, her first big heartbreak, which happened when her mum was still alive. Shan leaving Caitlin and turning up at home with a suitcase.

'Oh, Shan-Shan.' Her mum had hugged her tight. They sat and talked over hot chocolate and banana bread.

'Why so sudden?'

'I don't know,' Shan said. 'She didn't seem very into me anymore. I didn't want her to dump me.'

'Did you talk to her about it?' her mum said.

'No.'

'Did you try and tell her how you were feeling?'

'No.'

'So you left Caitlin because you were worried she might dump you,' her mum said.

'It's stupid, I know.'

Her mum had given a small smile and brushed Shan's hair back from her face. 'I think it makes a certain sort of sense.'

'Why?'

'Oh darling. Because you were rejected, abandoned as a baby.' Her mum's eyes glistened. 'Any hint of rejection is bound to be very, very hard for you. So you jump first. You'll go a long way not to have to deal with anything like that again.'

Is Shan doing that now? Starting that pattern all over again?

A pang in her back makes her shuffle. She feels hot. The storm still hasn't broken. Maybe she's coming down with something. Aches and pains and sweating.

'We can finalise the files in the morning,' Leo says. 'Send them through before lunch.'

And then?

Leo keeps impressing upon her that they have the slimmest of chances. But if there is any chance at all, she has to cling to that. She has to hope.

At the services Shan goes straight to the toilets. The cramping ache is still there. Maybe it's a bladder infection. She should've asked to use the toilet at Elizabeth's again instead of waiting. A lance-like pain digs in her left side.

In the cubicle, sheets of toilet paper litter the floor. Someone has defaced the advert for the domestic violence helpline with a *Keep Britain White* sticker. Someone else has scrawled an S over the W, so it now reads *Keep Britain Shite*. Shan thinks of Leo's son. But a woman must have stuck this up. Or someone cleaning at the station.

She sits to use the toilet and another cramp clutches at her bowels. She empties her bladder, wipes herself.

The tissue is red. Crimson. She is bleeding.

She peers into the bowl. Large clots like dark red jellyfish. More cramping. Sweat breaks over her.

Spotting is normal. She's read that, hasn't she? And breakthrough bleeding?

She feels another band of pain squeezing hard, like a period pain.

She can hear another woman using the sink, the noisy roar of the hand-dryer, the bang of the door.

Pulling more toilet paper free she holds it between her legs. When she draws it out there are a couple of lumps of jelly, formless, amorphous. Dark clots on the brighter blood. This isn't just spotting.

'You ready, Poppy?' a woman calls.

'Nearly.' A child's voice.

'Good girl.'

A siren screams past on the dual carriageway.

There's too much blood.

Panic rolls through her.

She's shaking. She hasn't picked a name. And she can't tell if that's a good thing or a bad thing.

* * *

Leo

Leo is by the car, tucking into a veggie sausage roll, flakes of pastry littering his shirt, when Shan comes back.

'Not bad.' He waves the pastry. 'Mushroom and veg.'

He notices her expression. She looks frightened. Anxious.

'What's up?' Leo says.

She hesitates. She's letting the case get to her. Is that it?

'I'm bleeding. I think I'm having a miscarriage.'

Christ! Leo's heart thumps in his chest. 'Oh, Shan.' He touches her shoulder. 'Look, we'll get you to hospital. Get in.'

'No.' She opens the car door. 'Take me home.'

'Well, wouldn't it be better . . .' He knows she doesn't like hospitals but—

'I've rung my doctor. She says I can go home if I want to. That it's okay, if that's what I want to do. There'll be tests to follow up,' she says. Her voice shakes.

'Are you sure, because—?'

'I'm sure.' She sounds definite.

'Okay.' Leo fumbles for something to say as he brushes the crumbs off his clothes. Sits and puts the key in the ignition.

'I'm sorry.' The best he can do.

She gives a curt nod in acknowledgement.

Leo wants to help. How can he help?

'Does it hurt? There's paracetamol in the glove compartment.'

'A bit. Thanks.' She takes two tablets.

'I just need to ring Ange,' Leo says. 'Tell her I'll see her a bit later.' Visiting Luke again.

While he's doing that Shan calls Erin. 'Ring me back,' he hears Shan say.

Calls made, a silence falls between them.

Shan breaks it. 'When's the prize thing for your wife's project.'

'Ah, it was Monday. She won.' The whole thing tarnished with the shock of Luke's accident and the Crusaders bollocks.

'Really? That's brilliant.'

'Yeah. She is pretty brilliant.'

'Have you been married long?'

'Twenty-five years. We were very young,' he says.

'And you've just the one son?'

'Yes.' Ange had miscarried her second pregnancy. Should he share that? Is it helpful or self-centred?

He'd found her in tears one morning when he got in from the night shift. Stripping the bed. Luke crying in his cot.

She was fifteen weeks along. They'd only just told everyone the week before.

It hit her hard. They agreed to wait until she felt keen to try again. But eventually she told him that she didn't want another child. That she was happy with Luke, with him. The three of them.

Leo had been disappointed, his fantasy of having a whole brood of kids, a busy, lively household, receding.

'It's my Irish roots,' he told her. 'Big families.'

'They'd no choice though, had they?' Ange pointed out. 'A baby every year. Eight, ten, thirteen kids. Those poor women.'

'True.' And he had gradually made peace with her decision. But now he thinks, would Luke have turned out any different with a sibling or two?

Shan's phone rings and she talks with her partner. Tears in her voice but being practical, relaying what the GP has advised. 'Any fever, high temperature or severe pain and I've got to go to the hospital. It might mean it's not complete and there's a risk of infection. But otherwise I can wait for the bleeding to stop and get a scan done to make sure it's all clear . . . Up to two weeks . . . Yes. I'll see you soon.'

As Leo pulls up outside Shan's house, he places his hand on her shoulder again. 'Take all the time that you need,' he says. 'Oh, but what about your car?' Still in Settle.

'We can fetch it tomorrow, thanks.'

'Seriously?'

'Yes. It'll be okay,' she says.

Their front door opens and Erin comes out. Her face full of concern.

What a shame, Leo thinks as he pulls away. What a crying shame.

CHAPTER FOURTEEN

Vicky
1997

Vicky opens her eyes but can see nothing.

Pain surges through her leg, her hip. Drilling white-hot. She bites her teeth together. Her tongue throbs. Blood coppery in her mouth. She spits.

She fell, yes. She's fallen.

Melanie?

Everything drops away.

* * *

Vicky wakes. The pain is spinning her. She must have broken her hip. Or her pelvis? She moans on each soft exhale.

She fell.

It's dark.

Call for help.

She inches on to her back, whimpering in agony.

'Melanie?' She tries to shout, but her voice is thready. Her tongue is swollen and clumsy and won't move properly.

As if she's had a long session at the dentist. 'Melanie.' The call resonates, bounces back to her.

She takes a few breaths, shouts again. 'Melanie. Help me.' Uses the cry to ride the waves of pain.

She waits. Listens. She can hear her breath, the thrum of blood in her ears and dripping water. Single drops. Sometimes near, sometimes far.

The smell of wet stone, intense, sterile.

She keeps calling 'Help' and 'Melanie'. But the only response is a faint echo.

Vicky rests, moaning again. Like someone in labour.

She tests the ground with her left hand. Rocky, uneven, lumps of loose stones under her fingers.

She fell.

When she looks upwards she can see no disc of daylight. Nothing but sparks of silver lights trailing comets. That must be her eyes playing tricks.

Lighter.

She fumbles in her coat pocket, digs past the cigarette packet and feels the metal tip, the tube of plastic.

She has to stop, pause, when the pain comes roaring.

Vicky tries to gather strength, summons the power to retrieve the lighter and flick it on.

The flame ignites.

She's in a sort of cave, almost round, a dark space narrowing above. As though she's at the bottom of an upturned funnel.

She moves the lighter and finds a gap leading off to the left. A tunnel?

She is still lying down. Moving slowly she holds the lighter over her middle. And tilts her head to look at her right leg. It is twisted to the side. It shouldn't be like that. Her thumb tires. She releases the button and the light goes out.

'I don't know what to do.' She says the words aloud.

Melanie might have gone for help, mightn't she?

Then why hasn't she called back, to let you know?

You passed out, she might have done it then. Told you to hold on, she'd get the mountain rescue out or whoever.

Robin will come find, her, won't he? But how will he know where she is? How will anyone unless Melanie tells them?

Bitch! Lying slag!

Terror grips her spine, clutches at her heart, as intense and overwhelming as the pain.

She gasps, panic disrupting her pulse. Hyperventilating.

Stop! Think!

She strikes the lighter again. She can't see any way to reach up the shaft. She doesn't think she can stand with her leg like that, never mind climb.

She wants her mum. She's afraid, so very afraid, and she wants her mum. Tears leak out of her eyes, sliding into her ears.

If no one comes . . .

So either you stay here and give up, or you can move, find another way out.

She looks at the tunnel to the left. Is it a pothole?

If it's a pothole it must go somewhere, right?

One of her dad's friends used to go potholing. Their boys' school had a trip as teenagers and the friend got the bug but her dad always said he hated it. Too claustrophobic.

She wants a cigarette.

She thinks there are two left. She can ration them. She'll have half of one now.

The smoke hurts her tongue, makes her mouth water, but then she feels the relief of the nicotine entering her system.

She smokes in the dark, eyes closed. Keening with the pain.

She replaces the tab in the packet then tries to work out how best to move. She pushes with her good foot hoping to slide on her back but the agony in her hip makes it impossible. The tide of pain seems even worse than before. Like something is burning her nerves, mining into her bones.

Vicky tries rocking on to her left side, yelling aloud, and on the third attempt manages to shift her weight. She lies there, her heart beating too fast and sweating everywhere.

263

She waits, summing up the courage to move.

Bending her knee, she uses her left hand and elbow, knee and foot to haul herself a few inches after groping ahead with her hand, to check for obstacles. She does it again.

It hurts too much. The pain is all consuming and she vomits. The acrid stench fills her nostrils. She spits to clear her mouth.

She wants to cry.

She will not lie here next to a pool of sick!

Move!

Keep going. A bit at a time.

She hauls herself forward. And again. Her groans ringing round the hollow space.

She will count. When she's done fifty moves, she will have another smoke.

Saying the words aloud, she plays word association with the numbers. 'Five gold rings, six — pick up sticks, seven deadly sins, eight, three times three is nine . . .' At eighteen, waving her hand, her fingers meet stone. A wall.

She's trapped.

She's stuck.

Horror rips through her. *I don't want to . . .* She won't say that word. She won't think it.

She flicks the lighter.

The passage turns almost ninety degrees. Thin streams of water snake down the wall. Vicky pulls herself close and presses her tongue to the stone. The water tastes of soil, of the earth, and the tang of something else, blood or metal.

'Help me,' she prays. 'Help.'

Her hand is scraped raw from dragging over the rock.

The flame gutters and dies.

'No, no, no!'

I hate you, Melanie. You left me. You fucking bitch. You watched me fall. You stepped away. Her rage is ice-cold.

Vicky sparks the flint once, twice. Shakes the lighter. Feels to checks the setting is on high. She strikes it again and a tiny flame ignites, the size of a match head, blue ringed with orange. She pulls out her cigarettes and lights the whole one. Before she finishes smoking, the flame dies.

Her last cigarette. Images flood in, mocking her: movie firing squads, death cells, blindfold executions.

Fear skitters in her bowels, and the back of her neck.

She lets the pain swamp her. Focuses only on that. It is an orange blade and a crushing black vice. It is a mouth, teeth like daggers dripping acid. A poker hot and heavy.

Go on, she tells herself. *Go on*. And she readies herself to edge round the corner and drag her body over the next few inches.

It takes a moment to remember where she was up to. 'Nineteen — song about Vietnam. Twenty. Twenty-one — key of the door. Two little ducks.' In between she whines and moans, answering the pain.

It isn't real. This can't be real.

She imagines waking up. Escape. She sees herself telling the tale of it at the pub. Then she sees Melanie there. Vicky's blood turns to ice, and the fantasy sours and fades.

* * *

Shan
2019

Shan wakes disorientated. Erin's side of the bed is empty. *I'm late!*

She remembers. *The baby*. The day takes on a new shape.

She puts her hand on her belly. Apparently she can take a pregnancy test for confirmation in a few days' time if she wishes. Salt in the wound.

That first test — the leap of joy mixed with disbelief as both lines turned pink. A rill of fear. Could she do this?

Short answer?

The cramps have eased. She only noticed a twinge or two in the night. She is surprised to have slept so well. How could she?

She can smell coffee.

Downstairs Erin sits at the table. Shan thinks for a moment she is reading then sees the hitch of her shoulders, and knows.

'Erin?'

Erin turns, drying her cheeks, mouth pressed tight, nose reddened.

Shan goes to hug her, feeling her own eyes prick in response.

'I'm sorry,' Erin says.

'Don't be daft.'

'It's just . . . oh, I don't know.'

'It happens a lot,' Shan says.' Something was probably wrong.'

'It doesn't make it any easier, though. Does it?' Erin looks at her, big blue eyes swimming.

'No.' Shan kisses her forehead. Her nose. She hadn't expected this, for Erin to be so upset.

A pause. 'Are you going to work?' Shan asks.

Erin nods. 'Yes. Unless you want me to stay.'

'No, no. You going to be okay?'

'Yes.'

Another moment goes by.

'How are you?' Erin asks.

Shan thinks. 'Sad,' she says. 'Just sad.' And ashamed that she's failed. That she's lost the baby.

She hugs herself. 'I'm going to have a cup of coffee. You want more?'

Erin shakes her head. 'I'll get ready.'

* * *

The house is quiet and Shan is at a loss. She empties the recycling into the outside bin and puts a load of washing on.

Her dad texts asking how she is. They spoke last night. She reassures him and says she might have a walk.

It's a lovely day out there. He encourages her. *If you want some company I could rearrange things at work and drive down? Xx.*

266

It's kind of him but she wants some time on her own. *No, don't do that. I'll be fine. Thanks though. xx.*

It is warm enough for shorts and a T-shirt. She puts sunscreen on too.

The walk through the castle woods by the canal is filled with dappled light. The air is busy with flies and bees and butterflies. The beck on the other side, slender and brown, winds between rocky banks stippled with moss and lichen.

She stops at the weir and stares at the billowing water, letting herself be mesmerised by the rhythm, the repeated patterns of light and shadow, the smooth mirror sheets that cascade then dissolve into foam.

She carries the sadness with her, knowing she needs to grow accustomed to it. Absorb it. All the people they need to tell, all the discussions and the arrangements that no longer matter. Birth plans and maternity leave. Cots and prams.

Shan skirts the castle grounds, which are full of visitors.

She hears American accents.

A little later a small group passes, Chinese or Japanese. Little flickers of curiosity directed her way. *We're the same but not the same.*

All the forms with their tick boxes, *our equal opportunity monitoring.* Choosing British-Chinese but not certain she really fits that box. Not sure where she fits.

She doesn't often think about her own birth. Her time as an orphan. And of course she has no memories of it.

The facts are scant. A date in October 1988, a baby wrapped in blankets in a box on the steps of a temple in a city called Shantou. Estimated to be a couple of weeks old.

Had they always known they would abandon her? Was there another child at home already? Or was it only decided at birth when they got a girl and not the longed-for son and heir?

Who was it wrapped her up, carried that box? Had her parents disagreed about it? Were they forced into it? Was she a problem to be palmed off on others?

A disappointment?

A shame?

She feels a lump in her throat. Blinks, watching a toddler hurl himself to the floor, heels drumming in a tantrum.

She cried for the loss of a baby no bigger than a peach. Did anyone cry for the loss of her?

She walks home feeling leaden.

'New day tomorrow.' Something her mum used to say.

She eats soup for lunch, can't be bothered to make a salad. Follows it with a banana, sitting on the sofa.

The place looks neat and tidy. She notices the book of names has gone. Erin must have hidden it away, not wanting it there as a reminder.

As if we'd forget, Shan thinks. *As if we'll ever be able to forget.*

* * *

Leo

'How are you?' Leo asks.

Shan shrugs. 'I wanted to come into work.'

'You sure?' He's worried about her but has to trust what she says.

'Yes. I was going spare at home. I even baked.' She raises her eyebrows. 'Coconut macaroons.'

'Yes please,' Leo says.

She shakes her head. 'I had to chuck them. Turned out like cinders.'

He smiles. 'Stick to the day job.'

'You're not wrong.'

He tries to think of something else to say, to stretch out the time before he has to break the news.

She helps him out. 'How's your son?'

'Home the day after tomorrow. They'll likely arrest him then. They've already arrested his pal.'

Jack Sherringham's mother had rung Leo the previous day. Jack had been arrested and charged, which, in her eyes, was ridiculous. 'It's just a bit of graffiti, for heaven's sake.'

268

'It's a hate crime,' Leo said.

'Well . . .' She sounded taken aback. 'What about Luke?'

'Luke's in hospital. A broken leg, wrist and collarbone.'

'Oh, I'm so sorry. I'd no idea. Jack said he wasn't answering his phone. What happened?'

Leo didn't feel like talking. 'Came off his bike, trying to avoid the police.'

She sighed. 'Will he be all right?'

'Hope so,' Leo said.

'You think they'd have enough to do, honestly. With all these drug gangs and terrorists everywhere,' Mrs Sherringham said.

Leo felt his teeth clench. 'It *is* terrorism. Peddling fear and division, making Muslims and Jews and Black people and anyone else they fancy into scapegoats.'

She retorted, 'I really don't think—'

Leo really did not need to know what she really didn't think and hung up.

'And Christopher Hirst?' Shan says.

'Not heard. But then I wouldn't necessarily.'

She takes a breath in and he knows she's going to ask about the case.

'Shan, the CPS came back to us.' He doesn't need to elaborate.

'No,' she says. 'No.'

'Insufficient evidence, no realistic prospect of a successful prosecution.'

'No,' she says again. 'So Melanie Quinn carries on like nothing ever happened. She gets to do her job, and see her kid, and move up the property ladder—'

'Hey.' Leo spreads his hands. 'It's not what we wanted but it's not unexpected.' He shares her disappointment, a weight between his shoulder blades. The burden of something unfinished, unsuccessful.

'Shit!' She shakes her head.

'You worked so hard,' Leo says. 'I know, and—'

269

'Not hard enough, obviously.' She sounds bitter. He doesn't blame her.

'The evidence wasn't there,' Leo says. 'We found everything we could but it wasn't enough.'

'Have you told Elizabeth?'

'Not yet. But we should. I should. You don't need to—'

'I'm coming,' she says.

* * *

Shan

'And that's it?' Elizabeth Mott says to Leo. She swipes away a lock of silver hair. 'I'm left in limbo?' Her voice shakes and she stares at the kitchen ceiling, shaking her head. She wears a faded linen shift, patterned blue and white, sandals on her feet.

'I'm sorry. The case will remain on file,' Leo says.

Food from the fridge is piled on the table. A clear-out, Shan guesses. Some of the stuff looks rotten. Liquefying cucumber, for a start.

'If anything new comes to light, that decision will be revisited,' Leo says.

'There won't be any new evidence, will there? Not from what you said. Not unless—' she stumbles over the name, adds 'Quinn' with vitriol in her tone — 'confesses.'

'It is extremely unlikely.'

Elizabeth casts her hands to the sky.

Shan realises her own fists are closed tight, nails digging into her palms. She flexes them, trying to be discreet.

'I'm sorry. It's not the outcome any of us wanted,' Leo says.

Elizabeth pulls out a chair and sits down.

'But you're sure?'

'Yes,' Shan speaks up. 'As sure as we can be. We just can't prove it.'

Elizabeth wraps her hands around her forehead, her eyes. They wait quietly. Shan and Leo still on their feet.

When Elizabeth moves, her face is wet with tears. She sniffs hard and says, 'Thing is, you found her for me. You brought her back. I don't have to wonder anymore. It's hard to think of her going through that, hurt and alone, frightened. But at least I know. That might sound strange.' She breaks off, finds a tissue in her pocket and wipes her nose. 'At least I know. The not knowing.' She nods. 'That was hard. That was so hard. At least I can say my goodbyes.'

Shan blinks fast, clears her throat. The sentiments are tough to hear. Would be difficult even if she wasn't already raw with her own sorrow.

'So thank you for that.' Elizabeth looks from Shan to Leo, her face working with emotion. 'Thank you so much.'

* * *

Vicky
1997

Vicky can hear a heartbeat, a *poum*, *poum*, *poum* that travels through her. Is it the earth?

She drags herself a little further forward.

It is so hot and she is weak, like a newborn, like a seedling. She's dissolving.

Water drips.

'Hello?' she says. Her voice is thin but it bounces off the space. It must be enormous, this theatre.

And they are all here for her. The dripping of applause swells and grows.

They are all on the front row of the stalls, her mum and dad, Usha and Robin and Melanie, her drama teacher from school, press photographers. A full house behind them.

Cameras flash.

Vicky poses, smiles, waves.

The crowd roars. They all stand, the stalls and the circle, even the people up in the gods. An ovation. Whistling and cheering. Clamouring for an encore.

271

She is so proud, she feels like she'll burst. Her mum and dad look up at her with such love.

The clapping goes on and on.

Vicky is high above them now, on a trapeze. She's swinging, soaring high above the festival stage. Caught in the spotlights.

Singing in her head.

The heartbeat rocking her.

Slower.

And slower.

And—

* * *

Elizabeth
2019

The detached house sits on a generous plot of land, the grounds are yet to be landscaped. The raw earth is rutted and uneven, strewn with builder's rubble. Tufts of wildflowers and weeds, dock and nettles, dandelions and couch grass, sprout here and there.

A large terrace, to the side of the house, has already been built, paved with the same York flagstones as at Elizabeth's. A young boy there. *Kieran.* Elizabeth's stomach contracts.

He's bouncing a basketball. He shoots, misses the hoop bracketed to the wall well away from the sliding glass doors.

Usha turns off the engine. 'You okay?' she says.

'No.' Elizabeth shakes her head. 'But we're here now.' Her throat is clotted with fear, head buzzing. She feels sick. She meets Usha's gaze and sees her own trepidation mirrored there. Elizabeth trusts what the police have told her but she needs to see the truth for herself.

'Ready?' Elizabeth says. Usha gives a nod, takes a steadying breath.

When they get out of the car, Kieran stops playing and turns to look at them, face open and curious. He runs towards them, bouncing the ball fast as he goes, arm bent at the elbow and parallel to the ground.

'Hello.' Elizabeth forces a smile for the boy. 'Is your mum in?'

'Yes.' His eyes are screwed up against the sun. He is skinny, like Melanie. Has sticklike ankles, the same blond hair.

'You winning?' Elizabeth nods to the ball.

He shrugs, probably not sure if it's a serious question. 'Just practising.'

Before they can move to the door, it opens.

Elizabeth's heart stutters in her chest.

The man in the doorway wears a linen shirt and shorts, with trek sandals on his feet. He has a deep tan. Silver stubble, short grey hair.

Melanie's husband.

'Hello,' he says. He doesn't recognise them. But then neither she nor Usha have ever met Graham.

'Is Melanie in?' Elizabeth asks.

He turns back to the house to call her but Melanie is there in an instant.

Melanie's face flashes surprise. A moment's apprehension, then she is all smiles. 'Elizabeth, Usha.' She turns to her husband. 'Darling, this is Vicky's mother.'

'Ah.' The man's expression changes to sympathy. 'I'm so sorry for your loss.'

Elizabeth wonders if he knows the police have interviewed his wife. That they suspect her of murder. There is no air of trauma or crisis between the couple that she can sense. Perhaps Melanie has kept it from him. She is a past master at keeping secrets.

'Can you check the sauce?' Melanie says to him. *Getting rid.* 'Come in, come in. We can sit through here.'

They follow her into the room that runs alongside the terrace.

Two large sofas dominate the space, upholstered in a floral print, a folk-art style, vivid pinks and blues, greens and oranges on a white background. There are also a couple of teak recliners. The walls are plain white, the floor white-washed boards. An upright piano sits against one internal wall.

Two enormous palms in square, charcoal-coloured planters stand either side of the patio doors.

'You want tea, a cold drink?' *The perfect host.*

'No, thank you,' Elizabeth says.

Elizabeth and Usha sit on one of the sofas. Melanie perches on the edge of the other. There's a nervousness in her pose, back stiff, hands on her knees.

You haven't asked us why we're here.

Elizabeth recalls the times she disciplined children in school. There were the ones who instantly launched into denials and protests, anxious that their side of the story be heard, knowing they might be in trouble. Then the others who kept quiet, pretending innocence or puzzlement. Not acknowledging anything about the incident, hoping to get away with it.

'It's ridiculous, isn't it?' Melanie says into the silence. 'I'm thinking of putting in an official complaint.'

A thud against the outside wall sends her to her feet. 'For heaven's sake!'

She opens the sliding door. 'Kieran! Leave the ball, it's too noisy,' she snaps.

'But—'

'Leave it.' She's firm but has modulated her tone.

She comes back in. 'Sorry about that.'

Elizabeth doesn't speak. She waits, eyes on Melanie, while Melanie reclaims her seat.

Melanie takes a breath, thumb and fingers of her right hand gripping the sides of her left wrist, the bony spur on the outside there.

'I know what you did,' Elizabeth whispers.

Melanie is ostensibly shocked, mouth opening, blinking. A blush rises up her neck.

'You can't . . . you don't believe . . . it's not true, Elizabeth. Any of it. Vicky was my friend.' She leans forward,

274

her palms up, inviting understanding. 'Usha, you know that. You were there.'

Usha is trembling lightly, Elizabeth can see the tremors in her hands, around her mouth. 'Col kept talking about it, about Robin and Vicky,' Usha says. 'At the cottage and after, back in Leeds. He knew something was going on between them.'

'There was nothing going on!' Melanie hisses. 'Col was raving, he was ill. He said the water was poisoned and we were being spied on. He said all sorts of things. Psychosis involves a loss of touch with reality. He was talking rubbish. I would never have done anything that hurt Vicky. You know that. This — the police, it's a witch hunt. Just because they can't find—'

The internal door opens. Kieran. 'Mum, can I go and—'

'Out! Now! Outside,' Melanie says.

'Sorr-eee!' he retorts. He slams the door.

Melanie's cheeks flush red.

'You've just the one,' Elizabeth says. 'Like me.' She holds eye contact and Melanie does the same, but the expression in her eyes falters, fractures, and Elizabeth glimpses the flicker of guilt. It's enough. Enough for her to know the truth. Melanie looks away, looks down. 'Elizabeth, I swear—'

'Don't bother.' Rage seethes inside her, molten. As much for the years of deception, the years of betrayal, of lie upon lie, as for the act itself.

'You left her there to die.' Elizabeth says it as steadily as she is able. *She loved you.*

'I didn't. I didn't,' Melanie insists, voice rising. 'This is a complete nightmare.'

Welcome to my world.

'I never left the cottage. I was asleep all night. I've told the police.'

'That's not true.' Usha's voice quavers but she is determined to say her piece. 'I went to your room.' Usha casts a quick glance at Elizabeth who has already heard this from her. Elizabeth told Usha about Melanie and saw the horror

275

bloom on Usha's face as her memories took on new sinister meaning, as the light dawned. Realising she had information that could help to confirm Melanie's guilt, she'd gone straight to the police — only to be told they still couldn't bring charges.

'I had period pains, remember? And I knew you had some ibuprofen,' Usha says.

Melanie grimaces, eyes puzzled.

'You weren't there, and Robin wasn't there. He was sleeping downstairs.'

'Well, I was probably in the bathroom,' Melanie says. She swings her head, looking exasperated, fraught. Crosses her ankles. 'Honestly, if you think—'

'You weren't in the bathroom.' Usha speaks over Melanie. 'I went in there and found the tablets in your washbag.'

'So? I must have been downstairs.'

What happened to, 'I was asleep all night'?

Melanie bends forward again, hands pleading. 'Usha, this was twenty-two years ago and suddenly you dredge this up as some sort of accusation just because the police—'

Usha won't be derailed and Elizabeth loves her for it. 'It was just getting light. I didn't need to put the lights on in the hall. I remember that.'

'So?' Melanie presses her fingers to her forehead.

'It was dawn and you'd gone out. You'd gone after Vicky.'

'No,' Melanie says.

'How could you?' Usha bursts out. Her voice cracks with emotion.

'No! Look, please, listen to yourselves. This is paranoia. I didn't *do* anything. How many more times? You have to believe me. My lawyer says there's no real evidence. The police can't prosecute because there's nothing—'

'No, but we can.' Elizabeth cuts her off.

'What?'

'Private prosecution.' Shan Young had rung her and suggested it, the detective furious that the police could take things no further.

'You can't,' Melanie says.

'Just watch us. Usha, me, Dee — even Robin.'

'That's ridiculous.'

'It'll be difficult, take years and lots of money, but then the Westwoods have very deep pockets. We will drag you through the courts,' Elizabeth says.

'And the court of public opinion.' Usha waves her phone.

Elizabeth rises. Usha too.

'Listen, wait,' Melanie begs.

They do neither.

Outside Kieran rides a go-kart over the terrace. They all watch. When he drives out of view, Elizabeth says, 'You killed my girl. I know you did. You lied to me for years. I know. Don't you ever forget that. I know. And I will do everything in my power to make sure the whole world knows, too. Or die trying.'

'Usha?' Melanie whimpers. A last desperate cry for her support.

Usha shakes her head.

Melanie takes a step towards her.

'Stay away from me!' Usha touches Elizabeth's arm and they walk to the car.

The sun is too bright, the sky too blue, the day too beautiful.

From the side of the house, Kieran waves goodbye.

And they wave back.

* * *

Shan

They file out of the chapel and wait in the queue to greet Elizabeth. All the mourners wear bright colours at her request.

Usha and Elizabeth's friend Pam, who'd come to the mortuary when Elizabeth viewed Vicky's remains, have read out poems and there was music: 'Imagine' by John Lennon and 'Sit Down' by James. Then a young couple, a singer and violinist, performed 'Will Ye Go Lassie Go', which made Shan weep.

She hid it as best she could, breathing steadily and clenching her mouth shut, staring up at the arched ceiling, but she's sure her eyes must give it away now. And there are probably tear tracks on her cheeks.

It doesn't matter, she tells herself. But she feels as if it's not her place to mourn. She never knew Vicky. She's a police detective doing her job. A professional.

'Thank you.' Elizabeth takes Shan's hands in hers. 'And thank you for coming.'

'Thank you.' Usha, beside Elizabeth, echoes her.

Shan moves away, through the groups talking, to the edge of the crowd.

The graves stretch away in all directions, the pathways shaded by forest trees. These are old graves, grey most of them. No balloons or plastic windmills here. No gaudy colours.

We should make wills, Shan thinks. *Erin and me, say what we want to happen.*

We should do that if we're going to stay together. If.

The thought unnerves her, as if simply considering they might not, that they might separate, will bring it about. Jinx everything. They haven't talked really, not yet, not talked about the future. Whether to try for another baby. Shan's not ready to think about that yet. Still coming to terms with what's happened. What's lost.

At her mum's funeral she was wretched with grief. She felt numb and raw and angry all at the same time. A zombie lurching into episodes of suppressed fury. For years afterwards she'd see her mum — in the street, on the bus, in the supermarket. Catch sight of her familiar shape, her gait, her hair, only to be disappointed.

'You good to go?' Leo is at her side.

'Yes,' she says.

'I was thinking of going up to Lund Seat later,' he says. She looks at him.

'It's something I like to do. Revisit the place where a case started.'

'Why?'

He looks slightly awkward, a half-smile on his lips. He raises his head to gaze across the cemetery. 'Something about closing the circle, measuring how far we've come. It's not in the handbook,' he adds.

She nods. Chuckles — he's dry as ever.

No one is parked by the bridge when they arrive.

The azure sky is dotted with pillowy clouds. A weak, warm breeze carries scents of grass and earth. From high above comes a skylark's song and, much closer by, the bleating of a sheep.

They pass through the kissing gate at the start of the footpath and begin the steep climb up the fellside to the moorland plateau.

* * *

Elizabeth

It is October when Elizabeth makes the trip to Littondale with Pam and Usha.

The nip of autumn is in the air and the first of the trees in the valley, the sycamores and maples, are turning golden and crimson.

After this they will go for lunch in one of the pubs in Grassington or Kettlewell. Drink a toast to her beloved girl.

They stop often, ostensibly for Pam to catch her breath. 'I never remember it being this steep,' she says at one point. 'Aren't things meant to look smaller when you revisit them?' at another. They laugh.

But the pace is also slow because there is no great desire to rush this. Because this day, this ceremony, has been such a long, long time coming.

At the summit by the trig point there are other walkers, taking selfies and snaps of the landscape.

Elizabeth points out the campsite to Usha, where they came so often. Usha, who has been a rock. Who is still troubled, haunted by the truth.

'Remember the shadow plays?' Pam says.

Elizabeth laughs. Remembers Vicky and Pam's son, Duncan, creating shows on the walls of their tents. An adult roped in, directing the torchlight. Adventures with rabbits and crocodiles, spider monsters, wooden-spoon people, tent pegs.

Vicky spinning her stories, weaving her magic.

Elizabeth's eyes fill.

The other ramblers have left.

The hill is theirs.

'Okay. You two first.' Elizabeth gets out the ashes already divided into paper bags.

'Rest in peace,' Pam whispers and scatters her portion on the grass.

'Vicky—' Usha chokes up. Elizabeth puts an arm around her. Usha empties her bag. A little pile of ashes. Speckled, like the colour of the gritty path, the limestone rock.

'Oh, no,' Usha says.

'It's fine,' Elizabeth says. *The wind will take her.*

Elizabeth steps forward, opens her bag and shakes, turning in a semicircle. Casting her daughter wide. *Go now, my love.*

To the skies, to the earth, to the sea.

Be free.

THE END

APOLOGY

I have taken outrageous liberties with the geography of the Dales, inventing places and changing some real locations for the sake of my story, but I hope I've managed to capture the beauty of the landscape that was the backdrop to so many childhood outings and holidays. My dad was a keen walker and would drag us off with him, often following the routes in the Wainwright guides. He usually filled in the log at the end of the book. While researching this novel in 2021 I revisited a walk the family had done together back in 1970. Fifty-one years ago! That felt pretty special — even if I did get lost this time.

ACKNOWLEDGEMENTS

Thank you so much to my writers' group — Livi Michael, Sophie Claire, Anjum Malik and Jennifer Nansubuga Makumbi — whose feedback always makes my work better. Our meetings are a real pleasure. Thanks to Lan, Xi Lei, Lynda and Joe whose stories gave me the spark for Shan's character. Thanks to my agent, Sara Menguc, and many thanks to Kate Lyall Grant and the whole team at Joffe — you're brilliant! Finally a huge thank you to everyone who campaigns to protect our precious wild places and open them up for us all to enjoy.

THE JOFFE BOOKS STORY

We began in 2014 when Jasper agreed to publish his mum's much-rejected romance novel and it became a bestseller.

Since then we've grown into the largest independent publisher in the UK. We're extremely proud to publish some of the very best writers in the world, including Joy Ellis, Faith Martin, Caro Ramsay, Helen Forrester, Simon Brett and Robert Goddard. Everyone at Joffe Books loves reading and we never forget that it all begins with the magic of an author telling a story.

We are proud to publish talented first-time authors, as well as established writers whose books we love introducing to a new generation of readers.

We won Trade Publisher of the Year at the Independent Publishing Awards in 2023. We have been shortlisted for Independent Publisher of the Year at the British Book Awards for the last four years, and were shortlisted for the Diversity and Inclusivity Award at the 2022 Independent Publishing Awards. In 2023 we were shortlisted for Publisher of the Year at the RNA Industry Awards.

We built this company with your help, and we love to hear from you, so please email us about absolutely anything bookish at feedback@joffebooks.com

If you want to receive free books every Friday and hear about all our new releases, join our mailing list: www.joffebooks.com/contact

And when you tell your friends about us, just remember: it's pronounced Joffe as in coffee or toffee!

Milton Keynes UK
Ingram Content Group UK Ltd.
UKHW010635290424
441924UK00005B/292